Collins

AQA GCSE 9-1
English Language & Literature

Revision Guide

Paul Burns

About this Revision & Practice book

Revise

These pages provide a recap of everything you need to know for each topic.

You should read through all the information before taking the Quick Test at the end. This will test whether you can recall the key facts.

Quick Test

Insert the correct punctuation:
1. Wheres my hamster Leo cried
2. He had gone there was no doubt about it
3. Maureen who lived next door searched her bins
4. Maureens son found Hammy in the kitchen

Practise

These topic-based questions appear shortly after the revision pages for each topic and will test whether you have understood the topic. If you get any of the questions wrong, make sure you read the correct answer carefully.

Review

These topic-based questions appear later in the book, allowing you to revisit the topic and test how well you have remembered the information. If you get any of the questions wrong, make sure you read the correct answer carefully.

Mix it Up

These pages feature a mix of questions for all the different topics, just like you would get in an exam. They will make sure you can recall the relevant information to answer a question without being told which topic it relates to.

Test Yourself on the Go

Visit our website at **collins.co.uk/collinsGCSErevision** and print off a set of flashcards. These pocket-sized cards feature questions and answers so that you can test yourself on all the key facts anytime and anywhere. You will also find lots more information about the advantages of spaced practice and how to plan for it.

Workbook

This section features even more topic-based questions as well as practice exam papers, providing two further practice opportunities for each topic to guarantee the best results.

ebook

To access the ebook revision guide visit

collins.co.uk/ebooks

and follow the step-by-step instructions.

Contents

Reading Task

Read the text below and answer the questions that follow.

From *Little Women* by Louisa May Alcott

nagging

'Christmas won't be Christmas without any presents,' grumbled Jo, lying on the rug.

scary

'It's so dreadful to be poor!' sighed Meg, looking down at her old dress.

'I don't think it's fair for some girls to have plenty of pretty things, and other girls nothing at all,' added little Amy, with an injured sniff. → *smelling*

in a way that express happiness/satisfied.

'We've got Father and Mother, and each other,' said Beth contentedly from her corner.

The four young faces on which the firelight shone brightened at the cheerful words, but darkened again as Jo said sadly, 'We haven't got Father, and shall not have him for a long time.' She didn't say perhaps never, but each silently added it, thinking of Father far away, where the fighting was. *shine*

Nobody spoke for a minute; then Meg said in an altered tone, 'You know the reason Mother proposed not having any presents this Christmas was because it is going to be a hard winter for everyone; and she thinks we ought not to spend money for pleasure, when our men are suffering so in the army. We can't do much, but we can make our little sacrifices, and ought to do it gladly. But I am afraid I don't.' And Meg shook her head, as she thought regretfully of all the pretty things she wanted. *past shake*

'But I don't think the little we should spend would do any good. We've each got a dollar, and the army wouldn't be much helped by our giving that. I agree not to expect anything from Mother or you, but I do want to buy *Undine and Sintram* for myself. I've wanted it so long,' said Jo, who was a bookworm.

'I planned to spend mine in new music,' said Beth, with a little sigh, which no one heard but the hearth brush and kettle holder.

home

'I shall get a nice box of Faber's drawing pencils. I really need them,' said Amy decidedly.

obviously

1 At the start of the extract which of the girls seems the happiest?

Support your answer with evidence from the text.

Beth, she was contentedly talking about having both of their parents around.

[3]

2 Why is the girls' father not living with them?

Because he is in the war.

[1]

3 **a)** What is it that the girls all think about their father but do not say?

They think that they may never see him again.

b) Why do you think they do not say it?

Because they don't want to make each other upset

[2]

4 What is meant by the following expressions?

a) Little sacrifices

Giving up small things for a good reason.

b) A bookworm

Someone that likes reading. [2]

5 Using your own words, explain Jo's argument for spending the money.

That if they spend one dollar it can make them really happy but giving the dollar to army won't be a big help [2]

6 Why does the writer use the past tense ('I planned') when Beth is talking about what she would like, and the future ('I shall') when Amy speaks?

Beth is talking about what her plan on spending money was before they were told there's no present this year but Amy is talking about her plan in the future about buying what. [3]

7 What do we learn about the characters and situation of the four girls?

Think about:

- the situation of the family as a whole
- how they behave and what they are interested in
- what they say and how they speak.

x This is family of four young girls which spending
different
Christmas during the war.

[5]

Writing Task

Thank-You Letter

Your grandfather lives abroad and was not able to come home for your birthday. However, he sent you a present. Here is part of the letter that came with it. You now want to reply to him, thanking him for the present and telling him all about your birthday.

> I decided to send you money because I don't really know what you like now and I want you to get something you really want. Please let me know what you decided to spend the money on – and send me one of those lovely letters full of news, that I so enjoy reading.
>
> Looking forward to hearing from you,
>
> Love, Grandad

Write your letter on a separate piece of paper. [20]

Spelling

You must be able to:

- Spell basic and regular words
- Spell complex and irregular words.

[handwritten notes: barry→ consonant + y + s ⇒ ie vowel + y + s ⇒ ys]

Spelling Rules

- A lot of English spelling is regular, meaning it follows rules or patterns. Here are some of the most useful rules.

'i' before 'e' except after 'c'

- achieve
- receive

Changing the 'y' to 'ie'

- Change the 'y' to 'ie' when adding 's' to a word ending in 'y'. *[handwritten: _y + s → ie]*
  - berry – berries
  - pity – pities

  but only if there is a **consonant** before the 'y'. If there is a **vowel** before the 'y', you just add 's'.
  - boy – boys
  - say – says
- Follow the same rule when you add 'ed'.
  - pity – pitied
  - play – played

- To form the **plural** of words that end in 'o', add 'es' (potatoes), except for words taken from Italian (pianos).
- If a word ends in 's' or a 'buzzing' or 'hissing' sound, add 'es' (glasses, dashes).
- You can also learn when to double a letter before 'ing' or 'ed'.
- Look for other patterns and rules that will help your spelling and learn them.

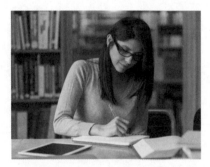

Homophones

- **Homophones** are words that sound the same but have different meanings. These cause a lot of problems. Here are some of the most common:
  - 'Here' means 'in this place': 'It's over here.'
  - You hear with your ears: 'I can hear you.'
  - 'There' means 'in that place': 'I put it over there.' It is also used in phrases such as 'there is' and 'there are'.
  - 'They're' is a **contraction** of 'they are': 'They're not really friends.'
  - 'Their' means 'belonging to them': 'They took all their things with them.'
  - 'Where', like 'here' and 'there', refers to place: 'Where do you think you're going?'

- 'Wear' is used about clothes etc.: 'You wear your earrings on your ears'.
- 'We're and 'were' are not homophones but they often get mixed up:
  * 'We're' is a contraction of 'we are': 'We're in the same class.'
  * 'Were' is the **past tense** of 'are': 'We were very happy there.'
- 'To' indicates direction: 'He went to the cinema.' It is also used as part of a **verb**: 'I want to do this now.'
- 'Too' means excessively: 'Too much' or 'too many'.
- 'Two' is the number 2: 'There were two questions to choose from.'

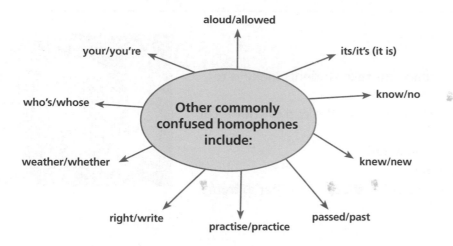

aloud/allowed

your/you're

its/it's (it is)

who's/whose

Other commonly confused homophones include:

know/no

weather/whether

knew/new

right/write

practise/practice

passed/past

- If you're not sure about any of these, look up their meanings and practise using them in sentences. You might be able to think of others that give you trouble.

Spelling Strategies

- **Mnemonics** are ways of remembering things. It can be useful to learn a phrase where the first letters of the words spell out the word you are trying to spell:
  - Big Elephants Can Always Upset Small Elephants (**because**).
- Another useful trick is to **isolate** the part of the word that causes you trouble:
  - There is a **rat** in sepa**rat**e.
- Or you might **associate** the spelling with the meaning of the word:
  - **Necessary** – it is necessary to wear one collar, two socks
- Some letters are not pronounced clearly, if at all (**silent letters**).
- Try splitting up the word and saying it slowly and carefully to yourself:
  - **en-vir-on-ment**
  - **k-now-ledge**.

Quick Test

Identify the correct spelling from the alternatives given in the following sentences:
1. We had know/no idea wear/where we were going. ✓
2. Its/it's Monday today. ✓
3. I can't decide weather/whether to/two/too buy it or not. ✓
4. Hurry up or you'll miss football practice/practise. ✗

Key Words

consonant
vowel
plural
homophone
contraction
past tense
verb
mnemonic
isolate
associate
silent letter

Punctuation

You must be able to:

- Clearly demarcate sentences
- Accurately use a range of punctuation.

Ending Sentences

- **Full stops** separate sentences. A common mistake students make is to use **commas** instead of full stops.
- **Question marks** can be used in direct speech or at the end of rhetorical questions:
  - 'Do you really want to do that?' she asked.
  - Are we ready to meet the challenge?
- **Exclamation marks** are used to show surprise, shock and other extreme emotions:
  - What a monstrosity!
  - That's amazing!

Commas

if clause

- Commas are used to separate subordinate clauses from main clauses. Subordinate clauses give extra information but are not necessary for the sentence to make sense:
  - Mina, having run the marathon, was exhausted. ←
  - After eating two puddings, Ali was full. ←
- They are used in lists:
  - I ordered fish, chips, mushy peas and a fizzy drink.
- Commas are also used to introduce and to end direct speech:
  - He shouted, 'Leave me alone!'
  - 'Nobody move,' ordered the policeman.

> 'having run the marathon' is the subordinate clause

> 'After eating two puddings' is the subordinate clause

Colons and Semi-colons

Colons:
1) before an explanation.
2) introduce quotation.
3) introduce lists.

- **Colons** are used before an explanation:
  - It took two hours: it was a difficult job.
- They introduce quotations:
  - Mercutio plays down his injury: 'Ay, ay, a scratch, a scratch.'
- They introduce lists:
  - The collection was wide and varied: historic manuscripts; suits of armour; ancient bones; and hundreds of old coins.
- Note that **semi-colons** are used to separate the items in the list above. Semi-colons separate items in a list that consist of more than one or two words. The semi-colon helps with clarity.
- Semi-colons are also used to show that two clauses are closely related, when the writer does not want to use a connective or a full stop:
  - The flowers are blooming; the trees are green.

Semicolons:
- separate items that consist more than one or two words.
- when you do not want to use a connective or a fullstop.

Key Point

Commas must not be used to link clauses (statements which could stand alone as sentences) unless a connective or relative pronoun is used:

I fed the cat, although it had already eaten.

I fed the cat, which had already eaten.

Brackets, Dashes and Ellipsis

- Brackets (**parentheses**) go around a bit of extra information:
  - A huge man (he was at least seven feet tall) dashed across the road.
- Dashes can be used to show an interruption in the train of thought:
  - I finished the meal – if you could call it that – and quickly left.
- **Ellipsis** (…) indicates the omission of words from a sentence. It can be used to show a thought trailing off or to make the reader wonder what comes next:
  - I realized that I was not alone…

Inverted Commas

- **Inverted commas** can also be referred to as **speech marks** or **quotation marks**.
- Speech marks surround the actual words spoken:
  - 'Never again!' she cried.
- Similarly, when quoting from a text, you put the inverted commas (quotation marks) around any words taken from the original:
  - Tybalt refers to Romeo as 'that villain'.
- Inverted commas are also used for titles:
  - Shelley's 'Ozymandias' is about power.

Apostrophes

- **Apostrophes** are used to show **omission** (also called contraction), or **possession**.
- Only use apostrophes for omission when writing informally. In formal writing you should write all words in full. When you do use an apostrophe, put it where the missing letter or letters would have been:
  - You **shouldn't** have done that.
  - **Malik's** finished but **Rachel's** still working.
  - Let's go home.
- Apostrophes for possession show ownership. If the owner is singular, or a plural that does not end in 's', add an apostrophe and an 's' to the word that indicates the 'owner':
  - the cat's tail
  - the class's teacher
  - the children's toys
  - James's hat.
- The only time you have to do anything different is for a plural ending in 's'. In this case, simply add an apostrophe:
  - the cats' tails
  - the boys' team.

> **Quick Test**
>
> Insert the correct punctuation:
> 1. Where's my hamster Leo cried
> 2. He had gone there was no doubt about it
> 3. Maureen who lived next door searched her bins
> 4. Maureen's son found Hammy in the kitchen

Key Point

Punctuation matters because writing does not make sense without it. Incorrect punctuation can change the meaning of your writing or even turn it into nonsense, confusing the reader.

Key Words

full stop
comma
question mark
exclamation mark
colon
semi-colon
parenthesis
ellipsis
inverted commas
speech marks
quotation marks
apostrophe
omission
possession

Sentence Structure

You must be able to:

- Use sentence structures accurately
- Use a variety of sentence structures for effect.

Simple Sentences *one verb*

- Every sentence must contain a **subject** and a main verb. The subject is the person or thing (a **noun**) that the sentence is about. The verb is the doing, feeling or being word:

  > Ronnie ate
  >
  > subject · verb

- **Simple sentences** often include an **object** (also a noun).

  > Ronnie ate an apple
  >
  > subject · verb · object

  'An apple' is the direct object. You can also use an indirect object:

  > Ronnie ate at the table
  >
  > subject · verb · preposition · object

  The **preposition** explains Ronnie's relationship to the table.

- You can vary simple sentences, and other sentence forms, by changing the verb from the **active** to the **passive voice**:

  > The apple was eaten by Ronnie
  >
  > subject · verb · preposition · agent

  Here the apple, by being put at the start of the sentence, becomes the subject.

Minor Sentences *no verb*

- A **minor sentence**, also known as a **fragment**, is not really a sentence at all because it does not contain a main verb. These are very short and are used for effect. They are often answers to questions or exclamations:
  - Oh my word!
  - Just another boring day.
- They should be used rarely or they will lose their impact.

Compound Sentences *two verbs (two complete sentence)*

Compound sentence: simple sentence + conj + simple sentence.

- To make a **compound sentence** you join together two **clauses** of equal importance using a **conjunction**. Clauses are phrases that could stand alone as simple sentences.
- You can use 'and', 'but' or 'or' to form compound sentences:
  - Lucia left the room and [she] went to the shops.
  - Lucia left the room but Mark stayed in the house.

> **Key Point**
>
> Try to vary the length and type of sentences you use. The examiner is looking for a range of sentence types being used.

- You can join more than two clauses in this way, though the result often appears clumsy:
  - Lucia left the room and went to the shops and bought a banana.

Complex Sentences

- A **complex sentence** also has two or more clauses joined together. The main clause should make sense on its own but the **subordinate clause**, which adds detail or explanation, does not need to.

main clause: should make sense on it's own

Subordinate clause: adds detail or explanation and does not need to make sense on it's own.

- Some complex sentences are formed by joining two clauses with a conjunction. In these sentences the two clauses are not equal. Examples of conjunctions you might use are:

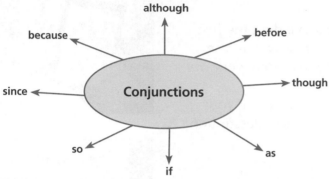

although

because

before

since

Conjunctions

though

so

as

if

- The conjunction tells you what the relationship between the two clauses is: *main clause*   *subordinate clause*
  - Charlie left school **because** he had moved house.
  - Charlie left home **after** he had moved house.

In the first sentence moving house is the reason for Charlie leaving school, whereas the second simply tells us the order in which the events happened.

- Sometimes the conjunction is placed at the beginning of the sentence rather than between the two clauses:
  - Although he felt ill, Dan ate an apple.
- Conjunctions are not needed to form complex sentences:
  - Maria, who loved shopping, left the house immediately.
  - Having left the house quickly, Maria went shopping.
- The first of these examples uses a **relative pronoun** (who) to connect the clauses, while the second changes the verb form to a past participle (having left).
- You can build even longer sentences by using several clauses and joining them in an appropriate way:
  - Dan was ill for several days so he stayed in bed, sometimes reading and sometimes watching television, but mostly bored and grumpy.

> **Key Point**
>
> Complex sentences can give more information and express more complex ideas.

> **Key Words**
>
> subject
> noun
> simple sentence
> object
> preposition
> active voice
> passive voice
> minor sentence
> fragment
> compound sentence
> clause
> conjunction
> complex sentence
> subordinate clause
> relative pronoun

> **Quick Test**
>
> Which of the following is (a) a simple sentence, (b) a compound sentence, (c) a complex sentence and (d) a minor sentence?
> 1. Never again. *m / d*
> 2. The hamster was found safe and well. *s / a*
> 3. She liked sheep but she hated cows. *c / b*
> 4. Although she had been there before, the girl could not remember where she was. *c / c*

Text Structure and Organization

You must be able to:

- Organize your writing in coherent paragraphs
- Use a range of discourse markers.

Paragraphs

- The traditional way of starting a new **paragraph** is to **indent** the first line of the new paragraph, that is, start a centimetre or two in from your margin. This is usual in most books, and in handwritten work. Try to do it in your exams.
- There is no set length for paragraphs. Try to vary the length of your paragraphs. You might use long paragraphs for a detailed description or explanation and short paragraphs for impact.

Starting a New Paragraph

- When you start writing about something new, you should start a new paragraph. This could be a change of:
  - **speaker** – when using direct speech, start a new paragraph when a new person speaks:

    > 'I didn't see anything,' added Marco.

  - **person** – introducing a new character:

    > Julie was quite the opposite…

  - **place**:

    > Toppington is also worth a visit…

  - **time**:

    > A week later, Roland realized that all was not well…

  - **topic or idea** – moving from one aspect of your subject to another or introducing a different opinion:

    > Another cause of concern is the local bus shelter…
    > Some residents disagree with this view…

> **Key Point**
>
> Paragraphs help you to organize your text so that it makes sense, follows a logical order and is easier to read.

- Paragraphs often start with **topic sentences**, which introduce the topic or subject of the paragraph:

  > When we left, there was nobody else on the boat.

  ← The topic of the paragraph is the boat and whether or not it was empty.

  > Laurie Grantham, 17, has her own take on fashion.

  ← This paragraph is about Laurie's attitude to fashion.

Opening and Closing Paragraphs

- Opening and closing paragraphs can make a big difference to the impact of your writing. How you approach them depends on the form and purpose of your writing.
- Beginnings and endings in descriptive and narrative writing are dealt with on pages 40–43. Beginnings and endings in non-fiction are dealt with on page 30 and pages 53–55.

Discourse Markers

- **Discourse markers** connect sentences and paragraphs. They guide readers through the text, showing how one sentence relates to another and how one paragraph relates to another.
- They can be single-word **connectives**, such as 'however', or phrases, such as 'in addition to this'. A discourse marker can also be a phrase which picks up on an idea from the previous paragraph:
  - This kind of behaviour is common throughout Europe.
- Not all discourse markers (for example, 'however' and 'therefore') have to be used at the beginning of a sentence. They can be more effective a little way in.
- Discourse markers have many different purposes:

To add information or ideas	In addition; As well as; Furthermore; Moreover	The new building, moreover, will ruin the view from Huntington Hill.
To point out a similarity	Similarly; In the same way	Similarly, the owl hunts at night.
To introduce a contrasting idea or point of view	Nevertheless; On the other hand; In spite of; Alternatively	Some good points have been made in favour of the plan. Nevertheless, I still think it's a bad idea.
To express cause and effect	As a result; Consequently; In order to; Therefore	I have had no objections so far. I will, therefore, continue as planned.
To give order or to sum up	Firstly; Finally; In conclusion; Basically	Finally, I'd like to thank Josh for making all this possible.
To express passing time	Subsequently; Later; As soon as; Meanwhile	The police took an hour to arrive. Meanwhile, Archie had escaped.

> ### Key Point
>
> You do not have to use a discourse marker in every sentence or even every paragraph, especially in descriptive and narrative writing.

Quick Test

Identify the discourse markers in the following sentences and explain their purpose.

1. First, I will consider Ken's proposal.
2. Tom's idea, on the other hand, is ridiculous.
3. Before the bus shelter was built, there was no vandalism.
4. I suggest, therefore, that we demolish the bus shelter.

> ### Key Words
>
> paragraph
> indent
> topic sentence
> discourse marker
> connective

Standard English and Grammar

You must be able to:

- Use Standard English
- Use correct grammatical structures.

Standard English

- **Standard English** is the version of English that is widely accepted as being correct.
- You may not always have to write in Standard English. Characters in a story might use **dialect** or **slang**. If you are writing for teenagers or children, you might use the sort of language they would use with their friends.
- For all other purposes write in Standard English, using correct **grammar** and spelling.

Personal Pronouns: First Person

- The most common misuse of **personal pronouns** is the confusion of 'I' and 'me'. 'I' is the subject of the sentence; 'me' is the object:
  - 'Ikram and me were late' is clearly wrong because you would not say: 'Me was late.' You would say: 'I was late.' So, logically, it must be: 'Ikram and I were late.'
  - Similarly you should not say: 'They gave prizes to Lucy and I.' The correct form is: 'They gave prizes to Lucy and me.'

Personal Pronouns: Second Person

- 'You' is both the **singular** and **plural** form of the second person. You could say, 'Thank you for coming' to one person or to hundreds. There is no such word as 'yous'.
- Do not use the Americanism 'you guys'. 'Guys' is not Standard English.

Words and Phrases to Avoid

- Be aware of any words or phrases that are common in your area but are not Standard English, and avoid using them in formal writing.
- The same applies to current slang used by young people (such as 'sick' for 'good') and Americanisms, for example, using 'lay' instead of 'lie' or 'period' rather than 'full stop'.

Modal Verbs

- Do not use the word 'of' instead of 'have' after **modal verbs** such as would, could, should and might:
  - If I'd known, I would **have** told you.

> **Key Point**
>
> Standard English is the form of English which is most widely understood. You need to be able to use it so that your audience can understand what you are saying.

Verbs: Agreement and Tenses

- There are three basic tenses – past, **present** and future. This section focuses on the past tense because that is where most errors occur.
  - A common error is to confuse the first and **third person** of the verb, for example, using 'you was' instead of 'you were'.
  - Another is the confusion of the **simple past tense** and the **perfect tense**, which expresses a completed action (for example, using 'done' instead of 'did' or 'has done'). The perfect tense is formed by adding the past participle to 'have' or 'has'.
- Most verbs follow this pattern:

	Singular	Plural
Simple past	I/you/he/she/it walked.	We/you/they walked.
Perfect	I/you have walked. He/she/it has walked.	We/you/they have walked.

- Many of the most commonly used verbs are irregular, among them the verb 'to be'. These are its correct forms:

	Singular	Plural
Simple past	I was.	We were.
	You were.	You were.
	He/she/it was.	They were.
Perfect	I/you have been.	We/you have been.
	He/she/it has been.	They have been.

- Some other irregular verbs which cause problems are shown here.

Simple Past	Perfect	Simple Past	Perfect
ate	have/has eaten	sang	has/has sung
did	have/has done	saw	have/has seen
drove	have/has driven	spoke	have/has spoken
gave	have/has given	taught	have/has taught
got	have/has got	went	have/has gone
lay	have/has lain	woke	have/has woken

- If you are writing in the past tense and you want to refer to something that happened before the events you are describing, use the **past perfect tense**, which is formed using 'had' and the past participle:
  - She had eaten before she arrived.
- If you are writing about an event in the past which continued for some time, use the **past continuous**, formed by the past tense of the verb 'to be' and the present participle:
  - She was eating for the whole journey.

> ## Key Point
>
> The subject and verb of your sentence must agree in number and person.

> ## Key Words
>
> **Standard English**
> **dialect**
> **slang**
> **grammar**
> **personal pronoun**
> **singular**
> **plural**
> **modal verb**
> **present tense**
> **third person**
> **simple past tense**
> **perfect tense**
> **past perfect tense**
> **past continuous tense**

> ## Quick Test
>
> Rewrite the following sentences in Standard English:
> 1. Me and Jay was put on detention. *Jay and I* *we've*
> 2. I seen you guys on Saturday. ~~I have seen~~ *I saw*
> 3. You was the bestest player we had. *were*
> 4. After we had sang the first number, we ~~done~~ a dance. *danced* ✗

1 The following paragraph includes 10 incorrect spellings. Find them and rewrite them correctly.

We where hoping for good whether for Sports Day. Unfortunately, on Friday morning it was poring with rain. Luckily, by ten o'clock it was clear and sunny. I was very exited when I got to the stadium but I had a long weight for my race, the 200 meters. Their were eight of us in the final. I was in the inside lane, witch I don't usually like, but I ran well round the bend and was second comming into the straight. As I crossed the line I was neck and neck with Jo. It wasn't until the teacher congratulated me that I knew I had definately won.

_____

_____ [10]

2 The following five sentences have been written without punctuation.
Insert the correct punctuation.

a) Peter Kowalski who was the tallest boy in the class easily won the high jump.

_____

b) What are you doing in the sand pit shouted Miss O'Connor get out of there at once.

_____

c) Francesca won medals for the long jump the high jump and the relay.

_____

d) I wasnt entered in any of the races because Im hopeless at running.

_____

e) Jonathan finished last however he was pleased with his time.

_____ [5]

3 a) Change each of the following pairs of sentences into single sentences, using conjunctions.

i) Julia stayed off school. She had a stomach ache.

_____

ii) He might be in the changing rooms. He might have already left.

_____

b) Change the following pairs of sentences into single sentences using relative pronouns.

i) Michael announced the results. He has a really loud voice.

_____

ii) The form with the best results won a cup. The cup was presented by Mr Cadogan.

_____

c) Turn the following three sentences into a single sentence.

  i) Maria had won the discus competition. ~~but~~ She went home early. ~~because.~~ She was feeling sick.

  Maria had won the discus co   **[5]**

4 Rewrite the following sentences using Standard English.

a) Me and Hayley is going to town tomorrow.

  Hayley and I are going to town Tomorrow.

b) You guys can come wiv us if youse want.

  You can come with us if you want.

c) We ~~was well chuffed~~ with what we bought.

  were very pleased

d) I don't know nothing about what they done at school.

  ✗ *I don't know anything about what they have done at school*

check again

✗ **e)** I aint skiving off again cöz I wanna get my GCSEs.

  cause want to   **[5]**

5 Insert each of the following five connectives or discourse markers in the text below to help it to make sense.

however   **as well as**   **also**   **as a result of**   **consequently**

I am disgusted by the plan to close our library. (1) ~~as a result of~~ *well as* having a massive impact on our community, this act of vandalism shows how little interest the council has in education. (2) *as a result of* this attitude, our children are being deprived of a wonderful resource. Adults, especially older people, (3) ✗ *consequently* benefit greatly from the library. The council says we can use Hartington Library, but that is much too far away for most pensioners. (4) *however* ✗, they will lose what has become for many a real lifeline, making them feel part of the community. (5) *also* ✗, it does not have to be like this. There are other ways for the council to save money: we could start with cutting down on the Mayor's free trips to America! **[5]**

6 Rewrite the following paragraph on a separate piece of paper, correcting errors in spelling, punctuation and grammar.

My first experiance of Bingley Park Library was when I was five. My grandmother, who were an avid reader, visitted the library every week and always borrowed four books. She read more or less anything but she especially liked detective story's, gardening books, and film star's biografies. Naturally, she wanted the rest of her family to be as enthusiastic as she was about books therefore, as soon as I could read, me and her marched down to bingley park. It was an imposing and rather frightening edifice for a child of five, the librarian, Miss Maloney, was just as imposing and twice as intimidating. **[10]**

Explicit Information and Ideas

You must be able to:

- Identify and interpret explicit information and ideas.

Explicit Information

- **Explicit** information is information that is openly stated. You will find it in the text.
- When answering questions it does not matter whether you think what the writer says is true or plausible. You are required to find the information and repeat it, either in the writer's words or in your own.
- Questions about explicit information normally ask you to list a number of things you can find in the text, for example:
  - List four things the writer tells you about the garden.
  - What do you learn about butterflies from the text?
- Read the text below and list four things the writer tells us about Griselda the cat:

> There were only two places where Griselda would sit in the garden: in the middle of the lawn (to catch the sun) and (if the sun was too hot) in the shade of the plum tree. She sometimes hunted at night and would return in the morning with little presents for us, mice or birds, which she always left in the middle of the kitchen floor to make sure we got them.

- You could say:
  - She would only sit in two places in the garden.
  - She liked to sit in the middle of the lawn.
  - If it was hot she sat under the plum tree.
  - She hunted at night.
  - She brought back mice and birds.
  - She left mice and birds in the kitchen.
    There are six points made here. You can get marks for any four of them but if you put more than four you will not get any extra marks.
- You would not get marks for:
  - She was a cat – you are told this in the question, not in the text.
  - She was friendly – there is no mention of this in the text.
  - There was a plum tree in the garden – true, but it is not about Griselda. It would be a good answer if you were told to 'list four things about the place where Griselda lived'.

Explicit Ideas

- Explicit ideas are ideas and **opinions** that are openly stated.
- You could be asked, for example:
  - List four ways in which people react to the news.

Key Point

You may be directed to a section of the text. Make sure you take your information only from that part of the text.

- – List four reasons given for the start of the war.
- Read the text below and **identify** four ideas that, according to the writer, would improve the park:

> Bilberry Recreation Ground is an eyesore. It is time for radical action. Let's start by getting rid of the graffiti – it's not art; it's vandalism. The Victorian benches are also in a sad state – let's restore them. There used to be beautiful flower beds. It's time we planted some new ones. Let's encourage families to return by building a new and exciting playground. What about a kiosk selling cups of tea and ice cream? Finally, may I suggest a change of name? 'Recreation Ground' sounds old-fashioned and dreary. Let's call it Bilberry Park from now on.

- You would get marks for:
  - – Get rid of the graffiti.
  - – Restore the park benches.
  - – Plant new flower beds.
  - – Build a playground.
  - – Build a refreshment kiosk.
  - – Change the name.
- You would not get marks for:
  - – It is an eyesore – this is not an idea for improvement.
  - – Put a fence round the park – you might think this is a good idea but the writer does not mention it.
  - – Take radical action – this is too vague.

> ### Key Point
>
> It does not matter whether you agree with what the writer says. You are being asked to identify the writer's ideas, not yours.

Quick Test

1. What does 'explicit' mean?
2. Can you quote from the text?
3. Can you put the answer in your own words?
4. If you are asked to list four points, do you get an extra mark for giving five?

> ### Key Words
>
> explicit
> opinion
> identify

Implicit Information and Ideas

You must be able to:

- Identify and interpret implicit information and ideas.

Implicit Information

- **Implicit** information is not stated openly. It is **implied**, so you have to 'read between the lines' to **infer** it from the text.
- Sometimes information is implied by saying what is not true:
  - He was not a happy child.
  This implies that he was sad.
- One piece of information can be implied by giving another:
  - They painted their garden shed blue.
  We can infer from this that they had a garden. Otherwise it would not be a 'garden' shed.

Implicit Ideas

- Similarly, writers can make their views and feelings clear without openly stating them:
  - I would rather stick pins in my eyes than sit through another maths lesson.
  This implies that the writer does not like maths.
- When you infer meaning and explain what you have inferred, you are **interpreting** implicit information or ideas.
- Sometimes we infer a writer's views or feelings by putting together a number of pieces of **evidence**. Read the following text:

> One thing that really annoys me is the way they constantly scratch themselves. And every dog I've ever met has had smelly breath. As for the constant barking and yapping! Give me a nice quiet cat or hamster any day.

If you were asked whether the writer likes dogs, you could only answer 'no'. He or she does not ever say 'I don't like dogs', but gives three negative opinions about them and no positive ones.

True or False?

- You might get a question in the form of a tick box exercise, for example: 'Choose four statements below that are TRUE'.
- Read the following passage:

I Left My Heart on Bilberry Rec

by Mary Goodenough

Bilberry Rec is a part of my past. It didn't have wonderful facilities or beautiful vistas. There were no rose gardens or tea shops, no adventure playgrounds and certainly no 'wild meadows'. There were a few trees and hedges, the 'swing park' and a football pitch.

It was what it said it was: a recreation ground, a place where people of all ages went for recreation. Small children played on the swings and didn't often bash their heads on the concrete floor. Bigger children played football or cricket – or just fought. Courting couples walked hand in hand along the muddy paths or snogged on the broken benches. Pensioners walked their dogs and everyone used it as a short cut.

I know times have changed. And my head tells me the new Bilberry Park will be much nicer (and cleaner and safer) than the old Rec, but my heart wants it left just as it is. It's a sure sign of getting older – an attack of illogical nostalgia.

- Which of the following statements are true?
  1. Mary Goodenough has happy memories of Bilberry Rec.
  2. There was a rose garden in Bilberry Rec.
  3. The new park will have better facilities than the old Rec.
  4. Goodenough didn't feel safe in the Rec.
  5. Bilberry Rec was a beautiful place.
  6. Sometimes there were accidents in the swing park.
  7. Goodenough understands why things should change.
  8. Bilberry Rec is going to be built on.
- Numbers 1, 3, 6 and 7 are true.
  - 1 is implied by references to her 'heart' and nostalgia.
  - 3 is implied by referring to what the old Rec didn't have and calling the new park 'nicer...cleaner and safer'.
  - 6 is implied by saying that it didn't happen 'often'.
  - 7 is implied by saying that her 'head' tells her it will be better and that her nostalgia is 'illogical'.

> ### Key Point
>
> When completing a 'true or false' exercise, make sure you fill in the correct number of boxes.

Quick Test

1. Who implies, the writer or the reader?
2. Who infers?
3. Should you give your opinion?
4. What happens if you tick/shade too many boxes?

> ### Key Words
>
> **implicit**
> **imply**
> **infer**
> **interpret**
> **evidence**

Synthesis and Summary

You must be able to:

- Select and synthesize evidence from different texts
- Summarize the content of texts.

Synthesis

- **Synthesis** is the bringing together of parts to make a whole. In exams this usually takes the form of writing about two different texts.
- In Paper 2 of the English Language exam you will have to compare the **content** of two non-fiction texts.
- The texts will be about similar subjects but one will have been written in the nineteenth and one in the twenty-first century, so it is likely that there will be differences in attitudes as well as in the things and people described.

Summary

- A **summary** is a shortened version of something, keeping the main points but leaving out unnecessary detail.
- When you write a summary do not add your own thoughts or comment on the writers' style or techniques.
- You should use evidence from the text in the form of short quotations but most of the answer should be in your own words. Do not copy out huge chunks of the text.
- Remember you are being asked to summarize two texts, so write about them both at equal length.
  - Do not write about one and then the other.
  - Write about both throughout your answer, summarising different aspects of the texts as you go.

Approaching the Question

- Read the question carefully. It will not just ask you to summarize the texts; it will have a particular focus, for example:
  - Write a summary of the differences between Mary and Jordan.
  - Summarize the different feelings of the writers about school.
- **Skim read** both texts.
- Underline or highlight the main points in the texts.
- You might want to do a (very quick) plan, listing **differences** (and **similarities** if asked for).
- Focus on the question.
- Don't repeat yourself.
- Don't waste time on an introductory and concluding paragraph.
- Write in proper sentences and paragraphs, using connectives.

> ### Key Point
>
> Remember to look for both explicit and implicit information and ideas.

Example

- Below are two short extracts from texts about sea voyages. Think about what you would include if you were asked to write a summary of the differences between the voyages:

Daily Southern Cross, 21 October 1859

The *Mermaid* […] arrived in harbour on Wednesday at 4 a.m. She left Liverpool on 11th July at 5 p.m. Passengers have been very healthy during the voyage; three infants died, and one birth occurred. The passengers speak highly of Captain White and officers.

Southern Star, 19 July 2014

After three weeks the luxury liner *Ariadne* finally arrived home and the passengers disembarked from the journey one of them described as 'a floating nightmare'. For the last week almost a quarter of the passengers had been confined to their cabins with mild food poisoning and many are now demanding their money back.

- You could pick out the following differences:

Mermaid	Ariadne
Journey over three months	Three-week journey
Passengers 'healthy' – three infants died	Food poisoning
Passengers praise captain and crew	Passengers demand money back

- A paragraph summarizing the differences might read:

The **Mermaid's** journey lasted over three months; **Ariadne's** took three weeks. The **Mermaid's** passengers are 'healthy' but the **Ariadne's** have food poisoning. However, 'three infants died' on the **Mermaid**, suggesting that not everyone was healthy. Nevertheless, it would seem that the Victorian passengers were happier than the modern ones, as they 'speak highly' of the crew rather than complaining.

> **Key Point**
>
> Bear in mind that this is a short answer question, attracting only 8 marks of the total of 80 for the paper, so you should aim to spend no more than 9 minutes on it.

> **Key Words**
>
> synthesis
> content
> summary
> skim read
> difference
> similarity

> **Quick Test**
>
> 1. Should the summary be shorter than the original text?
> 2. Should you use quotations in your summary?
> 3. Can you write about just one of the texts?
> 4. Should you discuss the writers' use of language in your answer?

Referring to the Text

You must be able to:

- Select appropriate and relevant examples from texts
- Use textual references to support and illustrate your interpretation of the texts.

Referring to the Text

- You can **refer** to a text by **paraphrasing** the text or by **quoting** from the text.
- For all Language questions and some Literature questions, you will have a text in front of you from which you can take your examples.
- For other Literature questions you will have to rely on your memory, so it is a good idea to learn some significant quotations.

Paraphrasing

- Paraphrasing means putting something into your own words. It is useful for summing up, for example:

The writer gives us a number of examples of cruelty to animals such as neglect and physical violence, which he describes in very vivid terms.

- When you are writing about a longer text, such as a novel, you might not need to quote because you are writing about events or feelings and the exact wording is not important:

Lydia clearly does not think much about her family's reputation. When she returns from London she does not express any shame at her behaviour but boasts about being married.

> **Key Point**
>
> It is very important to refer to the text in your answers, both in English Language and English Literature exams.

Using Quotations

- A **quotation** is a word or phrase taken directly from the text. Indicate that you are quoting by putting inverted commas (or quotation marks) around the quotation.
- There are three main ways to set out your quotations.
- If your quotation consists of just a few words (or even one word) and fits naturally into your sentence, you simply put it into inverted commas (quotation marks):

At the start of the soliloquy Juliet refers to 'love-performing night' but later it becomes a 'sober suited matron all in black'.

This is called **embedding**. Examiners like you to embed and it should be the method you use most often.

- If the quotation will not fit easily into your sentence but is fairly short (no more than 40 words of prose or one line of verse), put a colon (:) before it, continue on the same line and use inverted commas:

> Benvolio passionately asserts that he is not lying: 'This is the truth or let Benvolio die.'

- If you want to use a longer quotation, leave a line and indent. You must indent the whole quotation. When quoting verse, end the lines where they end in the original. Do not use inverted commas:

> This opposition will inevitably cause problems for the lovers and Juliet expresses her dilemma:
>
>> My only love sprung from my only hate!
>> Too early seen unknown and known too late!
>
> The use of paradox emphasizes her confusion.

> **Key Point**
>
> Only put words taken directly from the text inside the quotation marks. Spell and punctuate exactly as in the text.

Using PEE

- Remember to use PEE (Point, Evidence, Explanation).
- First make your **point**, saying what you want to say about the text.
- Then give your **evidence**, either in the form of a paraphrase or a quotation.
- Finally, **explain** or explore the evidence you have given.

> The writer is very concerned about what he sees as widespread cruelty to domestic animals. He mentions the 'heartless neglect' of some dogs by their owners. The use of this emotive adjective paints the owners as villains and appeals to the compassion of the readers.

Here the first sentence makes the point, the second gives the evidence in quotation marks, and the third explains/explores the evidence.

> **Quick Test**
>
> 1. What are the two different ways of using evidence from the text?
> 2. When you quote, what goes inside the inverted commas?
> 3. When should you not 'embed' a quotation?
> 4. What does PEE stand for?

> **Key Words**
>
> refer
> paraphrase
> quote (verb)
> quotation (noun)
> embed

Analysing Language 1

You must be able to:

- Explain, comment on and analyse how writers use language
- Use relevant subject terminology to support your views.

Diction and Register

- **Diction** and **register** both refer to the writer's choice of words or **vocabulary**.
- Most texts you read will be in Standard English. Sometimes, however, you will come across a text that uses a lot of non-standard words, for example slang and dialect words (see pages 14–15).
- Their use can tell you something about the writer, the narrator, certain characters or the audience at which the text is aimed.
- Writers might use specialized diction: for example, a lot of scientific or medical terms. The use of such language shows that the text is aimed at people who are interested in the subject and probably already know quite a lot about it.
- Writers might use words and expressions associated with a particular subject – for example, war or nature – for rhetorical or figurative purposes. Sometimes their word choice is referred to as a **semantic field**. We can often infer their attitude to the subject from their choice of semantic field.

Parts of Speech (Word Classes)

- **Nouns** are naming words.
  - **Concrete nouns** name objects (chair, mountain).
  - **Abstract nouns** name ideas and feelings (love, suspicion).
  - **Proper nouns** have capital letters and name individual people (Jelena), places (Warsaw), days of the week (Saturday), months (April) etc.
  - A 'noun phrase' is a group of words built around a noun.
- **Adjectives** describe nouns (the **red** house; his **undying** love).
- **Verbs** are doing, feeling and being words. You might comment on whether verbs are:
  - in the past tense (she walked; he was thinking)
  - in the present tense (she is walking; he thinks)
  - or in the future tense (we are going to walk; you will go).
- **Adverbs** describe verbs, telling us how something is being done, for example, she spoke **slowly**; he writes **carefully**.
- **Pronouns** stand in for other words, usually nouns. Whether the writer uses first person (I/we), second person (you) or third person (he/she/they) can make a difference to how we read the text. 'I' makes the text more personal to the writer. 'We' and 'you' aim to involve the reader more in the text. There are different types of pronouns.

Key Point

When we talk about 'parts of speech' or 'word class' we are referring to what words do in sentences. It is important that you can identify these so that you can refer easily to them in a way that shows you understand their function: for example, 'The writer uses a lot of adjectives associated with war to describe the scene.'

Personal pronouns	Relative pronouns
I/me	who
we/us	whom
you	whose
he/him	that
she/her	which
it	
they/them	

- **Prepositions** are used to express the relationship between nouns (or noun phrases) and other parts of the sentence or clause:
  - We went **to** the cinema.
  - The cat is **under** the table.
- **Conjunctions** join words, phrases and clauses: for example, 'and', 'but', 'although', 'because'. A conjunction is a type of connective but the two words are not interchangeable. Other types of word and phrase, including relative pronouns and adverbs, can also act as connectives (see Sentence Structure, pages 10–11).
- **Determiners** come before nouns and help to define them. The most common are the definite article (the) and the indefinite article (a/an). Other examples of determiners are 'this', 'both' and 'some'.

Key Point

If you are not confident about identifying parts of speech it is better to avoid mentioning them. Using incorrect terminology will not impress the examiner.

Key Words

diction
register
vocabulary
semantic field
noun
concrete noun
abstract noun
proper noun
adjective
verb
adverb
pronoun
preposition
conjunction
determiner

Quick Test

Read this sentence:
The old horse was munching thoughtfully on his oats.
Identify:
1. Two nouns
2. A verb
3. An adjective
4. A preposition
5. An adverb

Analysing Language 2

You must be able to:

- Explain, comment on and analyse how writers use language
- Use relevant subject terminology to support your views.

Connotation

- A **connotation** is an implied meaning. Words can have associations other than their literal meanings. For example, red indicates danger or anger. 'Heart' has connotations of love and sincerity.

Emotive Language

- Writers often seek to arouse certain feelings or emotions in the reader, for example, pity or anger. This can be done by using **emotive language**: words and phrases that have certain connotations.
- A reporter writing about a crime could write:

> Burglars stole some jewellery from Mr Bolton's house.

This just tells us the facts. A writer who wanted to influence our emotions might write:

> Heartless burglars stole jewellery of great sentimental value from frail pensioner Albert Bolton.

Rhetorical Language

- **Rhetoric** is the art of speaking. Effective speakers have developed ways of influencing their audiences. Writers also use rhetorical techniques to affect readers.
- **Hyperbole** is another word for exaggeration:

> Councillor Williams is the most obnoxious man ever to disgrace this council chamber.

- Lists of three are used to hammer home a point:

> Friends, Romans, countrymen.

- **Repetition** is used to emphasize the importance of the point being made:

> Victory at all costs, victory in spite of all terror, victory however long and hard the road may be; for without victory there is no survival.

- **Rhetorical questions** are questions which do not need an answer. Sometimes the writer gives an answer:

> Can we do this? Yes, we can.

Sometimes they are left unanswered to make the reader think about the answer:

> What kind of people do they think we are?

Key Point

Writers use language to affect and influence their readers.

The adjective 'heartless' makes the burglars sound deliberately cruel, and 'frail' emphasizes the weakness of the victim, while the phrase 'of great sentimental value' tells us how important the jewellery was to Mr Bolton. This increases our sympathy for him.

Sound

- The sound of words can make a difference to their meaning and effect.
- **Onomatopoeia** is the use of words which sound like their meaning:

  The door creaked open and clunked shut.

- **Alliteration**, the use of a series of words starting with the same sound, is common in newspaper headlines as well as in poetry and other literary texts:
  - Brave Bella battles burglars.
  - Storm'd at with shot and shell.
- When you see alliteration, think about why the writer uses a particular sound. Some consonants ('d', 'k', 'g') are hard. Others ('s', 'f') are soft. 'P' and 'b' have an explosive quality.
- The repetition of 's' sounds is also referred to as **sibilance**.
- **Assonance** is the use of a series of similar vowel sounds for effect:

  From the bronzey soft sky…Tipples over and spills down.

Imagery

- Literal **imagery** is the use of description to convey a mood or atmosphere. A description of a storm might create an atmosphere of violence and danger.
- Figurative imagery uses an image of one thing to tell us about another.
  - **Similes** compare one thing to another directly, using 'like' or 'as':

    Straight and slight as a young larch tree.

  - **Metaphors** imply a comparison. Something is written about *as if it were* something else:

    Beth was a real angel.

  - **Personification** makes a thing, idea or feeling into a person:

    At my back I always hear
    Time's winged chariot hurrying near.

  - The personification of nature, giving it human qualities, is also called **pathetic fallacy**:

    The clouds wept with joy.

    This term can also be applied to a literal description in which nature or the weather reflects the feelings of characters.
  - A **symbol** is an object which represents a feeling or idea, for example a dove to represent peace.

> ## Key Point
>
> Imagery is usually associated with literary texts, such as poems. However, non-fiction texts also use imagery to paint pictures in the readers' minds.

> ## Key Words
>
> connotation
> emotive language
> rhetoric
> hyperbole
> repetition
> rhetorical question
> onomatopoeia
> alliteration
> sibilance
> assonance
> imagery
> simile
> metaphor
> personification
> pathetic fallacy
> symbol

> ## Quick Test
>
> Of which literary techniques are the following examples?
> 1. Macbeth doth murder sleep.
> 2. Ill met by moonlight.
> 3. I wandered lonely as a cloud.
> 4. You were sunrise to me.

Analysing Form and Structure

You must be able to:

- Explain, comment on and analyse how writers use form and structure
- Use relevant subject terminology to support your views.

Form and Structure

- The structure of a text is the way in which it is organized: for example, the order in which information is given or events described.
- The terms 'structure' and 'form' are both used to describe how a text is set out on the page.

Openings

- The beginning (**opening**) of a text is very important as it has to draw in the readers and encourage them to continue reading.
- Some texts begin by giving an overview of the subject, indicating what the text is going to be about:

> There are thousands of varieties of butterfly. In this article I will discuss some of the most common.

- A writer might explain why he or she has decided to write:

> Lewis's views about youth unemployment are fundamentally wrong.

- Fiction writers can use their openings to introduce characters or settings:

> 'I shall never forget Tony's face,' said the carrier.

- Texts can also start with dramatic statements, designed to shock, surprise or intrigue:

> It was a bright cold day in April, and the clocks were striking thirteen.

Endings

- Fiction writers might give a neat **conclusion**: for example, with the solving of a crime or a marriage:

> Reader, I married him.

- They might prefer to leave us with a sense of mystery or suspense:

> 'Who are they?' asked George [...]
> *'Wolves.'*

- Writers of essays and articles usually end by drawing together their main points and reaching a conclusion.
- Some texts end with a question or even an instruction:

> Get out there now and use your vote!

Key Point

You should consider why the writer has decided to arrange things in a particular way and the effect of this on the reader.

Chronological Order

- **Chronological order** gives events in the order in which they happened. This is the most common way of ordering fiction, and non-fiction texts such as histories, biographies and travel writing.
- Writers might, however, start at the end of the story or somewhere in the middle before going back to recap previous events in 'flashbacks'.
- **Reverse chronological order** means starting with the latest event and working backwards. You will see this in **blogs** and discussion forums.

Other Ways of Ordering Texts

- Some texts start with general information and move on to more detailed information and explanation.
- A text giving a point of view might build up to what the writer thinks are the most persuasive arguments.
- Information can be arranged in **alphabetical order**, as in dictionaries and encyclopaedias.
- Texts sometimes rank things or people in order of importance or popularity, as in a music chart, either starting with the best and working down or starting with the worst and working up.

Divisions

- Books are usually divided into **chapters**, sometimes with titles or numbers.
- Most prose is arranged in **paragraphs** (see pages 12–13), while verse is often divided into **stanzas** (see pages 102–103). Make sure you use the correct terminology.
- Other devices used to divide up text include **bullet points**, numbering and **text boxes**. Headlines and subheadings help to guide readers through the text.

Analysing Structure

- When analysing a short text, or an extract from a longer text, think about how and why the writer changes focus from one paragraph or section to another, perhaps moving from a general description to something more detailed, from a group of people to a particular character, or from description to action or speech.

> **Key Point**
>
> Texts, especially longer texts, are often divided into sections. These give order to their contents and help readers find their way through the text.

> **Key Words**
>
> opening
> conclusion
> chronological order
> reverse chronological order
> blog
> alphabetical order
> chapter
> paragraph
> stanza
> bullet point
> text box

> **Quick Test**
>
> Put the following in:
> 1. chronological order
> 2. reverse chronological order
> 3. alphabetical order
>   a) December 2014
>   b) January 2002
>   c) April 2011
>   d) November 2011

1. Insert the correctly spelled word in each of the following pairs of sentences.

   a) **except/accept**

   I did them all _____ the last one.

   I _____ your apology.

   b) **affect/effect**

   The weather seemed to have a bad _____ on everyone's mood.

   I don't think the weather will _____ the result.

   c) **aloud/allowed**

   Nobody is _____ in here at lunchtime.

   Mo really likes reading _____ in class.

   d) **write/right**

   Nobody got the _____ answer.

   I'll _____ a letter and explain.

   e) **who's/whose**

   He couldn't return it because he didn't know _____ coat it was.

   Tell me _____ going and then I'll decide.   [5]

2. Rewrite the following passage on a separate piece of paper using the correct punctuation.

   dont you think we should wait for him asked Eve

   not at all Henry replied he never waits for us

   well that's true Eve replied but he doesn't know the way

   [10]

3. Rewrite the following passage on a separate piece of paper, using a variety of simple, compound and complex sentences (and adding words if necessary) to make it more effective.   [10]

   Henry and Eve waited for another ten minutes. Joel did not arrive. They left without him. They walked to the bus stop. There was no-one there. This suggested they had just missed the bus. Henry was very annoyed with Joel. Eve told him to calm down. She told him to forget about Joel. The journey was uneventful. They got off the bus by the lake. It looked eerie in the moonlight. They sat down on a grassy bank. They took their sandwiches and drinks out of the bag. Henry felt a hand on his shoulder.

   [10]

4. Pick the five sentences in which the correct forms of the verb are used.

   a) You was really good tonight.   ☐

   b) Ms Greenall taught me how to boil an egg.   ☐

c) They've gotten two more kittens. ☐

d) I knew the song because we had sung it in class. ☐

e) I rung the bell twice but nobody come. ☐

f) She lay on the sofa until she felt better. ☐

g) I done my homework at break. ☐

h) He says he won't come because he's already seen it. ☐

i) I have done what you asked. ☐

j) I'm going to lay down here for a while. ☐ [5]

5 Put the following nouns into their plural forms.

a) pizza _____   f) stadium _____

b) latch _____   g) quality _____

c) mosquito _____   h) church _____

d) sheep _____   i) woman _____

e) donkey _____   j) hypothesis _____ [5]

6 Rearrange the following paragraphs so that the whole letter makes sense.

a) The next thing I knew two young girls were leaning over me. I'm sorry to say I thought the worst when I saw the rings through their noses. But they asked me if I was all right and very gently helped me to stand up. One of them stayed with me while the other went into the shop and fetched a chair. Then I noticed there were two boys carefully collecting all my shopping and bagging it up.

b) When it was all collected in, they called a taxi to take me home. I'm sorry to say I didn't ask their names, so I'd like to give them a big thank you through your newspaper. Whoever you are, you're a real credit to Bilberry and to your generation!

c) I was in town on Wednesday to do my usual shop in the supermarket. I got a little more than usual so my bags were rather heavy. As I came out of the shop I lost my balance and keeled over, spilling all my shopping.

d) I wasn't badly hurt but it was quite a shock. I just sat there on the pavement, stunned and not knowing what to do.

e) I am writing to express my thanks to a group of young people I met last week. It isn't often we hear good things about teenagers. We read so much about crime and vandalism, drinking and bad manners that we can easily end up thinking the worst of all teenagers.

a) ☐   b) ☐   c) ☐   d) ☐   e) ☐   [5]

1 Read the passage below. List four reactions that people have to Scrooge. [4]

From *A Christmas Carol* by Charles Dickens

Nobody ever stopped him in the street to say, with gladsome looks, 'My dear Scrooge, how are you? When will you come to see me?' No beggars implored him to bestow a trifle;[1] no children asked him what it was o'clock; no man or woman ever once in all his life inquired the way to such and such a place, of Scrooge. Even the blindmen's dogs appeared to know him; and when they saw him coming on, would tug their owners into doorways and up courts; and then would wag their tails as though they said, 'No eye at all is better than an evil eye, dark master!'

[1] *bestow a trifle* – to give a small amount

_____

_____

_____

_____

2 How does Dickens use language to give us an impression of Scrooge's character? You could comment on his use of:
- words and phrases
- language feature and techniques
- sentence forms. [8]

Write your answer on a separate piece of paper.

3 Read the passage below.

From a letter written by Charles Lamb to William Wordsworth

London, January 30, 1801

I ought before this to have replied to your very kind invitation into Cumberland. With you and your sister I could gang[1] anywhere. But I am afraid whether I shall ever be able to afford so desperate a Journey. Separate from the pleasure of your company, I don't much care if I never see a mountain in my life. I have passed all my days in London […] The lighted shops of the Strand and Fleet Street, the innumerable trades, tradesmen and customers, coaches, waggons, playhouses, all the bustle and wickedness round about Covent Garden, the very women of the Town, the Watchmen, drunken scenes, rattles;[2]—life awake, if you awake, at all hours of the night, the impossibility of being dull in Fleet Street, the crowds, the very dirt & mud, the Sun shining upon houses and pavements, the print shops, the old *Book* stalls, […] coffee houses, steams of soup from kitchens, the pantomimes, London itself a pantomime and a masquerade, all these things work themselves into my mind and feed me without a power of satiating me. The wonder of these sights impels me into night walks about the crowded streets, and I often shed tears in the motley Strand from fullness of joy at so much *Life*.—All these emotions must be strange to you. So are your rural emotions to me […]

My attachments are all local, purely local.—I have no passion […] to groves and valleys.—The rooms where I was born, the furniture which has been before my eyes all my life, a book case which has followed me about (like a faithful dog, only exceeding him in knowledge) wherever I have moved, old tables, streets, squares, where I have sunned myself, my old school,—these are my mistresses. Have I not enough, without your mountains?

[1] *gang* – a dialect word for 'go'
[2] *rattles* – constant chatterers

Which of the following statements are TRUE? Tick the correct boxes.

    a) Charles Lamb hates London. ☐

    b) He has always lived in London. ☐

    c) He finds life in the city exciting. ☐

    d) He does not like going out after dark. ☐

    e) He thinks Wordsworth will find it strange that he does not like the countryside. ☐

    f) He likes to spend time with Wordsworth and his sister. ☐

    g) He loves climbing mountains. ☐

    h) He is thinking of buying some new furniture. ☐   **[4]**

4 Now read this article and write a summary of the differences between Weston's and Lamb's attitudes to city life.   **[8]**

I'm a City-Hater – Get Me out of Here!

by Malcolm Weston

I've had enough. I'm leaving. Who was it who said that when a man is tired of London he's tired of life? Well, I don't think I'm tired of life – I'd like to go on living as long as I can – but I'm fed up to the back teeth with London. It's dirty. It's noisy. You can barely move in Oxford Street sometimes. Everything's expensive (how can anyone afford to live here?). And everyone is so bad-tempered. I know it's meant to be terribly lively and exciting but, frankly, I'm bored with it. Sorry, Londoners. It's nothing personal: I don't really like any cities – or towns. So I'm off home. And this time next week you'll find me (if you can – it's a bit off the beaten track) halfway up a mountain somewhere in the Lake District, looking up at the sky and listening to the sound of silence.

Creative Reading 1

You must be able to:

- Read and understand a range of literature
- Critically evaluate literature texts.

Story Structure

- Most novels and stories begin by 'setting the scene', introducing characters or places and giving us a sense of the world we are entering.
- That world might be very like our own world but it could be unfamiliar, perhaps because the story is set in a different country or a different time.
- The writer might even, like Tolkien, have invented a complete fantasy world.
- This part of a story is called **exposition** and can take a chapter or more, or maybe just a few lines.
- The event that really gets the story going is sometimes called the **inciting incident**. This can be dramatic and shocking, like Pip's encounter with the convict at the beginning of *Great Expectations*, or it can be a seemingly ordinary event, like Darcy coming to stay with Bingley in *Pride and Prejudice*.
- Inciting incidents change the lives of the protagonists (the main characters) for ever.

> **Key Point**
>
> Every story has a beginning, a middle and an end. The extracts you will be given might come from any part of the story.

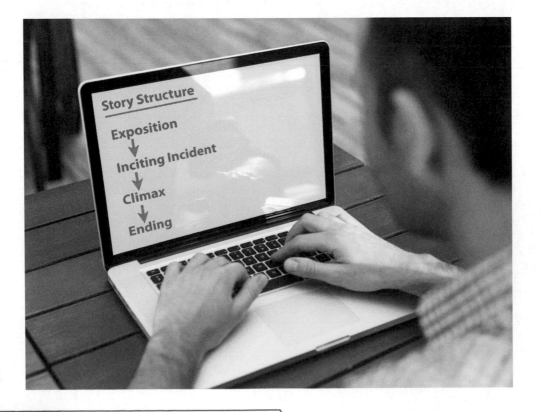

- During the course of a story there are usually several **turning points**. Turning points are events which change the direction of the story for good or ill. Sometimes we can see them coming; sometimes they are unexpected and surprising 'twists' in the plot.
- Towards the end, most stories reach a **climax**, or denouement, when things come to a conclusion, sometimes happily as in a fairy tale, sometimes not. This is the event the whole story has been building up to.
- The climax is not always at the end of the story. Most writers take some time to reflect on how things have turned out.
- Endings quite often refer back to openings, giving a sense of how things have changed.

Narrative Perspectives

- Many stories are told in the first person singular ('I'), so that we see the story through the eyes of one of the characters, usually the **protagonist**, for example, Jane in *Jane Eyre* or Harri in *Pigeon English*. This encourages us to empathize with them.
- Sometimes the **narrator** is another character, acting more as an observer and putting some distance between the reader and the protagonist. Dr Watson in the Sherlock Holmes stories is an example of this.
- Each narrator has his or her own 'voice'. In *Pigeon English*, for example, the kind of language the narrator uses tells us about his background and culture.
- A writer might use different several narrators so that we get different characters' experiences and points of view: Mary Shelley does this in *Frankenstein*.
- In a 'third-person **narrative**' the narrator is not involved in the story at all. If there is a sense of the narrator's 'voice', it is the voice of the author. This gives the writer the opportunity of sharing with us the thoughts, feelings and experiences of many characters.
- A narrator who can see everything in this way is called an **omniscient narrator**.
- Sometimes omniscient narrators comment on characters and action using the first person. If so they are called **intrusive**. Dickens uses this technique in *A Christmas Carol*.

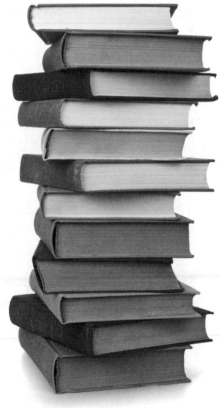

> **Key Point**
>
> When analysing a literary text, always consider the 'narrative voice' and your reaction to it.

> **Key Words**
>
> **exposition**
> **inciting incident**
> **turning point**
> **climax**
> **protagonist**
> **narrator**
> **narrative**
> **omniscient narrator**
> **intrusive narrator**

> **Quick Test**
>
> 1. Does the exposition come at the beginning or end?
> 2. When the narrator is part of the action is it a first-person or third-person narrative?
> 3. Which comes first: the climax or the inciting incident?
> 4. What is an omniscient narrator?

Creative Reading 2

You must be able to:

- Read and understand a range of literature
- Critically evaluate texts.

Character

- We learn about **characters** in different ways.
- The narrator can directly describe a character. In this example (from *The Strange Case of Dr Jekyll and Mr Hyde*) we can infer something about the man's character from his appearance.

> …the lawyer was a man of a rugged countenance, that was never lighted by a smile.

Key Point

Descriptions of people make the characters seem more real and can tell us a lot about them.

- We can learn about characters from what they say and how they say it, as well as from what other characters say about and to them. In this quotation from *Pride and Prejudice* Mr Bennet gives his opinion of his daughters:

> 'They are all silly and ignorant like other girls; but Lizzy has something more of quickness than her sisters.'

We can infer from this that Lizzy is the only daughter that Mr Bennet is interested in and that he can be quite blunt and dismissive. However, we might get a slightly different impression if we know that he is talking to his wife. It could be that he is trying to provoke her and/or that his remark about the girls being 'silly and ignorant' is intended as a joke.

- Most importantly, you should consider how characters behave and how others react to them. Dickens leaves us in no doubt about Scrooge's character:

> Even the blindmen's dogs appeared to know him; and when they saw him coming on, would tug their owners into doorways and up courts.

This comes at the beginning of *A Christmas Carol* and gives us a strong first impression, which is built on by descriptions of his treatment of his clerk, his nephew and the men who come collecting for charity.

Description

- This description (from *The Withered Arm* by Thomas Hardy) is fairly simple:

  > …it was not a main road; and the long white riband of gravel that stretched before them was empty, save for one moving speck.

  This tells us that the story is set in a remote place and sets up the encounter between the people in the carriage and the boy, whom they first see as a 'moving speck'.

- In the first chapter of *Great Expectations*, Dickens describes the **setting** in a way that gives us information about the landscape while creating an **atmosphere** that prepares us for the frightening event that is about to happen:

  > …and that the dark flat wilderness beyond the churchyard, intersected with dykes and mounds and gates, with scattered cattle feeding on it, was the marshes; and that the low leaden line beyond, was the river; and that the distant savage lair from which the wind was rushing, was the sea…

  Dickens uses adjectives like 'dark', 'low' and 'leaden' to give us a sense of an unattractive, featureless landscape, but adds words like 'wilderness' and 'savage' to make it seem dangerous and threatening.

- The description above uses **literal imagery** to create **mood** and atmosphere, the lonely, rather frightening place reflecting the feelings of the protagonist Pip.
- **Figurative imagery**, too, is often used in descriptive writing. In *The Withered Arm* Hardy uses a simile to describe one of his characters:

  > Her face too was fresh in colour, but it was of a totally different quality – soft and evanescent, like the light under a heap of rose-petals.

  The imagery helps us to picture her complexion and gives us a sense of her beauty and fragility.

Key Point

Writers describe places to root their stories in a time and place, and to create mood and atmosphere.

Quick Test

Identify what kind of imagery is being used in these sentences:
1. The lake shone like a silver mirror.
2. Angry crags surrounded us.
3. A veil of snow hid it from view.
4. There was a cluster of jagged black rocks.

Key Words

character
setting
atmosphere
literal imagery
mood
figurative imagery

Narrative Writing

You must be able to:

- Write clear and imaginative narratives.

Narrative

- A **narrative** is an account of events – a story, whether real or imagined.
- One of the writing tasks in Paper 1 will ask you to write a story or part of a story. This gives you the opportunity to use your imagination and be creative.
- You may be asked to write for a particular audience. If so, it is most likely to be for people of your own age.
- You will be given a 'stimulus' for your story. This could be a picture or just a brief instruction:
  - Write the opening of a story suggested by the picture above.
  - Write a story about someone whose life changes suddenly.

  These instructions are deliberately vague, so you can develop your own ideas in your own style.

Planning

- Before you start to write, spend a few minutes planning, making decisions about the main elements of your story.

Character and Voice

- Decide whether you are going to write in the first or third person. If you opt for the first person, is the narrator the **protagonist** or an observer?

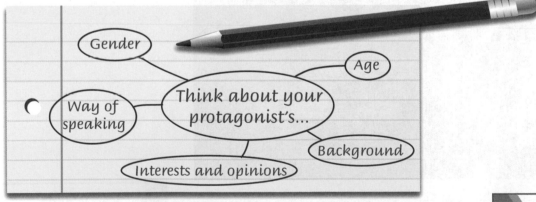

- The protagonist could be a version of you, but it can be much more interesting to write about someone who is completely different.
- There may also be an **antagonist**, someone who stands in the way of or opposes the protagonist.
- Think about other, minor characters – but beware of inventing too many. You don't want to make things too complicated.

> **Key Point**
>
> You can tell a story in your own voice or you can invent a character (persona) to tell the story.

Structure

- The same applies to the plot. If you are writing a complete story, keep it fairly simple.
  - You need an inciting incident, a climax and at least one turning point, but not too many.
  - You need to establish your 'world,' but don't spend too much time on exposition.
  - You might end with a shock or surprise. It has been said that writers should give their readers what they want but not in the way they expect.
- If you are only writing the opening, make sure something interesting or dramatic happens that would make a reader want to know what happens in the rest of the story. You should know how the story would develop and end.
- It is less likely that you would be asked to write the end of a story, but if you are asked to do this, you need to know what happened before the point at which you start your story.
- Stories are normally written mainly in chronological order but you might want to use 'flashbacks'.

Language and Style

- Normally you would write in Standard English but if you use a first-person narrator, you should write in that person's **voice**. Think about its tone – formal or chatty? – as well as whether to use dialect or slang.
- Stories are usually written in the past tense. Using the present tense can make the action seem more immediate and vivid, though. You can use either, but stick to one.
- **Direct speech** can help to move on the story and tell us about character, but use it sparingly. Think about whether it adds anything – and make sure you set it out properly. Sometimes **indirect** (or **reported**) **speech** can be more effective.
- Write in paragraphs. These should usually be linked by discourse markers, particularly ones that relate to time:
  - After they left, he sank to his knees.
- Use a variety of sentence structures, for example using complex sentences for descriptions and simple or even minor sentences for dramatic impact:
  - It was her.
  - A gun beneath the leaves.
- Use a range of punctuation but avoid using a lot of exclamation marks.

Key Point

Be careful not to just tell the 'bare bones' of the story. You also need to describe people and places.

Key Words

narrative
protagonist
antagonist
voice
direct speech
indirect speech
reported speech

Quick Test

What is meant by the following?
1. The protagonist.
2. The antagonist.
3. The inciting incident.
4. A turning point.

Descriptive Writing

You must be able to:

- Write clear and imaginative descriptions.

Description

- One of the tasks in Paper 1 will be to write a description, possibly based on a picture. If there is a picture, you are not limited to describing what is actually in the picture. It is there to stimulate your imagination.
- When writing a description you can draw on your memories of real people, places or things.
- You might also be inspired by something you've read.
- Think about different aspects of your subject – and not just positive ones. This is especially important when describing a person – there is only so much you can write about how lovely someone is.
- Think about all five senses: sight, hearing, smell, taste and touch. When you have decided what you want to describe, it is a good idea to jot down what you experience through each sense. If you were describing a beach you might put:

Taste	Touch	Hearing	Smell	Sight
Sandwiches with sand in	Slimy seaweed	Waves crashing	Salty water	Rocks, sand

- Another useful way of approaching description is 'big to small', starting with what something is like from a distance and moving in like a camera:

the panoramic view	→	sand, rocks and people	→	children playing in rock pool	→	shells and seaweed

Language and Style

- Consider whether to use the first or third person – you may or may not want to describe personal feelings:

  I feel a huge sense of regret as the train leaves.

- Decide whether to write in the present or past tense: they can be equally effective but you should stick to one.
- Use **imagery** and figurative language, including metaphors and similes:

  The train roared like an angry lion.

> **Key Point**
>
> When you describe something, remember that you can use all five senses.

- Use adjectives and adverbs:

  - *The deep mysterious sea*
  - *The engine spluttered fitfully.*

- Be adventurous in your choice of vocabulary. Use words that have precise, rather than general, meanings. Does the man walk across the road? Or does he amble, trot, stride or even swagger?
- Use techniques such as alliteration, assonance and onomatopoeia:

  - *sparkling, shining sea*
  - *gloomy blue rooms*
  - *the fizz and pop of the fireworks*

- Use both active and passive voices:

  - A *dark forest surrounded the cottage.*
  - *The cottage is surrounded by a dark forest.*

- Write in paragraphs. Vary their length and link them with a variety of discourse markers:

  - *Beyond this lies a flat, wide bog.*
  - *But these sights were as nothing to what lay beyond.*

- Vary your sentence lengths and use techniques such as **parallel phrasing**. This is the use of phrases constructed in the same way and arranged in pairs or sequences:

  - *Tiny rivulets run down the lane; a massive lake covers the fields.*

> **Key Point**
>
> If the task is to write a description, do not write a story.

Example
- This description of a person uses some of the techniques described above.

> George lived alone. Gnarled and weather-beaten, he looked older than his sixty years: his skin was sun-baked and blemished; his forehead grooved with deep furrows; his few remaining teeth black and crooked, like ancient gravestones. His teeth were rarely seen, for he had few reasons to smile. His one companion was his terrier Barney, whom he loved. In return Barney offered unquestioning love, loyalty and apparent affection.

It is written in the past tense and the third person.

It describes George's appearance but also gives us some background.

The imagery is mainly literal but figurative imagery is also used.

Both active and passive voices are used.

There is a variety of sentence structures.

> **Quick Test**
>
> Look at the example above. Find examples of:
> 1. A simple sentence.
> 2. A simile.
> 3. Alliteration.
> 4. The passive voice.

> **Key Words**
>
> imagery
> parallel phrasing

1 Read the passage below (Source A), in which Charlotte Brontë describes how she and her sisters, Anne and Emily, went about publishing their poems.

From Charlotte Brontë's *Biographical Notice of Ellis and Acton Bell*

We agreed to arrange a small selection of our poems, and, if possible, get them printed. Averse to personal publicity, we veiled our own names under those of Currer, Ellis, and Acton Bell; the ambiguous choice being dictated by a sort of conscientious scruple at assuming Christian names positively masculine, while we did not like to declare ourselves women, because – without at that time suspecting that our mode of writing and thinking was not what is called 'feminine' – we had a vague impression that authoresses are liable to be looked on with prejudice [...]

The bringing out of our little book was hard work. As was to be expected, neither we nor our poems were at all wanted; but for this we had been prepared at the outset; though inexperienced ourselves, we had read the experience of others. The great puzzle lay in the difficulty of getting answers of any kind from the publishers to whom we applied. Being greatly harassed by this obstacle I ventured to apply to the Messrs. Chambers, of Edinburgh, for a word of advice; they may have forgotten the circumstance, but I have not, for from them I received a brief and business-like, but civil and sensible reply, on which we acted, and at last made a way.

The book was printed; it is scarcely known, and all of it that merits to be known are the poems of Ellis Bell. The fixed conviction I held, and hold of the worth of these poems has not indeed received the confirmation of much favourable criticism; but I must retain it notwithstanding.

Which of the following statements are TRUE? Tick the correct boxes.

a) All three sisters contributed poems to the book. ☐

b) They wrote under their own names. ☐

c) They felt that critics were prejudiced against female authors. ☐

d) They were not keen on publicity. ☐

e) They had lots of replies from publishers. ☐

f) Charlotte Brontë found the advice of Chambers sensible and useful. ☐

g) The book was a great success. ☐

h) Emily's (Ellis's) poems were the worst thing about the book. ☐

i) Bringing out the book was simple, easy work. ☐

j) The sisters were all very experienced at working with publishers. ☐ [4]

2 Now read this article (Source B) and write a summary of the differences between Brontë's and Fordyce's experience.

How I Made My Own Luck

by Lily Fordyce

People often ask me for advice about writing, which really means they want me to give them the magic key that opens the door to publication, fame and fortune. I can't promise any of that. All I can do is say how it was for me, and that what worked for me won't work for everyone. There are two essential ingredients: hard work and luck. Some people say you make your own luck. If that's true, this is the luck I made:

1. I started reading out my poetry in public. It wasn't that hard for me. I'm one of life's show-offs. I was welcomed with enthusiasm, especially because I'm a woman. 'We don't get enough women' was a cry I heard again and again.

2. I sent my poems to every poetry magazine going, whether they pay or not (mostly they don't) and very soon I was seeing my work in print.

3. I entered almost every competition I could find.

And finally, I won a competition, which led to my first book, which did very well – and here I am: a hardworking and very lucky poet.

_____

_____

_____

_____

_____

_____

_____

_____ [8]

3 Look again at Source B. How does Fordyce use language to convey her feelings about becoming a poet? You could include her choice of:

- words and phrases
- language features and techniques
- sentence forms.

Write your answer on a separate piece of paper. [12]

Reading

Read the passage below, which is the opening of *The Withered Arm* by Thomas Hardy, and then answer the questions.

It was an eighty-cow dairy, and the troop of milkers, regular and supernumerary, were all at work; [...] The hour was about six in the evening, and three-fourths of the large, red, rectangular animals having been finished off, there was opportunity for a little conversation.

'He do bring home his bride tomorrow, I hear. They've come as far as Anglebury today.'

The voice seemed to proceed from the belly of the cow called Cherry, but the speaker was a milking-woman, whose face was buried in the flank of that motionless beast.

'Hav' anybody seen her?' said another.

There was a negative response from the first. 'Though they say she's a rosy-cheeked, tisty-tosty little body enough,' she added; and as the milkmaid spoke she turned her face so that she could glance past her cow's tail to the other side of the barton,[1] where a thin fading woman of thirty milked somewhat apart from the rest.

'Years younger than he, they say,' continued the second, with also a glance of reflectiveness in the same direction.

'How old do you call him, then?'

'Thirty or so.'

'More like forty,' broke in an old milkman [...]

The discussion waxed so warm that the purr of the milk streams became jerky, till a voice from another cow's belly cried with authority, 'Now then, what the Turk do it matter to us about Farmer Lodge's age, or Farmer Lodge's new mis'ess? [...] Get on with your work, or 'twill be dark afore we have done. The evening is pinking in a'ready.' This speaker was the dairyman himself, by whom the milkmaids and men were employed.

Nothing more was said publicly about Farmer Lodge's wedding, but the first woman murmured under her cow to her next neighbour.[1] ''Tis hard for she,' signifying the thin worn milkmaid aforesaid.

'O no,' said the second. 'He ha'n't spoke to Rhoda Brook for years.'

When the milking was done they washed their pails and hung them on a many-forked stand made as usual of the peeled limb of an oak-tree, set upright in the earth, and resembling a colossal antlered horn. The majority then dispersed in various directions homeward. The thin woman who had not spoken was joined by a boy of twelve or thereabout, and the twain[2] went away up the field also.

Their course lay apart from that of the others, to a lonely spot high above the water-meads, and not far from the border of Egdon Heath, whose dark countenance was visible in the distance as they drew nigh to their home.

'They've just been saying down in barton that your father brings his young wife home from Anglebury tomorrow,' the woman observed. 'I shall want to send you for a few things to market, and you'll be pretty sure to meet 'em.'

'Yes, Mother,' said the boy. 'Is Father married then?'

'Yes...You can give her a look, and tell me what she's like, if you do see her.'

---

[1] *barton* – cowshed

[2] *twain* – two

1 This text is the opening of a short story. How has the writer structured the text to interest you?

You could write about:

- what the writer focuses on at the beginning
- how and why the writer changes this focus as the extract develops
- any other structural features that interest you. [8]

_____

_____

_____

_____

_____

2 Halfway through this extract the writer introduces Rhoda Brook. What impression do you get of her?

In your response you could:

- write about the attitude of the other characters to her
- evaluate the ways in which the writer describes her
- support your answer with quotations from the text. [20]

_____

_____

_____

_____

_____

_____

_____

_____

Writing

3 Write the opening of a story about a mother and her son. Write on a separate piece of paper.

[24 marks for content and organization; 16 marks for technical accuracy; total 40]

Reading Non-fiction 1

You must be able to:

- Read and understand a range of non-fiction texts
- Compare writers' ideas and perspectives.

Viewpoints and Perspectives

- Paper 2 of the English Language exam requires you to compare two non-fiction texts.
- The exam is called 'Writers' Viewpoints and Perspectives'. In order to understand **viewpoints** and **perspectives** you are expected to consider writers' opinions, ideas and feelings.

Form, Purpose and Audience

- Your texts could come from a number of **non-fiction forms** and **genres**. The most likely are discussed below.
- Think about the writer's purpose. It could be to describe, to inform and explain, to argue, to persuade or to advise. Remember that a text can have more than one purpose.
- Think about the intended audience. It might be aimed at people of a certain age (children, teenagers, older people). It could be intended for people in a particular job or with particular interests: for example, doctors, gardeners, cyclists. It might, however, be written for a general audience or with no audience in mind.

> ### Key Point
>
> Non-fiction is any writing that is not made up by the writer. It is not necessarily fact but it is what the writer believes to be true.

Diaries

- Diaries and **journals** are very personal. They are written by people who want to keep a record of what they have done and to express their opinions and feelings about what is happening around them.
- They can seem very immediate and spontaneous. We expect to get a genuine, uncensored and sincere point of view.
- They also give us an insight into what people really did and thought in the past.
- However, many diaries have been edited. We can still learn what the writer thought at the time of writing but it may not be exactly what he or she wrote.
- Some diaries may have been written with publication in mind by writers conscious of giving their 'version' of events.
- Diaries can vary a lot in style. Some use chatty, **informal language**. Others are quite formal.
- Some **diarists** jot down impressions and thoughts in a quite disorganized way. Other diaries are considered and crafted.

Letters

- Letters can give us an insight into people's everyday lives. Their style and tone depend a lot on their purpose.
- Letters give news and opinions, discuss ideas and express feelings. Letters might also be asking for something (like a job), complaining about something, or thanking someone for something.
- Unlike diarists, letter writers are always conscious of their audience. A letter to a close friend would be different in tone, style and content from a letter to a grandmother. It would be very different from a letter to a newspaper about current events, or to a prospective employer.
- The tone of a letter – friendly, angry, ironic, cold – will tell you a lot about the relationship between the writer and the **recipient** at the time of writing.

Autobiography and Biography

- **Biography** means writing about life. **Autobiography** means writing about one's own life.
- An autobiography can be reflective, even 'confessional', as the writer considers his or her past actions. It may also be self-justifying, naive or untrue. Autobiographies written by current celebrities (or their 'ghostwriters') are often written with the purpose of promoting the subject's career.
- Biographies range from what are known as 'hatchet jobs', designed to ruin their subjects' reputations, to 'hagiographies' (originally written about saints), which have nothing but good to say. Most are something in between.
- A biographer's point of view may come from his or her own relationship with the subject. On the other hand, it might be based on a careful consideration of the evidence.

> **Key Point**
>
> An autobiography is written by someone looking back on events, and so has the benefit of hindsight.

> **Key Words**
>
> viewpoint
> perspective
> non-fiction
> form
> genre
> journal
> informal language
> diarist
> recipient
> biography
> autobiography

> **Quick Test**
>
> Where are you most likely to find the following?
> 1. An account of someone's whole life.
> 2. Thanks for a present.
> 3. The writer's secret feelings.
> 4. How the writer became a megastar.

Reading Non-fiction 2

You must be able to:

- Read and understand a range of non-fiction texts
- Compare writers' ideas and perspectives.

Travel Writing

- Travel writing includes newspaper and magazine **articles** about places to visit, which give readers opinions and advice about a place. These are similar to reviews.
- You are more likely to be given **autobiographical** accounts of more adventurous trips – a journey down the Amazon or climbing a mountain in the Himalayas. These contain information about the places described but are more concerned with the personal experience of challenge and adventure.
- Some writers might seem awestruck and/or delighted by everything they encounter. Others are more critical, especially when writing about people and their way of life. They might even give opinions on political or other controversial issues.
- Some writers use the techniques of fiction writers to build suspense and involve readers. Others go in for colourful, even poetic description. Some write wittily about their reactions to new experiences.
- Some writers are experts, perhaps using a lot of unfamiliar terminology, for example, about mountaineering. Others see themselves as naive travellers – 'innocents abroad' – who tell jokes at their own expense.

Key Point
Many non-fiction texts use 'literary' techniques associated with fiction.

Journalism

- **Journalism** is anything that is published in a newspaper or magazine.
- Newspaper **reports** give the news and are mainly factual. **Features** – in both newspapers and magazines – look at issues in more depth. Sometimes they are balanced discussions. They can, however, strongly argue for a point of view.
- Articles can be serious or amusing. Most newspapers have regular feature writers. Some of them write about themselves and their families in a way that encourages readers to empathize with them. Others focus on more controversial issues.
- Most magazines are aimed at particular readerships – for example, women, men, teenagers, older people.
- Newspapers are aimed at a general, adult audience. However, different newspapers have different readerships, often associated with particular political views.

Reviews

- A **review** is an article that gives a point of view about, for example, a film, book, concert, game or restaurant.

- Reviews give information, such as venue, date, time and price. Their main purpose, however, is to give the writer's point of view.
- Some reviews are quite balanced, giving positive and negative views, though they usually do arrive at a judgement. Others express their views very strongly, sometimes in a witty way.

Comparing Points of View

- The two **sources** you are given will be about similar subjects but written from different points of view:
  - Compare how the writers convey different attitudes to the environment.
- You should discuss what these attitudes are:

Smith feels that we need to save rural areas, whereas Jones is happy for towns to expand.

- The attitudes shown in the sources might be directly stated or implied:

While Williams is shocked at the idea of women doing 'men's work', Roberts seems not to share the view as she does not comment on the fact that the engineer is a woman.

- Think about the impression you get of the writer:

Jones is clearly an expert on the subject, while Smith writes as a confused voter.

- Consider the general tone:

Williams uses humour to make his point, but Roberts writes seriously about her emotions.

- And remember to comment on structure and language:

Jones's use of subheadings breaks the article into clear 'points', making it more accessible.

Smith uses slang, trying to appeal to young readers, whereas Jones uses formal, quite technical language.

> **Key Point**
>
> Remember that you are being asked to compare the writers' views, not to give your own.

> **Quick Test**
>
> In which of the following are you least likely to find the writer's point of view?
> 1. A review.
> 2. A news report.
> 3. A feature.
> 4. Travel writing.

> **Key Words**
>
> article
> autobiographical
> journalism
> report
> feature
> review
> source

Writing Non-fiction 1

You must be able to:

- Communicate clearly, effectively and imaginatively
- Adapt your writing for different forms, purposes and audiences.

The Task

- Paper 2 of the English Language exam includes one writing task. It gives you the opportunity to express your views on a theme explored in the reading section of the exam.
- You will be given a statement or scenario, and instructions which include details of purpose, form and audience:

> School holidays create problems for parents and damage children's education.
>
> Write an article for a student website in which you argue for or against this view.

Audience

- Sometimes the task specifies an **audience**:

> Write a letter to your head teacher.

- Sometimes the audience is implied by the form:

> – Write an article for your school website.

- Your intended audience determines what sort of language you use. Think about whether a formal or informal tone is called for.
- You would write informally for people you know well, using the sort of language that you use when chatting with them. However, you should avoid using 'text language' (**abbreviations**, emoticons etc.) in the exam.
- It can be appropriate to write informally for people you don't know, as if you were their friend, for example, in a magazine article aimed at teenagers.
- For almost everything else use a formal tone and write in Standard English (see pages 14–15).
- Whether you are writing formally or informally, be aware of your audience's interests and points of view. For example, if you were writing for a local audience you would focus on known local concerns:

> Here in Bingley, we have always been proud of our green spaces.

- – You would expect school governors to be concerned about the school's reputation:

> I know that you are just as concerned as I am about recent complaints of unsocial behaviour.

Key Point

You are free to agree or disagree with the stimulus you are given. The important thing is to try to convince the reader of your view.

– And a little flattery can go a long way:

> *I have always been impressed by your commitment to our community.*

Purpose

- The purpose of your writing is to express your point of view. The wording of the task might give a slightly different emphasis. For example, 'argue' sounds more passionate than 'explain', while 'persuade' suggests more emphasis on the audience.

Constructing Your Argument

- In constructing your **argument**, start with a powerful opening paragraph, which grabs your audience and makes your point clear.
- Make sure you offer a number of points in support of your argument, starting a new paragraph for each.
- Acknowledge other points of view but then give your **counter-arguments**, pointing out why you think they are wrong:

> *Some people argue that school uniforms stifle individuality. However,...*

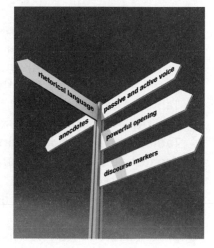

- Structure your argument in a logical order, using **discourse markers** to 'signpost' the development of your argument:

> *Another point I would like to make is...*

- Back up your points with evidence if you can. You can use the sources for the reading question to help you with this.
- Give appropriate examples, including **anecdotes**:

> *Only last week, I encountered such behaviour...*

- Address your audience directly (**direct address**), using 'you', and show your own involvement by using 'I' and 'we'.
- Use a full range of **rhetorical devices**, including lists of three, repetition and **hyperbole** (see pages 28–29).
- Use humour if you think it is appropriate.
- Use a variety of sentence structures, and use the passive as well as the active voice.
- Finish with a strong conclusion, summing up the main points and strongly stating your opinion.

> **Key Point**
>
> Spend a few minutes (but only a few!) planning your answer, using whatever method works best for you.

> **Key Words**
>
> audience
> abbreviation
> argument
> counter-argument
> discourse marker
> anecdote
> direct address
> rhetorical device
> hyperbole

> **Quick Test**
>
> Your head teacher has banned packed lunches. You want to write to the governors giving your reaction. What would be the:
> 1. purpose?
> 2. audience?
> 3. form?

Writing Non-fiction 2

You must be able to:

- Communicate clearly, effectively and imaginatively
- Adapt your writing for different forms, purposes and audiences.

Form: Articles

- You could be asked to write an article for a newspaper, magazine or website.
- If it is a newspaper, the task might specify whether it is a **broadsheet**, **tabloid** or local newspaper.
- Broadsheets are 'serious' newspapers, which look at news in more detail and depth, such as the *Daily Telegraph* and *The Guardian.*
- Tabloids, like *The Sun* and the *Daily Mirror*, cover news in less depth and devote more space to things like celebrity gossip.
- Tabloids use short paragraphs and sentences, and simple vocabulary. Broadsheets use longer paragraphs and sentences, and more sophisticated vocabulary.
- Do not try to make your answer look like a newspaper or magazine. There are no marks for design. Do not include:
  - a masthead (the newspaper's title)
  - columns
  - illustrations
  - any articles apart from the one you have been asked to write.
- You can, however, include organizational devices such as:
  - a **headline** – perhaps using alliteration ('Ban this Beastly Business'), a **pun** or a play on words ('A Tale of Two Kitties'). But don't put it in huge coloured letters!
  - a **strapline,** under the headline, expanding on or explaining the headline ('Why We Should Boycott Cosmetics')
  - **subheadings** – to guide the reader through the text.
- You must write in paragraphs.
- Magazine and website articles are similar to newspaper articles in form.

> ### Key Point
>
> You are not likely to be asked to write a tabloid article: it would not give you enough scope to demonstrate your skills.

Form: Letters

- There are a number of 'rules' or conventions that are used in letter-writing. These are often not used in informal letters.
- If you are asked to write a letter in the exam, it will probably be quite formal.

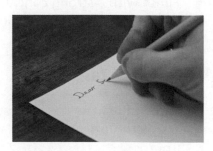

Example of How to Open a Letter

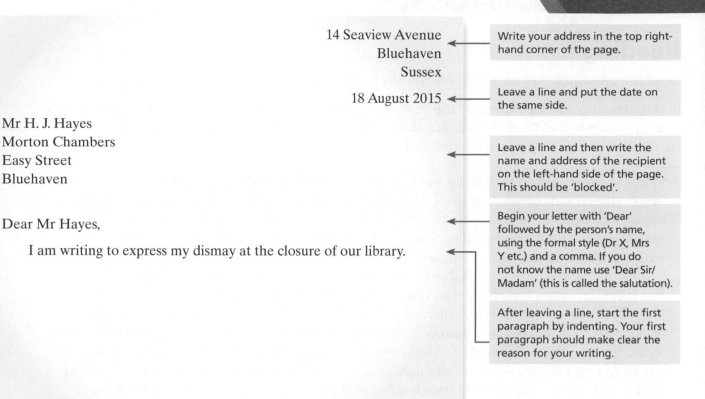

14 Seaview Avenue
Bluehaven
Sussex

Write your address in the top right-hand corner of the page.

18 August 2015

Leave a line and put the date on the same side.

Mr H. J. Hayes
Morton Chambers
Easy Street
Bluehaven

Leave a line and then write the name and address of the recipient on the left-hand side of the page. This should be 'blocked'.

Dear Mr Hayes,

Begin your letter with 'Dear' followed by the person's name, using the formal style (Dr X, Mrs Y etc.) and a comma. If you do not know the name use 'Dear Sir/Madam' (this is called the salutation).

I am writing to express my dismay at the closure of our library.

After leaving a line, start the first paragraph by indenting. Your first paragraph should make clear the reason for your writing.

- Continue with paragraphs that make further relevant points before ending with one that tells the reader what you would like to happen next.
- Connect your paragraphs with discourse markers.
- If you have addressed the reader by name, sign off with 'Yours sincerely'. If you haven't, use 'Yours faithfully'.
- Remember the 'five Cs':
  - Clear – Say what you mean in good English.
  - Complete – Include everything necessary, giving enough detail and explaining your points properly.
  - Concise – Don't 'ramble'. Do not include irrelevant information or ideas.
  - Correct – Say what you believe to be true.
  - Courteous – Be polite. Consider the recipient and his or her possible reaction to your letter.

> **Key Point**
>
> Unless you are writing informally for young people, avoid slang or dialect words, contractions and abbreviations.

> **Quick Test**
>
> How should you end a letter beginning with the following salutations?
> 1. Dear Mr Blenkinsop
> 2. Dear Principal
> 3. Dear Madam
> 4. Dear Sir Arthur

> **Key Words**
>
> broadsheet
> tabloid
> headline
> pun
> strapline
> subheading

Reading

Read the passage below and then answer the questions.

In this extract from *The Hound of the Baskervilles* by Sir Arthur Conan Doyle, Dr Mortimer is telling Sherlock Holmes and Dr Watson about the death of Sir Charles Baskerville, who believed his family was cursed and haunted by a mysterious beast.

'It was at my advice that Sir Charles was about to go to London. His heart was, I knew, affected, and the constant anxiety in which he lived, however chimerical[1] the cause of it might be, was evidently having a serious effect upon his health. I thought that a few months among the distractions of town would send him back a new man. Mr Stapleton, a mutual friend who was much concerned at his state of health, was of the same opinion. At the last instant came this terrible catastrophe.

'On the night of Sir Charles's death Barrymore, the butler who made the discovery, sent Perkins the groom on horseback to me, and as I was sitting up late I was able to reach Baskerville Hall within an hour of the event. I checked and corroborated all the facts which were mentioned at the inquest. I followed the footsteps down the yew alley, I saw the spot at the moor-gate where he seemed to have waited, I remarked the change in the shape of the prints after that point, I noted that there were no other footsteps save those of Barrymore on the soft gravel, and finally I carefully examined the body, which had not been touched until my arrival. Sir Charles lay on his face, his arms out, his fingers dug into the ground, and his features convulsed with some strong emotion to such an extent that I could hardly have sworn to his identity. There was certainly no physical injury of any kind. But one false statement was made by Barrymore at the inquest. He said that there were no traces upon the ground round the body. He did not observe any. But I did – some little distance off, but fresh and clear.'

'Footprints?'

'Footprints.'

'A man's or a woman's?'

Dr Mortimer looked strangely at us for an instant, and his voice sank almost to a whisper as he answered:

'Mr Holmes, they were the footprints of a gigantic hound!'

[1] *chimerical* – fanciful or imagined

1 This extract comes from the end of the second chapter of *The Hound of the Baskervilles*, a detective story featuring Sherlock Holmes.

How has the writer structured the text to interest you as a reader?

You could write about:

- how Dr Mortimer builds up to the discovery of the body
- how the information about the footprints is revealed
- any other structural features that interest you.

_____

_____

_____

_____

_____

_____ [8]

2 Look at the whole text.

What impression do you get of the narrator and his story?

- Write about your impressions of Dr Mortimer and his story.
- Evaluate how the writer has created these impressions.
- Support your opinions with quotations from the text.

Write your answer on a separate piece of paper. [20]

Writing

3 You have been asked to write a creative piece for your school magazine or website.

Either

Write a description suggested by this picture.

Or

Write the opening of a story set in a wild, isolated place. Write on a separate piece of paper.

[24 marks for content and organization; 16 marks for technical accuracy; total 40]

Reading

Source A

Source A is an article from *The Times* newspaper, 15 May 1914.

The Cult of Little Dogs: An Irresistible Appeal by Our Correspondent

There is a certain melancholy attaching to shows of toy dogs. Not that toy dogs are themselves melancholy – indeed it is their sprightly unconsciousness of their degeneracy that most confounds the moralist – but that they suggest melancholy reflections. The Englishman, perhaps alone among the peoples of the world, understands fully the great soul of the dog; he feels his own kinship with it – as he did in former days with that of the fighting cock; and he has accepted with pride the bull-dog as the type of his national qualities. It is not, then, without misgiving that he watches the process of minimizing the dog, or a large proportion of him, in an eager competition to crib, cabin, and confine the great soul in the smallest possible body, until, in place of the dignified friend and ally of man, there will be left nothing but, at worst, a pampered toy; at best, a pathetic creature, all eyes and nerves, whose insurgent soul frets the puny body to decay.

Where will the process end? Already we have held up to the admiration of the world a Pomeranian puppy which, at the age of three months, can be comfortably bestowed in a tumbler, over the edge of which his picture shows him looking, with shy eyes and apprehensively, at the disproportionate scheme of things. Presently, maybe, we shall have a childhood's dream realized and really see the little dog of the fairy-story who was hidden in a walnut and, when the shell was cracked, leapt forth barking and wagging his tail to the delight of all the noble company.

Source B

Source B is a letter to a newspaper

14 Raglan Terrace
Tillingbourne

12 July 2015

Dear Editor,

I was saddened to read yet more negative coverage of so-called 'purse pets' in your paper. What is it about celebrities who own small dogs that inspires such vitriol?

I know some people think celebrities use their pets as fashion accessories – and this is questionable. But it is not, as you suggest, cruel. We like to think of our four-legged friends as free and independent spirits – equal companions on life's journey – but they're not. Dogs depend on us for food, shelter and love.

This is the case whether they are tiny little chihuahuas that can fit in a Versace handbag or massive Afghans – or even breeds like pit bulls. Now, I don't want to be accused of the kind of prejudice I'm criticizing others for, but let's just reflect for a moment. Which is crueller? Pampering your pet with little treats or training her to fight and kill other dogs?

Of course, I'm not saying that all Staffie owners do this. But you should not imply that everyone who owns a little dog is cruel. Taking dogs shopping for little doggy clothes is a bit silly, but it does not damage their health or well-being. On the contrary, it shows that the owners care about their pets. In fact, many celebrity dog owners go further to show they care. Actress Kristin Chenoweth has even founded a charity, named after her tiny Maltese, to help homeless pets.

These dogs are beautiful, loyal and lovable. I know. I've got one. I don't keep her in my handbag or take her to canine boutiques, but I love and cherish her – and I wouldn't be without her. I don't think you'd write an article castigating me for those feelings, so why aim your vitriol at Paris Hilton and Mariah Carey, whose only crime is to love their pets?

Yours faithfully

Joanna P. Hanlon

1 Refer only to Source A. How does the writer use language to express his feelings about small dogs?

_____

_____

_____

_____

_____

_____

_____ [12]

2 Refer to both Source A and Source B.

Compare how the two writers convey different attitudes to small dogs.

In your answer you should:
* compare their attitudes
* compare the methods they use to convey their attitudes
* support your ideas with quotations from both texts.

Write your answer on a separate piece of paper. [16]

Writing

3 'A dog is for life, not just for Christmas.'

Write an article for a magazine aimed at people your own age, inspired by this quotation, in which you give your views about dogs, dog owners, or both.

Write on a separate piece of paper.

[24 marks for content and organization, 16 marks for technical accuracy. Total 40]

Context

You must be able to:

- Understand the social, historical and cultural context of a Shakespeare play
- Use this understanding to evaluate the play.

History

- The historical **context** in which Shakespeare lived was very different from ours.
- He lived from 1564 to 1616 and started writing during the reign of Queen Elizabeth I, a time of great prosperity for England, when explorers were discovering and colonizing new lands across the world. Such adventures inspired *The Tempest.*
- There was also a great flowering of literature and theatre, inspired by the Renaissance in Italy.
- In 1603 Elizabeth I was succeeded by King James I, who was already King of Scotland. He became patron of Shakespeare's theatre company and *Macbeth* was written in his honour.

Religion

- England was an overwhelmingly Christian country. The official church was the Church of England, but many people were still Roman Catholics, while others (like Puritans) had stricter Protestant beliefs.
- Most people believed that after death God would judge them and decide whether they should spend eternity in Heaven or Hell. The idea of Hell is ever-present in *Macbeth.*
- The general attitude to non-Christians is reflected in the way other characters treat Shylock in *The Merchant of Venice*, although some would say that Shakespeare's writing causes the audience to question their assumptions.
- Many people also believed in astrology. The tension between the popular belief that everything is mapped out in the stars and the Christian belief in free will is present in many plays. We see this in *Romeo and Juliet.* Astrology is also prominent in *Julius Caesar*.

> **Key Point**
>
> Elizabethans and Jacobeans would have recognized the many biblical references found in Shakespeare.

Morality

- Society's moral and ethical standards were rooted in Christian teaching and the Ten Commandments.
- Most people shared similar ideas about sexual **morality**. Chastity, especially among women, was much more highly prized than in today's society and marriage was for life. This idea is central to *Much Ado About Nothing* and *Romeo and Juliet*.

Social Order

- Many people believed that the **social order**, with the King or Queen at the top, was derived from God and should not be tampered with.
- King James believed in 'the **divine right** of kings'.
  - This is a major theme in *Macbeth*.
  - The rights and wrongs of opposing rulers are also a theme of *Julius Caesar* and *The Tempest*.
- The **authority** of parents over children might also be seen as sacred, although this authority is challenged in *Romeo and Juliet*.

Society

- Although there was a parliament, England was not democratic in the modern sense.
- Political power centred on the **court**, around the Queen or King. Here, aristocrats competed for the monarch's favour.
- There was a growing middle class. Shakespeare was the son of a well-off glover from Stratford-upon-Avon. He benefited from a good education at the local grammar school. In these schools boys studied ancient history and Latin literature, the source of *Julius Caesar*.
- Most people, however, were illiterate. Many worked on the land, although cities were expanding. London's thriving port attracted merchants and travellers from all over the world.
- Women were usually dependent on their husbands or fathers, so making the right marriage was important. However, there were examples of rich and powerful women.
  - Portia in *The Merchant of Venice* has inherited her wealth from her father but she still cannot choose her own husband.
- Many of Shakespeare's female characters, like Beatrice in *Much Ado About Nothing*, show themselves to be equal to men. However, both Portia, in disguising herself as a man, and Lady Macbeth, in her desire to be 'unsexed', are conscious of taking on a 'man's role'.

> **Key Point**
>
> It is important to understand the differences between Shakespeare's society and ours.

> **Quick Test**
>
> True or False?
> 1. *Macbeth* was written for Queen Elizabeth.
> 2. Astrology is a Christian belief.
> 3. Divorce was common in Shakespeare's time.
> 4. James I believed that his authority came from God.

> **Key Words**
>
> context
> morality
> social order
> divine right
> authority
> court

Themes

You must be able to:

- Identify themes in a Shakespeare play
- Write about how Shakespeare presents themes.

Themes and Ideas

- A **theme** is part of the subject matter of a text – a concern that runs through the play.
- Shakespeare's plays are full of ideas about relationships, morality and society.
- Your exam question could focus on themes and ideas:
  - Write about how Shakespeare presents ideas about kingship in *Macbeth.*
  - Write about how Shakespeare explores ideas about love in *Romeo and Juliet.*

Identifying Themes

- Throughout his career, Shakespeare would return to the same themes. Here are some themes that occur frequently in his plays:

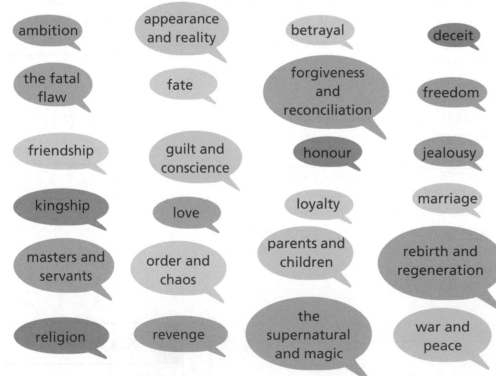

ambition

appearance and reality

betrayal

deceit

the fatal flaw

fate

forgiveness and reconciliation

freedom

friendship

guilt and conscience

honour

jealousy

kingship

love

loyalty

marriage

masters and servants

order and chaos

parents and children

rebirth and regeneration

religion

revenge

the supernatural and magic

war and peace

- You may think of more themes. In over 30 plays Shakespeare looked at almost every aspect of human life.
- Write down some themes that occur in the play you have studied. Try to find at least five. Here are some to get you started:
  - *Macbeth* – marriage…
  - *Much Ado About Nothing* – misunderstandings…

- *The Merchant of Venice* – the outsider...
- *The Tempest* – forgiveness...
- *Romeo and Juliet* – betrayal...
- *Julius Caesar* – ambition...
- Now write a sentence or two about each theme:

> *Ambition is an important theme in 'Julius Caesar' because Caesar is killed when he achieves his ambition to rule Rome alone. The conspirators are also ambitious and their ambitions also destroy them.*
>
> *Forgiveness and reconciliation are central to 'The Tempest'. Prospero has his enemies at his mercy but chooses not to have his revenge on them.*

How Themes are Presented

- Shakespeare's plays have been interpreted in many different ways over the past 400 years. You must come to your own conclusions about his themes by considering the evidence.
- Think about the **plot** – what happens in the play:
  - Macbeth's murder of Duncan brings together the themes of ambition and kingship.
  - The theme of friendship comes to the fore in *Much Ado About Nothing* when Beatrice asks Benedick to kill his friend Claudio because of how he has treated Hero.
- Theatre is a visual medium. Shakespeare presents powerful **images**:
  - The appearance of Banquo's ghost in *Macbeth* speaks volumes about betrayal and guilt.
  - Juliet's appearance on a balcony above Romeo demonstrates the kind of love that he has for her.

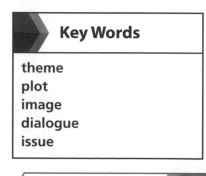

- **Dialogue** can give us insight into themes by presenting more than one point of view:
  - The trial scene in *The Merchant of Venice* gives us both Shylock's and Antonio's views about business ethics.
  - In *Julius Caesar* idealist Brutus and pragmatist Cassius debate the rights and wrongs of their actions. We might side with one or the other, or feel that there is a middle way.
- Characters can raise themes and **issues** when they speak directly to the audience in a soliloquy or aside. When they do this they reveal what they really think:
  - Macbeth shares his doubts about killing Duncan. His soliloquies draw us into a consideration of the themes of kingship, loyalty and ambition.
  - In *The Tempest* Prospero tells us he intends to give up his 'rough magic', making us think about power and old age.

Key Point

Shakespeare does not tell us what he thinks or what we should think. There are more questions than answers.

Quick Test

Give a single word defined by the following:
1. A speech made to the audience.
2. Speech between two or more people.
3. What happens in the play.
4. A concern that runs through the play.

Key Words

theme
plot
image
dialogue
issue

Characters

You must be able to:

- Write about how Shakespeare presents characters.

Characters

- Shakespeare is known for his huge range of characters and his understanding of human psychology.
- Your exam question might focus on a character, for example:
  - Write about how Shakespeare presents Brutus as an idealist.
  - Write about how far you think Shakespeare presents Shylock as a victim.
- You will get an extract from the play as a starting point. Look at what this reveals about the character before considering what else you know about him/her and how s/he develops in the rest of the play.
- When revising, think about each character's:
  - background
  - personality
  - relationships
  - **motivation**
  - function in the plot.
- Identify the main characters in your play and draw up a chart like the (partially completed) one below:

Key Point

When looking at characters, consider their historical and social context.

Character	Background	Personality	Relationships	Motivation	Function
Romeo	The son of the Montagues			Wants to be with Juliet whatever the cost	
Juliet		Innocent but very determined			
Capulet			Loves his family but expects obedience		
Nurse		Chatty, bawdy, devoted, pragmatic			Juliet's confidante – but advises her to forget Romeo

- The main characters all find themselves in different situations by the end of the play. How did they get there and how did their experiences change them?
- Try tracing your characters' development through events that have influenced them. Here is an example for Macbeth.

What happens?	What effect does it have?
He meets the witches.	He starts to think about his future and possibly becoming king.

He kills Duncan.	He becomes king. He has power but fears losing it and turns against Banquo.
He sees Banquo's ghost.	He feels guilty and acts strangely.
He visits the witches.	He fears losing his crown, which makes him more ruthless.
Malcolm invades Scotland.	Thinking he is invincible, he becomes defiant and brave.

How Characters are Presented

What They Say

- A **soliloquy** is a speech to the audience, usually with no other characters on stage. Soliloquies let us into characters' thought processes, revealing a lot about their character and motivation:
  - Juliet shows her excitement and impatience when waiting for the Nurse to return from seeing Romeo.
- Sometimes characters comment briefly on what others are saying and doing in an **aside**. We can assume they mean what they say.
- Characters do not always tell the truth. All Shakespeare plays include people who lie to others.
- We do not, however, have to guess who is lying. It is clear when someone cannot be trusted:
  - Lady Macbeth tells Macbeth to 'look like the innocent flower / But be the serpent under't'.

What Others Say

- We learn about characters through what others say to and about them.
- Sometimes we get a consensus of opinion:
  - Macbeth changes from being universally praised for his bravery and loyalty to being hated and feared as a 'devil' and 'fiend'.
- A difference of opinion can give us something to think about:
  - The violent Tybalt in *Romeo and Juliet* is a favourite of both Lady Capulet and the Nurse. This tells us about both his character and theirs.
- Always be aware of who the speaker is:
  - Antony's description of Brutus, in *Julius Caesar*, as 'the noblest Roman of them all' carries more weight because of their enmity.

How They Act and React

- We learn about characters by their actions:
  - When Bassanio chooses the lead casket in *The Merchant of Venice* we know he is genuine.
- Their reactions also reveal a lot:
  - Benedick's reaction to Beatrice's command to 'kill Claudio' reveals his growing feelings for her, and tells us about his sense of honour.

> **Key Point**
>
> When Shakespeare wants us to know what characters are really thinking and feeling, they speak to the audience.

> **Quick Test**
>
> True or False?
> 1. Everyone tells the truth.
> 2. Characters never address the audience.
> 3. Characters can change.
> 4. We can get differing views of a character.

> **Key Words**
>
> motivation
> soliloquy
> aside

Language and Structure

You must be able to:

- Analyse Shakespeare's use of language and structure
- Use relevant terminology.

Verse and Prose

- Shakespeare wrote in a mixture of **verse** and **prose**. Most of his verse is in **iambic pentameter**. 'Pentameter' means there are five stressed syllables on every line. 'Iambic' refers to the stress falling on every second syllable:

  O, **she** doth **teach** the **torch**es **to** shine **bright**.

- It is often said that the iambic pentameter follows the natural rhythms of speech and that it resembles a heartbeat.
- Sometimes Shakespeare varies the **metre** to emphasize certain words: for example, stressing the first syllable in a line or adding an extra syllable. He might create a pause (known as a **caesura**) in the middle of the line.
- **Rhyming couplets** might end a scene or emphasize an important thought.
- Other metres are occasionally used in Shakespeare, for example in songs.
- Verse tends to be used for higher-status characters when discussing serious things. However, much of the banter in *Much Ado About Nothing* is in prose. Characters such as servants usually speak in prose, but there are exceptions, as in Caliban's description of the island.

Structure

- Shakespeare's plays are divided into five acts. The first introduces the characters and their concerns. Then something happens that changes the characters' lives. In the third act things become more complicated. The fourth act tends to be about the complications being sorted out. The final act brings a resolution and the play ends with the restoration of order.
- When focusing on an extract think about which part of the play it comes from and how it fits into the play as a whole.
- Think about how Shakespeare uses contrasting scenes. He sometimes uses comic scenes to release tension before building to a tragic climax: for example, the 'porter scene' in *Macbeth*.

> ### Key Point
>
> You can tell verse from prose just by looking at it. Verse has definite line endings and a rhythm, often in a regular pattern or metre.

Imagery

- Shakespeare's imagery tells us about characters, creates mood and underlines key themes. His techniques include simile, metaphor and personification.

- Sometimes characters use **extended metaphors** or **conceits**. Romeo and Juliet use the **sonnet** form to develop the idea of Romeo being a pilgrim and Juliet a saint.
- Look for patterns of imagery in your play. Animal imagery, much of it connected to the Bible, runs through *The Merchant of Venice*:

> Why he hath made the ewe bleat for the lamb.

Rhetorical Language

- Rhetorical questions are common when characters are wondering what to do:

> I have railed so long against marriage, but doth not the appetite alter?

- Repetition emphasizes important ideas or feelings:

> Tomorrow and tomorrow and tomorrow.

- The 'rule of three' is used by characters trying to convince others:

> Friends, Romans, countrymen, lend me your ears.

- Shakespeare uses rhetorical techniques in situations where they might be used in life, for example in the trial scene in *The Merchant of Venice*.

Playing with Words

- Elizabethans loved experimenting with words. Shakespeare shows this in characters like Romeo, who uses **oxymoron** to express his confusion:

> Feather of lead, bright smoke, cold fire, sick health.

- Romeo also uses puns (double meanings), as do Beatrice and Benedick when they pit their wits against each other.
- Double meanings are often used to make sexual innuendoes.
- Shakespeare also uses techniques such as alliteration and assonance to create feelings and mood:

> Full fathom five thy father lies.

> ### Key Point
>
> Whatever the focus of the question, you must write about Shakespeare's language in your answer.

> ### Key Words
>
> verse
> prose
> iambic pentameter
> metre
> caesura
> rhyming couplet
> extended metaphor
> conceit
> sonnet
> oxymoron

> ### Quick Test
>
> Of what are the following examples?
> 1. What, must I hold a candle to my shames?
> 2. Pure impiety and impious purity.
> 3. O mighty Caesar! Dost thou lie so low?
> 4. Hence will I to my ghostly sire's close cell,
>   His help to crave and my dear hap to tell.

Reading

Source A

An Extract from the Journal of Dorothy Wordsworth

Thursday 15 April 1802

It was a threatening, misty morning, but mild. We set off after dinner from Eusemere. Mrs Clarkson went a short way with us, but turned back. The wind was furious and we thought we must have returned. We first rested in the large boat-house, then under a furze bush opposite Mr Clarkson's. Saw the plough going into the field. The wind seized our breath. The lake was rough. There was a boat by itself floating in the middle of the bay below Water Millock. We rested again in the Water Millock Lane. The hawthornes are black and green, the birches here and there greenish, but there is yet more of purple to be seen on the twigs. We got over into a field to avoid some cows – people working. A few primroses by the roadside – woodsorrel flower, the anemone, scentless violets, strawberries, and that starry yellow flower which Mrs C. calls pile wort. When we were in the woods beyond Gowbarrow Park we saw a few daffodils close to the water-side. We fancied that the lake had floated the seeds ashore, and that the little colony had so sprung up. But as we went along there were more and yet more; and at last, under the boughs of the trees, we saw that there was a long belt of them along the shore, about the breadth of a country turnpike road. I never saw daffodils so beautiful. They grew among the mossy stones about and about them; some rested their heads upon those stones as on a pillow for weariness; and the rest tossed and reeled and danced, and seemed as if they verily laughed with the wind that blew upon them over the lake; they looked so gay, ever glancing, ever changing.

Source B

Blog Entry

Betsy's Blog, 2nd June

Yesterday was a complete washout. First, it was a two-hour trip in the rickety school minibus squashed in with rucksacks, suitcases and sweaty bodies.

We made it – just – and were decanted from ancient minibus into even more ancient, more rickety and smellier youth hostel. Six in a room! It's like the workhouse in Dickens. We were barely given time to unpack – although time enough to notice that Anoushka O'Reilly had brought six pairs of high-heeled shoes and eight towels – before the Camp Commandant, alias Miss Frobisher, marched in with her whistle round her neck.

'Right, girls! Gentle walk round the lake before lunch!' Gentle! It was like one of those forced marches they do in boot camps. Hours of wading through mud and getting soaked to our skins. As for the wonderful scenery we were promised. What scenery? We could barely see six inches in front of our faces through the driving rain.

Thankfully, today's been a huge improvement – they took us to an assault course thing, swinging on ropes and stuff, which is a lot better than boring walking. And there was actually a shop and a café – so I was able to replace my lost energy with a massive dose of CAKE. So now I'm feeling maybe the country's not so bad – as long as we don't have to stay much longer.

1 Refer only to Source A.

How does the writer use language to express the feelings inspired by her walk? [12]

_____

_____

_____

_____

_____

_____

_____

_____

_____

_____

_____

_____

2 Refer to both Source A and Source B.

Compare how the two writers convey different attitudes to the countryside.

In your answer you should:

- compare their attitudes
- compare the methods they use to convey their attitudes
- support your ideas with quotations from both texts.

Write your answer on a separate piece of paper. [16]

Writing

3 'School trips are a waste of time and money.'

Write an article for a magazine aimed at people your own age giving your views on this statement.

Write your answer on a separate piece of paper.

[24 marks for content and organization, 16 marks for technical accuracy; total 40]

Answer the question on the play you have studied.

Write your answer on a separate piece of paper.

 1 *Romeo and Juliet* – Read the extract specified and answer the question below.

In this extract, Juliet is waiting for the Nurse to return.

Act 2 Scene 5

From

JULIET   The clock struck nine when I did send the nurse;

To

              She would be as swift in motion as a ball.

How does Shakespeare present Romeo and Juliet's love in this speech?

Write about:

- the feelings that Juliet expresses in this speech
- how Shakespeare uses language to describe Juliet's feelings.   [30]

2 *Macbeth* – Read the extract specified and answer the question below.

In this extract, Macbeth has just been told by the witches that he will be king.

Act 1 Scene 3

From

MACBETH   Two truths are told

              As happy prologues to the swelling act

              Of the imperial theme.

To

              My thought, whose murder yet is but fantastical,

              Shakes so my single state of man that function

              Is smothered in surmise, and nothing is

              But what is not.

How does Shakespeare present Macbeth's feelings about power and ambition in this speech?

Write about:

- Macbeth's feelings about power and ambition
- how Shakespeare uses language to convey Macbeth's feelings.   [30]

3 *The Tempest* – Read the extract specified and answer the question below.

In this extract, Ariel has just reported to Prospero that he has carried out his orders and caused the shipwreck.

Act 1 Scene 2

From

ARIEL   Is there more toil?

To

PROSPERO   Dost thou forget

            From what a torment I did free thee?

Write about how Shakespeare presents Ariel and Prospero's relationship in this extract.

Write about:

- the relationship Ariel has with Prospero
- how Shakespeare uses language to present this relationship.   [30]

4 *The Merchant of Venice*

Explore how Shakespeare presents Shylock's relationship with Jessica. Refer to the whole of the play. Write about:

- the sort of relationship they have
- the methods Shakespeare uses to present their relationship.   [30]

5 *Julius Caesar*

Explore how Shakespeare presents the attitudes of Brutus and Cassius to Caesar. Refer to the whole of the play. Write about:

- the attitudes Brutus and Cassius have towards Caesar
- the methods Shakespeare uses to present their attitudes.   [30]

6 *Much Ado About Nothing*

To what extent does Shakespeare present Beatrice as an independent woman? Refer to the whole of the play. Write about:

- how far and in what ways you think Beatrice can be described as 'independent'
- the methods Shakespeare uses to present Beatrice.   [30]

Context

You must be able to:

- Understand the social, historical and cultural context of a nineteenth-century novel
- Use this understanding to evaluate the text.

Religion and Morality

- In the nineteenth century, Britain was a Christian country, with many more churchgoers than now; religion was part of the fabric of most people's lives. Ministers of religion feature in *Jane Eyre* and *Pride and Prejudice.*
- People tended to share similar ideas about what was acceptable, particularly sexually. Deviations from the norm, like Lydia eloping with Wickham in *Pride and Prejudice*, are shocking.
- Many novels are concerned with right and wrong. Dr Jekyll wants to separate his 'evil' and 'good' sides. In *A Christmas Carol*, Dickens asks his readers to think about what Christmas and Christianity really mean.

Society

- Britain was a very wealthy country with a worldwide empire. Some people made huge fortunes, giving them as much power as the old aristocrats.
- There was a growing middle class of people who had comfortable homes and money to spend – including on novels.
- However, there was also great poverty, especially in towns and cities. With no welfare state and low wages, many people lived in terrible conditions.
- Social reformers fought against inequality. Dickens's work made people think about social issues.

Gender

- Women did not have a vote (although neither did most men) and their career options were limited. *Pride and Prejudice* is based on the need of middle-class women to find husbands. Jane Eyre has to earn her living as a governess.
- Many writers and thinkers supported women's rights. Mary Shelley's mother, Mary Wollstonecraft, was an early feminist.

Race

- It is unusual to find characters who are not white. Some modern readers are shocked by the attitudes shown to ethnic minorities. They are often seen as wild or savage, like Tonga in *The Sign of Four*, or as exotic and mysterious.

Key Point

The nineteenth century was a time of great change in Britain. Literature reflected this.

Science

- There were many scientific discoveries and advances. Shelley in *Frankenstein* and Stevenson in *The Strange Case of Dr Jekyll and Mr Hyde* use science as a starting point to consider 'what if', as science fiction writers do today. Frankenstein harnesses the power of electricity to create his monster, while Dr Jekyll mixes chemicals to find his formula.
- Sherlock Holmes uses a range of methods to solve his cases. Some of his **deductions** might seem fanciful but Conan Doyle was knowledgeable about forensics and Holmes is ahead of his time in using this new science.
- Many writers took an interest in new ideas about **psychology**. Shelley's work reflects current discussion of 'nature and nurture'. Stevenson explores ideas about behaviour and responsibility.

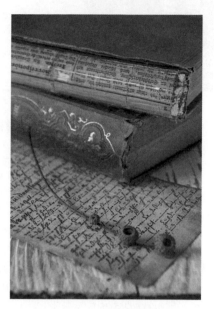

Literature: Movements and Genre

- Novelists were influenced by the Romantic movement, led by poets like Wordsworth. This movement rejected the eighteenth-century taste for order and rationality in favour of an emphasis on personal feelings and nature.
- While Jane Austen belongs more to the eighteenth-century tradition, her characters do reflect the fashion for **sentiment** and poetry.
- Mary Shelley was the wife of the Romantic poet Percy Bysshe Shelley, and her work can be described as Romantic. However, *Frankenstein* is more often described as Gothic, a genre related to Romanticism but more sensational, thrilling its readers with horror and the **supernatural**.
- Brontë, Dickens and Stevenson use elements of the Gothic. *A Christmas Carol* and *The Strange Case of Dr Jekyll and Mr Hyde* both cashed in on the popular taste for ghost stories. *The Strange Case of Dr Jekyll and Mr Hyde* also owes something to the increasingly popular detective story, of which Sir Arthur Conan Doyle was the best-known exponent.

> **Key Point**
>
> Whatever aspect of a text you are looking at, consider its context.

> **Quick Test**
>
> True or False?
> 1. All men had the vote.
> 2. Nobody cared about social injustice.
> 3. Romantic poets thought feelings mattered.
> 4. Britain changed a lot during the nineteenth century.

> **Key Words**
>
> deduction
> psychology
> sentiment
> supernatural

Themes

You must be able to:

- Identify themes in a nineteenth-century novel
- Write about how themes are presented.

Identifying Themes

- Here are some themes you will find in the set books.
- Look at the themes of the books you have not studied and think about whether they are also present in your novel.
- *Pride and Prejudice*
  - Marriage: marrying well is vital for the women. They want to marry for love but they also think in practical terms.
  - Class: the class system seems rigid and there is a lot of snobbery but Elizabeth breaks through it.
- *Frankenstein*
  - The pursuit of knowledge: Frankenstein's intellectual curiosity has terrible results.
  - Nature and nurture: the monster's potential for good is destroyed because of the way he is treated.
- *A Christmas Carol*
  - The spirit of Christmas: the 'spirit of Christmas' is the true message of Christianity.
  - Ignorance and Want: the monstrous children are a warning of what will happen if society does not tackle poverty and improve education.
- *Jane Eyre*
  - Women's roles: Jane does not accept an inferior role. She is independent, determined and outspoken.
  - Integrity: Jane remains honest and true to herself, and is rewarded by true love.
- *Great Expectations*
  - Money and ambition: Pip's money creates more problems than it solves.
  - Friendship: affection and loyalty are not always valued, but true friendship wins through.
- *The Strange Case of Dr Jekyll and Mr Hyde*
  - Good and evil: Jekyll's attempts to separate the good and evil parts of himself are doomed to failure.
  - Secrets: Victorian London is not as respectable as it seems, but is full of dark secrets.
- *The Sign of Four*
  - Crime: what makes people commit crimes?
  - Truth: detective stories are about finding the truth, thus making the world safer and better.

> ### Key Point
>
> Novels often focus on issues of personal morality, but they are also concerned with society as a whole.

How Themes are Presented

- Consider events in the novel:
  - In *Great Expectations* Pip suddenly acquires great wealth. The rest of the novel is about how it changes him.
  - The creation of the monster in *Frankenstein* raises questions about science and people trying to 'play God'.
- Narrators might discuss themes:
  - In *A Christmas Carol* Dickens uses his **authorial voice** to give us his views on social problems.
  - The opening lines of *Pride and Prejudice* tell us straightaway that the novel will be about courtship and marriage.
- Characters can embody themes:
  - Edward Hyde is evil personified.
  - The character of Bertha Rochester in *Jane Eyre* brings together themes of madness and duty.
- Characters discuss themes and **issues**:
  - Elizabeth in *Pride and Prejudice* discusses money, class, love and marriage with her sister Jane, and with Darcy, who has a quite different **perspective** on life.
  - Dr Watson disagrees with Sherlock Holmes about women, Watson being shocked at his friend's misogyny.
- It can be helpful to look for **motifs** in a novel. A motif is an image, idea or situation that recurs through a work, suggesting a theme:
  - Characters in *Frankenstein* find comfort and healing in natural beauty.
  - Fire is a recurring motif in *Jane Eyre*, symbolizing passion as well as moving on the story.
- **Settings** can encapsulate themes:
  - Satis House in *Great Expectations* could symbolize the emptiness of wealth and the gloom of lovelessness.
  - The London of *The Strange Case of Dr Jekyll and Mr Hyde* gives us a sense of the dark side of life.

> ## Key Point
>
> A novel's themes emerge in many ways. Think about the themes of your novel. How do you know they are there?

Quick Test

1. Can a novel have more than one theme?
2. What is a motif?
3. Can a narrator discuss themes and ideas?
4. Can a writer give us differing perspectives on a theme?

> ## Key Words
>
> authorial voice
> issue
> perspective
> motif
> setting

Characters

You must be able to:

- Write about how characters are presented in a nineteenth-century novel.

Characters

- Your exam question might focus on a character.
- It could be about a character's personality:
  - How does Austen present Elizabeth as a strong-minded woman?
- Or attitudes and feelings:
  - Explore how Stevenson conveys Jekyll's feelings about good and evil.
- Or relationships:
  - Write about how Conan Doyle presents Watson and Holmes's relationship.

Protagonists

- When the protagonist is also the narrator, we are invited to share the character's thoughts and feelings.
- Jane Eyre, and Pip in *Great Expectations*, speak to the readers as if they are looking back over their past, sharing feelings and thoughts as well as experiences.
- Pip can be seen as a **naive narrator**, as he does not understand what is going on. Jane Eyre is more perceptive, even though she does not fully understand everything she experiences.
- Both these novels are accounts of growing up. This sort of novel is known by the German word **Bildungsroman**.
- Victor Frankenstein relates most of his own story, but we do get other perspectives. Part of *The Strange Case of Dr Jekyll and Mr Hyde* is narrated by Jekyll, giving us some insight into his mind and a degree of empathy for him.
- Sherlock Holmes is seen through the eyes of Dr Watson. Conan Doyle keeps him distant, to be admired by the readers as he is by Watson.
- Although Elizabeth in *Pride and Prejudice* and Scrooge in *A Christmas Carol* do not tell their own stories, the writers give us access to their thoughts and feelings. However, the third-person narrative allows authors to stand aside and comment on their characters.

> ### Key Point
>
> Questions on character are most likely to be about the protagonists, but you should not neglect other characters.

Other Characters

- You could be asked to focus on other characters as individuals or as a group.
- Look at these in terms of:
  - their relationship to the protagonist: for example, Elizabeth Bennet's relationship with her sisters
  - their **function** in the novel, perhaps as a way of looking at

themes: for example, Shelley's use of the monster to present ideas about nature and nurture.

– their **significance** in terms of plot: for example, Miss Havisham's influence on Pip's life.

How Characters are Presented

What They Say

- Characters who are also narrators have plenty to say about their ideas and feelings.
- Those who are not main narrators sometimes express themselves in letters.
- Characters reveal themselves in conversation with other characters. Sometimes this is by giving an opinion or expressing feelings, as when the monster confronts Frankenstein. Sometimes it is by the way they talk. Mr Collins, in *Pride and Prejudice*, reveals his snobbery by constantly referring to Lady Catherine de Burgh.

What the Narrator Says

- Narrators describe characters' personalities as well as their appearance. In *Great Expectations* Pip, as narrator, describes Estella as 'beautiful and self-possessed'. We see her through his eyes.
- In a third-person narrative, however, we can take comments on characters as being trustworthy and neutral, as when Stevenson describes Mr Utterson as having 'an approved tolerance for others'.
- A narrator might go further and describe a character's thoughts and feelings. Jane Austen often takes us into her characters' heads.

How They Act and React

- As in life, character is best seen through actions. In *Pride and Prejudice* Wickham charms everyone, including Elizabeth and the reader, but when he runs away with Lydia, we can all see him for what he is.
- Reactions are just as important. Darcy's reaction to the elopement of Lydia and Wickham makes Elizabeth and the reader see his true character.

Key Point
Look for what one character says about another and think about what this tells you about both.

Quick Test
1. Without looking at your novel or your notes, write down the names of as many characters as you can in 10 minutes.

Key Words
naive narrator Bildungsroman function significance

Language and Structure

You must be able to:

- Analyse the use of language and structure in a nineteenth-century novel
- Use relevant terminology.

Structure

- *Jane Eyre* starts near the beginning of the protagonist's life and tells her story in chronological order. The novel starts at Gateshead (her aunt's house), moves to Lowood school, then Thornfield Hall, on to Moor House and back again to Thornfield. These places represent five stages in Jane's development.
- Dickens divides Pip's 'expectations' into three stages, coinciding with the three volumes in which it was published: his childhood in Kent, his life in London as a young man, and his 'growing up' from the return of Magwitch to the end.
- In *A Christmas Carol* each chapter (Stave) is devoted to a different spirit. Dickens uses the power of his spirits to introduce 'flashbacks' to Scrooge's past life and 'flash forwards' to show how things might turn out.
- *Pride and Prejudice* uses letters as a form of flashback, filling in details about events in London, for example, which have previously been kept from the reader.
- *Frankenstein* starts with a series of letters from Walton, which lead us to Frankenstein's narrative, which in turn includes the creature's narrative. At the end we return to Walton's letters to bring the story up to date. This use of multiple narratives is quite common in the Gothic tradition and 'distances' the story, making it seem almost mythical.
- This technique is also used in *The Strange Case of Dr Jekyll and Mr Hyde*. The third-person narrative focuses on Mr Utterson, the reader knowing only what he knows, until the events leading up to Jekyll's death are revealed in his own and Dr Lanyon's narratives.
- The story told by Jonathan Small in *The Sign of Four* performs a similar function, fully explaining the mystery to the reader as well as to the narrator, Dr Watson.

> ### Key Point
>
> Although all stories follow more or less the same structure (see page 36), novelists arrange their narratives in very different ways.

The Narrative Voice

- Narrators in nineteenth-century novels always use Standard English. However, narratives can be very different in **tone**. In a first-person narrative this can reflect the character of the protagonist. In other novels, we can still detect a distinctive authorial voice.
- Is your narrator's tone:
  - friendly?
  - **colloquial**?
  - **formal**?
  - **ironic**?
  - **authoritative**?
- As you are reading, do you feel the narrator is talking to you personally?
- In *A Christmas Carol* Dickens tells the story as if we were in a room with him.
- Jane Austen's authorial voice is more detached – amused and ironic.

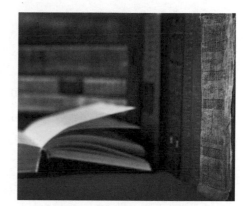

Speech

- Different characters can use language in different ways, adding to our understanding of them.
- They might:
  - use dialect or slang
  - use language in a comic way
  - have oddities or peculiarities of speech
  - use over-formal language
  - use language others might not understand.
- Magwitch's language, in *Great Expectations*, tells us a lot about him instantly. His pronunciation 'pint', 'wittles' places him in a different social class from Pip, and his cursing scares Pip.
- Sherlock Holmes uses technical terms to dazzle his listeners.

Descriptive Language

- Novelists use techniques in the same way as poets do to create mood and atmosphere. You might find that your novelist uses:
  - detail
  - varied sentence structures
  - alliteration, assonance and onomatopoeia
  - imagery
  - symbolism.
- Stevenson uses detail to build a vivid picture of Soho, where Hyde lives.
- In *Jane Eyre*, Brontë's description of the chestnut tree is hugely **symbolic**.

> ### Key Point
>
> The question in the exam will include a short extract from your novel. You should analyse the language used in it in detail.

> ### Quick Test
>
> What is meant by the following terms?
> 1. Dialect
> 2. Colloquial
> 3. Symbol
> 4. Flashback

> ### Key Words
>
> tone
> colloquial
> formal
> ironic
> authoritative
> symbolic

Answer the question on the play you have studied.

Write your answer on a separate piece of paper.

1 *Julius Caesar* – Read the extract specified and answer the question below.

In this extract, Cassius is trying to persuade Brutus to join him in conspiring against Caesar.

Act 1 Scene 2

From

CASSIUS	Ye gods, it doth amaze me
	A man of such a feeble temper should
	So get the start of the majestic world
	And bear the palm alone.

To

	Brutus and Caesar: what should be in that 'Caesar'?
	Why should that name be sounded more than yours?

Explore how Shakespeare presents the attitude of Cassius to Caesar in this extract.

Write about:

- the attitudes and feelings shown in this extract
- how Shakespeare uses language to present them. [30]

2 *Much Ado About Nothing* – Read the extract specified and answer the question below.

In this extract, the marriage between Hero and Claudio has just been arranged.

Act 2 Scene 1

From

BEATRICE	Good Lord, for alliance! Thus goes everyone to the world but I, and I am sunburnt. I may sit in a corner and cry, 'Heigh-ho for a husband!'

To

BEATRICE	No, sure, my lord, my mother cried. But then there was a star danced, and under that was I born.

How does Shakespeare present Beatrice in this extract?

Write about:

- the ideas and feelings expressed by Beatrice
- how Shakespeare uses language to present her in this extract. [30]

3 *The Merchant of Venice* – Read the extract specified and answer the question below.

In this extract, Tubal has brought Shylock news about his daughter, who has eloped with Lorenzo.

Act 3 Scene 1

From

TUBAL   Your daughter spent in Genoa, as I heard, one night fourscore ducats.

To

SHYLOCK Out upon her! Thou torturest me, Tubal. It was my turquoise; I had it of Leah when I was a bachelor. I would not have given it for a wilderness of monkeys.

Explore how Shakespeare presents Shylock's relationship with Jessica in this extract.

Write about:

- the nature of the relationship presented in this extract
- how he uses language to present the relationship.   [30]

4 *Romeo and Juliet*

Explore how Shakespeare presents the growing love of Romeo and Juliet. Write about the whole of the play. Write about:

- how their love develops during the play.
- the methods Shakespeare uses to present their love.   [30]

5 *Macbeth*

How does Shakespeare present Macbeth's feelings about power and ambition? Write about the whole of the play. Write about:

- Macbeth's feelings about power and ambition
- the methods Shakespeare uses to present Macbeth's feelings about power and ambition.   [30]

6 *The Tempest*

Write about how Shakespeare presents Ariel as a spirit and a slave. Write about the whole of the play. Write about:

- Ariel's relationship with Prospero and his position as a spirit and a slave
- the methods Shakespeare uses to present him as a spirit and a slave.   [30]

Answer the question on the novel you have studied.

 1 Robert Louis Stevenson: *The Strange Case of Dr Jekyll and Mr Hyde*

> **Read Chapter 4**
>
> *From*
>
> When they had come within speech (which was just under the maid's eyes) the older man bowed and accosted the other with a very pretty manner of politeness.
>
> *To*
>
> And next moment, with ape-like fury, he was trampling his victim under foot and hailing down a storm of blows, under which the bones were audibly shattered and the body jumped upon the roadway.

In this extract, the murder of Sir Danvers Carew has been witnessed by a maid.

In this extract, how does Stevenson convey a sense of horror?

Write about:

- the sense of horror conveyed in the extract
- how he uses language, structure and form to convey a sense of horror in the extract. [30]

2 Charles Dickens: *A Christmas Carol*

> **Read Stave (Chapter) 1**
>
> *From*
>
> 'Are there no prisons?' asked Scrooge.
>
> *To*
>
> 'It's not my business', Scrooge returned. 'It's enough for a man to understand his own business, and not to interfere with other people's. Mine occupies me constantly. Good afternoon, gentlemen!'

In this extract, two gentlemen have just asked Scrooge to make a contribution to charity to help the poor.

In this extract how does Dickens present Scrooge's attitude to other people? Write about:

- Scrooge's attitude in the extract
- how Dickens uses language, structure and form to present Scrooge's attitude in the extract. [30]

3 Jane Austen: *Pride and Prejudice*

> **Read Chapter 3**
>
> *From*
>
> Elizabeth Bennet had been obliged, by the scarcity of gentlemen, to sit down for two dances; and during part of that time, Mr Darcy had been standing near enough for her to overhear a conversation between him and Mr Bingley, who came from the dance for a few minutes to press his friend to join it.
>
> *To*
>
> 'You had better return to your partner and enjoy her smiles, for you are wasting your time with me'.

In this extract, Mr Darcy and his friend Mr Bingley are attending a ball at Meryton, where they meet the Bennet family.

In this extract, how does Austen present Mr Darcy's 'pride'?

Write about:

- the impression we get of Mr Darcy in the extract
- how Austen uses language, form and structure to present his pride in the extract.   [30]

4 Charles Dickens: *Great Expectations*

Read Chapter 21

From

'So you were never in London before?' said Mr Wemmick to me.

To

We had got to the top of Holborn Hill before I knew that it was merely a mechanical appearance, and that he was not smiling at all.

In this extract, Pip has just arrived in London.

In this extract, how does Dickens present Pip's arrival in London?

Write about:

- the impressions we get of London and Pip's feelings about it in the extract
- how Dickens uses language, form and structure to present Pip's arrival in London in the extract.   [30]

5 Mary Shelley: *Frankenstein*

How does Shelley present Frankenstein's feelings about his creation?

Write about the whole novel. Write about:

- Frankenstein's feelings about the monster
- the methods Shelley uses to present Frankenstein's feelings about the monster.   [30]

6 Sir Arthur Conan Doyle: *The Sign of Four*

Write about how Conan Doyle presents Sherlock Holmes as a great detective.

Write about the whole novel. Write about:

- what makes Holmes a great detective
- the methods Conan Doyle uses to present Holmes in the novel as a whole.   [30]

7 Charlotte Brontë: *Jane Eyre*

Write about how Brontë presents Jane's feelings for Mr Rochester.

Write about the whole novel. Write about:

- Jane's changing feelings about Rochester
- the methods Brontë uses to convey Jane's feelings towards him.   [30]

Context

You must be able to:

- Understand the social, historical and cultural context of a modern text
- Use this understanding to evaluate the text.

Context

- You need to consider the social and historical context of your text. Think about the kind of society presented in the text.
- Think about 'cultural context', including genre and intended audience.

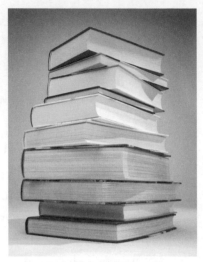

Time

- British society has changed a lot over the last 100 years. The set texts were written over a period of more than 60 years.
- The Britain portrayed in them ranges from the hypocritical, class-conscious world of 1912 shown in *An Inspector Calls* to the violent, morally confused twenty-first-century world shown in *Pigeon English* and *DNA*.
- *An Inspector Calls*, written in 1945, looks back on an earlier **period**. This is 1912 seen from the perspective of a country that had experienced two world wars and in which many were looking forward a new, fairer society. Someone writing in 1912 would have seen things differently.
- Other texts set in earlier periods include:
  - *Blood Brothers* (written 1983, set 1950s–1970s)
  - *The History Boys* (written 2004, set 1980s)
  - *Anita and Me* (written 1996, set 1960/1970s).

  If you have studied one of these texts, think about why the writer has chosen the period and how his or her view of it is coloured by the events, ideas and attitudes of later years.
- *Animal Farm* (1945) and *Lord of the Flies* (1954) are not set at a particular time but they are the product of their time. *Animal Farm* is based on the Russian Revolution of 1917 and written at a time of great concern about totalitarianism. *Lord of the Flies* picks up on post-war concerns about what is meant by civilization.
- Other texts – from *A Taste of Honey* (1956) to *Pigeon English* (2011) – reflect the world at the time they were written.

> ### Key Point
>
> Think about how your text reflects the concerns, attitudes and assumptions of the time and how these might differ from those of today.

Place

- The place where a text is set can help to give it a distinctive tone and atmosphere.
- Regional differences come out most strongly in the way characters speak:
  - Meera Syal presents the way people from a Black Country village speak by writing their speech phonetically, imitating the way they pronounce words.

- Helen in *A Taste of Honey* uses dialect expressions, such as 'I'd sooner be put on't street', reflecting the play's Lancashire setting.
- Some texts establish a sense of place by referring to specific **locations**:
  - *Blood Brothers* references places in and around Liverpool. The family's move from the city to a 'new town' marks the end of Act 1.
- Factors such as whether the setting is urban or rural, in the inner city or the suburbs, can be more important than the exact location:
  - *An Inspector Calls* takes place in a 'large suburban house' in a fictional industrial city.
- Some texts are set within a particular community or communities:
  - *Anita and Me* is about two very different communities co-existing: the village of Tollington and Meena's 'family' of Indians, who visit her house.

Cultural Context

- If you are studying a play, think about where and for whom it was/is performed.
  - *Blood Brothers* is a musical. In **musical theatre** characters use songs to express emotion and to move the story on.
  - *DNA* was written to be performed by and for young people.
- With prose, too, genre can be important:
  - *Never Let Me Go* is sometimes categorized as science fiction. It is about what could happen as a result of science.
  - Golding has called *Lord of the Flies* a **fable**, and *Animal Farm* is subtitled 'A fairy story'. What are the implications of these descriptions?

> **Key Point**
>
> Think about whether the place where your text is set makes a difference and, if so, how.

> **Quick Test**
>
> True or False?
> 1. A text's setting can determine how characters speak.
> 2. Characters in musicals express emotion by singing.
> 3. Science fiction is about things that have really happened.
> 4. Some texts are set in imaginary places.

> **Key Words**
>
> period
> location
> musical theatre
> fable

Themes

You must be able to:

- Identify themes in a modern text
- Write about how themes are presented.

Identifying Themes

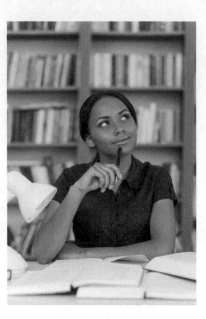

- Think about:
  - what the writer is saying
  - what the text makes you think about.
- Try answering, in one sentence, the question, 'What is the text about?'

Lord of the Flies is about a group of boys stranded on an island.

- Ask yourself why the writer might want us to read about this situation and what it makes us think about. You are now moving from the situation to the themes.
- Try to come up with some new answers to the question. 'What is the text about?' You could make a spider **diagram** or a list:

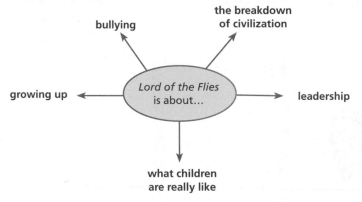

- Some themes crop up again and again in the set texts. Here are some questions that might get you thinking about themes and ideas in your text:

- Write down as many questions as you can that might come out of your text. Then try to find more than one answer to each, backing up your answer with evidence from the text.

> ## Key Point
>
> Themes in modern texts reflect current concerns, as well as issues that have always interested writers.

How Themes are Presented in Novels and Short Stories

Modern **prose** presents themes:

- through events:
  - In *Animal Farm*, a pig walks on its hind legs, showing that the pigs have become like the humans they replaced.
- through the narrator:
  - In *Anita and Me*, Meena draws lessons from her experiences about culture, friendship and growing up.
- through characters:
  - Steve in 'My Polish Teacher's Tie' represents identity and new possibilities to Carla.
- through what characters say:
  - In *Lord of the Flies*, the boys discuss issues like responsibility and survival.
- through motifs and symbols:
  - In 'The Odour of Chrysanthemums', the symbolism of the chrysanthemums is **ambiguous**. They represent unhappiness and death to Elizabeth, but she also associates them with happy memories.

How Themes are Presented in Plays

- The stage is a visual **medium**. It is about showing, not telling. Look in the stage directions for striking **images** which encapsulate themes:
  - The image of Mickey and Edward lying dead at the end of *Blood Brothers* brings together many of the play's themes.
  Remember, though, that play **scripts** can be interpreted differently by different **directors**, designers and actors. The images of one production may not be the same as those of another.
- Characters sometimes speak directly to the audience, bringing our attention to themes and issues:
  - In *The History Boys*, Scripps occasionally steps out of the action to reflect on the meaning of the boys' experiences.
- Mostly, we encounter themes and ideas through dialogue. There can be as many different points of view about an issue as there are characters on stage:
  - In *DNA* different ideas about guilt and honesty emerge as the characters discuss their actions.
- Some writers present us with several viewpoints and leave us to make up our own minds. Others give their preferred point of view to a character who is presented as being wiser or more trustworthy than others:
  - Inspector Goole in *An Inspector Calls* stands apart from the action, and his **interpretation** of what has happened can be seen as that of the writer.

> **Key Point**
>
> Our interpretation of themes and ideas can depend as much on our background and opinions as on those of the writer.

> **Key Words**
>
> diagram
> prose
> ambiguous
> medium
> image
> script
> director
> interpretation

Quick Test

In the theatre, which of the following influence how themes are presented?
1. The writer.
2. The director.
3. The actors.
4. The designer.

Characters

You must be able to:

- Write about how characters are presented in a modern text.

Prose: First-Person Narratives

- *Never Let Me Go*, *Anita and Me* and *Pigeon English* are first-person narratives, as are most of the stories in *Telling Tales*.
- Kathy in *Never Let Me Go* and Meena in *Anita and Me* write as adults looking back on their past. Harrison in *Pigeon English* tells us the story as it happens, like a diary.
- We might expect the adult narrators to have a greater understanding of their stories. Kathy (like the narrator in 'A Family Supper') seems quite detached and thoughtful. She writes as if she is trying to work out the meaning of the things she remembers.
- We can get an idea of what other characters think of the narrators, but this is always filtered through the narrator's perspective:
  - In *Never Let Me Go* Kathy does not always understand how others are responding to her, but the reader can make inferences from what she reports.
- Readers might draw conclusions about narrators which the narrators (and possibly writers) do not foresee:
  - Some readers might think Meena in *Anita and Me* comes across as a snob who looks down on her old friends.
- We might draw our own conclusions, different from those of the narrator, about other characters:
  - The narrator in 'Chemistry' is **naive** and his naivety makes him **unreliable**. At the end his assessment of other characters is called into question.

Prose: Third-Person Narratives

- Although it is a third-person narrative, the action in 'The Darkness Out There' is seen through the eyes of Sandra, so we learn about her thoughts and feelings. Similarly, in 'The Odour of Chrysanthemums' we share Elizabeth's thoughts.
- Golding is an **omniscient** narrator in *Lord of the Flies*. The character we are given most insight into is the protagonist, Ralph, but he also takes us into the minds of other characters.
- In *Lord of the Flies* there is a strong antagonist in Jack. Other characters, like Piggy and Simon, are important because of what they do in the story and because of what they represent.
- The characters in *Animal Farm* are different from conventional characters. Most of them are animals, which fits with the novel being called a 'fairy tale' or 'fable'. Some of them can be identified with real

Key Point

Modern novelists tell us about characters in the same ways as nineteenth-century novelists did.

historical figures, such as Lenin and Trotsky, but they can also be seen as 'types': for example, the honest worker, the spy, the tyrant.

Drama

- Sometimes **playwrights** tell us about characters in stage directions:
  - Arthur Birling in *An Inspector Calls* is described as 'a heavy-looking, rather portentous man in his middle fifties, with fairly easy manners but rather provincial in his speech'.
- Characters can reveal themselves, either directly to the audience or to other characters. Judy in *The Curious Incident of the Dog in the Night-Time* gives her side of things through letters:

> And your father is really patient, but I'm not. I get cross, even though I don't mean to […] and I felt really lonely.

- We learn about characters through dialogue. When Dakin and Scripps converse in *The History Boys* we hear their differing points of view, and we see that they are both intellectually, if not emotionally, mature as they can express themselves well, using sophisticated diction:

> No more the bike's melancholy long withdrawing roar as he dropped you off at the corner, your honour still intact.

Key Point

Always remember when writing about a play, that it is a script to be performed. Actors can interpret characters in different ways.

- What really matters is what characters do:
  - Mrs Johnstone in *Blood Brothers* gives away one of her children. Why? And what are the consequences?

Quick Test

Rearrange the letters to find a useful term:
1. TSGNROAPTOI
2. RRRTNAOA
3. GIDOULEA
4. GATES TIRODENIC

Key Words

naive narrator
unreliable narrator
omniscient narrator
playwright

Language and Structure

You must be able to:

- Analyse the use of language and structure in a modern text
- Use relevant terminology.

Prose

The Narrative Voice

- In *Pigeon English* the narrator appears to be speaking to the reader. Because of his age and background, he does not use Standard English. His use of dialect and slang ('donkey hours', 'hutious') gives a sense of where he lives and where he comes from.
- Some narrators, like Kathy in *Never Let Me Go*, adopt a colloquial tone while using Standard English, as if explaining things to a friend:

> I suppose that might sound odd.

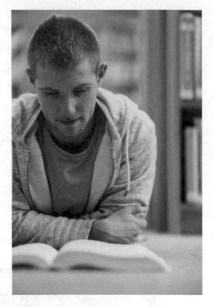

- Others, like the boy in 'Chemistry', write about their lives in a more detached, adult way, also using Standard English.

Speech

- The language characters use adds to our understanding of them and the world they inhabit.
- Most of the boys in *Lord of the Flies* speak in Standard English, but in the rather clipped manner of public schoolboys in the 1950s:

> 'Give him a fourpenny one!'

Piggy is shown to be from a different class:

> 'I got the conch, ain't I Ralph?'

- In *Anita and Me*, the local people use dialect and their **accent** is shown phonetically:

> 'Ay up, Mr K! Havin a bit of a do then?'

The Indian characters use Standard English except when speaking Punjabi.

Structure

- Most of the set texts are written in chronological order, although some of them (*Anita and Me*, *Never Let Me Go*) jump backwards and forwards as one event reminds the narrator of another.
- Think about how the text is divided. Why does the writer decide to start a new chapter at a certain point?

> **Key Point**
>
> In first-person narratives, the language of the narration can reflect the background of the narrator.

- Look for anything different or odd about your text's structure:
  - Some sections of *Pigeon English* start with the pigeon narrating, distinguished from the rest of the text by being in italics.

Drama

Language

- **Dialogue** can reflect where the play is set and also tell us about the characters.
- The class divisions of *Blood Brothers* are shown in the contrast between the way the Johnstone and Lyons families speak:

> EDWARD: Do you…Do you really? Goodness, that's fantastic.

> MICKEY: Come on, bunk under y'fence, y'Ma won't see y'.

- Christopher in *The Curious Incident of the Dog in the Night-Time* speaks in a deliberate, rather impersonal way:

> I remember 20 July 2006. I was 9 years old. It was a Saturday.

Structure

- Most plays are in two **acts**, with an **interval** between them. Because of this, writers usually build up to a **turning point** at the end of Act 1, leaving the audience wanting to know what happens next.
- When *An Inspector Calls* was written, most plays had a three-act structure, so both Act 1 and Act 2 end with turning points.
- *An Inspector Calls* and *A Taste of Honey* have clear act and **scene** divisions. Within each section, action is continuous and happens in one place.
- In other, more recent plays the action flows from one short scene to another, time and place changing frequently.
- Look for anything unusual about your play's structure, for example:
  - At the end of *An Inspector Calls*, it looks as though the play is about to start all over again.
  - In *The History Boys* characters seem to jump out of the 'past' to speak to us and then return seamlessly.

Key Point

When we discuss language in a play we are discussing the language the characters use.

Key Words

accent
dialogue
act
interval
turning point
scene

Quick Test

1. Can a narrator use a colloquial tone and Standard English?
2. In the same play, which is longer, a scene or an act?
3. What would the use of dialect tell us about a character?
4. Are the events in a play or novel always in chronological order?

Answer the question on the novel you have studied.

 1 Mary Shelley: *Frankenstein*

> **Read Chapter 5**
>
> *From*
>
> It was on a dreary night of November that I beheld the accomplishment of my toils.
>
> *To*
>
> His yellow skin scarcely covered the work of muscles and arteries beneath; his hair was of a lustrous black, and flowing; his teeth of a pearly whiteness; but these luxuriances only formed a more horrid contrast with his watery eyes, that seemed almost of the same colour as the dun white sockets in which they were set, his shrivelled complexion and straight black lips.

In this extract, Victor Frankenstein describes seeing the monster he has created.

In this extract, how does Shelley present Frankenstein's feelings about his creation?
Write about:

- Frankenstein's reaction to the monster in this extract
- how Shelley uses language, form and structure to convey Frankenstein's feelings about the monster in this extract.

[30]

2 Sir Arthur Conan Doyle: *The Sign of Four*

> **Read Chapter 6**
>
> *From*
>
> He held down the lamp to the floor, and as he did so I saw for the second time that night a startled, surprised look come over his face.
>
> *To*
>
> 'What then?' I asked.
>
> 'Why, we have got him, that's all', said he.

In this extract, Holmes and Watson are searching Pondicherry House for clues about the murder of Bartholomew Sholto.

In this extract, how does Conan Doyle present Sherlock Holmes as a great detective?
Write about:

- what Sherlock Holmes does and says in this extract
- how Conan Doyle uses language, form and structure to present Holmes as a great detective in this extract.

[30]

3 Charlotte Brontë: *Jane Eyre*

> **Read Chapter 12**
>
> *From*
>
> I was in the mood for being useful, or at least officious, I think, for I now drew near him again.
>
> *To*
>
> He looked at me when I said this; he had hardly turned his eyes in my direction before.

In this extract, Jane meets Mr Rochester for the first time.

In this extract, how does Brontë present Jane's feelings about Mr Rochester?
Write about:

- how Jane describes and reacts to Rochester in this extract
- how Brontë uses language, structure and form to convey Jane's feelings towards Rochester in this extract. [30]

4 Robert Louis Stevenson: *The Strange Case of Dr Jekyll and Mr Hyde*

How does Stevenson convey an atmosphere of mystery and horror?
Write about the whole novel. Write about:

- the atmosphere of mystery and horror in the novel
- the methods Stevenson uses to convey an atmosphere of mystery and horror. [30]

5 Charles Dickens: *A Christmas Carol*

How does Dickens present Scrooge's attitude to other people?
Write about the whole novel. Write about:

- Scrooge's attitude to other people
- how Dickens presents Scrooge's attitude. [30]

6 Jane Austen: *Pride and Prejudice*

How does Austen present Mr Darcy's 'pride'?
Write about the whole novel. Write about:

- to what extent and in what ways Darcy is proud
- the methods Austen uses to present his 'pride'. [30]

7 Charles Dickens: *Great Expectations*

Write about how Dickens presents Pip's journey into adulthood.
Write about the whole novel. Write about:

- the stages in Pip's journey into adulthood
- the methods Dickens uses to present Pip's journey into adulthood. [30]

Answer the question on the text you have studied.

Your answer should be in note form, using bullet points.

1 J. B. Priestley: *An Inspector Calls*

Make notes on the character and significance of Inspector Goole in *An Inspector Calls*.

Write down five statements about the character and give evidence from the text in support of each one.

[10]

2 Willy Russell: *Blood Brothers*

Make notes on the character and significance of Mrs Lyons in *Blood Brothers*.

Write down five statements about the character and give evidence from the text in support of each one.

[10]

3 Alan Bennett: *The History Boys*

Make notes on the character and significance of Dakin in *The History Boys*.

Write down five statements about the character and give evidence from the text in support of each one.

[10]

4 Dennis Kelly: *DNA*

Make notes on the character and significance of Leah in *DNA*.

Write down five statements about the character and give evidence from the text in support of each one.

[10]

5 Simon Stephens: *The Curious Incident of the Dog in the Night-Time*

Make notes on the character and significance of Christopher in *The Curious Incident of the Dog in the Night-Time*.

Write down five statements about the character and give evidence from the text in support of each one.

[10]

6 Shelagh Delaney: *A Taste of Honey*

Make notes on the character and significance of Jo in *A Taste of Honey*.

Write down five statements about the character and give evidence from the text in support of each one.

[10]

7 William Golding: *Lord of the Flies*

Make notes on the character and significance of Simon in *Lord of the Flies*.

Write down five statements about the character and give evidence from the text in support of each one.

[10]

8 AQA Anthology*: Telling Tales*

Make notes on the character and significance of Carla in 'My Polish Teacher's Tie'.

Write down five statements about the character and give evidence from the text in support of each one. [10]

9 George Orwell: *Animal Farm*

Make notes on the character and significance of Boxer in *Animal Farm*.

Write down five statements about the character and give evidence from the text in support of each one. [10]

10 Kazuo Ishiguro: *Never Let Me Go*

Make notes on the character and significance of Tommy in *Never Let Me Go*.

Write down five statements about the character and give evidence from the text in support of each one. [10]

11 Meera Syal: *Anita and Me*

Make notes on the character and significance of Anita in *Anita and Me.*

Write down five statements about the character and give evidence from the text in support of each one. [10]

12 Stephen Kelman: *Pigeon English*

Make notes on the character and significance of Harrison in *Pigeon English.*

Write down five statements about the character and give evidence from the text in support of each one. [10]

Context

You must be able to:

- Understand the social, historical and cultural context of poetry
- Use this understanding in your evaluation of texts.

Time and Place

- Many of the 'Love and Relationships' poems focus on personal memories, and the poets evoke a sense of the time and place they are remembering:
  - Carol Ann Duffy's memories of her mother in 'Before You Were Mine' include specific references that 'place' her mother in terms of time (Marilyn), place (Portobello) and even religion (Mass).
  - Charles Causley freezes his parents in time, with references to their clothes and their picnic (Thermos, HP Sauce bottle), although he ends by teasing the reader with his assertion that the place is made up.
- Some 'Power and Conflict' poems, such as 'Poppies', can also be seen in a personal context, but more often they are about historical events, and some knowledge and understanding of these events can be helpful:
  - 'Exposure' is both personal and historical as it is based around Owen's own experiences in the First World War. His reactions are personal and immediate.
  - 'Remains' is inspired by the memories of a soldier who fought in the recent war in Iraq.
- The attitudes of the poets to their subjects should be seen in the context of their own time:
  - 'The Charge of the Light Brigade', inspired by a newspaper article, reflects popular sentiment at the time by criticizing the orders given to the Brigade but glorifying the soldiers themselves.
- When a poet writes about something in the past, consider both the time when it was written and the time it was written about.
  - Browning's **dramatic monologues** use historical settings to present characters that must have been shocking as well as fascinating to his huge Victorian readership, reflecting an interest in psychology.
  - 'Kamikaze' presents the attitudes of Japanese people in the Second World War to a modern audience.

The Romantic Movement

- Blake, Byron, Shelley and Wordsworth were all part of the Romantic **movement** in literature. An understanding of Romanticism will inform your reading of their poetry.
- In the eighteenth century most English poets admired and imitated Greek and Latin poetry. Intellectuals valued logic and reason above feelings.

> **Key Point**
>
> When comparing poems from the anthology, you must think about similarities and differences between their contexts.

- The Romantics rebelled against this. They used more traditional forms of poetry, such as the **ballad**, using simpler rhythms and rhyme schemes and more everyday language. They sometimes wrote about ordinary people.
- Most of their poetry, whether **lyric** poetry (short poems about feelings) like 'Love's Philosophy' or the lengthy autobiographical 'Prelude', focuses on emotions, which they often associated with nature.
- They could also be political, inspired by events like the French Revolution to write anti-establishment poems like 'London'.
- Later poets continued to be influenced by the Romantics. You can see this in Hardy and Mew, and modern poets like Sheers and Hughes.

Social Issues

- Gender is important in several of the poems:
  - The relationship between the farmer and his bride in Charlotte Mew's poem seems to have more to do with power than love. The traditional roles the man and woman are given create misery for both.
  - To the Duke in 'My Last Duchess', his wife is just a possession.
- Ideas about cultural identity are central to 'Checking Out Me History'. The poet is angry about being given a 'white' version of history when growing up in the British Empire.
- 'London' is concerned with the poverty, disease and inequality of its time.

> **Quick Test**
>
> True or False?
> 1. Romantic poets were not political.
> 2. When a poem is set does not matter.
> 3. Wordsworth is a Romantic poet.
> 4. Lyric poetry is about feelings.

Themes

You must be able to:

- Identify themes in poetry
- Compare how themes are presented.

Themes and Ideas in the Anthology

- The poems in the anthology have been grouped together under two broad themes, 'Love and Relationships' and 'Power and Conflict'. You will have studied one of these 'clusters'.
- Consider what aspect of the main theme the poet is writing about.
- Look for other themes, ideas and issues that might be present.
- Consider the poet's **attitudes** to these themes.
- Connect the poems through their treatment of themes, looking for both similarities and differences.

How Themes are Presented in Poetry

- Because most poems are quite short, they tend not to explore themes and ideas in great depth or detail.
- Poems often focus on an incident or moment in life, perhaps an anecdote or a snapshot of someone's feelings at a certain time.
- Poems that tell a story include 'My Last Duchess', 'The Charge of the Light Brigade' (Power and Conflict), 'Porphyria's Lover' and 'The Farmer's Bride' (Love and Relationships).
- Some poems, like 'The Charge of the Light Brigade', tell a story and then reflect on its meaning. Others, like 'Porphyria's Lover', do not include the poet's thoughts, leaving readers to infer meaning.
- Many poems have no story but tell us directly about the poet's thoughts and feelings. Some poets express strong views and feelings, as in 'Checking Out Me History' and Sonnet 29 'I think of thee!'.
- Others, like 'Neutral Tones', present us with images and experiences, leaving us to infer the poet's attitudes and feelings.
- At times it is impossible to 'work out' what the poet's feelings are, as the poem is **ambiguous**. The poet might not have the answer or might want readers to come up with their own answers.

> **Key Point**
>
> The same poem can mean different things to different people. Your response and interpretation is as valid as anyone else's – and it is your response that the examiner wants to read.

Connections

- In the exam you are required to compare two poems (one named) from the cluster you have studied. Here are some questions you could ask when comparing poems during revision.

Love and Relationships
- What sort of relationship is it?

Lovers   Husband and wife   Parents and children   Other family relationships   Friends

- What else is the poem about?

Time passing Culture and identity Nature Death

Betrayal Hope Possession Power

- What feelings does the **voice** or **persona** in the poem have about the subject of the poem?

Love Jealousy Indifference Disgust

Gratitude Obsession Admiration Anger

What are the feelings of the subject?

Power and Conflict

- What kind of conflict is it?

A battle An argument A war A psychological conflict

- What kind of power is it?

Power over one person Power over many people The power of a government or state

The power of an individual Physical power Mental power

- Or is it about lack of power?
- What else is the poem about?

Loss Death Love Relationships Nature Memory

- What does the poet feel about the subject of the poem?

Anger Sorrow Fear Disgust Regret Confusion

- If there are other people in the poem, how do they feel?
- How does it make you feel?

> **Key Point**
>
> You will also need to think about and comment on themes and ideas when writing about unseen poetry.

> **Quick Test**
>
> 1. Can a poem be about conflict and relationships?
> 2. Can the title of the cluster help you think about themes?
> 3. Should you write about your response to the poems?
> 4. Will you always know what the poet's feelings are?

> **Key Words**
>
> attitude
> ambiguous
> voice
> persona

Language

You must be able to:

- Analyse poets' use of language, using appropriate terminology
- Compare how poets use language.

Sound

- Look at the ways poets use sound. Read the poems out loud or listen to someone else reading them.
- The most obvious way in which sound reflects meaning is through **onomatopoeia**:
  - Elizabeth Barrett Browning uses the phrase 'rustle thy boughs' to convey the sound of the wind in the trees (Sonnet 29).
- **Alliteration** can convey different moods, according to the sound used:
  - In 'Kamikaze' Beatrice Garland uses 's' sounds (also known as sibilance) to reflect the peaceful mood, as she describes fish 'flashing silver as their bellies swivelled toward the sun'.
  - She adds 'sh' within words as well as at the beginning of them ('shoals of fishes flashing'), adding to the mood.
- Browning uses plosive sounds to sinister effect, almost as if he were spitting, in 'Porphyria's Lover':

  Blushed bright beneath my burning kiss.

- **Assonance** is the use of a series of similar vowel sounds to create patterns and atmosphere:

  but as we moved on through the afternoon light ('Winter Swans')

- Poets often repeat not just sounds, but whole words and phrases, emphasizing their importance, as in Blake's 'London':

  In every cry of every Man

  Or reflecting the repetition of an action and its impact, as in 'The Charge of the Light Brigade':

  Cannon to the right of them.
  Cannon to the left of them.

- A phrase which is repeated at the end of each stanza is often called a **refrain**.

Diction

- When poets use a **persona**, their choice of words helps to create the character. Browning, in 'My Last Duchess', uses colloquial language to make it seem as if the persona is having a conversation:

> A heart – how shall I say? – too soon made glad

- In 'Singh Song!' Daljit Nagra changes the spelling of words to reflect his persona's accent:

> But ven nobody in, I do di lock.

- In 'Checking Out Me History', John Agard speaks as himself but he uses the dialect of his childhood to convey both character and situation:

> Dem tell me bout de man who discover de balloon

- Other poets use specialized or technical vocabulary to give us a sense of a character, as Seamus Heaney does in 'Follower':

> He would set the wing
> And fit the bright steel-pointed sock.

- You might see self-consciously 'poetic' or even **archaic** (outdated) words used for effect, as in Barrett Browning's use of 'thee' rather than 'you'.

Key Point

Think about the 'voice' in the poem. Is the poet writing as him/herself or as a character – a 'persona'?

Imagery

- Imagery is central to our understanding of how poets create meaning. When a poet compares something to something else, think about why that comparison has been made.
- In 'The Farmer's Bride' Charlotte Mew's persona uses a series of **similes** to describe his bride:

> Straight and slight as a young larch tree,
> Sweet as the first wild violets, she.

He compares her to things that he, as a farmer, would be familiar with, and he describes her as a wild thing, part of nature.

- In 'Winter Swans' Owen Sheers uses the **metaphor** of 'porcelain' to convey the fragility and beauty of the swans.
- In 'Love's Philosophy' Shelley uses pathetic fallacy, personifying nature:

> See the mountains kiss high heaven.

- In 'Ozymandias' his description of the statue can be read as a **symbol** of the futility of power and the passing of time.

Key Words

onomatopoeia
alliteration
assonance
refrain
persona
archaic
simile
metaphor
symbol

> **Quick Test**
>
> Give the correct term for:
> 1. The use of a word that sounds like what it describes.
> 2. Writing about a thing or idea as if it were a person.
> 3. Starting a series of words with the same sound.
> 4. A character in a poem who speaks in the first person.

Form and Structure

You must be able to:

- Analyse poets' use of form and structure, using appropriate terminology
- Compare how poets use form and structure.

Stanzas

- Look at how many **stanzas** there are and whether they are equal in length.
- Hardy's 'Neutral Tones' is divided into four stanzas of four lines each. This is the traditional form of the ballad, a poem that tells a story. It is about strong feelings, so you might expect the poet to lose control. Instead he imposes order on his emotions. What effect does the tension between form and content have on the reader?
- Other poets, like Tennyson in 'The Charge of the Light Brigade', vary the length of their stanzas. If this is the case, think about what is happening in the poem when a poet adds an extra line or includes a very short stanza.
- Think about when the poet starts a new stanza. Is there a new idea being introduced? Or is there a change in place or time?
- Where a poem is not divided into stanzas, think about why this might be. Browning's 'Porphyria's Lover' is a dramatic monologue, in which the poet gives the impression that the persona is speaking to us spontaneously. Perhaps he does not stop to think.
- Single-stanza poems can have their own internal structure. Sonnets, such as Sonnet 29, follow strict rules, in this case those of the **Petrarchan sonnet**. These consist of an **octave** (8 lines) followed by a **sestet** (6 lines). Traditionally the change from the octave to the sestet reflects a turn (called the **volta**) or change in the argument or mood. You may also come across **Shakespearean sonnets**, which consist of three **quatrains** followed by a rhyming couplet.
- If a line ends with a punctuation mark, it is called **end-stopping**. If a poet continues across lines or even stanzas without a pause, it is called **enjambment**. Think about why the poet would choose one or the other.

Key Point
'Stanza' is Italian for 'room', so if a poem is a house the stanzas are its rooms.

Rhyme

- **Rhyme** is easy to spot but can be difficult to comment on. It can be used to make us laugh, to emphasize something, or to give a sense of order.
- The simplest form of rhyme is the **rhyming couplet**, rhyming one line with the next. This is an almost childish use of rhyme, so when it is used in a poem like 'The Farmer's Bride' it could be telling us something about the persona.
- Rhyming couplets are also used to underline important points.

- The traditional rhyme scheme of the ballad is *abab.* This is used in 'London'. Although 'Neutral Tones' has the shape of a ballad, the rhyme scheme is different.
- Some poets use more complex rhyme schemes, while others use rhyme occasionally for effect, sometimes within lines (internal rhyme).
- You might come across sight or eye rhymes, where the words look as if they should rhyme but do not, for example, 'rough' and 'bough'.
- Many poets use 'half rhyme' (also known as 'slant rhyme' and 'pararhyme'), where the final consonants agree but the vowel sounds do not match, softening the effect of the rhyme. Heaney rhymes 'pluck' and 'sock' in 'Follower'.

Rhythm

- A poem's **rhythm** comes from its pattern of **stressed** and unstressed **syllables**. You can get a sense of this by reading a poem aloud.
- Some poems have a very strong rhythm. 'The Charge of the Light Brigade' is written in dactyls (a stressed syllable followed by two unstressed syllables), giving a sense of the pounding of horses' hooves and cannons:

> **Half** a league **half** a league

- One of the most commonly used **metres** is the iambic pentameter. This is quite a gentle rhythm, often compared to a heartbeat. Wordsworth uses it in 'The Prelude':

> And **as** I **rose** up**on** the **stroke**, my **boat**

- Contemporary poets are less likely to use strong rhythmical patterns, though there are exceptions like 'Checking Out Me History'. However, if you listen carefully you should still hear a rhythm.
- If you hear a rhythm, think about how the poet uses it to create the mood and tone of the poem.
- Poetry that has a regular metre but no rhyme is called **blank verse**.
- Poetry that has no regular pattern, either of rhyme or metre, is called **free verse**.

Key Point

When looking at rhyme and metre, look for patterns and variations in patterns.

Key Words

stanza
Petrarchan sonnet
octave
sestet
volta
Shakespearean sonnet
quatrain
end-stopping
enjambment
rhyme
rhyming couplet
rhythm
stress
syllable
metre
blank verse
free verse

Quick Test

Give the correct term for:
1. A set of two lines that rhyme.
2. A rhyme within a line.
3. A poem that tells a story in four-line stanzas.
4. Poetry that has no regular pattern.

Unseen Poetry

You must be able to:

- Respond to and analyse a poem you have not seen before
- Compare two unseen poems.

Approaching an Unseen Poem

- In Section C of Paper 2 you will be given two poems you have never seen before. You will have to answer a question about one of them, before comparing them.
- Start by reading the poem to gain a general sense of its themes, mood and atmosphere. Then use your knowledge of poetry to 'interrogate' the text. Here are some questions you could ask yourself when reading an unseen poem.

Title	What does it make you think about?
	Does it tell you what the poem is about or is it ambiguous?
Speaker	Is the voice in the poem that of the poet or a persona?
	Who, if anyone, is being addressed?
Setting	Where and when is it set?
	Does the place change?
	Does the time change?
Form and structure	How is it arranged?
	When and why does the poet start a new stanza?
	Is there a strong regular rhythm? If so, what effect does it have?
	Does it rhyme? If so, is there a regular rhyme scheme? What is the effect of the rhyme?
Language	How does the poet use sound?
	What kind of vocabulary/register does the poet use?
	What sort of imagery does the poet use?
	Is there anything else interesting about the language?
Themes and ideas	Is there a story? If so, what is it?
	What do you think the poem is really about?
	Is more than one theme touched on?
	What do you think is the poet's attitude / point of view?
Personal response	What does the poem make you think about?
	How does it make you feel?

> ### Key Point
>
> To answer the questions, you will need all the skills you have learned studying poems from the anthology.

Comparing Unseen Poems

- You will be asked to compare a poem which you have already written about with another poem on a similar theme.
- Be careful not to repeat everything you have already said about the first poem. Focus on the second poem but make sure that every point you make refers back to the first one.
- You could go through the new poem line by line, linking it to the first poem as you go.
- Or you could take different aspects of the poem in turn, starting a new paragraph for each.
- Whichever way you approach the comparison, consider:

> **Key Point**
>
> Remember to comment on both similarities and differences.

Structure and form	Brown's structure is regular, the four stanzas of four lines giving a sense of order and logic, whereas Smith's stanzas vary in length, as if her memories are random and disordered.
Language	Brown's use of harsh-sounding words such as 'rough' and 'dour' contrast with the softness of Smith's 'silken voice' and 'shuffling step'.
Imagery	Both poets use imagery connected with nature but in very different ways...
How the poets approach the theme	Both poems focus on the child's relationship with her father.
The poets' feelings and attitude	Unlike Brown, Smith remembers her father with affection.
Your response to the poems	Brown conveys a sense of regret and anger, whereas the way Smith describes her feelings, although sad, is somehow comforting.

- Back up every point you make with short quotations from both poems.
- Try to use correct **terminology** but remember that you do not get marks just for 'spotting' things like alliteration and metaphors. You must show that you understand how they are used and their effect on the reader.

> **Quick Test**
>
> Would you use the following connectives to express a similarity or a difference?
> 1. Both...and
> 2. whereas...
> 3. On the other hand...
> 4. Neither...nor

> **Key Word**
>
> terminology

Answer the question on the text you have studied.

Your answer should be in note form, using bullet points.

1 J. B. Priestley: *An Inspector Calls*

How does Priestley write about attitudes to women in *An Inspector Calls*?

Write down five statements and give evidence from the text to support each statement. **[10]**

2 Willy Russell: *Blood Brothers*

How does Russell write about fate in *Blood Brothers*?

Write down five statements and give evidence from the text to support each statement. **[10]**

3 Alan Bennett: *The History Boys*

How does Bennett write about history in *The History Boys*?

Write down five statements and give evidence from the text to support each statement. **[10]**

4 Dennis Kelly: *DNA*

How does Kelly write about guilt and responsibility in *DNA*?

Write down five statements and give evidence from the text to support each statement. **[10]**

5 Simon Stephens: *The Curious Incident of the Dog in the Night-Time*

How does Stephens explore ideas about families in *The Curious Incident of the Dog in the Night-Time*?

Write down five statements and give evidence from the text to support each statement. **[10]**

6 Shelagh Delaney: *A Taste of Honey*

How does Delaney present ideas about love in *A Taste of Honey*?

Write down five statements and give evidence from the text to support each statement. **[10]**

7 William Golding: *Lord of the Flies*

How does Golding explore ideas about civilization in *Lord of the Flies*?

Write down five statements and give evidence from the text to support each statement. **[10]**

8 AQA Anthology: *Telling Tales*

How does Lawrence write about death in 'The Odour of Chrysanthemums'?

Write down five statements and give evidence from the text to support each statement. **[10]**

9 George Orwell: *Animal Farm*

How does Orwell present ideas about oppression in *Animal Farm*?

Write down five statements and give evidence from the text to support each statement. [10]

10 Kazuo Ishiguro: *Never Let Me Go*

How does Ishiguro write about friendship in *Never Let Me Go*?

Write down five statements and give evidence from the text to support each statement. [10]

11 Meera Syal: *Anita and Me*

How does Syal write about living in two cultures in *Anita and Me*?

Write down five statements and give evidence from the text to support each statement. [10]

12 Stephen Kelman: *Pigeon English*

How does Kelman present ideas about violence in *Pigeon English*?

Write down five statements and give evidence from the text to support each statement. [10]

Answer the question on the cluster you have studied. You will need your copy of the Anthology.

Either

1 Look at how Owen describes conflict in 'Exposure' and answer the following questions.

a) What person is it written in? _____

b) What tense is used? _____

c) What effect do the person and tense have? _____
_____

d) Briefly describe where and when it is set. _____

e) How is it organized? _____

f) What is the effect of having four equal lines followed by a shorter line in each stanza?
_____

g) Look at the last line of each stanza and explain how and why the refrain changes.
_____

h) Find two examples of personification / pathetic fallacy in the first three stanzas. Explain their effect.
_____
_____

i) Find an example of onomatopoeia and explain its effect. _____
_____

j) What is the significance of the scene Owen describes in stanza 6, beginning 'Slowly our ghosts drag home'?

_____ [20]

Or

2 Look at the way Hardy presents a relationship in 'Neutral Tones' and answer the following questions.

a) What person is it written in? _____

b) What tense is used? _____

c) What effect do the person and tense have? _____
_____

d) Briefly describe where and when it is set. _____

e) How is it organized? _____

f) Describe the rhyme scheme and explain its effect.
_____

g) Identify the simile in the second stanza. What does it tell us about how the woman feels about the speaker? _____
_____

h) What is the effect of the ellipsis at the end of the third stanza? _____

_____

i) Find an example of alliteration and explain its effect. _____

_____

j) What does the description of the scene in the first stanza tell us about the relationship?

_____

_____ [20]

3 Read the poem below and answer the questions that follow.

> **The Song of the Old Mother by W. B. Yeats**
>
> I rise in the dawn, and I kneel and blow
> Till the seed of the fire flicker and glow;
> And then I must scrub and bake and sweep
> Till stars are beginning to blink and peep;
> And the young lie long and dream in their bed
> Of the matching ribbons for bosom and head,
> And their day goes over in idleness,
> And they sing if the wind but lift a tress:
> While I must work because I am old,
> And the seed of the fire gets feeble and cold.

a) Is the voice in the poem that of the poet or a persona? What sort of person is speaking?

_____

b) Where and when is it set? _____

c) Is there a strong, regular rhythm? If so, what effect does it have? _____

_____

d) Does it rhyme? If so, is there a regular rhyme scheme? What is the effect of the rhyme?

_____

e) What sort of imagery does the poet use? _____

f) Is there a story? If so, what is it? _____

g) What is the significance of the line 'And the seed of the fire gets feeble and cold'?

_____

h) What do you think the poem is really about? _____

i) What do you think is the poet's attitude / point of view? _____

_____

j) How does the poem make you feel? _____

_____ [20]

1 **Answer the question on the cluster you have studied.**

Write your answer on a separate piece of paper.

Either

a) Compare the way poets present the effect of war on people in 'Kamikaze' and one other poem from 'Power and Conflict'. [30]

Or

b) Compare the way poets present ideas about love in 'Love's Philosophy' and one other poem from 'Love and Relationships'. [30]

2 Read the two poems below and answer both questions.

Sonnet

by John Clare

I love to see the summer beaming forth

And white wool sack clouds sailing to the north

I love to see the wild flowers come again

And Mare drops stain with gold the meadow drain

And water lilies whiten on the floods

Where reed clumps rustle like a wind shook wood

Where from her hiding place the Moor Hen pushes

And seeks her flag nest floating in bull rushes

I like the willow leaning half way o'er

The clear deep lake to stand upon its shore

I love the hay grass when the flower head swings

To summer winds and insects happy wings

That sport about the meadow the bright day

And see bright beetles in the clear lake play.

The Eagle

by Alfred Tennyson

He clasps the crag with crooked hands;

Close to the sun in lonely lands,

Ring'd with the azure world he stands.

The wrinkled sea beneath him crawls;

He watches from his mountain walls,

And like a thunderbolt he falls.

a) How does Clare present his feelings about nature in 'Sonnet'?
Write your answer on a separate piece of paper. [24]

b) Both 'Sonnet' and 'The Eagle' describe aspects of nature. What are the similarities
and differences between the way the poets present feelings about the natural world?

[8]

English Language

Read the passage below and answer the questions that follow.

In this extract from 'Tickets, Please', D. H. Lawrence describes the trams of an English mining area, and the people who work on them, during the First World War.

To ride on these cars is always an adventure. Since we are in war-time, the drivers are men unfit for active service: cripples and hunchbacks. So they have the spirit of the devil in them. The ride becomes a steeple-chase.[1] Hurray! We have leapt in a clear jump over the canal bridges – now for the four-lane corner. With a shriek and a trail of sparks we are clear again. To be sure, a tram often leaps the rails – but what matter! It sits in a ditch till other trams come to haul it out. It is quite common for a car, packed with one solid mass of living people, to come to a dead halt in the midst of unbroken blackness, the heart of nowhere on a dark night, and for the driver and the girl conductor[2] to call, 'All get off – car's on fire!' Instead, however, of rushing out in a panic, the passengers stolidly reply: 'Get on – get on! We're not coming out. We're stopping where we are. Push on, George.' So till flames actually appear.

The reason for this reluctance to dismount is that the nights are howlingly cold, black, and windswept, and a car is a haven of refuge. From village to village the miners travel, for a change of cinema, of girl, of pub. The trams are desperately packed. Who is going to risk himself in the black gulf outside, to wait perhaps an hour for another tram, then to see the forlorn notice 'Depot Only', because there is something wrong! Or to greet a unit of three bright cars all so tight with people that they sail past with a howl of derision. Trams that pass in the night.

This, the most dangerous tram-service in England, as the authorities themselves declare, with pride, is entirely conducted by girls, and driven by rash young men, a little crippled, or by delicate young men, who creep forward in terror. The girls are fearless young hussies.[3] In their ugly blue uniform, skirts up to their knees, shapeless old peaked caps on their heads, they have all the *sang-froid*[4] of an old non-commissioned officer. With a tram packed with howling colliers, roaring hymns downstairs and a sort of antiphony[5] of obscenities upstairs, the lasses are perfectly at their ease. They pounce on the youths who try to evade their ticket-machine. They push off the men at the end of their distance. They are not going to be done in the eye – not they. They fear nobody – and everybody fears them.

'Hello, Annie!'

'Hello, Ted!'

'Oh, mind my corn, Miss Stone. It's my belief you've got a heart of stone, for you've trod on it again.'

'You should keep it in your pocket,' replies Miss Stone, and she goes sturdily upstairs in her high boots.

'Tickets, please.'

---

[1] *steeple-chase* – a horse race over fences

[2] *conductor* – someone who sells tickets on a tram, bus or train

[3] *hussies* – cheeky or immoral girls

[4] *sang-froid* – coolness

[5] *antiphony* – singing in responses (usually in hymns)

1 According to the passage, which of the following statements are TRUE?
Tick the correct answers.

   a) The trams are driven by women. ☐

   b) Trams often come off the rails. ☐

   c) Passengers are reluctant to leave the trams when told there's a fire. ☐

   d) The girls are easily shocked. ☐

   e) People are afraid of the girl conductors. ☐

   f) Riding on the trams is a very boring experience. ☐

   g) Not many people use the trams. ☐

   h) The kind of people who work on the trams has changed because of the war. ☐   [4 marks]

2 Look in detail at the first paragraph. How does the writer use language here to describe the atmosphere on the trams?

You could include the writer's choice of:
- words and phrases
- language features and techniques
- sentence forms.

Write your answer on a separate piece of paper.   [8 marks]

3 Now think about the whole text.

This extract comes near the beginning of a short story.

How has the writer structured the text to interest you as a reader?

You could write about:
- what the writer focuses on at the beginning
- how and why he changes this focus
- any other structural features that interest you.

Write your answer on a separate piece of paper.   [8 marks]

4 Think about the whole text.

What impression do you get of the people who work on the trams and who use them?
- Write about your own impressions of the people.
- Evaluate how the writer has created these impressions.
- Support your opinions with quotations from the text.

Write your answer on a separate piece of paper.   [20 marks]

5 You are going to enter a creative writing competition.

Either

Write a description suggested by this picture.

Or

Write the story of a bus, tram or train journey.

[24 marks for content and organization and 16 marks for technical accuracy; total 40 marks]

Read the sources below and answer the questions that follow.

Source A

In the extract below, taken from *Pictures from Italy*, Charles Dickens describes his visit to Florence in the 1840s.

But, how much beauty of another kind is here, when, on a fair clear morning, we look, from the summit of a hill, on Florence! See where it lies before us in a sun-lighted valley, bright with the winding Arno, and shut in by swelling hills; its domes, and towers, and palaces, rising from the rich country in a glittering heap, and shining in the sun like gold!

Magnificently stern and sombre are the streets of beautiful Florence; and the strong old piles of building make such heaps of shadow, on the ground and in the river, that there is another and a different city of rich forms and fancies, always lying at our feet. Prodigious palaces, constructed for defence, with small distrustful windows heavily barred, and walls of great thickness formed of huge masses of rough stone, frown, in their old sulky state, on every street. In the midst of the city – in the Piazza of the Grand Duke, adorned with beautiful statues and the Fountain of Neptune – rises the Palazzo Vecchio, with its enormous overhanging battlements, and the Great Tower that watches over the whole town. In its courtyard – worthy of the Castle of Otranto[1] in its ponderous gloom – is a massive staircase that the heaviest waggon and the stoutest team of horses might be driven up. Within it, is a Great Saloon, faded and tarnished in its stately decorations, and mouldering by grains, but recording yet, in pictures on its walls, the triumphs of the Medici and the wars of the old Florentine people. The prison is hard by, in an adjacent court-yard of the building – a foul and dismal place, where some men are shut up close, in small cells like ovens; and where others look through bars and beg; where some are playing draughts, and some are talking to their friends, who smoke, the while, to purify the air; and some are buying wine and fruit of women-vendors; and all are squalid, dirty, and vile to look at. 'They are merry enough, Signore,' says the jailer. 'They are all blood-stained here,' he adds, indicating, with his hand, three-fourths of the whole building. Before the hour is out, an old man, eighty years of age, quarrelling over a bargain with a young girl of seventeen, stabs her dead, in the market-place full of bright flowers; and is brought in prisoner, to swell the number.

---

[1] *Castle of Otranto* – the setting of a popular Gothic horror story of the same name

Source B

In this article for *The Times* (13 October 1982) Joyce Rackham discusses the problems caused by tourism in the Italian city of Florence.

FLORENCE: A city of dilemma

by Joyce Rackham

The bust of Benvenuto Cellini looks down sternly on the tourists littering the Ponte Vecchio. The younger ones loll – even sleep beneath him. Graffiti, although rarer than in the past, still scar some walls, and there is a very ugly souvenir stall. Yet the bridge is lined with fine shops, including jewellers whose best work follows Cellini's tradition of superb craftsmanship.

This scene reflects the dilemma of contemporary Florence – a matchless medieval city which has to stand up to the pressures, dirt and overcrowding of life in the 1980s.

Dr Silvio Abboni, a heart specialist who is also cultural assessor of the municipality, told me: 'We are victims of our big tourist boom. Florence was built as a fortress to withstand invaders. Now we must defend ourselves against too much mass tourism and potential speculators.'

Among his solutions are promoting itineraries off the beaten track, which will be published for visitors, as well as out of season attractions, both artistic and musical. He said that traffic jams could be intolerable in Florence and pointed to a new map showing plans to restrict car and bus parking and extend pedestrian precincts 'to allow city life to unfold in an orderly and pleasant manner'.

Dr Giorgio Chiarelli, Director of the Florence Tourist Board, said: 'We are a Renaissance city with about half a million inhabitants and an annual influx of around two million tourists.' He admitted that traffic pollution, litter and policing had been neglected, but said that this was changing.

Off-season tourism, with special art weekends from November to March, as well as extended shop and museum hours and more accommodation for young tourists, are intended to help ease pressures. The great Uffizi Gallery, the first public museum in the world, built by the Medici, celebrates its 400th anniversary this year. Professor Luciano Berti, its director since 1969, is also superintendent of the artistic and historic patrimony of Florence. 'Restoration is a continuous necessity and costs a great deal of money, and we don't have enough', he told me. 'We are most anxious that people see far more than the Uffizi. We cannot cope with a further growth of crowds. Since 1975 their volume has doubled.' He explained that dust from clothes and tramping feet, humidity from breath and wet clothes all have an adverse effect on paintings, many of which are now protected by glass. Crowd control measures are helping, as are the extended hours. Since August the Uffizi and most important museums, which used to close at 2pm, have been open until 7pm.

6 Read again the first five paragraphs of Source B (from 'The bust' to 'changing').

According to the article, which four of the following statements are TRUE?

- Shade the boxes of the ones you think are true.
- Choose a maximum of four statements.

a) The souvenir stall at the Ponte Vecchio is very attractive. ☐

b) There are shops on the bridge. ☐

c) There is no pollution in Florence. ☐

d) Dr Abboni believes the increase in tourists has been bad for Florence. ☐

e) Florence is a modern city. ☐

f) The jewellers produce some very good work. ☐

g) The authorities in Florence are encouraging tourists to go to less well-known parts of the city. ☐

h) Dr Abboni wants to ban tourists from Florence. ☐ [4 marks]

7 You need to refer to Source A and Source B for this question.

Use details from both sources.

Write a summary of the differences between the two descriptions of Florence. [8 marks]

8 You need only to refer to Source A for this question.

How does Dickens use language to convey his impressions of Florence? [12 marks]

9 For this question you need to refer to the whole of Source A together with the whole of Source B.

Compare how the two writers convey their different reactions to the city of Florence.

In your answer you should:
- compare their different reactions
- compare the methods they use to convey their reactions
- support your ideas with quotations from both texts. [16 marks]

10 'Travel might broaden the mind, but tourism is destroying some of the world's most beautiful places. It is time we put the good of the planet before our own pleasure.'

Write an article for a broadsheet newspaper in which you explain your point of view on this statement.

[24 marks for content and organization; 16 marks for technical accuracy; total 40]

English Literature: Shakespeare

• **Answer the question on the play you have studied.**

11 *Julius Caesar*

Read the extract specified and answer the question below.

Here, Antony addresses the Roman people after the death of Caesar.

> **Act 3 Scene 2**
>
> *From*
>
> ANTONY   Friends, Romans, countrymen, lend me your ears.
>
> *To*
>
> Come I to speak in Caesar's funeral.

Starting with this speech, explore how Shakespeare presents Antony as a politician.
Write about:

• how Shakespeare presents Antony as a politician in this speech

• how Shakespeare presents Antony as a politician in the play as a whole. [30 marks + AO4 4 marks]

12 *Much Ado About Nothing*

Read the extract specified and answer the question below.

Here, Benedick approaches Beatrice after Hero has been rejected by Claudio.

> **Act 4 Scene 1**
>
> *From*
>
> BENEDICK   Lady Beatrice, have you wept all this while?
>
> *To*
>
> BEATRICE   It is a man's office but not yours.

Starting with this conversation, write about how Shakespeare presents ideas about honour.
Write about:

• how Shakespeare presents ideas about honour in this dialogue

• how Shakespeare presents ideas about honour in the play as a whole.   [30 marks + AO4 4 marks]

13 *Macbeth*

Read the extract specified and answer the question below.

Here, Macbeth has murdered Duncan, and has returned with the blood-stained daggers.

> ## Act 2 Scene 2
>
> *From*
>
> LADY MACBETH   Infirm of purpose!
>
> *To*
>
> LADY MACBETH   I hear a knocking
>
>   At the south entry. Retire we to our chamber.
>
>   A little water clears us of this deed.

Starting with this dialogue, write about how Shakespeare presents the relationship of Macbeth and Lady Macbeth.
Write about:

- how Shakespeare presents their relationship in this dialogue
- how Shakespeare presents their relationship in the play as a whole.   [30 marks + AO4 4 marks]

14 *Romeo and Juliet*

Read the extract specified and answer the question below.

Here, Romeo has just seen Juliet for the first time.

> ## Act 1 Scene 5
>
> *From*
>
> ROMEO   O, she doth teach the torches to burn bright.
>
> *To*
>
>   Did my heart love till now? Forswear it sight.
>
>   For I ne'er saw true beauty till this night.

Starting with this speech explore how Shakespeare presents Romeo's love for Juliet.
Write about:

- how Shakespeare presents Romeo's feelings in this speech
- how Shakespeare presents Romeo's feelings in the play as a whole.   [30 marks + AO4 4 marks]

15 *The Tempest*

Read the extract specified and answer the question below.

Here, Prospero has just discovered Miranda talking to Ferdinand and has cast a spell on him.

Act 1 Scene 2

From

MIRANDA   Beseech you, father!

To

MIRANDA   My affections

            Are then most humble. I have no ambition

            To see a godlier man.

Starting with this extract, how does Shakespeare present Prospero as a father?
Write about:

- how Shakespeare presents Prospero as a father in the extract
- how he presents him as a father in the whole of the play.   [30 marks + AO4 4 marks]

 16 *The Merchant of Venice*

Read the extract specified and answer the question below.

Here, Portia, disguised as a man, pleads with Shylock to be merciful.

Act 4 Scene 1

From

PORTIA   The quality of mercy is not strained.

To

            And earthly power doth then show likest God's

            When mercy seasons justice.

Starting with this speech, explore how Shakespeare presents ideas about justice and mercy.
Write about:

- how Shakespeare writes about justice and mercy in this speech
- how Shakespeare writes about justice and mercy in the play as a whole. [30 marks + AO4 4 marks]

English Literature: The Nineteenth-Century novel

• **Answer one question from this section on your chosen text.**

17 **Mary Shelley:** *Frankenstein*

• **Answer both parts of the question.**

In this extract, Victor Frankenstein has been confronted by the creature in the mountains.

> **Re-read Chapter 10**
>
> *From*
>
> 'Abhorred monster! Fiend that thou art! The tortures of hell are too mild a vengeance for thy crimes. Wretched devil! You reproach me with your creation; come on, then, that I may extinguish the spark which I so negligently bestowed.'
>
> *To*
>
> 'Begone! I will not hear you. There can be no community between you and me; we are enemies. Begone, or let us try our strength in a fight, in which one must fall.'

Starting with this extract, explore to what extent and how Shelley makes the monster sympathetic. Write about:
• whether and how Shelley presents the monster sympathetically in this extract
• whether and how she presents the monster sympathetically in the novel as a whole.   [30 marks]

18 **Sir Arthur Conan Doyle:** *The Sign of Four*

• **Answer both parts of the question.**

In this extract, Miss Morstan has come to Sherlock Holmes for help.

> **Re-read Chapter 2**
>
> *From*
>
> Miss Morstan entered the room with a firm step and an outward composure of manner.
>
> *To*
>
> I relapsed into my chair.

Starting with this extract, write about how Conan Doyle presents Miss Morstan and about her role in the novel.
Write about:
• how he presents Miss Morstan in this extract
• how he presents Miss Morstan in the novel as a whole.   [30 marks]

Mixed Exam-Style Questions

19 **Charlotte Brontë: *Jane Eyre***

- **Answer both parts of the question.**

In this extract, Jane has been locked in the Red Room by her aunt.

> **Re-read Chapter 2**
>
> *From*
>
> 'Unjust! – unjust!' said my reason, forced by the agonising stimulus into precocious though transitory power: and Resolve, equally wrought up, instigated some strange expedient to achieve escape from insupportable oppression – as running away, or, if that could not be effected, never eating or drinking more, and letting myself die.
>
> *To*
>
> It must have been most irksome to find herself bound by a hard-wrung pledge to stand in the stead of a parent to a strange child she could not love, and to see an uncongenial alien permanently intruded on her own family group.

Starting with this extract, explore how Brontë presents Jane as an outsider.
Write about:
- how Brontë presents Jane in this extract
- how she presents Jane as an outsider in the novel as a whole. [30 marks]

20 **Jane Austen: *Pride and Prejudice***

- **Answer both parts of the question.**

In this extract, Austen describes Elizabeth's visit to Pemberley.

> **Re-read Chapter 43 (Volume 3, Chapter 1)**
>
> *From*
>
> The housekeeper came; a respectable-looking, elderly woman, much less fine, and more civil, than she had any notion of finding her.
>
> *To*
>
> 'Perhaps we might be deceived.'
>
> 'That is not very likely; our authority was too good.'

Starting with this extract, explore how Austen describes Elizabeth's changing feelings towards Darcy.
Write about:
- how she writes about Elizabeth's feelings in this extract
- how she writes about Elizabeth's changing feelings in the novel as a whole. [30 marks]

21 **Charles Dickens:** *Great Expectations*

- **Answer both parts of the question.**

In this extract, Pip is visiting Miss Havisham for the first time. She has asked him to call for Estella.

> **Re-read Chapter 8**
>
> *From*
>
> 'Call Estella,' she repeated, flashing a look at me. 'You can do that. Call Estella. At the door.'
>
> *To*
>
> 'You shall go soon,' said Miss Havisham, aloud. 'Play the game, out.'

Starting with this extract, write about how Dickens portrays Pip's relationship with Estella.

Write about:
- how he writes about their relationship in this extract
- how he writes about their relationship in the novel as a whole. **[30 marks]**

22 **Robert Louis Stevenson:** *The Strange Case of Dr Jekyll and Mr Hyde*

- **Answer both parts of the question.**

In this extract, Stevenson describes one of Mr Utterson's Sunday walks with his cousin, Mr Enfield.

> **Re-read Chapter 1 ('The Story of the Door')**
>
> *From*
>
> No doubt the feat was easy to Mr Utterson; for he was undemonstrative at the best, and even his friendship seemed to be founded in a similar catholicity of good-nature.
>
> *To*
>
> 'Indeed?' said Mr Utterson, with a slight change of voice, 'and what was that?'

Starting with this extract, write about how Stevenson uses Utterson to explore 'the strange case'.
Write about:
- how he writes about Utterson and his walk in this extract
- how he writes about and uses Utterson in the novel as a whole. **[30 marks]**

23 **Charles Dickens:** *A Christmas Carol*

- **Answer both parts of the question.**

In this extract, the Ghost of Christmas Present has taken Scrooge to observe the Cratchits' Christmas.

> **Re-read Stave 3 (Chapter 3) ('The Second of the Three Spirits')**
>
> *From*
>
> 'And how did little Tim behave?' asked Mrs Cratchit, when she had rallied Bob on his credulity and Bob had hugged his daughter to his heart's content.
>
> *To*
>
> 'I see a vacant seat,' replied the Ghost, 'in the poor chimney-corner, and a crutch without an owner, carefully preserved. If these shadows remain unaltered by the Future, the child will die.'

Starting with this extract, explore how Dickens writes about the 'spirit of Christmas'.

Write about:
- how he writes about the spirit of Christmas in this extract
- how he writes about the spirit of Christmas in the novel as a whole. **[30 marks]**

Mixed Exam-Style Questions

English Literature: Modern Prose or Drama

- **Answer the question on the text you have studied.**
  (In your exam you will have a choice of two questions on your text.)

24 **J. B. Priestley:** *An Inspector Calls*

How does Priestley present the character of Mr Birling in *An Inspector Calls*?
Write about:
- the character of Mr Birling
- how Priestley presents the character of Mr Birling.   [30 marks + AO4 4 marks]

25 **Willy Russell:** *Blood Brothers*

How does Russell use the narrator in *Blood Brothers*?
Write about:
- what the narrator does and says
- the purpose and significance of the narrator.   [30 marks + AO4 4 marks]

26 **Alan Bennett:** *The History Boys*

How does Bennett present Irwin as a teacher in *The History Boys*?
Write about:
- what Irwin does and says
- how Bennett presents Irwin in the play.   [30 marks + AO4 4 marks]

27 **Dennis Kelly:** *DNA*

How does Kelly present ideas about friendship in *DNA*?
Write about:
- what characters say and do
- how Kelly presents friendship in the play.   [30 marks + AO4 4 marks]

28 **Simon Stephens:** *The Curious Incident of the Dog in the Night-Time*

How does Stephens present the character of Siobhan in *The Curious Incident of the Dog in the Night-Time*?
Write about:
- what Siobhan does and says
- how Stephens presents Siobhan.   [30 marks + AO4 4 marks]

29 **Shelagh Delaney:** *A Taste of Honey*

How does Delaney present attitudes to sex in *A Taste of Honey*?
Write about:
- the different attitudes presented in the play
- how Delaney presents these attitudes.   [30 marks + AO4 4 marks]

30 **William Golding:** *Lord of the Flies*

How does Golding use symbols in *Lord of the Flies*?
Write about:
- symbols used in *Lord of the Flies*
- how Golding uses symbols to explore ideas and themes.   [30 marks + AO4 4 marks]

31 **AQA Anthology:** *Telling Tales*

How do writers explore relationships between men and women in 'Chemistry' and one other story
from *Telling Tales*?
Write about:
- relationships between men and women in the two stories
- how the writers present relationships between men and women.   [30 marks + AO4 4 marks]

32 **George Orwell:** *Animal Farm*

Explore how the pigs change in *Animal Farm*.
Write about:
- the ways in which the pigs change
- how Orwell presents the ways in which the pigs change.   [30 marks + AO4 4 marks]

33 **Kazuo Ishiguro:** *Never Let Me Go*

How does Ishiguro present the character of Tommy in *Never Let Me Go*?
Write about:
- what Tommy does and says
- how others react to Tommy.   [30 marks + AO4 4 marks]

34 **Meera Syal:** *Anita and Me*

How does Syal write about Meena's relationship with her parents in *Anita and Me*?
Write about:
- Meena's relationship with both parents
- how Syal presents these relationships.   [30 marks + AO4 4 marks]

35 **Stephen Kelman:** *Pigeon English*

How does Kelman present gang culture in *Pigeon English*?
Write about:
- how gangs and gang members behave in *Pigeon English*
- how Kelman presents gangs and gang members.   [30 marks + AO4 4 marks]

Mixed Exam-Style Questions

English Literature: Poetry

 36 Answer the question on the Anthology cluster you have studied.

Either

a) Compare the way poets present danger in 'The Charge of the Light Brigade' and one other poem from 'Power and Conflict'.

Or

b) Compare the way poets present parting in 'When We Two Parted' and one other poem from 'Love and Relationships'.

[30 marks]

37 Read the two poems below and answer both questions.

The Man He Killed

by Thomas Hardy

'Had he and I but met
By some old ancient inn
We should have sat us down to wet
Right many a nipperkin!

'But ranged as infantry
And staring face to face,
I shot at him as he at me,
And killed him in his place.

'I shot him dead because –
Because he was my foe,
Just so: my foe of course he was;
That's clear enough; although

'He thought he'd 'list, perhaps,
Off-hand like – just as I –
Was out of work – had sold his traps –
No other reason why.

'Yes; quaint and curious war is!
You shoot a fellow down
You'd treat if met where any bar is,
Or help to half-a-crown.'

The Soldier

by Rupert Brooke

If I should die, think only this of me:
That there's some corner of a foreign field
That is for ever England. There shall be
In that rich earth a richer dust concealed;
A dust whom England bore, shaped, made aware,
Gave, once, her flowers to love, her ways to roam,
A body of England's, breathing English air,
Washed by the rivers, blest by suns of home.

And think, this heart, all evil shed away,
A pulse the eternal mind, no less
Gives somewhere back the thoughts by England given;
Her sights and sounds; dreams happy as her day;
And laughter, learnt of friends; and gentleness,
In hearts at peace, under an English heaven.

a) How does Hardy present the speaker's feelings about being a soldier in 'The Man He Killed'?

[24 marks]

b) Both 'The Man He Killed' and 'The Soldier' are about being a soldier and going to war. What are the similarities and differences between the way the poets present feelings about war?

[8 marks]

Answers

GCSE Grades

Please note that we cannot give GCSE grade equivalents for numerical marks, as these are determined by the exam board after the exam has been taken.

Pages 4–5 Review Questions

1. Beth [1]; she is described as speaking 'contentedly'. The other girls 'grumbled', 'sighed' or sniffed. [2]
2. He is away in the army. [1]
3. a) That he might get killed. [1]
   b) They might not want to upset each other (or any reasonable answer). [1]
4. a) Giving up small things for a reason. [1]
   b) Someone who likes reading. [1]
5. They have very little money and even if they gave it to the government it would not make a lot of difference. [2]
6. Beth is saying what she wanted to spend her money on before they were told there were to be no presents, [1] implying she is not now going to spend it. [1] Amy tells us what she is planning to spend her money on. [1]
7. Suggested content:
   * They are poor so will not get any Christmas presents.
   * There are four sisters. They live with their mother, and their father seems to be in the army, fighting in a war.
   * Jo likes reading, Beth music and Amy drawing. Meg just seems to like 'pretty things'.
   * It is Meg who expresses their problem, but it is Jo who argues logically that they should still buy presents.
   * Beth is the most placid of the girls, Amy might be seen as selfish as she is so quick to take up Jo's idea and says she 'shall' get the pencils, but she could just be more decisive.
   [5 marks – 1 for one or two of these or similar points, 3 for about half of them, 5 for most of them and perhaps some original points]

   Possible ideas for your letter:
   Thank your grandfather for the money. Describe what you have spent it on / what you will spend it on. Explain why you decided to buy it. Say what your family/friends think about it. Mention that it will remind you of him. Tell him what you have been doing in school / after school / during the holidays. Say something about your family. Mention things that he might remember. Ask about his life and send your best wishes to other family members.

   An excellent answer (17–20 marks) will:
   * Show a full awareness of purpose (thanks), audience (grandfather) and form (informal letter).
   * Engage the reader's interest throughout, perhaps using humour and/or emotive language.
   * Include a full range of techniques, such as correct use of first and second

person, modal verbs, conditionals, questions.
   * Present a variety of ideas, using a sophisticated range of vocabulary and sentence structure.
   * Use paragraphs and connectives effectively.
   * Achieve a high level of accuracy in punctuation and grammar.
   * Achieve a high level of accuracy in spelling.

Pages 6–15 Revise Questions

Page 7 Quick Test
1. no, where 2. It's. 3. whether, to.
4. practice.

Page 9 Quick Test
1. 'Where's my hamster?' Leo cried.
2. He had gone. There was no doubt about it.
3. Maureen, who lived next door, searched her bins.
4. Maureen's son found Hammy in the kitchen.

Page 11 Quick Test
1. d   2. a   3. b   4. c

Page 13 Quick Test
1. First – to give order.
2. On the other hand – to introduce a contrasting idea or point of view.
3. Before – to express passing time.
4. Therefore – to express cause and effect.

Page 15 Quick Test
1. Jay and I were put on detention.
2. I saw you on Saturday.
3. You were the best player we had.
4. After we had sung the first number, we did a dance.

Pages 16–17 Practice Questions

1. were, weather, pouring, excited, wait, metres, There, which, coming, definitely.
   [1 mark for each correct spelling – maximum 10]
2. a) Peter Kowalski, who was the tallest boy in the class, easily won the high jump.
   b) 'What are you doing in the sand pit?' shouted Miss O'Connor. 'Get out of there at once!'
   c) Francesca won medals for the long jump, the high jump and the relay.
   d) I wasn't entered in any of the races because I'm hopeless at running.
   e) Jonathan finished last. However, he was pleased with his time.
   [1 mark for each sentence – maximum 5]
3. a) (i) Julia stayed off school because she had a stomach ache.
      (ii) He might be in the changing rooms or he might have already left.
   b) (i) Michael, who has a really loud voice, announced the results.
      (ii) The form with the best results won a cup, which was presented by Mr Cadogan.
   c) (i) Maria, who had won the discus competition, went home early because she was feeling sick.
   [1 mark for each – maximum 5]

4. a) Hayley and I are going to town tomorrow.
   b) You can come with us if you want to.
   c) We were very pleased with what we bought.
   d) I do not (don't) know anything about what they did at school.
   e) I am not truanting again because I want to get my GCSEs.
   [1 mark for each – maximum 5]
5. (1) As well as (2) As a result of (3) also (4) Consequently (5) However [5]
6. experience [1] was [1] visited [1] stories [1] stars' [1] biographies [1] Therefore [1] she and I [1] Bingley Park [1] The [1]
   [Maximum 10]

Pages 18–31 Revise Questions

Page 19 Quick Test
1. Openly stated. 2. Yes. 3. Yes. 4. No.
Page 21 Quick Test
1. The writer. 2. The reader. 3. No.
4. You get no marks.
Page 23 Quick Test
1. Yes. 2. Yes. 3. No. 4. No.
Page 25 Quick Test
1. Quotation and paraphrase.
2. Everything that is in the original text.
3. When it does not fit easily into the sentence.
4. Point Evidence Explanation (or exploration).
Page 27 Quick Test
1. Horse and oats. 2. Was munching.
3. Old. 4. On. 5. Thoughtfully.
Page 29 Quick Test
1. Personification. 2. Alliteration.
3. Simile. 4. Metaphor.
Page 31 Quick Test
1. b, c, d, a 2. a, d, c, b 3. c, a, b, d

Pages 32–33 Review Questions

1. a) except, accept   b) effect, affect
   c) allowed, aloud   d) right, write
   e) whose, who's
   [1 mark for each pair – maximum 5]
2. 'Don't you think we should wait for him?' asked Eve.
   'Not at all,' Henry replied. 'He never waits for us.'
   'Well, that's true,' Eve replied, 'but he doesn't know the way.'
   [½ mark for each correct punctuation mark – maximum 10]
3. This is a suggested answer only. There are other ways of doing it:
   Henry and Eve waited for another ten minutes but Joel did not arrive, so they left without him and walked to the bus stop. There was no-one there, suggesting they had just missed the bus. Henry was very annoyed with Joel. However, Eve told him to calm down and forget about Joel. After an uneventful journey, they got off the bus by the lake, which looked eerie in the moonlight. Having sat down on a grassy bank, they took their sandwiches and drinks out of the bag. Henry felt a hand on his shoulder. **[Maximum 10 marks]**

4. b, d, f, h, i [Maximum 5 marks]
5. a) pizzas b) latches c) mosquitoes
   d) sheep e) donkeys f) stadia
   g) qualities h) churches i) women
   j) hypotheses [½ mark for each – maximum 5]
6. e, c, d, a, b [Maximum 5 marks]

Pages 34–35 **Practice Questions**

1. • Nobody greeted him cheerfully.
   • People did not ask him to come and see them.
   • Beggars did not beg from him.
   • Children did not ask him for the time.
   • Nobody asked him the way anywhere.
   [Maximum 4 marks]

2.

Marks	Skills	Examples of possible content
7–8	• You have analysed the effects of the choice of language. • You have used an appropriate range of quotations. • You have used sophisticated subject terminology appropriately.	The first complex sentence seems quite light-hearted, the direct speech reflecting a polite greeting, such as people might make in the street, but the sentence starts with 'Nobody', so we know Scrooge is not like others. The next sentence builds a list of those who avoid Scrooge, starting each clause with 'no' before giving an innocuous phrase such as 'what it was o'clock'. The last sentence gives us a sense of evil, 'even the blindmen's dogs' implying that a dislike of Scrooge is natural and instinctive.
5–6	• You have clearly explained the effects of the choice of language. • You have used a range of relevant quotations. • You have used subject terminology appropriately.	In three sentences, each one longer than the last, the writer gives lists of different sorts of people, starting phrases with the repeated 'no', to give a general negative impression. When he imagines what the dogs might say he uses the adjectives 'dark' and 'evil' to show that Scrooge is feared.

[Maximum 8 marks]

3. b, c, e, f [Maximum 4 marks]
4.

Marks	Skills	Examples of possible content
7–8	• You have given a perceptive interpretation of both texts. • You have synthesized evidence from texts. • You have used appropriate quotations from both texts.	Although the writers have opposite views – Weston is a 'city-hater' but Lamb never wants to 'see a mountain in my life' – they are both careful not to insult people who have the opposite view ('I could gang anywhere'; 'Sorry, Londoners'). Lamb lists things like 'crowded streets' that he likes. These are the things Weston hates, calling it 'dirty' and 'noisy'. Weston knows 'it's meant to be…exciting' and this is clearly Lamb's view.
5–6	• You have started to interpret both texts. • You have shown clear connections between texts. • You have used relevant quotations from both texts.	Lamb explains that he has always lived in London so cannot see the attraction of the countryside. Weston, on the other hand, calls the country 'home' and thinks this is why he is bored with the city. Lamb loves the shops, the theatre and even the 'wickedness', but Weston can only see how 'expensive' it is and how everyone is 'bad-tempered'.

[Maximum 8 marks]

Pages 36–43 **Revise Questions**

Page 37 Quick Test
1. The beginning. 2. First.
3. The inciting incident.
4. One who knows everything.
Page 39 Quick Test
1. Simile.
2. Personification/pathetic fallacy.
3. Metaphor. 4. Literal imagery.
Page 41 Quick Test
1. The main character.
2. A character who opposes the protagonist.
3. Something that happens to get the story going.
4. An event that changes the direction of the story.
Page 43 Quick Test
1. George lived alone.
2. Like ancient gravestones.
3. Love loyalty/apparent affection.
4. His teeth were rarely seen.

Pages 44–45 **Review Questions**

1. a, c, d, f [Maximum 4 marks]
2. See 'Skills' column of table above (for pages 34–35 Practice Questions, Q4).

Marks	Examples of possible content
7–8	It took Brontë a long time to get published. She had to work out the 'puzzle' of why no-one was interested and look for advice. Fordyce, on the other hand, was published quickly and is often asked for advice by other poets. They also had very different experiences of being a woman poet. Brontë had a 'vague impression' that her sex would be a disadvantage, but Fordyce, who was 'welcomed with enthusiasm' by other poets, feels it was a positive thing for her.
5–6	The Brontës thought they might be 'looked on with prejudice' because they were women, whereas Fordyce thinks her gender was an advantage ('we don't get enough women'). Fordyce wrote to magazines and performed her poetry live, but for Brontë the only way was to write to publishers, who did not reply.

[Maximum 8 marks]

3.

Marks	Skills	Examples of possible content
10–12	• You have analysed the effects of the choice of language. • You have used an appropriate range of quotations. • You have used sophisticated subject terminology appropriately.	Fordyce gives advice in a clear, colloquial tone, as if she is talking to a friend: 'All I can do is say'. She is also modest, using the noun 'luck' three times and the adjective 'lucky' once, though this is balanced by the repetition of references to 'hard work'. She uses short, often simple sentences – 'It wasn't that hard for me' – which helps make the process seem simple. Using the metaphor 'magic key' in the first paragraph could make readers think she is saying she can't help, but this impression is contradicted by the rest of the passage, as she does try to help.

Marks	Skills	Examples of possible content
7–9	• You have clearly explained the effects of the choice of language. • You have used a range of relevant quotations. • You have used subject terminology appropriately.	Fordyce writes in a chatty, straightforward way, getting straight to the point with 'People often ask me'. She uses a metaphor, 'magic key', to show that there is no easy answer, but her tone is helpful. She emphasizes that this is her personal experience by constant use of the first person.

[Maximum 12 marks]

Pages 46–47 **Practice Questions**

1.

Marks	Skills	Examples of possible content
7–8	• You have analysed the use of structural features. • You have chosen an appropriate range of examples. • You have used a range of subject terminology accurately.	The text is written to gradually reveal to the reader who the 'thin woman' is and what her situation is. It starts by setting the scene in the 'barton', giving us an idea of the kind of people the story is about, just mentioning Rhoda briefly. The direct speech of the milkers tells us (and Rhoda) about the farmer's bride. When the dairyman tells them to stop, two brief lines of dialogue bring Rhoda into focus as having an interest in the farmer. At the end the focus shifts to Rhoda and her son. Through their dialogue, the writer reveals why she has an interest in the farmer, and the last thing she says leaves us wondering why she is so keen to hear about the bride and what might be the result of her curiosity.
5–6	• You have clearly explained the effect of structural features. • You have chosen relevant examples. • You have used subject terminology accurately.	At the beginning the focus is on the milking shed and we get an idea of their daily lives. The writer uses direct speech to tell us about the farmer getting married, and the last bit of dialogue tells us it has something to do with the 'worn milkmaid'. Then the focus changes to the worn milkmaid as she meets her son after work. Their conversation reveals to us that the farmer is the boy's father.

[Maximum 8 marks]

2.

Marks	Skills	Examples of possible content
16–20	• You have critically evaluated the text in a detailed way. • You have used examples from the text to explain your views convincingly. • You have analysed a range of the writer's methods. • You have used a range of relevant quotations to support your views.	Rhoda Brook is introduced as a 'thin fading woman'. She is a milkmaid, indicating her rural working-class background, but the writer's use of the phrase 'apart from the rest' suggests that she is somehow different. Perhaps she thinks she is better than the others or perhaps they look down on her. It may be a mixture of both, as the conversation between the milkers hints that she had a relationship with the farmer. The writer tells us she also lives 'apart' from others, emphasizing her solitary nature. The personification of the heath's 'dark countenance' suggests sadness and maybe mystery. This is reflected in Rhoda's nature and situation.
11–15	• You have clearly evaluated the text. • You have used examples from the text to explain your views clearly. • You have clearly explained the effect of the writer's methods. • You have used some relevant quotations to support your views.	The writer makes us interested in Rhoda Brook by not explaining anything about her but giving us hints. She is first described as 'a thin fading woman of thirty' and she does not work with the others. Perhaps she does not get on with the others or she just prefers to be alone. Because the others look at her when talking about the farmer, we can infer that she had a relationship with him. Later we find out that she had a son by him. This is scandalous and might explain why she is 'apart'.

[Maximum 20 marks]

3.

Content and Organization		
22–24	Content:	• You have communicated convincingly and compellingly throughout. • Your tone, style and register assuredly match purpose, form and audience. • You have used an extensive and ambitious vocabulary with sustained crafting of linguistic devices.
	Organization:	• Your writing is highly structured and developed, including a range of integrated and complex ideas. • Your paragraphs are fluently linked with integrated discourse markers. • You have used a variety of structural features in an inventive way.
19–21	Content:	• You have communicated convincingly. • Your tone, style and register consistently match purpose, form and audience. • You have used an extensive vocabulary with evidence of conscious crafting of linguistic devices.
	Organization:	• Your writing is structured and developed, including a range of engaging and complex ideas. • You have used paragraphs consistently with integrated discourse markers. • You have used a variety of structural features effectively.
16–18	Content:	• You have communicated clearly and effectively. • Your tone, style and register match purpose, form and audience. • You have used an increasingly sophisticated vocabulary with a range of appropriate linguistic devices.
	Organization:	• Your writing is engaging, including a range of engaging and detailed connected ideas. • You have used paragraphs coherently, with integrated discourse markers. • You have used structural features effectively.
13–15	Content:	• You have communicated clearly. • Your tone, style and register generally match purpose, form and audience. • You have used vocabulary for effect with a range of linguistic devices.
	Organization:	• Your writing is engaging, including a range of connected ideas. • You have usually used paragraphs coherently, with a range of discourse markers. • You have usually used structural features effectively.

Technical Accuracy	
13–16	• You have consistently demarcated sentences accurately. • You have used a wide range of punctuation with a high level of accuracy. • You have used a full range of sentence forms for effect. • You have used Standard English consistently and accurately, with secure control of grammatical structures. • You have achieved a high level of accuracy in spelling, including ambitious vocabulary. • Your use of vocabulary is extensive and ambitious.
9–12	• You have usually demarcated sentences accurately. • You have used a range of punctuation, usually accurately. • You have used a variety of sentence forms for effect. • You have used Standard English appropriately, with control of grammatical structures. • You have spelled most words, including complex and irregular words, correctly. • Your use of vocabulary is increasingly sophisticated.

[Maximum 40 marks]

Pages 48–55 Revise Questions

Page 49 Quick Test
1. Biography. 2. Letter.
3. Diary. 4. Autobiography.

Page 51 Quick Test
2 (news report).
Page 53 Quick Test
1. To argue your point of view.
2. The governors. 3. Letter.

Page 55 Quick Test
1. Yours sincerely.
2. Yours faithfully.
3. Yours faithfully.
4. Yours sincerely.

Pages 56–57 Review Questions

1. See 'Skills' column of table on p. 129 (for p. 46–47 Practice Questions, Q1).

Marks	Examples of possible content
7–8	The writer wants to create an air of mystery and to keep the reader curious. He distances the death of Sir Charles by describing it in Dr Mortimer's speech. In his first paragraph he talks about Sir Charles's health, which the reader might think explains his death, but he ends with the word 'catastrophe'. This makes us want to know what the awful thing was. The next paragraph is about his experience on the night of the death and builds up to his revelation that there was more to it than was revealed at the inquest. This adds to the mystery but he still does not reveal his information. Holmes asks him questions that might be in the reader's mind, while delaying the shock revelation.
5–6	The doctor builds up to a revelation by describing following Sir Charles's footprints. At the end he mentions that he knows something no-one else has noticed but keeps back the information until Holmes questions him. This makes the fact that 'they were the footprints of a gigantic hound' have more impact on the reader.

[Maximum 8 marks]

2. See 'Skills' column of table on p. 129 (for p. 46–47 Practice Questions, Q2).

Marks	Examples of possible content
16–20	We are not told anything about the doctor's character, but the fact that he is a professional, scientific man implies he is a reliable witness. This is confirmed by his suspicion that Sir Charles's illness was 'chimerical', suggesting he is not easily convinced of things. He describes how he 'checked and corroborated' the evidence from the inquest, implying that he is both thorough and independent-minded. The fact that he has done this, and the careful and detailed description he gives, make the reader more inclined to accept his story than if it had been told in a sensational way.
11–15	The story of finding the footprints is far-fetched but the use of Dr Mortimer to tell it makes it more believable. This is because he is a doctor and he tells the story in a calm way, remembering details: 'I noted that there were no other footsteps save those of Barrymore on the soft gravel.' When the writer says 'his voice sank almost to a whisper', the reader gets the impression that he is scared and shocked.

[Maximum 20 marks]

3. Look at the mark scheme for Question 3 on pages 46 and 47, decide which description is closest to your answer and then decide which mark to give yourself. This task is marked for content and organization, and for technical accuracy.

Pages 58–59 Practice Questions

1. Look at the mark scheme below, decide which description is closest to your answer and then decide which mark to give yourself.
See 'Skills' column of table on p. 128 (for pages 44–45 Review Questions, Q3).

Marks	Examples of possible content
10–12	The writer's tone is quite serious and authoritative. The expression 'confounds the moralist' suggests that he is dealing with a moral problem. He uses hyperbole to show he loves dogs ('the great soul'). Other rhetorical devices he uses include the rhetorical question ('Where will the process end?') and the list of three, combined with alliteration ('crib, cabin, and confine'). He uses emotive language to make us feel sorry for the small dogs: 'frets the puny body to decay'.
7–9	The writer uses Standard English and sounds as if he knows what he's talking about. He uses impressive phrases like the 'great soul' to show he loves dogs and feels sad that they are made into 'puny' animals. He uses a rhetorical question ('Where will the process end?') to make us think about the consequences of breeding these dogs.

[Maximum 12 marks]

2. Look at the mark scheme below, decide which description is closest to your answer and then decide which mark to give yourself.

Marks	Examples of possible content	
13–16	• You have compared ideas and perspectives in a perceptive way. • You have analysed methods used to convey ideas and perspectives. • You have used a range of appropriate quotations.	Both these writers are very passionate about their subject. The first writer attacks those who breed small dogs by making the dogs sound like victims ('all eyes and nerves') but also calls them 'pampered'. Hanlon picks up on this but cannot see what's wrong with pampering – she sees it as love. Her tone is chatty and personal, while his is impersonal and authoritative.

| 9–12 | • You have compared ideas and perspectives in a clear and relevant way.
• You have explained clearly methods used to convey ideas and perspectives.
• You have used relevant quotations from both texts. | The writer in *The Times* uses rhetorical devices to convince his readers. He claims to love dogs but is against breeding small dogs and treating them like toys. Hanlon defends people who have small dogs, saying those who attack them are just having a go at celebrities. She too uses rhetorical questions. |

[Maximum 16 marks]

3. Look at the mark scheme for the answer to Question 3 on pages 46 and 47, decide which description is closest to your answer and then decide which mark to give yourself. This task is marked for content and organization, and for technical accuracy.

Pages 60–67 **Revise Questions**

Page 61 Quick Test
1. False. 2. False.
3. False. 4. True.

Page 63 Quick Test
1. Soliloquy. 2. Dialogue.
3. Plot. 4. Theme.
Page 65 Quick Test
1. False. 2. False. 3. True. 4. True.

Page 67 Quick Test
1. Metaphor/Rhetorical question.
2. Oxymoron. 3. Rhetorical question.
4. Rhyming couplet.

Pages 68–69 **Review Questions**

1. Look at the mark scheme below, decide which description is closest to your answer and then decide which mark to give yourself.
   See 'Skills' column of table on p. 128 (for pages 44–45 Review Questions, Q3).

Marks	Examples of possible content
10–12	Most of the passage is a quite straightforward account of the walk, which is what you would expect from a diary entry – it is written in the first person and the past tense and just describes what she saw, often using simple sentences ('The lake was rough'), and fragments ('A few primroses by the roadside'). The effect of this is to make it seem fresh and immediate. When she describes the daffodils she uses more 'literary' language, personifying them: they 'rested their heads' and 'reeled and danced'.
7–9	She does not always used complete sentences ('Saw the plough…') which makes it seem like she's writing notes for herself. She describes nature in great detail – 'The hawthornes are black and green' – so you can picture it. The simple sentence 'I never saw daffodils so beautiful' emphasizes her strong emotion.

[Maximum 12 marks]

2. See 'Skills' column of table on p. 130 (for pages 58–59 Review Questions, Q2).

Marks	Examples of possible content
13–16	Wordsworth seems to be writing for herself, reflecting on her day, whereas Betsy is very aware of her audience. She uses hyperbole, 'complete washout' and 'like the workhouse', for comic effect. She writes in a colloquial way, as she might talk to her friends – 'ropes and stuff'. She also describes other members of the party in a critical yet amusing way (the Camp Commandant…with her whistle round her neck'), while Wordsworth makes no comment about her companions.
9–12	While Wordsworth clearly gets a lot of pleasure from observing nature, Betsy hates walking round the lake. Betsy is quite sarcastic and exaggerates everything for humour – 'It's like the workhouse'. Wordsworth's writing is serious and descriptive, not saying much about her feelings, but Betsy only thinks about herself.

[Maximum 16 marks]

3. Look at the mark scheme for the answer to Question 3 on pages 46 and 47. This task is marked for content and organization, and for technical accuracy.

Pages 70–71 **Practice Questions**

For all questions, look at the mark scheme below.

Marks	Skills
26–30	• You have responded to the task in an exploratory and critical way. • You have used precise, appropriate references to support your interpretation. • You have analysed the writer's methods using subject terminology appropriately. • You have explored the effects of the writer's methods. • You have explored links between text and ideas/context.
21–25	• You have responded to the task in a thoughtful, developed way. • You have used appropriate references to support your interpretation. • You have examined the writer's methods using subject terminology effectively. • You have examined the effects of the writer's methods. • You have thoughtfully considered links between text and ideas/context.

[Maximum 30 marks]

Your answers could include some of the following points.
1. *Romeo and Juliet*
   • Juliet's impatience with the Nurse – references to time.
   • Use of the soliloquy.
   • Her thoughts jumping about – use of caesura.
   • Personification of love.
   • Allusions to classical mythology.

   • Contrast of old and young – her belief that the old cannot understand.
   • Imagery of light and dark.
   • Her dependence on the Nurse, reflecting social context.
2. *Macbeth*
   • He sees power as good and desirable – 'happy prologues'.
   • He uses a metaphor of music to express how he sees things developing.

   • He immediately has doubts because of the source of the prophecy.
   • Use of soliloquy.
   • Use of rhetorical questions.
   • The 'horrid' image is the idea of killing the king to gain power.
   • The prophecy has a physical effect on him.
3. *The Tempest*
   • Ariel is a slave who has to do as he is told.

- He is loyal to Prospero and does not rebel, but wants to hold him to his bargain.
- Prospero reacts angrily to mention of Ariel's 'freedom'.
- Use of questions, exclamations and caesura to show this.
- Prospero treats Ariel like a naughty child. Father/child relationship?
- Prospero feels Ariel is indebted to him and has to be reminded of his past.

4. *The Merchant of Venice*
- She is his only daughter.
- He is protective to the point of locking her up – his main fear is that she marries a gentile.
- There is no evidence of any affection between them.
- When she elopes he seems more concerned with the money she has stolen than with her.
- Her giving of the ring for a monkey indicates how little respect she has for him.
- The audience's sympathies may change.

5. *Julius Caesar*
- They both feel he has taken too much power.
- Cassius persuades Brutus to join the conspiracy.
- Cassius seems to have a personal grudge against Caesar.
- He describes him as physically weak and tells a story to prove it.
- Brutus is more interested in principles. He wants to defend Rome rather than attack Caesar.
- Caesar is shocked by Brutus's action ('Et tu, Brute?').

6. *Much Ado About Nothing*
- She is not married and is ambivalent about being single.
- She is witty, opinionated and happy to express her opinions to men.
- She does not like being told what to do – but the less assertive Hero can trick her.
- She has a strong sense of justice and family loyalty.
- She is dependent on her uncle.
- She marries but on her own terms.

Pages 72–79 **Revise Questions**

Page 73 Quick Test
1. False. 2. False. 3. True. 4. True.
Page 75 Quick Test
1. Yes. 2. An image or idea that recurs in a text. 3. Yes. 4. Yes.
Page 77 Quick Test
No definitive answer – check your notes.
Page 79 Quick Test
1. A variation of English spoken in a particular region. 2. The language of conversation. 3. An object that represents an idea or feeling. 4. Part of the story that takes place at an earlier time.

Pages 80–81 **Review Questions**

For mark scheme, see answers above to questions on pages 70 and 71. Your answers could include some of the following points.
1. *Julius Caesar*
   - He starts with an oath ('Ye gods') to express the strength of his feelings.
   - The contrast between Cassius's attitude and that of the people of Rome is underlined by the off-stage noises, which form a background.

- He compares Caesar to one of the wonders of the ancient world, the Colossus, describing his power in terms of physical size.
- He uses words like 'petty' and 'dishonourable' to emphasize that Caesar is 'great' only because others let him be.
- He argues against the idea that we're controlled by fate and can do nothing.
- He insists that Caesar is no better than anyone else.
- He hammers home his point with two rhetorical questions.

2. *Much Ado About Nothing*
- Beatrice's tone is light-hearted and jokey, although she is talking about a serious matter.
- The extract is written is prose.
- She feels that she is different – 'Thus goes everyone to the world but I'.
- She flirts with Don Pedro, making a joke from the double meaning of 'get' to imply that she would like to marry him.
- She uses the metaphor of clothes to express the difference in status between her and Don Pedro.
- She tries to avoid a serious conversation by saying she does not take things seriously – 'born to speak all mirth and no matter'.
- The last line sums up her ambiguous attitude to life.

3. *The Merchant of Venice*
- It would seem that Shylock is anxious about Jessica as he had asked for news of her.
- However, he is more concerned about the money she has spent than her whereabouts.
- This is what the Elizabethan audience might expect from a Jew. Modern audiences might think such a stereotype was anti-Semitic.
- The dramatic exclamation (using a metaphor) 'Thou stick'st a dagger in me' suggests pain.
- His attention is soon taken by news about Antonio and he uses violent language to show his delight.
- The revelation about the ring changes our perception again. Shylock cares for his wife's memory, even if Jessica does not.

4. *Romeo and Juliet*
- Romeo's love for Juliet can be compared to his feelings for Rosaline.
- Their use of a sonnet suggests mutual love.
- Religious imagery could show the love to be sacred or could suggest it is sacrilegious.
- In spite of her age, Juliet takes control and makes conditions, wanting to be sure.
- Constant references to 'the stars' suggest their tragedy is inevitable.
- Although the audience's sympathies are with the couple, some could feel they are in the wrong when they defy their parents.

5. *Macbeth*
- Macbeth starts off loyal and happy with his status, but the meeting with the witches gives him ideas.
- His soliloquies show us he is ambitious for power but has a conscience.

- He gives all the reasons for not killing Duncan and seizing power.
- Lady Macbeth taunts him and pushes him into killing Duncan.
- When he gains power he cannot enjoy it because of his conscience and his feelings of vulnerability.
- He commits more and more terrible acts to keep power, abuses power and ruins his country.

6. *The Tempest*
- Ariel is shown doing things that humans cannot, unseen by most characters.
- When he asks for liberty, we know he is a slave.
- Prospero tells the story of how he freed Ariel from Sycorax.
- Ariel is contrasted with Caliban, Prospero's other slave. They can be seen as two parts of humanity, or as two ways of being a slave.
- Ariel obeys Prospero and is rewarded with his freedom.
- An interest in discovery and colonization is reflected in Prospero and Ariel's relationship.

Pages 82–83 **Practice Questions**

For mark scheme, see answers above to questions on pages 70 and 71. Your answers could include some of the following points.
1. *The Strange Case of Dr Jekyll and Mr Hyde*
- The extract is in the third person but is seen through the eyes of a maid, distancing it from the narrator.
- The old man has a 'pretty manner' and 'an innocent and old-world kindness', contrasting with the cruelty of the attacker.
- There is some mystery about why he has 'accosted' Hyde in the street.
- The mention of Hyde's name halfway through alerts the reader to what might happen.
- The violence builds over a few sentences – from impatiently playing with the cane, to brandishing the cane 'like a madman', to attacking him with the cane.
- The expression 'ape-like fury' makes him seem inhuman.

2. *A Christmas Carol*
- The extract shows Scrooge refusing to give to charity.
- His questions show that he thinks the poor are being taken care of and it is none of his business.
- The gentleman mentions 'Christian cheer', reminding us that caring about others is central to Christianity.
- His manner is abrupt and aggressive.
- His language is quite extreme and shocking, suggesting people should die and 'decrease the surplus population'. He thinks of people as just statistics.
- At the end he sets out his philosophy, using the double meaning of 'business' to show both that money is the most important thing for him and that he does not think people like the gentleman should be concerned with others.

3. *Pride and Prejudice*
- The incident is seen through the eyes of Elizabeth, who overhears it, so the impression we get is the same as hers.

- The conversation is a private one with his friend, so we can take it to be his true feelings.
- He is contrasted with Bingley, who is enjoying dancing and is sociable.
- The phrase 'such an assembly as this' makes him sound very snobbish and is an insult to the others there.
- Austen uses Bingley to confirm this impression, calling him 'fastidious'.
- When Bingley suggests he dance with Elizabeth, Darcy shows himself to be bad-mannered as well as snobbish. The adverb 'coldly' sums up his attitude.
- He damns Elizabeth with faint praise, calling her 'tolerable; but not handsome enough to tempt me', asserting his sense of his own superiority.

4. *Great Expectations*
- We learn straightaway that Pip knows nothing about London and it is established that Mr Wemmick has been there some time.
- Pip's question about London being 'wicked' implies an assumption made by people outside London.
- However, he says it 'for the sake of saying something', which implies that he is not concerned or nervous.
- It seems as if Wemmick is more concerned about danger than Pip is, as Pip wants to 'soften' the idea of people being wicked.
- Mr Wemmick paints a picture of an amoral city, but again he does not see London as being different from anywhere else.
- Most of the extract is in dialogue, without much comment. We know nothing about Wemmick and, like Pip, do not know whether to take notice of his opinions.

5. *Frankenstein*
- For most of the novel Frankenstein is the narrator, so his changing feelings are shared with the reader.
- The description of the monster is shocking, causing fear in Frankenstein.
- Frankenstein is concerned about his safety and that of those he loves.
- He does not see beyond the appearance of the monster when he rejects him.
- The monster's actions are horrifying and Frankenstein feels both guilt and hatred.
- The monster can be seen as representing part of Frankenstein.
- His feelings change when the monster is given his own narrative, as do the feelings of the reader.
- Finally there is a sense of a shared tragedy.

6. *The Sign of Four*
- Holmes draws conclusions from seemingly trivial evidence.
- Watson's narrative puts the reader in Watson's place. We know only what Watson knows, not what Holmes knows.
- When Holmes explains his findings they seem logical and, to him, obvious.
- Holmes always keeps something back from Watson, teasing the reader.
- Holmes displays wide and detailed knowledge of what to most people are obscure things.
- In his use of forensics he is ahead of his time and ahead of the police.

- He is set apart from other people. His distrust of women and his drug-taking suggest a mysterious past.

7. *Jane Eyre*
- Brontë builds an air of mystery about Rochester before Jane meets him.
- Their first meeting is dramatic and, while he seems strong, it is she who helps him.
- The relationship between employer and governess is odd. She is neither a servant nor a family member.
- Jane and Rochester both seem to 'earn' each other's love.
- The fire and the discovery of Bertha turn her world upside down. She has been lied to and betrayed.
- The first-person narrative allows us to share Jane's knowledge of Rochester and her feelings about him.
- Symbolism and imagery are important – fire, the chestnut tree etc.
- Rochester's blindness might signify that he can finally see the truth.
- At the end Jane is in control. It is as if she needs Rochester to be weakened in order to truly love him.

Page 85 Quick Test
1. True. 2. True. 3. False. 4. True.
Page 87 Quick Test
All of them.
Page 89 Quick Test
1. Protagonist. 2. Narrator.
3. Dialogue. 4. Stage direction.
Page 91 Quick Test
1. Yes. 2. An act.
3. Where he/she comes from. 4. No.

For mark scheme, see answers above to questions on pages 70 and 71. Your answers could include some of the following points.
1. *Frankenstein*
- The time – 'a dreary night of November' – sets the tone. The description could be seen as pathetic fallacy – 'the rain pattered dismally'.
- His feelings are almost physical ('agony') and give us a feeling of dread rather than excitement.
- He has tried to create a man but does not describe him in human terms. It is a 'creature' and a 'thing'.
- Frankenstein is disgusted by its appearance – the skin and eyes are yellow; the complexion is shrivelled.
- He uses a rhetorical question – 'How can I describe my emotions?' – but then describes the creature, not his emotions.
- His feelings are implied by his description, using adjectives like 'horrid', 'shrivelled' and 'dun'.
- The first-person narrative makes us see the experience as Frankenstein sees it.

2. *The Sign of Four*
- The narrator, Watson, watches and listens carefully. He is in the same position as the reader, waiting for Holmes to act and speak.
- Watson and Holmes have similar reactions to the footprints, but Holmes is less emotional.
- Holmes sees the meaning almost immediately – 'the thing is quite natural'.

- Holmes does not share his conclusions with Watson, challenging him to 'try a little analysis' using his 'methods'. This and his 'offhand way' tell us that he has gifts which seem natural to him but extraordinary to others.
- He is described measuring and examining things, showing that his detection is based on science, not just luck or instinct.
- A simile, 'like…a trained bloodhound', is used to show his keenness and his sensitivity.
- When Watson asks questions – 'What then?' Holmes does not give full answers, keeping us wondering.
- He is confident about his conclusions – 'Why, we have got him, that's all.'

3. *Jane Eyre*
- Jane comes to his aid. He is the master and she the servant, but due to his fall he is in a weak position.
- Jane is the narrator, so we see what she sees and she shares her feelings.
- She does not fall for his looks but points out that he is not handsome or young and, from the point of view of someone writing about her younger self, mocks her own 'theoretical reverence'.
- She concentrates on what he is not rather than what he is, building an idea of an atypical hero.
- At the same time she sees this as something they have in common, because she sees herself as unattractive.
- It is paradoxical that his frown and roughness 'set me at my ease'.
- Fire and lightning might be associated with passion. Does she want to avoid sexual passion?

4. *The Strange Case of Dr Jekyll and Mr Hyde*
- Descriptions of London are central. It is a city of wealth and poverty side-by-side.
- Most events take place in the dark or half-light.
- The multiple narratives mean that the story is 'distanced' from us. Truth is revealed gradually.
- The sealed letters add suspense because we know they might contain answers.
- Many elements are typical of the Gothic tradition.
- Lots of characters have secrets or do things that are not fully explained.
- The narrators, Mr Utterson and Dr Lanyon, are logical, professional men, so they are sceptical. If they're afraid, it must be something awful.
- The physical descriptions of Hyde make him seem almost animal-like.

5. *A Christmas Carol*
- Scrooge is introduced with a description of his appearance, using imagery, and of how strangers react to him.
- In the first chapter, he is seen as having no interest in family, through his conversation with his nephew.
- He expresses his feelings about charity and caring for others in his

conversation with the charitable gentlemen.
- All these encounters are written in quite a comic way, with Dickens as narrator commenting on Scrooge's absurdity.
- The Ghost of Christmas Past is used to show how Scrooge became like he is, making him think about what might have been and gaining some sympathy for him.
- The Ghost of Christmas Present takes the idea of 'other people' beyond family and acquaintances, showing Scrooge that he cannot cut himself off from the world.
- The Ghost of Christmas Yet to Come shows the result of his attitudes.
- Other characters are used as a contrast with Scrooge, showing love and the 'spirit of Christmas' – his nephew, the Cratchits, Mr Fezziwig.

6. *Pride and Prejudice*
- Darcy is mostly seen through Elizabeth's eyes. If he is proud, she is prejudiced.
- His first appearance shows him to be snobbish and unsociable, in contrast with his friend Mr Bingley.
- Society is very class-conscious. Darcy and Lady Catherine de Burgh are the highest-status characters in the novel. Her attitudes are seen as being shared by him, though it turns out he is not really as snobbish.
- Some of his 'pride' could be reserve – perhaps the result of his social class or of his own nature.
- Those who know him best do not see him as proud, while those who criticize him, like Wickham, are not reliable.
- He is concerned about his reputation and that of his family, which can be seen as proud.
- His actions, especially with regard to Wickham, show his true nature.
- In his letter to Elizabeth he admits he did not want Bingley to marry Jane because of the 'connection' but claims this was not because of class but because of the way other family members behaved. Is this pride?

7. *Great Expectations*
- Pip as narrator. Is he naive? Is he unreliable?
- The novel as a 'Bildungsroman'. Pip makes mistakes but learns from his experiences.
- Pip's childhood is vividly portrayed. The atmosphere of the marshes adds to his sense of isolation and a general air of mystery.
- The journey is sometimes literal, as he goes from Kent to London and back again.
- His 'expectations' change him and he is seduced by money and false friends.
- Things change again when Magwitch reappears and he begins to unravel the past.
- His changing relationship with Joe shows how much he is changing, for the worse and then for the better.
- Dickens uses the excitement of the Magwitch story to show Pip taking control and acting as an adult.
- His changing emotions towards Estella reflect a growing maturity.

Give yourself 2 marks for each valid point supported by appropriate evidence. The points below are just suggestions. There are many other valid points to be made.

1. *An Inspector Calls*
- He comes from the 'future' so has the benefit of hindsight.
- He acts like a real detective, trying to solve a crime.
- However, he seems more interested in the other characters' attitudes to Eva – and is it really a crime that would be investigated?
- He is the mouthpiece for the writer, with his speech about the 'future'.
- He is an outsider.
- He sometimes shows his impatience with the responses he gets.

2. *Blood Brothers*
- She is middle-class and well-off.
- Despite her money, she is unhappy because she cannot have a baby, and it's her idea to take one of the babies.
- She seems to be aware that it will end tragically once Edward meets Mickey.
- Her wanting to get away from Mickey looks like snobbery but she is frightened of the secret getting out.
- She has mental health problems, maybe as a result of the secret.
- Her actions precipitate the tragic outcome.

3. *The History Boys*
- He could be seen as the leader of the group – others look up to him.
- He is sexually active and has an amoral attitude to sex.
- He is aware of his own attraction and quite vain – he uses it to bestow favours.
- His language can be very crude but he can also be eloquent.
- He does not understand why he is attracted to Irwin – although he himself sees everything in sexual terms, it is probably something else.
- He can adapt easily from one teacher's ways to another's.
- He realizes that he enjoys having power and using it.

4. *DNA*
- She talks constantly, unlike most of the other characters, in a 'stream of consciousness' style, giving access to her thoughts.
- Her speeches punctuate the action, giving context to the play.
- She comments on what's been going on 'off-stage', giving us an insight into developments.
- She gives her views on all sorts of subjects, some of them quite eccentric.
- She is discovering a lot of things for the first time and finds the world full of wonder.
- What is the meaning of her revelation that she killed her pet?
- What is the point of her relationship/non-relationship with Phil?

5. *The Curious Incident of the Dog in the Night-Time*
- He is the protagonist. It is the story of him growing up.
- He is 'different'. Many people would call him 'autistic' but this is not specifically mentioned.
- He takes things literally and speaks mostly of facts. He does not describe or speculate.
- The audience knows only what he knows, so we discover things with him.
- He proves to himself and others that he can cope, but in his own way.
- Is he the victim or the cause of his family's problems?

6. *A Taste of Honey*
- Her relationship with her mother is central – there is an element of role-reversal in it.
- In some ways she is mature for her age and in others naive.
- She might be seen as typical of a girl of her age and class at the time, but her circumstances are unusual.
- She is witty and honest, and shows signs of creativity.
- She is motivated by not wanting to be like her mother.
- Through her eyes we see a world that is quite prejudiced and repressive, but she is not part of it.

7. *Lord of the Flies*
- Simon is inherently good, the opposite of Jack.
- He is gentle, and kind to the little 'uns.
- He has the same sort of background as the other boys but, in his case, morality and civilization are not superficial.
- He sees what the 'beast' means.
- His hallucinations are almost mystical.
- His murder represents the ultimate triumph of evil and savagery.
- He can be seen as a sacrificial victim, perhaps like Jesus.

8. *Telling Tales*
- Carla is the narrator, so we see things through her eyes.
- She is the 'tea lady' in a staffroom, a person people do not really notice, so she can observe things without being part of them.
- She tells her story in a straightforward way, as if telling it to a friend.
- She is conscious of her status – not being a teacher – and keeps it from Steve.
- She is half-Polish and her friendship with Steve helps her rediscover that part of her identity.

9. *Animal Farm*
- Boxer represents the honest working class, exploited by others.
- He is hard-working and loyal – first to Mr Jones, and then to the pigs.
- His naivety and trusting nature mean he is easily exploited.
- He is drawn sympathetically, though some readers might find him dull and frustrating.
- His death illustrates how little regard the pigs have for other animals.
- Without him the farm could not operate but he is not valued.

10. *Never Let Me Go*
- Tommy is shown from the start to be different from the others.
- His fits of temper and lack of 'creativity' mark him out.
- He does not actively rebel but he does not seem able to conform.
- For most of the novel Kathy does not understand his attitude but (unlike Ruth) she listens to him.

- Tommy is interested in finding out about the 'gallery' and other aspects of Hailsham before Kathy is.
- Like the others, his value to society is only as a donor – but he inspires friendship and love in Kathy.

11. *Anita and Me*
- Anita, as the title suggests, is the focus of the novel, though not the protagonist.
- She could be seen as an antagonist, in some ways the opposite of Meena.
- The changes in Meena's attitude to her show that Meena is growing up.
- She represents the white working-class culture of Tollington, which Meena is part of and yet not part of.
- Her troubled family helps to make her more sympathetic.
- She is a leader, looked up to by other children.
- Her association with Sam brings the community's racism into focus.

12. *Pigeon English*
- He is protagonist and narrator. We see things through his eyes. Is he a reliable narrator?
- His narration resembles a diary; its tone is chatty and colloquial.
- He is a young boy, a recent immigrant from Ghana. His speech reflects his background.
- He is keen to 'solve' the murder, not realizing the danger he is in.
- His innocence leads him to see things in a positive light, treating most of life as a game, although he is in a very dangerous environment.

Pages 96–105 Revise Questions

Page 97 Quick Test
1. False. 2. False. 3. True. 4. True.
Page 99 Quick Test
1. Yes. 2. Yes. 3. Yes. 4. No.
Page 101 Quick Test
1. Onomatopoeia. 2. Personification (or pathetic fallacy) 3. Alliteration.
4. Persona.
Page 103 Quick Test
1. Rhyming couplet. 2. Internal rhyme.
3. Ballad. 4. Free verse.
Page 105 Quick Test
1. Similarity. 2. Difference.
3. Difference. 4. Similarity.

Pages 106–107 Review Questions

Give yourself 2 marks for each valid point supported by appropriate evidence. The points below are just suggestions. There are many other valid points to be made.

1. *An Inspector Calls*
- At the time the play is set, women did not have the vote.
- Eva, the working-class woman, represents different things in different people's eyes. Their ideas of her are shaped by gender and class.
- Mrs Birling fulfils the expected role of a middle-class wife, sitting on committees and giving charity.
- Sheila seems to do little but shop and get engaged – but she finds a voice at the end.
- There is a double standard in terms of sexual morality.

- The female characters are strong and opinionated.

2. *Blood Brothers*
- By starting with a tableau of the end, Russell shows the tragedy is inevitable.
- Mrs Johnstone is very superstitious: for example, she reacts angrily to seeing shoes put upon the table.
- Mrs Lyons does not believe in superstitions at first but becomes obsessed by escaping from fate.
- The narrator speaks about fate.
- The characters might think their lack of choice is because of fate, but is it the consequence of their actions?
- Or is it the result of economics and politics?

3. *The History Boys*
- Double/triple meaning in title – are the boys making history as well as studying history? Could this have happened only in the past?
- As far as the head teacher is concerned, the subject itself is not important. He just wants them to make the school look good.
- Mrs Lintott's approach to history is conventional and designed to equip pupils to pass exams.
- Irwin wants them to question everything – a different way of looking at history.
- However, Irwin's approach is also about passing exams – just different exams. He knows what they want.
- Irwin's idea that there is 'no need to tell the truth' can be applied to history, politics and life in general.
- Irwin ends up playing a part in history as a political adviser.

4. *DNA*
- When they think they are guilty of a crime, their reaction is to avoid blame.
- Some of the teenagers are nervous and scared but do not really accept their responsibility.
- They tend to look for 'leaders' – John Tate, Phil, Cathy to absolve them from responsibility.
- Not taking responsibility for the crime they haven't committed leads them to pin the guilt on the innocent postman. They have no qualms about this.
- Later they plan the actual murder of Adam. By this time some of them have drifted off. Only Leah objects.
- Although they do not express guilty feelings or take responsibility, Leah reveals how guilt might have affected some of them – Brian on medication and John 'finding God'.

5. *The Curious Incident of the Dog in the Night-Time*
- Christopher's family is shown as being unusual, as he lives with his widowed father. Like Christopher, the audience would probably admire his father.
- Our perceptions are changed when we find Ed has lied and Judy is alive.
- We learn this when Christopher does, through the sympathetic character of Mrs Alexander.
- Christopher's relationships with his parents are difficult as he does not like physical contact and does not express emotion. He does not realize this is a problem.

- We see the strain this has put on his parents in different ways.
- Judy's letters give a nostalgic account of a happier family, as well as explaining her point of view about the difficulties of family life.

6. *A Taste of Honey*
- Helen is not interested in love. She is described as a 'semi-whore' and marries Peter for a comfortable life.
- Jo's relationship with the Boy seems romantic, especially because of his race.
- Jo does not seem to be too bothered about his not coming back. Perhaps because of her background, she has no idea of long-term relationships.
- The only relationship that seems loving is with her homosexual friend Geof. Maybe she cannot connect love and sex.
- The central relationship is that between Jo and Helen – a 'love–hate' relationship.
- Jo's relationships are all unconventional for the time, but the play is part of the fashion for 'kitchen sink drama', trying to show 'real life' on the stage.

7. *Lord of the Flies*
- The boys' background – British, public school – suggests they are the epitome of Western civilization, so their savagery is shocking.
- They seek organization and order at first, but they are constructing an idea of order.
- Strong leadership emerges in the form of Jack, showing that the idea of 'leadership' as a force for good is misplaced.
- Civilization is a thin veneer. Given the opportunity, our instincts are to be savage, even evil.
- The beast is a symbol of savagery.
- The breakdown of 'civilization' on the island is no worse than the wars being fought by the apparently civilized world.

8. *Telling Tales*
- The story is set in a community where the reality of death is ever-present. Accidental deaths in the mines are not uncommon.
- Elizabeth's father's attitude is practical. His first wife has died so he needs another one. He is not sentimental.
- The reactions of Walter's wife and mother are very different. His mother is distraught, while his wife seems to feel little emotion.
- The bringing in and laying out of the body are described in detail, giving a sense of the physicality of death.
- His death makes Elizabeth reflect on their relationship – his death 'restored the truth'.
- The chrysanthemums are symbolic, their significance changing.
- Elizabeth has to 'submit' to life and carry on but she is now aware that death is her 'ultimate master'.

9. *Animal Farm*
- The animals escape one form of oppression only to find another.
- They allow the pigs to change into oppressors by looking to them for leadership and naively trusting them.
- The pigs use slogans and songs as instruments of oppression.

- They change and manipulate language in order to oppress the other animals.
- The oppressors depend on spies and traitors to survive.
- *Animal Farm* is based on the events after the Russian Revolution but it is a 'fable' and its lessons can be applied to all kinds of oppressive regimes.

10. *Never Let Me Go*
- The novel centres on Kathy's friendship with Ruth and Tommy, seen through her eyes.
- Friendship may be more important to them because they do not have families.
- Their friendships are in many ways like those of any teenagers/young adults, but they are more intense because of their being kept apart.
- Friendships often turn into sexual relationships. People want to be part of a couple.
- Kathy notices in the Cottages that behaviour is often copied from TV programmes. This might cast doubt on whether any of the clones really do have feelings for each other.
- The relationship between carer and donor is a form of friendship – Kathy is allowed to choose her donors.

11. *Anita and Me*
- Meena's family are a novelty in Tollington. As there are no other non-white children, Meena keeps her culture separate.
- Differences in culture are shown in dress and in food. Meena's mother and Mrs Worrall cook in completely different ways.
- The cultures are differentiated by language.
- Meena wants to belong and acts like the other children, exaggerating her accent to be accepted.
- There is an element of class difference as well as ethnic difference. Meena's family are well educated and middle-class.
- The visit of Nanima brings Meena closer to her Punjabi culture. She is protective of her grandmother and, by implication, her culture.
- Meena becomes aware of racism as she matures. When the novel

ends she moves away from Tollington and further into her Punjabi culture.

12. *Pigeon English*
- The novel focuses on the repercussions of a single violent act – a boy's murder.
- Harri is fascinated by the murder and tries to investigate it, treating it as an adventure rather than a dangerous reality.
- The school and area are dominated by gangs, who often commit violence.
- Harri's aunt has committed an act of violence on herself.
- Violence and petty crime seem to be part of everyday life on the estate.
- and drawn into the violence.
- The novel was inspired by a real-life murder and tries to understand the gang culture of Britain's cities.

Pages 108–109 Practice Questions

1. a) First person (plural).   b) Past.
    c) They make us feel as if he is recounting an experience shared with others.
    d) In the trenches during the First World War (winter).
    e) Eight stanzas of equal length, each five lines, the last line being shorter.
    f) It is as if he has an extra thought (after the quatrain) or as if his thought is unfinished. It makes the refrain stand out, leaving a pause for thought.
    g) The refrain changes between 'but nothing happens' and variations on 'dying'. The first 'what are we doing here?' is like a stifled cry to which there is no answer as Owen returns to 'but nothing happens'. Stanzas 5–7 look for answers, but after he says that the love of God is dying, he returns to the hopelessness of nothing happening.
    h) 'east winds that knife us' identifies nature with violence; 'the mad gusts tugging on the wire' calls to mind the mental effect of the conflict as well as physical dangers of the wire.
    i) 'Gunnery rumbles' reflects the deep ominous sound of the guns.
    j) It is as if they are dreaming or even hallucinating about being at home, returning as 'ghosts' when they have died. The warmth contrasts with cold reality, but even this image is sad, as the houses are empty.
    [2 marks for each point]

2. a) First person – includes both singular and plural, as well as the second person singular. b) Past.
    c) It is about personal memories, addressed to the person he shared them with.
    d) Winter, by a lake.
    e) Four stanzas of four lines each (quatrains).
    f) *abba* The regularity of the rhyme scheme makes the memories seem organized and calm.
    g) 'as eyes that rove over tedious riddles'. It suggests that she is bored and perhaps does not understand him.
    h) It marks the end of the memory and suggests that a lot of things have passed since, fading away from him.
    i) 'Wrings with wrong' gives a sense of the almost physical pain she has caused him.
    j) The literal imagery paints a depressing picture. Nature is dead – cold and dry – reflecting the state of the relationship.
    [2 marks for each point]

3. a) A persona. An old mother.
    b) In a house, probably in a poor rural area, during the course of a day.
    c) Yes. There are four stressed syllables per line, though the number of unstressed syllables varies. The regularity could reflect the routine of her day. In spite of her hard life, it gives the poem a cheerful tone.
    d) Yes. It is in rhyming couplets, regular and simple, reflecting a regular and simple life.
    e) Mostly, it is literal, describing what she sees, though the fire could be taken as a metaphor for life and the stars are personified as they 'blink and peep'.
    f) It is the story of an ordinary old woman's day and her life.
    g) Fire could be a symbol of life. Growing feeble and then cold is an image for old age.
    h) Old age. A woman's role. Death. Work. Envy of the young.
    i) He feels sympathy for the old woman. He sees life as pointless. He is saddened by the passing of time.
    j) All answers are valid.
    [2 marks for each point]

Pages 110–111 Review Questions

1.

Marks	Skills
26–30	• You have compared texts in an exploratory and critical way. • You have used precise, appropriate references to support your interpretation. • You have analysed the writer's methods using subject terminology appropriately. • You have explored the effects of the writer's methods. • You have explored links between text and ideas/context.
21–25	• You have made thoughtful, developed comparisons. • You have used appropriate references to support your interpretation. • You have examined the writer's methods using subject terminology effectively. • You have examined the effects of the writer's methods. • You have thoughtfully considered links between text and ideas/context.

[Maximum 30 marks]

a) Your answer might include:
- Ideas about who is affected by conflict and how – soldiers, relatives, civilians.
- Comparisons dealing with soldiers during and after the conflict: 'The Charge of the Light Brigade', 'Bayonet Charge', 'Exposure', 'Remains'.
- Comparisons of the effect on non-combatants: 'Poppies', 'The Émigrée', 'War Photographer'.
- Use of language, e.g. alliteration.

- Use of imagery and descriptions of nature.
- The use of the speaker to explore ideas and context.

b) Your answer might include:
- Ideas about what love means – 'I think of thee!',

'When We Two Parted', 'Winter Swans'.
- Different stages in love; the beginning and the end – 'Neutral Tones', 'Singh Song!', 'When We Two Parted'.
- The use of imagery of nature.

- Romantic ideas about love and relationships.
- Direct address to the loved one.
- Structure of a logical argument.

2. a)

Marks	Skills
21–24	• You have explored the text critically. • You have used precise references to support your interpretation. • You have analysed the writer's methods using appropriate subject terminology. • You have explored the effects of the writer's methods on the reader.
17–20	• You have responded thoughtfully to the text. • You have used appropriate references to support your interpretation. • You have examined the writer's methods using subject terminology effectively. • You have examined the effects of the writer's methods on the reader.

Your answer might include comments on:
- Clare's entirely positive view of nature.
- Repetition of 'I love'.
- Use of the sonnet form for a poem about nature.
- Hope and joy brought about by the season.
- Use of personification.
- Listing of all aspects of nature – animals, plants, the weather.
- The idea of nature being 'happy' and at 'play'.
- The lack of punctuation, giving a sense of freedom.
- Use of alliteration and onomatopoeia to create sounds – 'rustle like a wind shook wood'.

[Maximum 24 marks]

b)

Marks	Skills
7–8	• You have explored comparisons of the writers' use of language, structure and form, using appropriate subject terminology. • You have convincingly compared the effects of the writers' methods on the reader.
5–6	• You have thoughtfully compared the writers' use of language and/or structure and/or form, using effective subject terminology. • You have clearly compared the effects of the writers' methods on the reader.

Your answer might include comments on:
- Differing attitudes to nature.
- Difference in focus on one creature / all nature.
- Presence of speaker.
- Use of imagery.
- Use made of techniques such as alliteration.
- Differences in structure.

[Maximum 8 marks]

Pages 112–126 Mixed Exam-Style Questions

1. b, c, e, h [4]

2. See 'Skills' column of table on p. 128 (for pages 34–35 Practice Questions, Q2).

Marks	Examples of possible content
7–8	The writer writes at first as if he is explaining something to us, describing in detail something that is happening now. The phrase 'the spirit of the devil' makes us think of evil, and the descriptions of darkness and flames might also have connotations of hell and damnation. Yet there is a sense of excitement in the extended metaphor of the horse race. The paragraph ends with a comic contrast between the danger of the fire and the passengers' down-to-earth colloquial reaction: 'We're stopping where we are. Push on, George.'
5–6	He writes in the present tense and we can imagine ourselves there. The metaphor of the 'steeple-chase' makes the tram seem like a living thing and the experience like being on a horse. There is a contrast between the 'blackness' and 'heart of nowhere', which sound ominous, and the cheerful speech of the people.

[Maximum 8 marks]

3. See 'Skills' column of table on p. 129 (for p. 46–47 Practice Questions, Q1).

Marks	Examples of possible content
7–8	The writer moves from the general to the particular. The first three paragraphs move from describing the trams as something exotic and fantastical to telling us about particular people on them. The mood changes at the start of paragraph 2 with 'the reason for this', which leads into an account of what the trams are actually used for, contrasting with the fantastical imagery of the first paragraph…
5–6	At first the focus is on the tram ride and how exciting it is, at the same time telling us about the setting. The focus shifts to the passengers and how they feel about the tram service – more of the reality of it. In the third paragraph he gives a general description of drivers and conductors. Then we have some dialogue, which brings the focus to one conductor, Annie.

[Maximum 8 marks]

4. See 'Skills' column of table on p. 130 (for pages 56–57 Review Questions, Q2).

Marks	Examples of possible content
16–20	The writer only describes the men briefly, his main focus being the girl conductors. However, he gives a very vivid impression of the men in a few words. Although they are 'cripples and hunchbacks', who might be looked down on, especially because they are not at war, they have the 'spirit of the devil', a comparison which makes them seem exotic and exciting. The girls are introduced to us as 'fearless young hussies', implying that they do not behave in the way expected of women at the time. He goes on to compare them to non-commissioned officers. Coupled with a description of their unflattering uniform, this may not sound complimentary, but the tone of the description suggests admiration and respect…

Answers

137

| 11–15 | At first the people who work on the trams sound like misfits and are described in a quite insulting way – 'cripples and hunchbacks', but then the writer says they have 'the spirit of the devil in them'. This could mean they are wicked but, from what he then says, I think he means they are reckless and brave. The girls are different because they would not be at war anyway. They are young and very confident. He calls them 'fearless young hussies', which makes them sound attractive but a bit frightening. |

[Maximum 20 marks]

5. Look at the mark scheme for Question 3 on pages 46 and 47. This task is marked for content and organization, and for technical accuracy.
   [Maximum 40 marks]

6. b, d, f, g **[4]**

7. See 'Skills' column of table on p. 128 (for pages 34–35 Practice Questions, Q4).

Marks	Examples of possible content
7–8	Both writers say the city is beautiful. Dickens describes the view from outside the city and then the centre. Rackham describes tourist places, like the Ponte Vecchio, but says tourists are 'littering' it and also mentions graffiti and 'a very ugly souvenir stall'. Dickens does not say anything about other tourists. While Rackham focuses on the 'dilemma' facing the city, Dickens is most interested in the prison and the life of the 'blood-stained' inmates.
5–6	Dickens is very impressed by the 'magnificent' city and describes its beauty. Rackham also describes some of the attractions but talks about graffiti and an 'ugly' stall. Dickens sees a negative side of the city but for him it is the prison, next to the great castle, and the violence of a place where 'they are all blood-stained'. According to Rackham, the downside of Florence is all the tourists, who are spoiling what they come to see.

[Maximum 8 marks]

8. See 'Skills' column of table on p. 128 (for pages 34–35 Practice Questions, Q2).

Marks	Examples of possible content
10–12	In the first paragraph, Dickens uses images of light and richness to describe Florence: 'bright…glittering…like gold!' His exclamations and his use of the second person ('we') make us feel his wonder as if we were there with him. In the second paragraph, he moves into the city and his language reflects both the atmosphere and the architecture. He personifies the buildings, describing 'distrustful windows' and saying they 'frown, in their old sulky state'…
7–9	Dickens writes in the present tense and the first person ('we') as if he is telling us what happens as it happens. He describes the buildings as if they were people, saying they 'frown'. He contrasts the beautiful palaces with the prison, summing up how uncomfortable it is in the simile 'cells like ovens'.

[Maximum 12 marks]

9. See 'Skills' column of table on p. 130 (for pages 58–59 Practice Questions, Q2).

Marks	Examples of possible content
13–16	Dickens is writing about his personal experience of visiting Florence and the effect it had on him, whereas the purpose of Rackham's article is to examine the 'dilemma' of a city dependent on tourists being ruined by 'mass tourism and potential speculators'. Dickens uses hyperbolic, poetic images to describe the city 'shining in the sun like gold' but also 'stern and sombre'. Rackham starts almost by imitating Dickens as she describes a statue looking 'sternly', but for her this implies a judgement on the tourists, and from then on her focus is not on describing the city but on the issues.
9–12	Rackham writes about the issues of tourism and pollution and their effect on the city. Dickens does not mention this, perhaps because it was not a problem in his day. He describes the 'magnificent' city in detail, whereas she just sketches in a few details about the shops on the Ponte Vecchio in order to show us the 'dilemma of contemporary Florence'.

[Maximum 16 marks]

10. Look at the mark scheme for Question 3 on pages 46 and 47. This task is marked for content and organization, and for technical accuracy.
   [Maximum 40 marks]

Questions 11–16
For all questions, look at the mark scheme table on p.131 (for pages 70–71 Practice Questions).
[Maximum 30 marks]

This question is also marked for AO4 (spelling, punctuation and grammar).
For all questions, look at the mark scheme below.

Marks	Description of performance
4	• You have spelled and punctuated with consistent accuracy. • You have consistently used vocabulary and sentence structures to achieve effective control of meaning.
2–3	• You have spelled and punctuated with considerable accuracy. • You have consistently used a considerable range of vocabulary and sentence structures to achieve general control of meaning.

[Maximum 4 marks]

Your answers could include some of the following points.

11. *Julius Caesar*
   • Antony's use of rhetorical language.
   • His claim that he is not going to praise Caesar.
   • His praise of Brutus and the conspirators.
   • The way he seeks to portray himself as one of the people.
   • His position as Caesar's protégé.
   • His actions after he has got the people on his side.
   • His dealings with Octavius and Lepidus.

12. *Much Ado About Nothing*
   • Two meanings of honour – sexual reputation and the obligation to defend your reputation and that of your friends.
   • Benedick knows Hero has been 'wronged' and her honour questioned.
   • Benedick is not part of Hero's family so he is not obliged to defend her.
   • What Beatrice has in mind is 'a man's office' – different ideas of honour for men and women.
   • Defending Hero's honour shows Benedick's love for Beatrice.

- It also shows that he understands 'honour' as being a matter of right and wrong, not loyalty to friends.
- Honour is associated with the court and the aristocracy. Claudio has not acted as a man of his class should.

13. *Macbeth*
- Contrast between Macbeth's guilt and Lady Macbeth's lack of guilt.
- Lady Macbeth takes control.
- The knocking makes him nervous but she reacts in a practical way.
- She speaks to him as if telling off a child.
- She may be more ruthless, as she is happy to blame the grooms.
- Lady Macbeth persuades Macbeth to murder Duncan. She embraces evil; he knows he is doing wrong.
- He discusses his guilt but hers seems not to affect her until the sleepwalking scene.
- As a woman she can only have power through him, but she is dominant and taunts him about his role as a man.

14. *Romeo and Juliet*
- He falls in love at first sight.
- The audience might think he has got over Rosaline very quickly.
- Imagery of light and dark is used to express Juliet's beauty.
- Religious imagery is introduced.
- The effect of the soliloquy while the ball continues around him.
- Comparison with his ideas about love in the first scene.
- Mutual love is expressed in a sonnet.
- Portrayal of his love and their relationship in the balcony scene.
- His commitment to her and his actions after their marriage.
- Association of love and death.

15. *The Tempest*
- Prospero's power over Miranda is increased by his use of magic.
- Very unequal relationship – Miranda begs and kneels.
- Prospero is angry and not willing to listen.
- He uses her inexperience of the world to control her, lying to her.
- He is protective, has brought her up and educated her.
- He may be jealous of Ferdinand and/or unwilling to see Miranda grow up.
- However, he is won over by their love and welcomes Ferdinand – part of the general reconciliation at the end.
- Prospero seen as a father figure to Ariel and Caliban.
- Fatherhood as a metaphor for creativity/writing.

16. *The Merchant of Venice*
- Mercy seen as God-given and natural.
- Imagery used to express its 'quality'.
- Mercy contrasted with power, symbolized in the sceptre, but seen as necessary in a ruler.
- It is not the opposite of justice but 'seasons' it.
- Portia's use of rhetorical language to convince Shylock.
- The failure of her appeal to Shylock and what this says about him.
- Is the outcome of the trial just?
- How far would differences in Elizabethan and modern attitudes influence an audience's reaction to the trial?

Questions 17–23:
See mark scheme above for Questions 11–16. This question does not carry additional marks for spelling, punctuation and grammar. Your answers could include some of the following points.

17. *Frankenstein*
- Frankenstein's reaction and his language reflect his terror.
- The readers see the monster through Frankenstein's narration. They might think his reaction unfair.
- The monster's speech is calm, whereas we, like Frankenstein, might expect him to be aggressive.
- The monster is humble and even servile in his approach – 'I am thy creature'.
- He uses gentle language – 'mild', 'clemency' – contrasting with Frankenstein's violent language.
- He uses logic, and refers to ideas of justice and to the Bible, suggesting he is intelligent and educated.
- This chapter marks a turning point, leading to the monster's narration.
- His narrative helps us see him as a victim of Frankenstein.
- His story shows the potential he had for good and how this was destroyed.

18. *The Sign of Four*
- As Watson is the narrator, we see her through his eyes.
- He describes her appearance in great detail, as he would describe anything else in the book.
- He draws conclusions about her character, which do not have the logical basis of conclusions that Holmes might make, and show he is attracted to her.
- She is drawn as a sympathetic character and a victim who needs protecting: 'her lip trembled'.
- Watson declares his admiration in hyperbolic terms.
- Her main purpose is to introduce the plot. The note she has been sent leads into the mystery and adventure.
- Her romance with Watson forms a sub-plot, which contrasts with the main plot.
- The reactions of Watson and Holmes to her differ sharply – Watson is shocked at Holmes's misogyny; Holmes lacks Watson's empathy.
- The reader might suspect that Watson is foolish in falling for her and she could be tricking him, but he is proved right.

19. *Jane Eyre*
- The passage starts with 'Unjust!' Jane feels that she does not belong and is used as a scapegoat.
- Her adult narrator's voice analyses her position at Gateshead, seeing it partly as a result of the situation but also as owing to her own nature.
- Even as a child, Jane does not conform to her expected role.
- The Red Room is a powerful symbol of isolation from society, which Jane refers to throughout the novel.
- The description of the room and the weather build fear and mystery.
- This can be related to the Gothic tradition, although the supernatural elements are not real – here they are the result of a child's fears.

- Jane looks for love and substitute families throughout the novel – at Lowood, at Thornfield, with the Rivers family. Her position as governess is neither servant nor family.
- She thinks of herself as different – in her looks and her nature.

20. *Pride and Prejudice*
- The importance of the setting – Darcy's home, which reveals a lot about him.
- Pemberley is described as elegant, tasteful and beautiful. This says something about its owner which surprises Elizabeth.
- The idea of being its mistress appeals to her – she would not marry just for money but wants a 'good' marriage.
- The presence of the Gardiners reminds her why she refused Darcy.
- She had already begun to change her feelings after receiving Darcy's letter.
- Now she is given an account of his character by someone who can be seen as reliable and honest.
- The housekeeper maintains he is not proud and has other qualities.
- The way he treats and reacts to Wickham are central to Elizabeth's changing feelings. At first she was misled by Wickham. Now she sees Darcy's side.
- We are given access to Elizabeth's feelings through Austen's narrative style.

21. *Great Expectations*
- The strangeness of the setting and the contrast between Miss Havisham and Estella.
- How Dickens describes Estella's appearance.
- Pip as a naive/unreliable narrator.
- Estella's attitude towards Pip – her insults and her contempt for him – and how far this is due to Miss Havisham.
- Pip's love for Estella in spite of this.
- Issues of class and gender.
- Pip's reaction to Estella when he meets her after her marriage.
- The ending – is it ambiguous?

22. *The Strange Case of Dr Jekyll and Mr Hyde*
- Utterson is introduced as a reliable, logical, professional man.
- His profession gives him access to Lanyon, Jekyll and their documents.
- Utterson and Enfield are described as 'dull', making the contrast with the events Enfield describes greater.
- Stevenson uses their walk to describe the contrast between the 'thriving' street and 'sinister' building, like Jekyll and Hyde.
- Use of imagery to create atmosphere.
- Utterson is inquisitive but also discreet – information is gradually revealed to him.

23. *A Christmas Carol*
- The readers are taken with Scrooge to see an 'ordinary', poor family celebrate Christmas.
- The importance of family life and being with loved ones – contrast with Scrooge's situation.
- Dickens's characteristic use of lists to build descriptions of plenty.
- A sense of excitement and anticipation built.
- Bob refers to Tiny Tim's words about Christ.

- A sense throughout the novel that celebration and caring for others go together.
- The ghost shows Scrooge a range of people celebrating Christmas.
- Dickens's use of a popular genre to put across a serious message about society.

Questions 24–35

Use the mark scheme for Questions 19–23 (above). This question is also marked on your spelling, punctuation and grammar. Your answers could include some of the following points.

24. *An Inspector Calls*
- Description of Mr Birling in the opening stage directions.
- His physical presence and bombastic style of speech.
- His social position as a rich, self-made man.
- His views on politics, society and the future.
- His traditional role in the family and relations with his wife and children.
- His reaction to the Inspector's arrival.
- His contact with Eva Smith and what it tells us about industrial relations.
- The difference hindsight makes to an assessment of his character (both from the 1940s and a modern perspective).

25. *Blood Brothers*
- Narrator makes it sound like the re-telling of a legend or myth.
- Narrator comments on action.
- Narrator enters action as various minor characters.
- Comic effect of narrator's intervention.
- Narrator used to move story forward.
- Narrator's musings on fate, superstition etc.
- How the narrator becomes sinister.
- Does he control as well as comment on the action?
- Narrator as a Brechtian alienation (distancing) technique.

26. *The History Boys*
- Irwin as stereotypical young, keen supply teacher.
- Headmaster's use of Irwin to get results and to undermine Hector.
- Contrast with Mrs Lintott's approach to history.
- Comparison with Hector's teaching style and ideas.
- His disregard for the truth.
- His sexuality / interest in Dakin and comparisons with Hector's 'groping'.
- Significance of the revelation that he lied about his background.
- His subsequent career as 'spin doctor'.
- His use as a framing device to start the acts from the 'present'.

27. *DNA*
- Characters come mostly in pairs, in established friendships.
- Their action demands group loyalty.
- In the first part the focus is entirely on the friendship group – the outside world is not important.
- Reported sentimental outpouring of friendship and grief for the 'dead' boy.
- Contrast this with their responsibility and guilt.
- How friendships fall apart.
- How some are leaders and some followers – and how leadership of the group changes.

- What is meant by friendship? Is it meaningful in this context?
- Writer says performers can change names and even genders of characters – would this change the dynamics of the group?

28. *The Curious Incident of the Dog in the Night-Time*
- She is a special needs teacher – we know little about her beyond this.
- Scenes between her and Christopher show how he reacts to others in school.
- Her role shows us his personality/ character as a 'special need', which is how society sees it.
- She is a sounding board for Christopher's thoughts/ideas/plans.
- She has a professional understanding/ distance which helps her deal with him without the emotional frustrations of his parents.
- She reads out the letters and is therefore a channel through which we hear Judy's point of view.
- She tells him that he cannot live with her because she is not his mother.
- There is sympathy but maybe a lack of emotional attachment – this might make it easier for Christopher to deal with her.

29. *A Taste of Honey*
- Description of Helen as 'semi-whore' implies casual attitude to sex and society's disapproval.
- Helen more interested in money/ security than love – not certain if she is actually a prostitute.
- Jo has grown up without the usual parental attitudes to sex of the period.
- Unlike Helen she does associate sex with love – she craves affection.
- Characters discuss sexual matters openly, even quite crudely.
- Attitudes to pre-marital sex / single mothers and homosexuality then and now.

30. *Lord of the Flies*
- The Lord of the Flies – the sow's head – symbolizing evil and lack of civilization.
- Symbolism of the conch–democracy and civilization.
- How they come to worship the Lord of the Flies – its association with the devil through Beelzebub.
- The Beast – an imaginary thing that becomes a powerful symbol.
- Symbolism of place – the forest glade, the mountain, the beach, the island as a whole.
- Piggy's glasses, symbolizing intellect and reason, and the conch, symbolizing democracy and civilization, are both destroyed.
- Character can be symbolic of themes/ attitudes.
- Symbols related to the Bible / other literary sources and traditions.
- How the meaning of symbols can change and/or be ambiguous.

31. *Telling Tales*
- The narrator's version of his parents' happy family life.
- His interpretation of the relationship between Mother and Ralph, and what their relationship might really be like.
- Tensions between narrator and Ralph / Grandfather and Ralph – competing for Mother's affection?

- Compare Mother's reaction to husband's death with 'The Darkness Out There' / 'The Odour of Chrysanthemums' / 'A Family Supper'.
- Narrative viewpoint – compare with 'My Polish Teacher's Tie' – unreliable/ reliable viewpoint.
- Ideas about marriage – 'The Odour of Chrysanthemums', 'A Family Supper'.
- Use of symbolism and imagery – 'The Odour of Chrysanthemums'.

32. *Animal Farm*
- At the beginning the pigs are on the side of the other animals, opposed to the farmer, and act with them.
- From early on they are seen as leaders – more intelligent than others.
- Old Major's and Snowball's deaths change things. Napoleon is shown as power-hungry.
- Do they fill a power vacuum? Does someone have to take a lead in all societies?
- All power corrupts.
- Parallels with USSR and other totalitarian regimes.
- Symbolism of pigs walking on their hind feet.
- Final chapter where pigs are indistinguishable from humans and accepted by humans.
- Do they change or do they just show their true natures?

33. *Never Let Me Go*
- Tommy is seen through Kathy's eyes.
- She is tries to understand him, giving us anecdotes about him to try to work out why he behaves as he does.
- He is seen as different from other pupils – an outsider, picked on.
- His 'tantrums' seem to come from nowhere, expressions of anger that no-one understands.
- His conversations with Miss Lucy help him and Kathy to understand more about their situation.
- His relationship with Ruth and Kathy's view of it.
- How he changes as he gets older – what he is like as a donor.
- Kathy's love for him and her feelings after his 'completion'.

34. *Anita and Me*
- She lies to her parents and disobeys them. However, she loves and looks up to both of them.
- They allow her a lot of freedom, which she sometimes abuses.
- She is fascinated by their past lives in India and their love story.
- She sees them as devoted to each other – a love match, not an arranged marriage.
- She idealizes them – the only slight implied criticism is that they are a bit pushy and her mother wants to interfere in people's lives.
- The relationship changes a bit after the birth of her brother, when she does not get as much attention.
- They are seen as different from other parents in the village, because of their culture and their class.

35. *Pigeon English*
- Gang culture is seen through Harri's innocent eyes and its extent is gradually revealed to readers.
- Harri's desire to belong makes him want to join the Dell Farm Crew.

- At first he seems to see them just as a group who rule the school – it's like a game.
- Harri and Dean do not see the danger of 'investigating' the crime, not understanding what gangs are really about.

- Harri feels sick when he sees the reality of them attacking an old man.
- Tension between gang culture and the family and community's Christianity. Harri thinks gang members can be brought to God.

- Rules are important in gangs and in family life – gangs as perversion of family.
- Language used to show culture and membership of the group.
- Novel inspired by real-life crime – how this context influences its reception.

36. For both questions, look at the mark scheme table on p.136 (for pages 110–111 Review Questions, Q1).

a) Your answer might include:
- Who is in danger and from what? – 'Exposure', 'Bayonet Charge', 'Remains', 'Poppies'.
- Soldiers put in danger by those above them – 'Bayonet Charge', 'Exposure'.
- The brigade seen as one – other poems focus on individual reactions.
- Rhythm and metre.
- Sense of excitement and bravery – 'Remains'; contrast 'Bayonet Charge', 'Exposure'.

- Use of imagery, literal and figurative.
- Use of language, e.g. alliteration in 'Exposure'.
- Voice/speaker not in danger – 'War Photographer', 'Poppies'; contrast with 'Exposure', 'Remains'.

b) Your answer might include:
- The nature of the parting – here 'sorrow and tears', bitterness in 'Neutral Tones', death in 'Porphyria's Lover'.
- The nature of the relationship – parents in 'Eden Rock'.

- Reasons for the parting – she has broken her vows but the details are not given.
- The use of imagery of nature – 'Neutral Tones'.
- Romantic ideas about love and relationships.
- Direct address to the loved one.
- Feelings of poet/voice towards subject – 'love–hate relationship' or love turning to hate?
- Regular structure with simple rhyme scheme – apparent simplicity expresses deep feelings.

37. See mark scheme table on p.136 (for pages 110–111 Review Questions, Q2a).

a) Your answer might include comments on the following:
- He gives a voice to an ordinary soldier.
- Persona's motives for becoming a soldier – poverty, unemployment.
- The ballad form tells a story in a simple, traditional form – appropriate to subject.

- Rhythm and rhyme give it a cheerful tone in contrast with the subject.
- The language is colloquial, the voice working-class.
- His attitude to his enemy – he sees him as the same kind of man.
- References to the 'inn' and 'nipperkin' make it seem homely and everyday.

- Reference to 'traps' places him in the country, perhaps as gamekeeper, perhaps as poacher. He is used to killing animals.
- The nature of the deed contrasts with the friendly language.
- Makes a strong point about war through a naive voice who sees his 'foe' as an individual like himself.

b)

Marks	Skills
7–8	• You have explored comparisons of the writers' use of language, structure and form, using appropriate subject terminology. • You have convincingly compared the effects of the writers' methods on the reader.
5–6	• You have thoughtfully compared the writers' use of language and/or structure and/or form, using effective subject terminology. • You have clearly compared the effects of the writers' methods on the reader.

Your answer might include comments on:
- Differing situations – one going to war, the other having returned.
- Past tense / future tense.
- Difference in focus – one on killing, the other on dying.

- Contrast in language.
- Sense of patriotism in 'The Soldier' absent from 'The Man He Killed'.
- One matter-of-fact, the other emotional.

- Use of imagery in 'The Soldier'.
- Difference in tone created by rhythm/metre and language.

Glossary and Index

a

abbreviation   a shortened form of a word or phrase (52)

abstract noun   a noun which names something you cannot touch or feel, such as an idea or emotion (26)

accent   a way of pronouncing words, usually associated with a region or area (90)

act   a division of a play (91)

active voice   when the subject is the person or thing doing: for example, 'the dog bit the boy' (10)

adjective   a word used to describe a noun and add more detail (26)

adverb   a word used to describe verbs, often ending in 'ly', such as 'swiftly', 'anxiously' (26)

alliteration   repetition of a sound at the beginning of two or more words (29, 100)

alphabetical order   the arrangement of information according to the alphabet (A–Z) (31)

ambiguity   when something has more than one meaning (adjective – **ambiguous**) (87, 98)

anecdote   a short account of an interesting or humorous story, often used to reinforce a point being made (53)

antagonist   the person who opposes the protagonist (40)

apostrophe (')   punctuation mark used to show possession or omission (9)

archaic   old-fashioned, no longer in use (101)

argument   a reasoned point of view (53)

article   a short piece of writing, usually in a newspaper or magazine (50)

aside   a line or lines addressed to the audience while other actors are on stage (65)

associate   connect mentally (7)

assonance   repetition of a vowel sound within words (29, 100)

atmosphere   the tone or mood of the text (39)

attitude   a writer's feelings or opinions about something (98)

audience   a group of people who hear, watch or read something (52)

authorial voice   the writer speaking directly to the reader (75)

authority   power or influence, often because of knowledge or expertise (adjective – **authoritative**) (61, 79)

autobiographical   describes writing about the author's own experiences (50)

autobiography   the story of the author's life (49)

b

ballad   a form of poetry which tells a story, usually in quatrains with a regular metre and rhyme scheme (97)

Bildungsroman   a novel that tells the story of someone growing up (76)

biography   the story of someone's life (49)

blank verse   poetry which has a regular metre but does not rhyme (103)

blog   a dairy or journal published on the internet (short for weblog; **blogger** – a person who writes a blog) (31)

broadsheet   a 'serious' newspaper, so-called because they used to be published on large sheets of paper (54)

bullet point   a typographical symbol used to introduce an item in a list (31)

c

caesura   a pause in a line of poetry, sometimes denoted by a punctuation mark (66)

chapter   a division within a book (31)

character   a fictional person (38)

chronological order   order of time, starting with the earliest event (31)

clause   a phrase (group of words) which could stand alone as a sentence, having a main verb (10)

climax   the dramatic high point of a story, usually at the end (37)

colloquial   conversational or chatty (noun – **colloquialism**) (79)

colon (:)   a punctuation mark used to introduce a list or an explanation (8)

comma (,)   a punctuation mark used to separate clauses or items in a list (8)

complex sentence   a sentence containing more than one clause (but not a compound sentence) (11)

compound sentence   a sentence consisting of two clauses of equal importance, joined by a conjunction (10)

conceit   an elaborate or far-fetched simile or (extended) metaphor (67)

conclusion   end (30)

concrete noun   a noun that names something you can touch or feel (also **common noun**) (26)

conjunction   a word used to join two words, clauses or phrases and show the relationship between them: for example, 'and', 'but', 'because' (10, 27)

connective   any word or phrase used to join phrases, sentences or paragraphs (13)

connotation   a meaning that is suggested by the use of a word or phrase (28)

consonant   any letter that is not a vowel (6)

content   subject matter; what something contains (22)

context   circumstances (60)

contraction   making two words into one by leaving out letters and using an apostrophe: for example, 'doesn't', 'I'm', 'who's' (6)

counter-argument   an argument that answers one that has already been given (53)

court   the people surrounding a king or queen (61)

d

deduction   working something out or coming to a conclusion (73)

determiner   a short word that comes before a noun and helps to define it, including the definite article ('the') and indefinite article ('a') (27)

diagram   a plan, sketch, drawing, or outline designed to demonstrate or explain how something works (86)

dialect   words or phrases particular to a region (14)

dialogue   speech between two or more people; conversation (63, 91)

diarist   a person who writes a diary (48)

diction   the choice of words and phrases used (26)

difference   a way in which two or more things are not alike (22)

direct address   speaking directly to the audience, usually using 'you' (53)

direct speech   the actual words spoken, put in inverted commas (41)

director   a person who directs plays (87)

discourse marker   a word or phrase that connects sentences or paragraphs (13, 53)

divine right   the idea that the right to rule comes from God (61)

dramatic monologue   a long poem in which a fictional character speaks to a reader or an audience (96)

e

ellipsis (…)   punctuation indicating that something has been left out (9)

embed   with reference to a quotation, to place it within sentences so that the whole sentence makes sense (24)

emotive language   language used to provoke emotions, such as shock or pity, in readers (28)

end-stopping   ending a line of verse with a punctuation mark (also called lineation) (102)

enjambment   when lines are not end-stopped but the sense runs on between lines or even stanzas (102)

evidence   information referred to in order to support a point being made (21)

exclamation mark (!)   a punctuation mark used to denote extreme emotion (8)

explicit   open, obvious (18)

exposition   setting the scene or giving background information at the beginning of a story (36)

extended metaphor   a series of similar metaphors combining to create one image (67)

f

fable   a story, often about animals, that gives a moral lesson (85)

feature   a newspaper or magazine article that is not a news report (50)

figurative imagery   the use of an image of one thing to tell us about another (39)

form   a type of writing or the way it is presented (48)

formal language   language that is similar to Standard English and used in situations where it is not appropriate to be too conversational (79)

fragment   another word for a 'minor sentence', one which does not contain a main verb (10)

free verse   poetry that does not have a regular metre or rhyme scheme (103)

full stop (.)   a punctuation mark that marks the end of a sentence (8)

function   what something is used for (76)

g

genre   a kind or type of literature: for example, detective story or romance (48)

grammar   the study or rules of how words relate to each other (14)

h

headline   heading at the top of a newspaper or magazine article (54)

homophone   a word that sounds the same as another word but is spelled differently and has a different meaning (6)

hyperbole   exaggeration (adjective – **hyperbolic**) (28, 53)

i

iambic pentameter   a line of poetry consisting of ten syllables with the stress on every second syllable (66)

identify   select; name (19)

image   a picture, also used metaphorically of 'word pictures' (63, 87)

imagery   when words are so descriptive that they paint a picture in your mind. Imagery is used to allow the reader to empathize or imagine the moment being described. (29, 42)

imply   to suggest something that is not expressly stated (noun – **implication**; adjective – **implicit**) (20)

inciting incident   an event that starts the action of a story (36)

indent   to start writing a little way in from the margin: for example, to start a new paragraph (12)

indirect speech   speech that is reported rather than quoted: for example, He said that she was there (41)

infer   to deduce something that is not openly stated (noun – **inference**) (20)

informal language   conversational language that is spoken between people who are usually familiar with one another (48)

interpret   when you infer meaning and explain what you have inferred, you are interpreting implicit information or ideas (noun – **interpretation**) (20, 87)

interval   a break during a performance (91)

intrusive narrator   a narrator who is outside the action but comments on it (37)

inverted commas (' ')   punctuation marks used to indicate quotations, titles etc. (9)

irony   when words are used to imply an opposite meaning, or sarcastic language that can be used to mock or convey scorn (adjective – **ironic**) (79)

isolate   separate; place apart (7)

issue   a subject being discussed (63, 75)

j

journal   a form of diary (48)

journalism   writing in a newspaper or magazine (50)

l

literal imagery   the use of description to convey mood or atmosphere (39)

location   place (85)

lyric   a short poem about feelings (97)

m

medium   means of communication (plural – **media**) (87)

metaphor   an image created by directly comparing one thing to another, such as 'my brother is a little monkey' (29, 101)

metre   the pattern of stressed and unstressed syllables in poetry (66, 103)

minor sentence   a 'sentence' that does not contain a verb – also known as a 'fragment' (10)

mnemonic   a way of remembering information, especially spellings (7)

modal verb   a verb that shows the mood or state of another verb: for example, 'could', 'might' (14)

mood   the general feeling conveyed (see **atmosphere**) (39)

morality   ideas of good and bad behaviour, or right and wrong (61)

motif   an idea or image that is repeated at intervals in a text (75)

motivation   the reason(s) for doing something (64)

movement   a group of writers who share similar ideas about literature and/or write in a similar style (96)

musical theatre   a form of drama including music (85)

n

naive narrator   a narrator who does not understand what is going on, often a child (76, 89)

narrative   story (37, 40)

narrator   the person telling a story (37)

non-fiction text   a text that is mainly based on facts and not made up (48)

noun   a naming word (10, 26)

o

object   (in grammar) the thing or person to whom something is done (in the active voice) (10)

octave   a set of eight lines of verse (102)

omission   missing out (9)

omniscient narrator   a narrator who is outside the action and knows everything (37, 89)

onomatopoeia   the use of a word that sounds like what it describes (29, 100)

opening   start, beginning (30)

opinion   what someone thinks (18)

oxymoron   two contradictory words placed together: for example, 'bitter sweet' (67)

p

paragraph   a section of a piece of prose writing, shown by indentation or leaving a line (12, 31)

parallel phrasing   repeating the structure and some of the words, phrases, clauses or sentences (43)

paraphrase   to put something in your own words (24)

parenthesis   brackets; a word or phrase inserted into a sentence to explain something (plural – **parentheses**) (9)

passive voice   where the subject has the action done to him or her: for example, 'the boy was bitten by the dog' (10)

past continuous tense   the tense used to convey an action that continued for some time in the past, e.g. 'he was talking for hours' (15)

past perfect tense   the tense used to describe events that happened before those being described in the past tense, using 'had' (15)

past tense   the tense used to described something that has happened (7)

pathetic fallacy   either a form of personification, giving nature human qualities, or using a description of the surroundings to reflect the mood of a character (29)

perfect tense   a form of the past tense, using 'has' or 'have' (15)

period   an amount of time (84)

persona   a fictional voice used by a poet (98, 100)

personal pronoun   a pronoun that stands in for the names of people (14)

personification   when an inanimate object or idea is given human qualities (29)

perspective   point of view (48, 75)

Petrarchan or Italian sonnet   a form of sonnet consisting of an octave and a sestet (102)

playwright   a person who writes plays (89)

plot   the main events of a story (63)

plural   more than one (6, 14)

possession   belonging or ownership (9)

preposition   a short word showing the relationship of one thing to another: for example, 'to', 'under' (10, 27)

present tense   the tense used to describe things happening now (15)

pronoun   a short word which replaces a noun ('I', 'you', 'he', 'she' etc.) (26)

proper noun   a noun that names an individual person or thing, such as a place or day, and has a capital letter (26)

prose   any writing that is not poetry (66, 87)

protagonist   the main character, the person whom the story is about (37, 40)

psychology   the study of the human mind (73)

pun   word play, when words are organized in an amusing way to suggest other meaning (54)

q

quatrain   a set of four lines of verse (102)

question mark (?)   a punctuation mark used at the end of a question (8)

quotation   words or phrases taken directly from the text (verb – **quote**) (24)

quotation marks   inverted commas when used around a quotation (9)

r

recipient   the person who receives something, especially a letter (49)

refer   mention or allude to something (noun - **reference**) (24)

refrain   a repeated line or lines, usually at the end of stanzas, in poetry (100)

register   the form of language used in particular circumstances (26)

relative pronoun   a word such as 'who', 'which' or 'that', used to connect clauses (11)

repetition   when words, phrases, ideas or sentences are used more than once – this can be used to highlight key issues and make important sections more memorable (28)

report   an account of something that has happened, often in a newspaper (50)

reported speech   see **indirect speech** (41)

reverse chronological order   ordering events by putting the most recent first and working backwards (31)

review   an article that gives an opinion on, for example, a film, play or book (50)

rhetoric   the art of speaking (adjective – **rhetorical**) (28)

rhetorical device   a language technique used to influence an audience (53)

rhetorical question   a question that does not require an answer, used to make the reader think about the possible answer and involve them in the text (28)

rhyme   the use of words with the same endings to make patterns (102)

rhyming couplet   two successive lines of poetry that rhyme (66, 102)

rhythm   the beat of the writing, usually in poetry (103)

s

scene   a division of a play, often within an act (91)

script   the text of a play (87)

semantic field   the area from which words and phrases have been taken (26)

semi-colon (;)   punctuation mark used to connect clauses, also used in lists (8)

sentiment   feeling (73)

sestet   a set of six lines of verse (102)

setting   where and when the action takes place (39, 75)

Shakespearean or English sonnet   a form of sonnet popularized by Shakespeare, consisting of four quatrains and a rhyming couplet (102)

sibilance   repetition of 's' sounds (29)

significance   what something means or stands for (77)

silent letter   a letter within a word which is not pronounced (7)

similarity   a way in which two or more things are alike (22)

simile   a comparison of one thing to another using the words 'like' or 'as', such as 'the raindrops fell like tears' (29, 101)

simple past tense   the form of the past tense usually formed by adding '-ed' (15)

simple sentence   a sentence that only contains a main clause (10)

singular   one (14)

skim read   to read quickly in order to find something in the text (22)

slang   informal language, often local and changing quickly (14)

social order   where people are 'placed' in society, with some more important than others (61)

soliloquy   a speech to the audience, expressing a character's thoughts or feelings (plural **soliloquies**) (65)

sonnet   a form of poetry, usually a love poem, of 14 lines (67)

source   the origin of something, used by examiners to describe texts used in exams (51)

speech marks   inverted commas when used around direct speech (9)

Standard English   the variety of English generally accepted as the correct form for writing and formal speech (14)

stanza   a section of a poem, often called a verse (31, 102)

strapline   a subheading under a headline, which explains or expands on the headline (54)

stress   (in poetry) emphasis (103)

subheading   used to break up the text and guide the reader through various sections (54)

subject   the person or thing that a sentence is about (10)

subordinate clause   a clause that contains extra information (11)

summarize   give a shortened account of something, retaining the meaning (noun – **summary**) (22)

supernatural   not belonging to the natural world; magical (73)

syllable   a unit of pronunciation (103)

symbol   an object that represents something else: for example, an idea or emotion (adjective – **symbolic**) (29, 79, 100)

synthesis   the combining of two or more things (verb – **synthesize**) (22)

t

tabloid   a type of newspaper, less serious and easier to read than a broadsheet, traditionally in a smaller format (54)

terminology   use of appropriate, often specialized, words (105)

text box   a box which contains text (31)

theme   subject matter: what the text is about rather than what happens in it (62)

third person   he, she, it (singular); they (plural) (15)

tone   the overall feel or attitude of the writing (79)

topic sentence   a sentence, usually the first in the paragraph, which tells you what the paragraph is about (12)

turning point   an event that changes the direction of a story (37, 91)

u

unreliable narrator   a narrator who cannot always be trusted (89)

v

verb   a doing, thinking, feeling or being word (7, 26)

verse   poetry (66)

viewpoint   point of view (48)

vocabulary   words used (26)

voice   the narrator or speaker; his or her characteristic style (41, 98)

volta   a turn or change in a poem, especially between the octave and sestet in a Petrarchan sonnet (102)

vowel   a, e, i, o, u (6)

Collins

AQA GCSE 9-1 English Language & Literature

Workbook

Paul Burns

Contents

Key Technical Skills: Writing

Key Technical Skills: Reading

English Language 1

English Language 2

Shakespeare

The Nineteenth-Century Novel

Modern Texts

Contents

Poetry

Key Technical Skills: Writing

Spelling

1 Put the following words into their plural forms:

a) tomato ....

b) birthday ....

c) soliloquy ....

d) family ....

e) parenthesis ....

[5]

2 Insert the correctly spelled word in each of the following pairs of sentences:

a) Your/you're

.... not going out like that.

I asked .... sister to bring it.

b) There/they're/their

.... are twenty-five people in the class.

They have all done .... homework but .... not sitting in the right places.

c) Where/wear/we're

Turn it off or it will .... out.

We have no idea .... it is but .... going anyway.

d) Past/passed

I .... him in the street an hour ago.

He walked right .... me as if I wasn't there.

e) To/too/two

There were only .... exams .... sit but that was one .... many.

f) Practice/practise

If you don't go to the .... you'll be left out of the team.

If you want to improve you will have to .... every day.

[15]

3 The following passage includes ten incorrect spellings. Find them and circle them, then write the correct spellings below.

Last nite I went to the cinema with my friend Bob and his farther, Michael. The whole evening was not very succesfull. The cinema was very crouded and we had to sit seperately. Then, it turned out the film was in a forrein langauge and no-one could understand it. I think it was about the enviroment. Afterwards, Michael took us to a resturant were we had pizzas.

....

....

....

....

....

[10]

Total Marks .... / 30

Key Technical Skills: Writing

1 Punctuate the following passage using only commas and full stops. There should be a total of five punctuation marks.

> *Great Expectations* one of the best-known novels by Charles Dickens is the story of Pip a boy who grows up in the marshes of Kent at the beginning of the story he meets an escaped convict in the churchyard where his parents are buried

[5]

2 Add ten apostrophes, where necessary, to the following passage:

> At about ten o clock, we went to Romios for pizzas. Im not sure what Bobs pizza topping was but I had ham and pineapple. I wish I hadnt because later on I was sick in Michaels car. Its brand new and I thought hed be angry but he wasnt. Were not going there again.

[10]

3 Add a question mark, an exclamation mark, a colon, a semi-colon or parentheses (brackets) to the following clauses so that they make sense:

a)	Who was that masked man nobody knows.	
b)	The cat slept quietly on the mat the dog slept noisily on the step.	
c)	I don't believe it that's the first answer I've got.	
d)	Annie deserved the prize she was the best baker by far.	
e)	Jane and Elizabeth the two oldest Bennet sisters get married at the end.	

[5]

Total Marks _____ / 20

Key Technical Skills: Writing

Sentence Structure

1 Identify whether the sentences below are simple, compound, complex or minor sentences:

   a) I confess that I had my doubts when I reflected upon the great traffic which had passed along the London road in the interval. _____

   b) Very clearly. _____

   c) We all need help sometimes. _____

   d) Mr Collins was punctual to his time, and was received with great politeness by the whole family. _____

   e) Elizabeth smiled. _____   **[5]**

2 Combine the following sentences to form complex sentences, using the conjunctions **because**, **although** or **until**.

   a) I bought Anna a bunch of flowers. It was her birthday.

   _____

   _____

   b) He did not finish the race. They gave him a certificate.

   _____

   _____

   c) I kept going. I reached the finishing line.

   _____

   _____   **[3]**

3 Use the following sentences to form a complex sentence using a relative pronoun:

Joey was the oldest cat in the street. He never left the garden.

_____

_____

_____   **[1]**

4 Use the following sentences to form a complex sentence without using a connective:

I was walking down the street. I realized I had forgotten my phone.

_____

_____

_____   **[1]**

Total Marks _____ / 10

Key Technical Skills: Writing

Text Structure and Organization

1 Rearrange the following paragraphs so that the passage makes sense. Write the paragraphs in the correct order below.

a) As a result of this, the student body has decided to appeal to the governors. Jodie has written a letter to every governor, setting out the problems as the students see them.

b) As yet no replies have been received. The increasingly angry students are starting to consider taking 'direct action'.

c) Jodie Collins, a spokesperson for the students, has had several meetings about the issue with the Principal. Ms Rundle apparently listened to the students' points, but later sent an email claiming that nothing can be done because of lack of funds.

d) According to this letter, students' health and safety are at risk. Among other things, toilets are not properly cleaned and standards of hygiene in the kitchen leave a lot to be desired.

e) Students of Summerfield College have expressed concern about the environment they have to work in. They have a number of complaints.

[5]

2 Insert each of these five discourse markers or connectives into the passage so that it makes sense:

nevertheless   **when**   **subsequently**   **in spite of**   **however**

(a) _____ I read your letter I was shocked by its contents. **(b)** _____ being a governor of the college, I was completely unaware of the issues which you mention. I have **(c)** _____ been in touch with Ms Rundle to express my concern. She **(d)**, _____, has not responded to my letters. **(e)** _____, I shall continue to press her for answers.

[5]

Total Marks _____ / 10

Key Technical Skills: Writing

Standard English and Grammar

1 Insert the correct form of the verb 'to be' or 'to do':

Present tense

a) You _____ a great singer.

b) They _____ trying hard.

Simple past

c) We _____ waiting for you.

d) He _____ what they told him to do.

Perfect

e) She _____ my friend for years.

f) They _____ all their exams now.

Simple past + past perfect

g) We _____ happy because we _____ all the exercises.　　　**[7]**

2 Which of the following is correct in Standard UK English? Circle the correct word.

a) The defendant **pleaded/pled** guilty.

b) He's one of the **only/few** people who can do that.

c) He has **got/gotten** two coffees.　　　**[3]**

3 Change the following dialogue to Standard English:

Jo:　　　　Hey. How are you guys doing?

Arthur:　　Good. Real good.

Jo:　　　　Wanna drink?

Arthur:　　Can I get two coffees?

Jo:　　　　Sure. Where are you sat?

_____

_____

_____

　　　　　　　　　　　　　　　　　　　　　　　　　　　　　[5]

4 Rewrite the following passage in Standard English:

> I was stood in the street when Frankie come over. I give him a smile and opened me gob to speak. I was gonna ask him how he done in math. I never said nothing. Soon as I seen him I knew he done good.

_____

_____

　　　　　　　　　　　　　　　　　　　　　　　　　　　　　[5]

Total Marks	/ 20

Key Technical Skills: Reading

Explicit Information and Ideas

1 Read the passage below:

> The tower of St Peter's church was, until very recently, the tallest building in the town. On a clear day, it can still be seen from miles away. However, it is now overshadowed by a brutal example of modern architecture. Built two years ago, and twice as high as the church tower, the Kingsley Tower dominates the surrounding landscape.

Look at the statements below. Which of them are explicitly stated in the text? Tick the correct answers.

a) The church tower used to be the tallest building in town. ☐

b) Everyone hates the new building. ☐

c) The Kingsley Tower is taller than the church tower. ☐

d) The writer does not like modern architecture. ☐ [2]

2 Read the passage below:

List four things that we learn about the old gentleman's appearance.

> It was by the Green Dragon that the old gentleman travelled. He was a very nice looking old gentleman, and he looked as if he were nice, too, which is not at all the same thing. He had a fresh-coloured, clean-shaven face, and white hair, and he wore rather odd-shaped collars and a top hat that wasn't exactly the same kind as other people's. Of course the children didn't see all this at first. In fact, the first thing they noticed about the old gentleman was his hand.
>
> From *The Railway Children* by E. Nesbit

....

....

....

....

....

....

....

....

[4]

Total Marks .... / 6

Key Technical Skills: Reading

Implicit Information and Ideas

1 True or false?

Read the passage below and tick four statements below which are TRUE.

> Work experience is an established part of today's school calendar. All Year 10 pupils in all schools have to do it. But why? I decided to ask around and found the general opinion amongst the adults I asked was that it would prepare young people for the world of work. I have to say, though, that none of them sounded terribly convinced and I got the distinct impression that they were just following the party line.
>
> Assuming the object of the exercise is to prepare us for the world of work, does it? My placement was in my uncle's office. He is a solicitor and the rationale behind the placement was that I had expressed an interest in studying Law. That sounds logical. But what did I learn? I learned that you should dress smartly and be punctual. I learned how to answer the telephone politely. I learned that solicitors drink an awful lot of coffee. I could have found out all of that just by having a chat with my uncle.

a) Work experience is compulsory in Year 10. ☐

b) Most adults are against work experience. ☐

c) The writer thinks the adults did not give their true opinions. ☐

d) The writer questions the value of work experience. ☐

e) The writer does not want to be a solicitor. ☐

f) The writer found work experience challenging and stimulating. ☐

g) It is important to turn up to work on time. ☐

h) The writer thinks work experience is important. ☐

[4]

Total Marks _____ / 4

Key Technical Skills: Reading

Summary

1 Reduce each of the following sentences to five words to give the necessary information without losing sense.

a) Stunning trees stand like soldiers behind the shed.	
b) Charlotte Green, the girl with blonde hair, ate Lydia's chocolate.	
c) I demand that you tell me now who did it.	

[3]

2 Read this statement from the witness to a crime.

> I was walking down our street – Arbuckle Lane – at nine o'clock on Monday. I know it was nine o'clock because I was worried about being late for work and I looked at my watch. As I passed number eighteen, the big house with the yellow front door where Mrs Lightbody used to live, I heard a noise, so I stopped and turned around. There were two men on the step and one of them had something in his hand, which he was using to break the glass in the door. I shouted out and they turned. One of them was tall, about six foot, with a grey beard – he reminded me of someone on the television – and the other one was stocky with curly black hair. When they saw me the tall man dropped something and they both ran. It gave me quite a turn.

If you were investigating the crime, which FIVE of the following pieces of information would be relevant to solving it? Tick the correct answers.

a) Mrs Lightbody lived at number eighteen.

b) One of the men was six foot tall.

c) He used something to break the glass in the door.

d) The witness was worried about being late.

e) The witness lives in Arbuckle Lane.

f) The tall man dropped something.

g) One man had curly black hair.

h) It was nine o'clock.

[5]

3 On a separate piece of paper, write a summary of the statement. Aim for 70 words or fewer. [12]

Total Marks _____ / 20

Key Technical Skills: Reading

Synthesis and Summary

1 Read the two passages below.

Pick out as many differences as you can between the two girls' experiences of school and write them in the table below or on a separate piece of paper.

> **Mary Jane:** I grew up on a farm near Barrow. My parents were not at all happy about me going to school, but they were told it was the law and I had to go. They couldn't see the point of it. But I loved school and I never missed a day. The school was a low stone building in the centre of the village. There were two huge rooms, one for the juniors and one for the infants. There were forty pupils in my class and we sat in rows, facing the teacher. We worked really hard all day, except for playtime, and we were not allowed to speak at all unless spoken to. Miss Murdishaw was very strict. We did like her, though, and she only gave you the cane if you were very naughty.
>
> **Sarah:** I would never have gone to school at all if I'd had my way. But I was never allowed to stay off. 'Education, education, education', my mum used to say, 'that's what you need in life. Miss a day's school and you'll regret it'. My first school was in the village near where we lived. There were twenty-four children in our class and we used to sit around tables in groups of six. All my group did was talk, talk, talk all day long. I don't think we did much work at all. The teacher just wandered around the room smiling at us and telling us everything we did was brilliant. She never punished anyone really, not even telling them off. I think she thought we all loved her, but I certainly didn't.

Mary Jane	Sarah

[10]

2 Now sum up the differences between the girls' experiences of school, writing in proper sentences.

....

....

....

....

....

[8]

Total Marks .... / 18

Key Technical Skills: Reading

1 Match each statement (**a–c**) with its paraphrase (**d–f**):

   a) The modern apartments are situated close to all amenities.

   b) Six o'clock struck on the bells of the church that was so conveniently near to the solicitor's dwelling, and still he was digging at the problem.

   c) She suggested liaising outside the church at 18.05. I said yes.

   d) The lawyer was still trying to work it out in the evening.

   e) The flats are up-to-date and near shops and transport.

   f) We agreed to meet at about six o'clock by the church.

   [3]

2 The following sentences all include quotations from *Macbeth* which have not been set out correctly. Set them out correctly, using colons and/or quotation marks where appropriate.

a)	Macbeth refers to the prophecies as happy prologues.	
b)	He tells us that one of them has come true I am Thane of Cawdor.	
c)	Macbeth asks how the prophecies can be evil when the witches have told the truth If ill, Why hath it given me earnest of success Commencing in a truth?	

   [6]

3 The following sentences are an example of the use of PEE. Identify the point, the evidence and the explanation.

Frankenstein's response is negative from the start. Referring to the experiment as a 'catastrophe' and his creation as a 'wretch' suggests that he has rejected the creature and will not try to find any good in it.

Point	
Evidence	
Explanation	

   [3]

Total Marks _____ / 12

Key Technical Skills: Reading

1 How would you describe the register of the following sentences?

Choose from:

formal

technical

dialectical

colloquial

a) 'Appen he were took badly but he'll be all reet. _____

b) It may be that the gentleman was feeling ill. It is, however, likely that he will recover.

_____

c) Me mate wasn't feeling too good but he's OK now. _____

d) The patient suffered a brief episode of disequilibrium, which could be a symptom of a number of chronic conditions.

_____ [4]

2 Read the passage below and identify the word class (part of speech) of the highlighted words:

> Since the party, she had been more **eager** than ever, and had planned many ways of making friends **with** him; **but** he had not been seen lately, and Jo began to think he had gone away, when she one day spied a brown face at an upper **window**, looking **wistfully** down into their garden, where Beth and Amy **were snowballing** one another.
>
> From *Little Women* by Louisa May Alcott

a) eager		b) with	
c) but		d) window	
e) wistfully		f) were snowballing	

[6]

3 a) The passage above is only one sentence. What sort of sentence is it? _____

b) Give an example from the passage of a proper noun. _____

c) Is the clause 'he had not been seen lately' in the active or passive voice? _____

d) What tense is 'had planned' in the first line? _____

e) In what 'person' is the narrative written? _____ [5]

Total Marks _____ / 15

Key Technical Skills: Reading

Analysing Language 2

 1 State whether each of the following sentences contains a metaphor or a simile and describe the effect of the comparison.

	Metaphor or simile?	What is its effect?
a) He ran like the wind.		
b) An army of insects invaded the kitchen.		
c) Her heart was as cold as ice.		

[6]

2 Read the passage below. Find an example of each of the techniques listed in the table below.

> Time was not on their side. The fire fizzed and crackled around them as the brave Brown brothers entered the building. Inside, great flames came in waves.

a) personification	
b) onomatopoeia	

[2]

3 Read the passage below, from *The Hound of the Baskervilles* by Arthur Conan Doyle.

> October 16th – A dull and foggy day, with a drizzle of rain. The house is banked with rolling clouds, which rise now and then to show the dreary curves of the moor, with thin, silver veins upon the sides of the hills, and the distant boulders gleaming where the light strikes upon their wet faces. It is melancholy outside and in. The baronet is in a black reaction after the excitements of the night. I am conscious myself of a weight at my heart and a feeling of impending danger – ever-present, which is the more terrible because I am unable to define it.
>
> And have I not cause for such a feeling?

How does the writer use language to describe the thoughts and feelings of the narrator?

On a separate piece of paper, comment on:
- the writer's choice of words and phrases
- language features and techniques
- sentence form.

[8]

Total Marks _____ / 16

Key Technical Skills: Reading

Analysing Form and Structure

1 Here is the opening of a short story (*The Count and the Wedding Guest* by O. Henry).

> One evening when Andy Donovan went to dinner at his Second Avenue boarding-house, Mrs Scott introduced him to a new boarder, a young lady, Miss Conway. Miss Conway was small and unobtrusive. She wore a plain, snuffy-brown dress, and bestowed her interest, which seemed languid, upon her plate. She lifted her diffident eyelids and shot one perspicuous, judicial glance at Mr Donovan, politely murmured his name, and returned to her mutton. Mr Donovan bowed with the grace and beaming smile that were rapidly winning for him social, business and political advancement, and erased the snuffy-brown one from the tablets of his consideration.

a) What do we learn about the story's setting?

_____ [2]

b) What is your first impression of Miss Conway?

_____ [2]

c) What is the effect of the phrase 'shot one perspicuous, judicial glance'?

_____ [2]

d) What does the description of Andy Donovan's response tell us about him?

_____ [2]

e) What do you think might happen next?

_____ [2]

2 Match the endings **a–c** with the descriptions **x–z**.

a) Honour the charge they made! Honour the Light Brigade, Noble six hundred!		**x)** This ending draws a lesson from the story.	
b) ...the wishes, the hopes, the confidence, the predictions of the small band of true friends who witnessed the ceremony, were fully answered in the perfect happiness of the union.		**y)** This ending might inspire the reader.	
c) 'Was I not right?' said the little Mouse. Little friends may prove great friends.		**z)** A happy ending, leaving the reader satisfied.	

[3]

Total Marks _____ / 13

English Language 1

Creative Reading 1

1 Read the extracts below and state which is narrated by:

A naive/unreliable narrator	
An omniscient narrator	
A reliable first-person narrator	
An intrusive narrator	

[8]

A She told me to pray every day, and whatever I asked for I would get it. But it warn't so. I tried it. Once I got a fish-line but no hooks. It warn't any good to me without hooks. I tried for hooks three or four times, but somehow I couldn't make it work.

From *The Adventures of Huckleberry Finn* by Mark Twain

B The extract from my private diary which forms the last chapter has brought my narrative up to the 18th of October, a time when these strange events began to move swiftly towards their terrible conclusion.

From *The Hound of the Baskervilles* by Sir Arthur Conan Doyle

---

C As John Bold will occupy much of our attention, we must endeavour to explain who he is, and why he takes the part of John Hiram's beadsmen.

From *The Warden* by Anthony Trollope

D Mr James Duffy lived in Chapelizod because he wished to live as far as possible from the city of which he was a citizen and because he found all the other suburbs of Dublin mean, modern and pretentious.

From *Dubliners* by James Joyce

Total Marks _____ / 8

Creative Reading 2

1 Look at the quotations in the table. In the third column (or on a separate piece of paper) enter how we learn about character, choosing from:

a) Narrator's description

b) What the character says

c) What others say about/to the character

d) What the character does

e) How others react to the character

In the fourth column (or on a separate piece of paper) say what we learn about the character.

Character	Quotation	How we learn about the character	What we learn
Hyde's housekeeper *The Strange Case of Dr Jekyll and Mr Hyde*	She had an evil face, smoothed by hypocrisy; but her manners were excellent.		
Magwitch *Great Expectations*	'Hold your noise!' cried a terrible voice [...] 'Keep still, you little devil, or I'll cut your throat.'		
Darcy *Pride and Prejudice*	[Darcy] was looked at with great admiration for about half the evening, till his manners gave a disgust which turned the tide of his popularity.		
Mrs Reed *Jane Eyre*	Mrs Reed, impatient of my now frantic anguish and wild sobs, abruptly thrust me back and locked me in…		
Victor Frankenstein *Frankenstein*	'My dear Victor,' cried he, 'what, for God's sake, is the matter? Do not laugh in that manner. How ill you are!'		

[15]

Total Marks _____ / 15

English Language 1

Narrative Writing

Imagine you have been set the following task:

'Write a story about someone who wins a huge amount of money in the lottery.'

Use the following questions and points to help you create a plan for your writing.

1 Character and Voice

   a) What person will you write in? If first person, is the narrator also the protagonist?

   _____

   b) What kind of register will the narrator use?

   _____

   c) On a separate piece of paper, make notes on your protagonist's:

   • gender
   • age
   • appearance
   • background
   • relationships
   • way of speaking   [8]

2 Place and Time

   a) Where does it start?

   _____

   b) Does the setting change during the story?

   _____

   c) When is it set – now, in the past or in the future?

   _____

   d) How long does the story take?

   _____

   e) Will it be written in chronological order?

   _____   [5]

3 Structure

   On a separate piece of paper, make notes on your:

   • exposition
   • inciting incident
   • turning point(s)
   • climax
   • coda (ending)   [5]

Total Marks _____ / 18

English Language 1

Descriptive Writing

Choose one of the following tasks and answer the questions below:

Either

Describe someone who lives in your street.

Or

Describe a visit to a fairground.

Use the following questions and points to help you create a plan for your writing.

1 **a)** Are you going to use the first or third person? ....

    b) Are you going to use the past or present tense? .... **[2]**

2 Using an adjective and a noun for each, jot down at least two things you can:

    a) see ....

    b) hear ....

    c) smell ....

    d) taste ....

    e) touch .... **[10]**

3 Make notes on the scene/person from:

    a) long distance ....

    ....

    b) middle distance ....

    ....

    ....

    c) close up ....

    ....

    .... **[6]**

4 Imagery

Write down an appropriate:

    a) simile ....

    ....

    b) metaphor ....

    .... **[2]**

Total Marks .... / 20

English Language 2

Reading Non-fiction 1 and 2

1 Read the following short texts and use the table below to list differences in the writers' points of view and how they are expressed.

A

It's easy to miss Little Mickledon. It's a tiny village, with no shop or pub, nestling in a valley surrounded by fields of grazing sheep. It's a bit like stepping back in time to the Olde England of yore. It's charming and tranquil, cut off from 'civilization' by having no broadband and no mobile phone signal. But for visitors to Alf and Maisie's delightful bed and breakfast, that's a big attraction. 'People come here to relax', beams Maisie, 'and to rediscover a sense of inner peace and calm.'

B

The Bideaway B & B, Little Mickledon, was a massive disappointment. We were promised peace and quiet, sure, but we didn't expect to be totally cut off from the modern world. Be warned. There's no broadband and we couldn't get a mobile signal. When we complained – not our only complaint: the rooms were grubby and the breakfast pitiful – the hippy owners just shrugged their shoulders.

	Text A	Text B
What is the writer's attitude to Little Mickledon?		
What is the writer's opinion of the B & B?		
What impression do you get of the writer?		
How would you describe the general tone and style?		
Comment on language features.		

[20]

Total Marks _____ / 20

English Language 2

Writing Non-fiction 1 and 2

1 Imagine you have been asked to give your opinion on the statement 'Work Experience is a complete waste of time and should be abolished'.

Use the table below to list five arguments in favour of abolishing work experience (pro) and five against it (con).

Pros	Cons

[10]

2 The statement above was made in an article in your local newspaper. Decide whether you agree or disagree with it and write only **the opening paragraph** of a letter to the newspaper expressing your view.

[5]

3 Now write only **the opening paragraph** of an article for a teenage magazine expressing your views on the same statement.

[5]

Total Marks .... / 20

Shakespeare

Context and Themes

1 Think about the Shakespeare play you have studied and write a sentence to explain how each of the following aspects of social and historical context is reflected in it.

a) The play's setting — **Example: *Romeo and Juliet* is set in Italy, a country associated with romance and feuding families.**

_____

_____

b) History and politics

_____

_____

c) Religion

_____

d) Society

_____

e) Gender roles

_____

f) Cultural context

_____ [12]

2 Think about the play you have studied and write a sentence explaining how each of the following themes is reflected in it.

a) Marriage — Example: **In *Romeo and Juliet* Capulet sees it as his right and duty to choose Juliet's husband, but Romeo and Juliet see marriage as an expression of love.**

_____

b) Appearance and reality

_____

c) Power

_____

d) Revenge

_____

e) Loyalty and betrayal

_____

f) Parents and children

_____ [12]

Total Marks _____ / 24

Shakespeare

Characters, Language and Structure

1 Choose at least three characters from the play you have studied and find quotations (either something they say or something other characters say) which you feel tell us something about their characters.

Enter the characters' names and appropriate quotations, together with a brief explanation of what you think each quotation tells us, in the table below.

If you have studied *The Tempest* you could start with:

Character	Quotation	What it tells us
Caliban	The clouds methought would open and show riches Ready to drop upon me, that when I waked I cried to dream again (Act 3 Scene 2).	An unexpected, sensitive side of Caliban, showing him to be more than a monster.

[12]

2 Below are some quotations from Shakespeare which demonstrate his use of the following literary techniques: metaphor, oxymoron, pathetic fallacy / personification, rhetorical question.

For each one, state which technique is being used and explain its effect.

a) O brawling love, O loving hate (*Romeo and Juliet*, Act 1 Scene 1)

b) But since I am a dog, beware my fangs. (*The Merchant of Venice*, Act 3 Scene 3)

c) Brutus and Caesar: what should be in that 'Caesar?' (*Julius Caesar*, Act 1 Scene 2)

d) The winds did sing it to me [...] and the thunder [...] pronounced / The name of Prosper. (*The Tempest*, Act 3 Scene 3)

	Technique	Effect
a)		
b)		
c)		
d)		

[12]

Total Marks _____ / 24

The Nineteenth-Century Novel

Context and Themes

1 Look at these statements about life in the nineteenth century and write a sentence or two saying whether and how each one is reflected in the novel you have studied.

a) Christianity was part of the fabric of life and writers could assume their readers shared Christian ideas and values.

Example: **In *Great Expectations*, the moral values are those of Christianity. Virtues such as humility, self-sacrifice and love win out over vices like selfishness, greed and dishonesty.**

b) Nineteenth-century Britain was a rich country but many people were extremely poor.

c) Nineteenth-century women had far fewer rights than men and a more limited role in society.

d) The nineteenth century was a time of discovery, adventure and scientific advances.

e) Nineteenth-century writers wrote about both personal feelings and moral responsibility.

[10]

2 a) On a separate piece of paper, write down some themes that occur in the novel you have studied. Try to find five. Here are some examples to get you started:

Pride and Prejudice	social class
Frankenstein	nature and nurture
A Christmas Carol	poverty
Jane Eyre	integrity
Great Expectations	friendship
The Strange Case of Dr Jekyll and Mr Hyde	hypocrisy

[5]

b) Now write a sentence or two about each of these themes, for example:

In *Pride and Prejudice* awareness of social class can lead to misunderstanding and unhappiness, as well as being a source of humour.

[10]

Total Marks _____ / 25

The Nineteenth-Century Novel

Characters, Language and Structure

1 Identify the main characters in your novel and draw up a chart for each like the one below: Try to complete charts for five characters.

Name	
Background	
Personality	
Relationships	
Motivation	
Function	

[25]

2 Below are five quotations from nineteenth-century novels (**a–e**) and five descriptions of their use of language (**v–z**). Match each quotation to the appropriate description.

a) It is a truth universally acknowledged that a single man in possession of a good fortune must be in want of a wife. *Pride and Prejudice*, Chapter 1	**v)** The writer uses pathetic fallacy to create a mood.
b) Mud-coloured clouds drooped sadly over the muddy streets. *The Sign of Four*, Chapter 3	**w)** The first-person narrator uses a short, simple sentence for impact.
c) I pursued nature to her hiding places. *Frankenstein*, Chapter 4	**x)** The author uses irony to amuse the reader, making a statement that is clearly not true.
d) '…And it were my intentions to have had put upon his tombstone that Whatsume'er the failings on his part, Remember reader he were that good in his hart.' *Great Expectations*, Chapter 5	**y)** The writer uses personification, making an idea more real by writing as if it were a person.
e) Reader, I married him. *Jane Eyre*, Chapter 38	**z)** The writer uses non-standard English to reflect the origins of the speaker and amuse the reader.

[10]

Total Marks _____ / 35

Modern Texts

Context and Themes

1 Think about the social, historical and cultural context of the modern text you have studied. If you have studied the stories in the AQA Anthology, answer on one story. You might want to try further answers on other stories.

    a) Write a paragraph describing the 'world' of the prose text you have studied. Include information about when and where it is set, the lifestyle of the characters, their attitudes and the attitudes of society in general.

        [5]

    b) Write a paragraph explaining how this world differs from the world you live in today.

        [5]

    c) Now think about when the text was written, its genre and form, and its intended audience. Write a paragraph about how these elements are reflected in the text.

        [5]

2 **a)** In the table below, or on a separate piece of paper, write down some themes that occur in the text you have studied. Try to find four. **[4]**

    b) Now write a sentence or two about each theme, for example:

growing up	The young people in 'The Darkness Out There' grow up when they encounter the dark side of adult life in an unlikely place.

        [8]

Total Marks _____ / 27

Modern Texts

Characters, Language and Structure

Characters

1 Identify the main characters in your novel and draw up a chart for each like the one below:

Name	
Background	
Personality	
Relationships	
Motivation	
Function	

[25]

Language and Structure

2 If you have studied a novel or short stories, answer the following questions (**a–e**). If you have studied the stories in the AQA Anthology, answer on one story. You might want to try further answers on other stories.

a) How would you describe the narrator? _____

b) How would you describe the register used by the narrator? _____

c) Have you noticed anything interesting about the way in which any of the characters speak? _____

d) How is your text divided? _____

e) Give an example of the use of figurative language from your text. _____

_____

If you have studied a play, answer these questions (**f–j**):

f) What, if anything, do we learn from the stage directions? _____

_____

g) Do any of the characters speak directly to the audience? If so, which ones and why?

_____

h) Are there any interesting differences between the ways in which characters speak?

_____

i) How is the play divided? _____

j) Give an example of the use of figurative language from your text.

_____

[10]

Poetry

Context and Themes

Context

Think about the social, historical and cultural context of the poems you have studied. If you have studied the 'Love and Relationships' cluster, answer question 1. If you have studied 'Power and Conflict', answer question 2.

1 Match these descriptions of the context of poems to the appropriate poems.

   a) This poem is rooted in the poet's Irish heritage. ⎯⎯⎯⎯⎯⎯⎯⎯⎯⎯

   b) The poem's language reflects the speaker's Asian heritage. ⎯⎯⎯⎯⎯⎯⎯

   c) The poet uses a Petrarchan sonnet to express her feelings. ⎯⎯⎯⎯⎯ [3]

2 Match these descriptions of poems' context to the appropriate poems.

   a) In this Romantic poem the poet learns from nature. ⎯⎯⎯⎯⎯⎯⎯⎯⎯

   b) This poem reflects on the Japanese experience of the Second World War.

   ⎯⎯⎯⎯⎯⎯⎯⎯⎯⎯⎯⎯⎯⎯⎯⎯⎯⎯⎯⎯⎯⎯⎯⎯⎯⎯⎯⎯⎯⎯⎯⎯

   c) This poem considers the effect of his experiences on a soldier who has just returned from war. ⎯⎯⎯⎯⎯⎯⎯⎯⎯⎯⎯⎯ [3]

Themes

Now think about themes and ideas touched on in the poems you have studied. If you have studied the 'Love and Relationships' cluster, answer question 3. If you have studied 'Power and Conflict', answer question 4.

3 Which poems touch on the following aspects of the main theme (love and relationships)? Try to find at least three for each. You may list the same poem under more than one heading:

a) Parent/child relationships	
b) Loveless relationships	
c) Identity	
d) Lasting romantic love	

[12]

4 Which poems touch on the following aspects of the main theme (power and conflict)? Try to find at least three for each. You may list the same poem under more than one heading:

a) The experience of combatants (soldiers)	
b) The effect of war on non-combatants	
c) The abuse of power	
d) Memories	

[12]

Total Marks ⎯⎯⎯⎯⎯ / 30

Poetry

Language, Form and Structure

1 Below are some lines taken from poems which demonstrate poets' use of various language choices and literary techniques. Some are taken from 'Love and Relationships' and some from 'Power and Conflict'.

a) And a few leaves lay on the starving sod;   ('Neutral Tones')

b) Long, long shall I rue thee   ('When We Two Parted')

c) the waterlogged earth
gulping for breath at our feet   ('Winter Swans')

d) years between us. Anchor. Kite   ('Mother, any distance')

e) Dem tell me bout de man who discover de balloon
And de cow who jump over de moon   ('Checking Out Me History')

f) The only light is red and softly glows,
as though this were a church   ('War Photographer')

g) ..., the flung spray hits
The very windows, spits like a tame cat   ('Storm on the Island')

Some of the techniques below are used in more than one of these quotations, and some quotations include more than one technique. State which techniques are being used and explain their effect.

**alliteration   archaic language   assonance   caesura   dialect   end-stopping   enjambment
metaphor   pathetic fallacy/personification   repetition   rhyming couplet   simile   onomatopoeia**

	Technique	Effect
a)		
b)		
c)		
d)		
e)		
f)		
g)		

[40]

Total Marks _____ / 40

Poetry

1 Read the poem below and answer the questions that follow. (Use a separate piece of paper if necessary.)

Storm in the Black Forest, D. H. Lawrence

Now it is almost night, from the bronzey soft sky
jugfull after jugfull of pure white liquid fire, bright white
tipples over and spills down,
and is gone
and gold-bronze flutters bent through the thick upper air.

And as the electric liquid pours out, sometimes
a still brighter white snake wriggles among it, spilled
and tumbling wriggling down the sky:
and then the heavens cackle with uncouth sounds.

And the rain won't come, the rain refuses to come!

This is the electricity that man is supposed to have mastered
chained, subjugated to his use!
supposed to!

---

a) Where and when is it set?

b) Is there a strong regular rhythm or rhyme scheme? If so, what effect does it have? If not, what effect does this have?

c) Give an example of alliteration and explain its effect.

d) Give an example of assonance and explain its effect.

e) Give an example of the use of metaphor and explain its effect.

f) Explain the poet's repeated use of 'and'.

g) What is the significance of the final line 'supposed to!'?

h) What do you think the poem is really about?

i) How does the storm make the poet feel?

j) How does the poem make you feel? [20]

Total Marks ____ / 20

2 Read this poem. (Note that this poem is one stanza.)

The Vixen, John Clare

Among the taller wood with ivy hung,
The old fox plays and dances round her young.
She snuffs and barks if any passes by
And swings her tail and turns prepared to fly.
The horseman hurries by, she bolts to see,
And turns agen, from danger never free.
If any stands she runs among the poles
And barks and snaps and drives them in the holes.
The shepherd sees them and the boy goes by
And gets a stick and progs the hole to try.
They get all still and lie in safety sure,
And out again when everything's secure,
And start and snap at blackbirds bouncing by
To fight and catch the great white butterfly.

Re-read the poem on page 175 and compare the two poems using the chart below.

	'Storm in the Black Forest'	'The Vixen'
Setting (time and place)		The poem takes place in the woods on what seems to be a typical day for the vixen.
What happens in the poem		
Structure		
Rhythm and rhyme		
Vocabulary/register		
Use of sound		
Imagery		
Themes and poet's attitude		

[32]

Total Marks _____ / 32

Practice Exam Papers

English Language Paper 1

Explorations in Creative Reading and Writing

You should spend a total of 1 hour 45 minutes on this paper.
You are advised to spend about 15 minutes reading through the source and all five questions.
Answer **all** questions.
The marks for questions are shown in brackets.
There are 40 marks for **Section A** (reading) and 40 marks for **Section B** (writing). The maximum mark for this paper is 80.

Source A

This extract is the opening of 'The Invisible Man', a short detective story by G. K. Chesterton, first published in 1911.

In the cool blue twilight of two steep streets in Camden Town, the shop at the corner, a confectioner's,[1] glowed like the butt of a cigar. One should rather say, perhaps, like the butt of a firework, for the light was of many colours and some complexity, broken up by many mirrors and dancing on many gilt and gaily-coloured cakes and sweetmeats. Against this one fiery glass
5 were glued the noses of many gutter-snipes,[2] for the chocolates were all wrapped in those red and gold and green metallic colours which are almost better than chocolate itself; and the huge white wedding-cake in the window was somehow at once remote and satisfying, just as if the whole North Pole were good to eat. Such rainbow provocations could naturally collect the youth of the neighbourhood up to the ages of ten or twelve. But this corner was also attractive to youth at a
10 later stage; and a young man, not less than twenty-four, was staring into the same shop window. To him, also, the shop was of fiery charm, but this attraction was not wholly to be explained by chocolates; which, however, he was far from despising.

He was a tall, burly, red-haired young man, with a resolute face but a listless manner. He carried under his arm a flat, grey portfolio of black-and-white sketches, which he had sold with more
15 or less success to publishers ever since his uncle (who was an admiral) had disinherited him for Socialism, because of a lecture which he had delivered against that economic theory. His name was John Turnbull Angus.

Entering at last, he walked through the confectioner's shop to the back room, which was a sort of pastry-cook restaurant, merely raising his hat to the young lady who was serving there. She
20 was a dark, elegant, alert girl in black, with a high colour and very quick, dark eyes; and after the ordinary interval she followed him into the inner room to take his order.

His order was evidently a usual one. 'I want, please,' he said with precision, 'one halfpenny bun and a small cup of black coffee.' An instant before the girl could turn away he added, 'Also, I want you to marry me.'

[1] *confectioner* – a maker or seller of sweets and pastries

[2] *gutter-snipes* – 'street' children

Practice Exam Papers

Section A: Reading

Answer **all** questions in this section.
You are advised to spend about 45 minutes on this section.

1 Read again the first paragraph of Source A.

List four things that can be seen through the window of the confectioner's shop. **[4 marks]**

2 Look in detail at this extract from the first paragraph of the source (lines 1–9).

> In the cool blue twilight of two steep streets in Camden Town, the shop at the corner, a confectioner's, glowed like the butt of a cigar. One should rather say, perhaps, like the butt of a firework, for the light was of many colours and some complexity, broken up by many mirrors and dancing on many gilt and gaily-coloured cakes and sweetmeats. Against this one fiery glass were glued the noses of many gutter-snipes, for the chocolates were all wrapped in those red and gold and green metallic colours which are almost better than chocolate itself; and the huge white wedding-cake in the window was somehow at once remote and satisfying, just as if the whole North Pole were good to eat. Such rainbow provocations could naturally collect the youth of the neighbourhood up to the ages of ten or twelve.

How does the writer use language to describe how attractive the shop window is to children?

You could include the writer's choice of:
* words and phrases
* language features and techniques
* sentence forms. **[8 marks]**

3 Now think about the whole of the source.

This text is the opening of a short story.

How has the writer structured the text to interest you as a reader?

You could write about:
* what the writer focuses your attention on at the beginning
* how and why the writer changes this focus as the extract develops
* any other structural features that interest you. **[8 marks]**

4 Focus this answer on the latter part of the source, from line 9 ('But this corner was also attractive to youth at a later stage') to the end.

How does the writer bring to life the two characters, making the reader interested in them and their story?

In your response you should:
* write about your impressions of the characters.
* evaluate how the writer has created those impressions.
* support your opinions with quotations from the text. **[20 marks]**

Section B: Writing

You are advised to spend about 45 minutes on this section.
You are reminded of the need to plan your answer.
You should write in full sentences.
Leave enough time to check your work at the end.

5   You are going to enter a creative writing competition, judged by people of your own age.

EITHER

Write a description suggested by this picture.

OR

Write the opening of a story about a student who is doing a holiday job in a shop or cafe.

[24 marks for content and organization and 16 marks for technical accuracy]

[40 marks]

Practice Exam Papers

English Language Paper 2

Writers' Viewpoints and Perspectives

You should spend a total of 1 hour 45 minutes on this paper.
You are advised to spend about 15 minutes reading through the sources and all five questions.
Answer **all** questions.
The marks for questions are shown in brackets.
There are 40 marks for **Section A** (reading) and 40 marks for **Section B** (writing). The maximum mark for the paper is 80.

Source A

SAVE OUR LIBRARY

Local writer joins the fight against closure

By our Arts and Education Correspondent, Alfie Witherspoon

The campaign to save King's Park Library from closure has the backing of an array of local talent. Children's writer Mandy Frobisher says that without the library she would never have become a writer.

'I can't tell you how much that library meant to me,' she told me. 'It gave me a refuge, a place to do my homework, access to centuries of learning and a lifelong love of literature. It made me who I am.
5   Why should today's children be deprived of the opportunities which our generation took for granted?'

Actor Steve Gomez agrees wholeheartedly. 'When I was growing up, the library was the centre of our community. People from all walks of life and all ages used it. They still do. If it closes, there'll be a black hole at the heart of King's Park.' Steve may not mean this literally, but other locals are concerned about what will happen to the building itself, a purpose-built, generously proportioned,
10 roomy building beautifully decorated in the style of the Edwardian Arts and Crafts movement.

Campaigners have high hopes that the backing of Mary and Steve, and other well-known local figures, will help to publicize their campaign and maybe even persuade the Mayor and council to change their minds.

However, a spokesperson for the council claims that the facts simply don't justify keeping the
15 library open. Statistics show that there are now fewer than 300 regular borrowers, almost all of them pensioners, and that number is falling all the time. Figures for people using the references facilities are equally depressing, with only a handful of knowledge-seekers using the facilities each day.

Nevertheless, campaign leader Councillor Laurel Tompkins says she will continue to fight the closure 'every inch of the way'. According to her, the savings to be made by shutting King's Park
20 and five other local libraries are 'a drop in the ocean'. She acknowledges the government has made cuts in its funding – and that King's Park isn't the thriving, populous area it once was – but is convinced that it is not worth devastating the community for a comparatively small saving. 'And when new research is showing that one in three children in the UK does not own a book,' she adds, 'how can the Mayor deprive our kids of the chance of borrowing one and being turned on to
25 reading for life?'

Source B

A letter to *The Times*, written in 1891, about a vote on the issues of public libraries in the London district of Marylebone. Under the Public Libraries Act, people had to vote in favour of public libraries before they could be built by a local council. This letter is from representatives of a group that was running free libraries without public funding.

PUBLIC LIBRARIES IN MARYLEBONE: TO THE EDITOR OF *THE TIMES*

Sir,– May we be allowed, through your columns, to appeal to the ratepayers[1] of Marylebone to record their votes at the end of the present week in favour of the adoption of the Public Libraries Acts, and thus secure for this large and wealthy parish the inestimable social advantages of good libraries, free to all classes, in every district?

We do not make this appeal in order to expatiate upon these advantages, because, with free libraries springing
5   up in all directions, they are generally admitted. We would rather remind Marylebone of the work which our voluntary association has accomplished during the last three years – a work which must, in all probability, be brought to an end within the next year or so, unless the financial burden of maintaining the existing voluntary libraries be transferred from our association to the ratepayers at large.

The history of the Marylebone Free Library movement is briefly this:– An effort was made in 1887 to obtain
10   sufficient funds, £20,000, to erect a handsome central library, which should not only be a permanent Jubilee[2] memorial, but also serve as a stimulus to the inhabitants of Marylebone to adopt the Public Libraries Acts. The movement failed, only about £7,000 being promised, and an appeal to the ratepayers the following year failed also, not so much from opposition as from apathy on the part of the inhabitants. Our association, in no wise daunted, decided to establish small local reading rooms and libraries in two of the most populous parts of the
15   parish, in the hope that by these object-lessons demonstration amounting to proof would be given both of a great social need and a successful means of meeting it. We have not been mistaken in our calculations. The library in Lisson-grove, opened in 1889, has been an extraordinary success. The space is limited, and accommodation plain and insufficient, but notwithstanding these drawbacks no less than 219,000 persons of all sorts and conditions have used the news and reading room and the reference and lending libraries during the past year. A carefully
20   selected library of 4,000 volumes has attracted 1,200 borrowers, whilst the demand increases daily. Our second library in Mortimer-street, nearly opposite the Middlesex Hospital, was only opened nine months ago and is on a smaller scale. Its success, however, is proportionately greater. Funds, and funds only, are required to enable the association to multiply these useful institutions. One library is £300 in debt, and the funds of the second are running low. Unfortunately, many of our actual and also many of our would-be subscribers feel that the very
25   success of our movement relieves them of individual responsibility. That which exists, they say, for the good of all should be paid for by all, more especially when the maximum amount imposed upon each ratepayer by the 1d. rate[3] is so trifling. During the past few years no less than 28 metropolitan and suburban districts, some poor, some rich, have adopted the Public Libraries Acts. Others are about to follow, and our association hopes that Marylebone will be of the number. Much want of knowledge and indifference still exist on the subject of free
30   libraries, and we therefore appeal to you to give publicity to our case, and thus contribute to success at the poll.

We beg, Sir, to remain yours obediently,

JOHN R. HOLLOND Chairman

FRANK DEBENHAM Treasurer

Marylebone Public Libraries Association, 18 Baker-street. March 4.

[1] *ratepayers* – people who pay 'rates' or local taxes, the equivalent of Council Tax today
[2] *Jubilee* – the golden jubilee of Queen Victoria had taken place in 1887
[3] *1d. rate* – a one -penny tax; local councils could increase rates by up to a penny per pound for libraries and museums.

Section A: Reading

Answer **all** questions in this section.
You are advised to spend about 45 minutes on this section.

1 Read again **Source A** from lines 1 to 13.

Choose four statements below which are TRUE.

- Shade the boxes of the ones that you think are true.
- Choose a maximum of four statements.

A. King's Park Library is threatened with closure

B. Mandy Frobisher writes for children.

C. Steve Gomez is in favour of closing the library.

D. There is a big hole in the middle of the park.

E. The campaigners have given up hope.

F. Frobisher used to do her homework in the library.

G. Nobody in King's Park has heard of Mandy Frobisher or Steve Gomez.

H. Gomez thinks the whole community benefits from the library.

[4 marks]

2 You need to refer to **Source A** and **Source B** for this question.

Use details from **both** sources. Write a summary of the differences between King's Park Library now and the two Marylebone libraries in 1891.

[8 marks]

3 You now need to refer **only** to **Source B**, the letter written by John Hollond and Frank Debenham to *The Times.*

How do the writers use language to try to influence the reader?

[12 marks]

4 For this question you need to refer to **both Source A** and **Source B**.

Compare how the writers convey different attitudes to libraries.

In your answer you should:

- Compare the different attitudes (both those of the writers themselves and those that they report).
- Compare the methods they use to convey these attitudes.
- Support your ideas with quotations from both texts.   **[16 marks]**

Section B: Writing

You are advised to spend about 45 minutes on this section.
You are reminded of the need to plan your answer.
You should write in full sentences.
You should leave enough time to check your work at the end.

5 'Libraries are a thing of the past. You can get all the information you need from the internet at home. People who like books can buy them or download them. There are much more important things to spend public money on.'

Write an article for a broadsheet newspaper in which you explain your point of view on this statement.

[24 marks for content and organization; 16 marks for technical accuracy]

[40 marks]

Practice Exam Papers

English Literature Paper 1

Shakespeare and the Nineteenth-Century Novel

You should spend a total of 1 hour 45 minutes on this paper.
Answer one question from Section A and one from Section B.
The maximum mark for the paper is 64.
Spelling, punctuation and grammar will be assessed in Section A. There are four marks available
for AO4 in addition to 30 marks for answering the question.
There are 30 marks for Section B.

Section A

Shakespeare	Question	Page
Macbeth	1	185
Romeo and Juliet	2	185
The Tempest	3	186
The Merchant of Venice	4	187
Much Ado About Nothing	5	187
Julius Caesar	6	188

Section B

The nineteenth-century novel		Question	Page
Robert Louis Stevenson	*The Strange Case of Dr Jekyll and Mr Hyde*	7	189
Charles Dickens	*A Christmas Carol*	8	189
Charles Dickens	*Great Expectations*	9	190
Charlotte Brontë	*Jane Eyre*	10	190
Mary Shelley	*Frankenstein*	11	191
Jane Austen	*Pride and Prejudice*	12	191
Sir Arthur Conan Doyle	*The Sign of Four*	13	192

Section A: Shakespeare

Answer **one** question from this section on your chosen text.

1 *Macbeth*

Read the following extract from Act 5, Scene 5 of *Macbeth* and then answer the question that follows.

Here, Macbeth is preparing to meet the invading armies of Malcolm and Macduff.

MACBETH	I have almost forgot the taste of fears.
	The time has been my senses would have cooled
	To hear the night-shriek, and my fell of hair
	Would at a dismal treatise rise and stir
	As life were in't. I have supped full with horrors.
	Direness, familiar to my slaughterous thoughts,
	Cannot once start me.
Enter Seyton	
	Wherefore was that cry?
SEYTON	The Queen, my lord, is dead.
MACBETH	She should have died hereafter.
	There would have been a time for such a word.
	Tomorrow, and tomorrow, and tomorrow
	Creeps in this petty pace from day to day
	To the last syllable of recorded time,
	And all our yesterdays have lighted fools
	The way to dusty death. Out, out, brief candle.
	Life's but a walking shadow, a poor player
	That struts and frets his hour upon the stage,
	And then is heard no more. It is a tale
	Told by an idiot, full of sound and fury,
	Signifying nothing.

Starting with this extract, explore how Shakespeare presents Macbeth's changing character.

Write about:
- how Shakespeare presents Macbeth in this speech
- how Shakespeare presents Macbeth in the play as a whole. **[30 marks + AO4 4 marks]**

2 *Romeo and Juliet*

Read the following extract from Act 3, Scene 5 of *Romeo and Juliet* and then answer the question that follows.

Here, Romeo is leaving Juliet's room the morning after their secret wedding.

| JULIET | Wilt thou be gone? It is not yet near day. |
| | It was the nightingale, and not the lark, |

ROMEO
> That pierced the fear-full hollow of thine ear.
> Nightly she sings on yon pomegranate tree.
> Believe me, love, it was the nightingale.
> It was the lark, the herald of the morn,
> No nightingale. Look, love, what envious streaks
> Do lace the severing clouds in yonder east.
> Night's candles are burnt out, and jocund day
> Stands tiptoe on the misty mountain tops.
> I must be gone and live, or stay and die.

JULIET
> Yon light is not daylight; I know it, I.
> It is some meteor that the sun exhaled
> To be to thee this night a torchbearer
> And light thee on thy way to Mantua.
> Therefore stay yet. Thou need'st not be gone.

Starting with this extract, write about how Shakespeare presents ideas about love and marriage in *Romeo and Juliet*.

Write about:

- how Shakespeare presents Romeo and Juliet's relationship in this extract
- how Shakespeare presents ideas about love and marriage in the whole play.

[30 marks + AO4 4 marks]

3 | *The Tempest*

Read the following extract from Act 4, Scene 1 of *The Tempest* and then answer the question that follows.

In this scene Prospero punishes Caliban and his companions for plotting to kill him.

A noise of hunters is heard. Enter spirits in the shape of dogs and hounds. They hunt Caliban, Stefano and Trinculo, Prospero and Ariel setting them on

PROSPERO   Hey, Mountain, hey!
ARIEL   Silver! There it goes, Silver!
PROSPERO   Fury, Fury! There, Tyrant, there! Hark, hark!

Exeunt Stefano, Trinculo and Caliban, pursued by spirits
> Go, charge my goblins that they grind their joints
> With dry convulsions, shorten up their sinews
> With aged cramps, and shall more pinch-spotted make them
> Than pard or cat o' mountain.

Cries within
ARIEL   Hark, they roar!
PROPSERO   Let them be hunted soundly. At this hour
> Lies at my mercy all mine enemies.
> Shortly shall all my labours end, and thou
> Shalt have the air at freedom. For a little,
> Follow, and do me service.

Starting with this extract, explain how Shakespeare writes about revenge and forgiveness in *The Tempest*.

Write about:
- how Shakespeare presents ideas about revenge and forgiveness in this extract
- how Shakespeare presents ideas about revenge and forgiveness in the play as a whole.

[30 marks + AO4 4 marks]

4 | *The Merchant of Venice*

Read the following extract from Act 3, Scne 3 of *The Merchant of Venice* and then answer the question that follows.

Shylock has had Antonio put in prison for failing to repay the money he lent him.

SHYLOCK	Jailer, look to him. Tell me not of mercy.
	This is the fool that lent the money gratis.
	Jailer, look to him.
ANTONIO	Hear me yet, good Shylock.
SHYLOCK	I'll have my bond. Speak not against my bond.
	I have sworn an oath that I will have my bond.
	Thou called'st me a dog before thou hadst a cause,
	But since I am a dog, beware my fangs.
	The Duke shall grant me justice. I do wonder,
	Thou naughty jailer, that thou art so fond
	To come abroad with him at his request.
ANTONIO	I pray thee hear me speak.
SHYLOCK	I'll have my bond. I will not hear thee speak.
	I'll have my bond, and therefore speak not me more.
	I'll not be made a soft and dull-eyed fool
	To shake the head, relent, and sigh, and yield
	To Christian intercessors. Follow not.
	I'll have no speaking. I will have my bond.

Starting with this extract, write about how Shakespeare presents Shylock as an outsider.

Write about:
- how Shakespeare presents Shylock as an outsider in this extract
- how Shakespeare presents Shylock as an outsider in the play as a whole. **[30 marks + AO4 4 marks]**

5 | *Much Ado About Nothing*

Read the following extract from Act 1, Scene 1 of *Much Ado About Nothing* and then answer the question that follows.

The messenger has brought the news that Don Pedro is coming to Messina. Beatrice has asked him whether Benedick is with him.

LEONATO	Faith, niece, you tax Signor Benedick too much. But he'll be meet with you, I doubt it not.
MESSENGER	He hath done good service, lady, in these wars.

Practice Exam Papers

BEATRICE	You had musty victual, and he hath holp to eat it. He is a very valiant trencherman, he hath an excellent stomach.
MESSENGER	And a good soldier too, lady.
BEATRICE	And a good soldier to a lady, but what is he to a lord?
MESSENGER	A lord to a lord, a man to a man, stuffed with all honourable virtues.
BEATRICE	It is so, indeed. He is no less than a stuffed man. But for the stuffing – well, we are all mortal.
LEONATO	You must not, sir, mistake my niece. There is a kind of merry war betwixt Signor Benedick and her. They never meet but there's a skirmish of wit between them.

Starting with this extract, how does Shakespeare present the relationship between Benedick and Beatrice?

Write about:
- how Shakespeare presents their relationship in the extract
- how he presents their relationship in the whole of the play.   **[30 marks + AO4 4 marks]**

6 *Julius Caesar*

Read the following extract from Act 2, Scene 1 of *Julius Caesar* and then answer the question that follows.

Portia is concerned that her husband, Brutus, is keeping secrets from her.

BRUTUS	You are my true and honourable wife, As dear to me as are the ruddy drops That visit my sad heart.
PORTIA	If this were true, then should I know this secret. I grant I am a woman, but withal A woman that Lord Brutus took to wife. I grant I am a woman, but withal A woman well reputed, Cato's daughter. Think you I am no stronger than my sex, Being so fathered and so husbanded? Tell me your counsels; I will not disclose 'em. I have made strong proof of my constancy, Giving myself a voluntary wound Here in the thigh. Can I bear that with patience, And not my husband's secrets?
BRUTUS	O ye gods, Render me worthy of this noble wife!

Starting with this extract, explore how Shakespeare presents women and their role in *Julius Caesar*.

Write about:
- how Shakespeare writes about women in this speech
- how Shakespeare writes about women in the play as a whole.   **[30 marks + AO4 4 marks]**

Section B: The Nineteenth-Century Novel

Answer the question on the novel you have studied.

7 **Robert Louis Stevenson: *The Strange Case of Dr Jekyll and Mr Hyde***

Answer both parts of the question.

Re-read Chapter 8 ('The Last Night') from

> 'That's it!' said Poole. 'It was this way. I came suddenly into the theatre from the garden. It seems he had slipped out to look for this drug or whatever it is; for the cabinet door was open, and there he was at the far end of the room digging among the crates…'

to

> '…No, sir, that thing in the mask was never Doctor Jekyll – God knows what it was but it was never Doctor Jekyll; and it is the belief of my heart that there was murder done.'

In this extract, Poole, Dr Jekyll's servant, is telling Mr Utterson why he thinks that Jekyll has been murdered.

Starting with this extract, write about how Stevenson uses Jekyll's transformation to explore ideas about good and evil in *The Strange Case of Dr Jekyll and Mr Hyde*.

Write about:

* how Stevenson writes about what Poole has seen in this extract
* how he uses the transformation to explore ideas about good and evil in the novel as a whole.

[30 marks]

8 **Charles Dickens: *A Christmas Carol***

Answer both parts of the question.

Re-read Stave (Chapter) 3 ('The Second of the Three Spirits') from

> 'Forgive me if I am not justified in what I ask,' said Scrooge, looking intently at the Spirit's robe, 'but I see something strange, and not belonging to yourself, protruding from your skirts. Is it a foot or a claw?'

to

> 'Are there no prisons?' said the Spirit, turning on him for the last time with his own words. 'Are there no workhouses?'

In this extract, the children Ignorance and Want are revealed to Scrooge by the Ghost of Christmas Present. Starting with this extract, explain how Dickens writes about social problems in *A Christmas Carol*.

Write about:

* how Dickens writes about social problems in this extract
* how he explore ideas about social problems and social responsibility in the novel as a whole.

[30 marks]

Practice Exam Papers

9 **Charles Dickens:** *Great Expectations*

Answer both parts of the question.

Re-read Chapter 1 from

> Ours was the marsh country, down by the river, within, as the river wound, twenty miles of the sea. My first most vivid and broad impression of the identity of things, seems to me to have been gained on a memorable raw afternoon towards evening.

to

> I earnestly expressed my hope that he wouldn't, and held tighter to the tombstone on which he had put me; partly, to keep myself upon it; partly, to keep myself from crying.

In this extract, Pip meets the convict, Magwitch, for the first time.

Starting with this extract, write about how Dickens uses Pip as a narrator.

Write about:
* how Pip describes his encounter with Magwitch in this extract
* Pip's role as narrator in the novel as a whole. **[30 marks]**

10 **Charlotte Brontë:** *Jane Eyre*

Answer both parts of the question.

Re-read Chapter 15 from

> And was Mr Rochester now ugly in my eyes?

to

> Suppose he should be absent spring, summer, and autumn: how joyless sunshine and fine days will seem!

In this extract, Jane reflects on Mr Rochester's character, just before fire breaks out at Thornfield.

Starting with this extract, write about how Brontë presents the character of Mr Rochester and Jane's changing feelings towards him.

Write about:
* how Brontë writes about Rochester and Jane's feelings towards him in this extract
* how Brontë writes about Rochester and Jane's feelings towards him in the novel as a whole.

[30 marks]

11 Mary Shelley: *Frankenstein*

Answer both parts of the question.

Re-read Chapter 7 from

> We were soon joined by Elizabeth. Time had altered her since I last beheld her; it had endowed her with loveliness surpassing the beauty of her childish years.

to

> 'Dearest niece,' said my father, 'dry your tears. If she is, as you believe, innocent, rely on the justice of our laws, and the activity with which I shall prevent the slightest shadow of partiality.'

In this extract, Elizabeth, Victor Frankenstein and his father discuss the innocence of Justine, who has been arrested for murder.

Starting with this extract, write about how Shelley writes about attitudes to women.

Write about:
- how Shelley writes about women in this extract
- how Shelley writes about women and attitudes to women in the novel as a whole.   **[30 marks]**

12 Jane Austen: *Pride and Prejudice*

Answer both parts of the question.

Re-read Chapter 20 from

> 'An unhappy alternative is before you, Elizabeth. From this day you must be a stranger to one of your parents. – Your mother will never see you again if you do *not* marry Mr Collins, and I will never see you again if you *do*.'

to

> 'But I tell you what, Miss Lizzy, if you take it into your head to go on refusing every offer of marriage in this way, you will never get a husband at all – and I am sure I do not know who is to maintain you when your father is dead.'

In this extract, Elizabeth has just refused Mr Collins's proposal of marriage.

Starting with this extract, explore how Austen writes about attitudes to marriage in *Pride and Prejudice*.

Write about:
- how Austen writes about marriage in this extract
- how Austen writes about attitudes to marriage in the novel as a whole.   **[30 marks]**

13 **Sir Arthur Conan Doyle:** *The Sign of Four*

Answer both parts of the question.

Re-read Chapter 5 from

'There is something devilish in this, Watson,' said he, more moved than I had ever before seen him. 'What do you make of it?'

to

In the light of the lantern I read, with a thrill of horror, 'The sign of the four'.

In this extract, Holmes and Watson discover the body of the murdered man, Bartholomew Sholto, at Pondicherry Lodge.

Starting with this extract, explore how Conan Doyle writes about murder in *The Sign of Four*.

Write about:
• how Conan Doyle writes about murder in this extract
• how Conan Doyle writes about murder in the novel as a whole.　　　　　　　　　**[30 marks]**

English Literature Paper 2

Modern Texts and Poetry

You should spend a total of 2 hours 15 minutes on this paper.
Answer **one** question from **Section A, one** from **Section B** and **both** questions in **Section C**.
The marks for questions are shown in brackets.
The maximum mark for the paper is 96.
AO4 (Spelling, punctuation and grammar) will be assessed in Section A. There are four marks available
for AO4 in addition to 30 marks for answering the question. AO4 assesses the following skills: Use a range of vocabulary and sentence
structures for clarity, purpose and effect, with accurate spelling and punctuation.
There are 30 marks for **Section B** and 32 marks for **Section C**.

Section A

Modern prose or drama		Questions	Page
J. B. Priestley	*An Inspector Calls*	1–2	194
Willy Russell	*Blood Brothers*	3–4	194
Alan Bennett	*The History Boys*	5–6	194
Dennis Kelly	*DNA*	7–8	195
Simon Stephens	*The Curious Incident of the Dog in the Night-Time*	9–10	195
Shelagh Delaney	*A Taste of Honey*	11–12	195
William Golding	*Lord of the Flies*	13–14	196
AQA Anthology	*Telling Tales*	15–16	196
George Orwell	*Animal Farm*	17–18	196
Kazuo Ishiguro	*Never Let Me Go*	19–20	197
Meera Syal	*Anita and Me*	21–22	197
Stephen Kelman	*Pigeon English*	23–24	197

Section B

Poetry		Question	Page
AQA Anthology	Poems Past and Present		
	Love and Relationships	25	198
	Power and Conflict	26	199

Section C

Unseen texts	Question	Page
	27.1	200
	27.2	200

Practice Exam Papers

Section A: Modern Prose or Drama

Answer **one** question from this section on your chosen text.

J. B. Priestley: *An Inspector Calls*

EITHER

1 What is the significance of Eva Smith in *An Inspector Calls*?

Write about:
- what we learn about Eva Smith / Daisy Renton
- how Priestley uses the 'character' of Eva Smith / Daisy Renton.   **[30 marks + AO4 4 marks]**

OR

2 How does Priestley explore ideas about selfishness in *An Inspector Calls*?

Write about:
- the ideas about selfishness in *An Inspector Calls*
- how Priestley presents these ideas in the way he writes.   **[30 marks + AO4 4 marks]**

Willy Russell: *Blood Brothers*

EITHER

3 How does Russell use the characters of Edward and Mickey to write about social class in *Blood Brothers*?

Write about:
- how Russell presents Edward and Mickey
- how he uses Edward and Mickey to write about social class.   **[30 marks + AO4 4 marks]**

OR

4 How does Russell write about superstition and fate in *Blood Brothers*?

Write about:
- ideas about superstition and fate explored in *Blood Brothers*
- how Russell presents these ideas.   **[30 marks + AO4 4 marks]**

Alan Bennett: *The History Boys*

EITHER

5 How does Bennett present Hector as a teacher in *The History Boys*?

Write about:
- what Hector does and says
- how Bennett presents Hector in the play.   **[30 marks + AO4 4 marks]**

OR

6 How does Bennett explore attitudes to history in *The History Boys*?

Write about:
- attitudes to history explored in *The History Boys*
- how Bennett presents these attitudes.   **[30 marks + AO4 4 marks]**

Dennis Kelly: *DNA*

EITHER

7   How does Kelly write about bullying in *DNA*?

     Write about:
- examples of bullying behaviour in *DNA*
- how Kelly presents bullying in the play.   **[30 marks + AO4 4 marks]**

OR

8   How does Kelly present the character of John Tate in *DNA*?

     Write about:
- John Tate's behaviour and attitudes
- how Kelly uses John Tate to explore ideas about leadership and responsibility.

                                                    [30 marks + AO4 4 marks]

Simon Stephens: *The Curious Incident of the Dog in the Night-Time*

EITHER

9   How does Stephens present the character of Judy as a mother in *The Curious Incident of the Dog in the Night-Time*?

     Write about:
- what Judy does and says
- how Stephens presents Judy.   **[30 marks + AO4 4 marks]**

OR

10   How does Stephens present Christopher's experience of education in *The Curious Incident of the Dog in the Night-Time*?

     Write about:
- what Christopher's experience of education is and his attitude to it
- how Stephens presents Christopher's experience of education.   **[30 marks + AO4 4 marks]**

Shelagh Delaney: *A Taste of Honey*

EITHER

11   How does Delaney present the character of Jo as a daughter in *A Taste of Honey*?

     Write about:
- how Delaney presents the character of Jo
- how Delaney uses the character of Jo to explore parent/child relationships.

                                                    [30 marks + AO4 4 marks]

OR

12   How does Delaney write about responsibility in *A Taste of Honey*?

     Write about:
- ideas about responsibility in *A Taste of Honey*
- how Delaney presents these ideas.   **[30 marks + AO4 4 marks]**

Practice Exam Papers

William Golding: *Lord of the Flies*

EITHER

13 How does Golding present the character of Ralph as a leader in *Lord of the Flies*?

Write about:
- how Golding presents the character of Ralph
- how Golding uses the character of Ralph to explore ideas about leadership.

[30 marks + AO4 4 marks]

OR

14 How does Golding present ideas about the breakdown of civilization in *Lord of the Flies*?

Write about:
- ideas about the breakdown of civilization in *Lord of the Flies*
- how Golding presents these ideas.

[30 marks + AO4 4 marks]

AQA Anthology: *Telling Tales*

EITHER

15 How do writers explore ideas about identity in 'The Invisible Mass of the Back Row' and one other story from *Telling Tales*?

Write about:
- ideas about identity in the two stories
- how the writers present these ideas.

[30 marks + AO4 4 marks]

OR

16 How do writers use first-person narrators in 'My Polish Teacher's Tie' and one other story from *Telling Tales*?

Write about:
- the narrators in the two stories
- how the writers use these narrators to explore ideas and issues.

[30 marks + AO4 4 marks]

George Orwell: *Animal Farm*

EITHER

17 How does Orwell use the character of Boxer to explore ideas about the working class in *Animal Farm*?

Write about:
- how Orwell presents the character of Boxer
- how Orwell uses the character of Boxer to present ideas about the working class.

[30 marks + AO4 4 marks]

OR

18 How does Orwell present ideas about revolution in *Animal Farm*?

Write about:
- ideas about revolution in *Animal Farm*
- how Orwell presents these ideas.

[30 marks + AO4 4 marks]

Kazuo Ishiguro: *Never Let Me Go*

EITHER

19 How does Ishiguro present the guardians in *Never Let Me Go*?

Write about:
- the characters of the guardians in *Never Let Me Go*
- how Ishiguro presents the guardians and uses them to explore ideas and issues.

[30 marks + AO4 4 marks]

OR

20 What is the significance of the gallery in *Never Let Me Go*?

Write about:
- what the gallery is and what it represents to the characters in *Never Let Me Go*
- how Ishiguro uses the gallery to explore ideas and issues.   **[30 marks + AO4 4 marks]**

Meera Syal: *Anita and Me*

EITHER

21 How does Syal present racism in *Anita and Me*?

Write about:
- examples of racism in *Anita and Me*
- how Syal shows Meena becoming aware of racism.   **[30 marks + AO4 4 marks]**

OR

22 How does Syal present Nanima and Mrs Worrall as important influences in Meena's life?

Write about:
- the characters of Nanima and Mrs Worrall
- how they are significant in Meena's life.   **[30 marks + AO4 4 marks]**

Stephen Kelman: *Pigeon English*

EITHER

23 How does Kelman present ideas about culture and heritage in *Pigeon English*?

Write about:
- ideas about culture and heritage *Pigeon English*
- how Kelman presents these ideas.   **[30 marks + AO4 4 marks]**

OR

24 How does Kelman present school life in *Pigeon English*?

Write about:
- Harrison's experiences of school and his feelings about school
- how Kelman presents these attitudes and feelings.   **[30 marks + AO4 4 marks]**

Practice Exam Papers

Section B: Poetry

Answer **one** question from this section.

AQA Anthology: *Poems Past and Present*

EITHER

25 **Love and Relationships**

Compare the way poets present feelings of love in Sonnet 29 – 'I think of thee!' and **one** other poem from 'Love and Relationships'.

> **Sonnet 29 – 'I think of thee!'**, Elizabeth Barrett Browning
>
> I think of thee! – my thoughts do twine and bud
> About thee, as wild vines, about a tree,
> Put out broad leaves, and soon there's nought to see
> Except the straggling green which hides the wood.
> 5   Yet, O my palm tree, be it understood
> I will not have my thoughts instead of thee
> Who art dearer, better! Rather, instantly
> Renew thy presence; as a strong tree should,
> Rustle thy boughs and set thy trunk all bare,
> 10   And let these bands of greenery which insphere thee
> Drop heavily down, – burst, shattered, everywhere!
> Because, in this deep joy to see and hear thee
> And breathe within thy shadow a new air,
> I do not think of thee – I am too near thee.

[30 marks]

OR

26 **Power and Conflict**

Compare the way poets present suffering in 'London' and **one** other poem from 'Power and Conflict'.

London, William Blake

I wander through each chartered street,
Near where the chartered Thames does flow,
And mark in every face I meet
Marks of weakness, marks of woe.

5 In every cry of every man,
In every infant's cry of fear,
In every voice, in every ban,
The mind-forged manacles I hear:

How the chimney-sweeper's cry
10 Every black'ning church appals
And the hapless soldier's sigh
Runs in blood down palace walls.
But most through midnight streets I hear
How the youthful harlot's curse
15 Blasts the new-born infant's tear,
And blights with plague the marriage hearse.

[30 marks]

Practice Exam Papers

Section C: Unseen Texts

Answer **both** questions in this section.

Death the Leveller, James Shirley

The glories of our blood and state
    Are shadows, not substantial things;
There is no armour against Fate;
    Death lays his icy hand on kings:
5   Sceptre and Crown
        Must tumble down,
And in the dust be equal made
    With the poor crookèd scythe and spade.

Some men with swords may reap the field,
10   And plant fresh laurels where they kill:
But their strong nerves at last must yield;
    They tame but one another still:
        Early or late
        They stoop to fate,
15 And must give up their murmuring breath
    When they, pale captives, creep to death.

The garlands wither on your brow,
    Then boast no more your mighty deeds!
Upon Death's purple altar now
20   See where the victor-victim bleeds.
        Your heads must come
        To the cold tomb:
Only the actions of the just
    Smell sweet and blossom in their dust.

27.1 In 'Death the Leveller' how does the poet present his feelings about death? **[24 marks]**

Requiem, Robert Louis Stevenson

Under the wide and starry sky,
Dig the grave and let me lie.
Glad did I live and gladly die,
And I laid me down with a will.

5   This be the verse you gave for me:
Here he lies where he longed to be;
Home is the sailor, home from the sea,
And the hunter home from the hill.

27.2 In both 'Death the Leveller' and 'Requiem' the poets express their feelings about death. What are the similarities and/or differences between the ways the poets present their feelings?

[8 marks]

Answers

Key Technical Skills: Writing – pages 148–152

Page 148: Spelling

1. a) tomatoes   b) birthdays
   c) soliloquies   d) families
   e) parentheses   **[maximum 5]**
2. a) **You're** not going out like that. I asked **your** sister to bring it.
   b) **There** are twenty-five people in the class. They have all done **their** homework but **they're** not sitting in the right places.
   c) Turn it off or it will **wear** out. We have no idea **where** it is but **we're** going anyway.
   d) I **passed** him in the street an hour ago. He walked right **past** me as if I wasn't there.
   e) There were only **two** exams **to** sit but that was one **too** many.
   f) If you don't go to the **practice** you'll be left out of the team. If you want to improve you will have to **practise** every day.
       [1] for each correct answer up to a maximum of **[15]**
3. Last **night** I went to the cinema with my friend Bob and his **father**, Michael. The whole evening was not very **successful**. The cinema was very **crowded** and we had to sit **separately**. Then, it turned out the film was in a **foreign language** and no-one could understand it. I think it was about the **environment**. Afterwards, Michael took us to a **restaurant where** we had pizzas.
       [1] for each correct answer up to a maximum of **[10]**

Page 149: Punctuation

1. *Great Expectations,* **[1]** one of the best-known novels by Charles Dickens, **[1]** is the story of Pip, **[1]** a boy who grows up in the marshes of Kent. At **[1]** the beginning of the story he meets an escaped convict in the churchyard where his parents are buried. **[1]**   **[maximum 5]**
2. At about ten o'clock **[1]**, we went to Romio's **[1]** for pizzas. I'm **[1]** not sure what Bob's **[1]** pizza topping was but I had ham and pineapple. I wish I hadn't **[1]** because later on I was sick in Michael's **[1]** car. It's **[1]** brand new and I thought he'd **[1]** be angry but he wasn't **[1]**. We're **[1]** not going there again.   **[maximum 10]**
3. a) Who was that masked man? Nobody knows. b) The cat slept quietly on the mat; the dog slept noisily on the step. c) I don't believe it! That's the first answer I've got. d) Annie deserved the prize: she was the best baker by far. e) Jane and Elizabeth (the two oldest Bennet sisters) get married at the end.
       [1] for each correct answer up to a maximum of **[5]**

Page 150: Sentence Structure

1. a) complex   b) minor   c) simple
   d) compound   e) simple
       [1] for each correct answer up to a maximum of **[5]**
2. a) I bought Anna a bunch of flowers because it was her birthday. **[1]**
   b) He did not finish the race although they gave him a certificate. **[1]**
   a) and b) could be written with the conjunctions at the beginning of the sentence, but you would then need to add a comma after the first clause.
   c) I kept going until I reached the finishing line. **[1]**
3. Joey, who was the oldest cat in the street, never left the garden. **[1]**
4. Walking down the street, I realized I had forgotten my phone. **[1]**

Page 151: Text Structure and Organization

1. e) Students of Summerfield College have expressed concern about the environment they have to work in. They have a number of complaints.
   c) Jodie Collins, a spokesperson for the students, has had several meetings about the issue with the Principal. Ms Rundle apparently listened to the students' points, but later sent an email claiming that nothing can be done because of lack of funds.
   a) As a result of this, the student body has decided to appeal to the governors. Jodie has written a letter to every governor, setting out the problems as the students see them.
   d) According to this letter, students' health and safety are at risk. Among other things, toilets are not properly cleaned and standards of hygiene in the kitchen leave a lot to be desired.
   b) As yet no replies have been received. The increasingly angry students are starting to consider taking 'direct action'.   **[maximum 5]**
2. a) When   b) In spite of
   c) subsequently   d) however
   e) Nevertheless   **[maximum 5]**

Page 152: Standard English and Grammar

1. a) are   b) are   c) were   d) did
   e) has been   f) have done   g) were…had done
                          [maximum 7]
2. a) pleaded   b) few   c) got
                          [maximum 3]
3. Jo: Hello. How are you? **[1]**
   Arthur: Well. Very well, thank you. **[1]**
   Jo: Do you want (or would you like) a drink? **[1]**
   Arthur: May I have two coffees, please? **[1]**
   Jo: Of course. Where are you sitting? **[1]**
4. I was **standing** in the street when Frankie **came** over. **[1]** I gave him a smile and opened **my mouth** to speak. **[1]** I was **going to** ask him how he **did** in **maths** (or mathematics). **[1]** I **did not say anything. [1] As** soon as I **saw** him I knew he **had done well. [1]**

Key Technical Skills: Reading – pages 153–160

Page 153: Explicit Information and Ideas

1. a, c   **[maximum 2]**
2. **Any four from:** He was very nice looking. He had a fresh-coloured face. He was clean shaven. He had white hair. He wore odd-shaped collars. He wore a top hat.   **[maximum 4]**

Page 154: Implicit Information and Ideas

1. a, c, d, g   **[maximum 4]**

Page 155: Synthesis and Summary

1. a) Trees stand behind the shed. **[1]** b) Charlotte Green ate Lydia's chocolate. **[1]** c) Tell me who did it. **[1]**
2. b, c, f, g, h   **[maximum 5]**
3. The summary below is a suggestion only. You should have included details of where and when it happened, and a description of the men.
       [1] for each point up to a maximum of **[12]**.

   At nine o'clock on Monday I was in Arbuckle Lane. As I passed number eighteen, I heard a noise. There were two men on the step. One was breaking the glass in the door with something in his hand. I shouted and they turned. One was about six foot, with a grey beard. The other was stocky with curly black hair. The tall man dropped something and they ran.

Page 156: Synthesis and Summary

1.

Mary Jane	Sarah
Parents did not see the point of school	Mother thought education important
Loved going to school	Did not like going to school
40 in a class	24 in class
(Everyone) worked hard	Did not do much work
Teacher very strict	Teacher never told anyone off
Sat in rows	Sat in groups
Not allowed to talk	Talked all the time
Liked the teacher	Did not like the teacher
Respected the teacher	Did not respect the teacher
Appreciated/valued school	Did not appreciate/value school

[1] for each pair up to a maximum of **[10]**

2. Look at the mark scheme below, decide which description is closest to your answer and then decide what mark to give it up to a maximum of **[8]**.

Marks	Skills
7–8	You have given a perceptive interpretation of both texts. You have synthesized evidence from the texts. You have used appropriate quotations from both texts.
5–6	You have started to interpret both texts. You have shown clear connections between texts. You have used relevant quotations from both texts.

Page 157: Referring to the Text

1. a–e, b–d, c–f **[maximum 3]**
2. a) Macbeth refers to the prophecies as 'happy prologues'. **[2]**
   b) He tells us that one of them has come true: 'I am Thane of Cawdor.' **[2]**
   c) Macbeth asks how the prophecies can be evil when the witches have told the truth:

   If ill,
   Why hath it given me earnest of success
   Commencing in a truth? **[2]**

3.

Point	Frankenstein's response is negative from the start.
Evidence	Referring to the experiment as a 'catastrophe' and his creation as a 'wretch'
Explanation	suggests that he has rejected the creature and will not try to find any good in it.

[maximum 3]

Page 158: Analysing Language 1

1. a) dialectical (also colloquial)   b) formal
   c) colloquial   d) technical   **[maximum 4]**

2. a) adjective   b) preposition
   c) conjunction   d) (concrete) noun
   e) adverb   f) verb   **[maximum 6]**

3. a) complex   b) Jo, Beth or Amy
   c) passive   d) past perfect
   e) third person   **[maximum 5]**

Page 159: Analysing Language 2

1. a) Simile. It suggests he ran extremely quickly as the wind travels quickly. **[2]** b) Metaphor. It suggests that there are a lot of insects and that they are dangerous, violent and organized. **[2]** c) Both. 'Heart' is a metaphor for her feelings/emotions. Describing it as cold or frozen suggests that she feels nothing. **[maximum 6]**
2. a) time b) fizzed/crackled   **[maximum 2]**
3. Look at the mark scheme below, decide which description is closest to your answer and then decide what mark to give it up to a maximum of **[8]**.

Marks	Skills	Examples of possible content
7–8	You have analysed the effects of the choice of language. You have used an appropriate range of quotations. You have used sophisticated subject terminology appropriately.	The opening, which gives a date followed by a minor sentence describing the weather, gives the impression of a diary entry. This will clearly be an account of the narrator's private thoughts. His evocative description of the 'dull' and 'dreary' landscape uses pathetic fallacy (the boulders have 'faces') to imply his own 'melancholy'. The focus then moves to a more overt account of his feelings of dread: 'a weight at my heart and a feeling of impending danger'…
5–6	You have clearly explained the effects of the choice of language. You have used a range of relevant quotations. You have used subject terminology appropriately.	The passage looks like part of a diary. He starts with a short sentence and follows it with a long, descriptive sentence about the landscape. This sets a mood of 'melancholy', which is his mood. He feels the 'weight' of fear and responsibility and analyses why he feels like this, answering a rhetorical question: 'Have I not cause for such a feeling?'

Page 160: Analysing Form and Structure

1. Up to **[2]** for any reasonable answer to each question up to a maximum of **[10]**.
   a) A boarding house / in a city / a place where single people rent rooms / Second Avenue (New York / America).
   b) 'Small and unobtrusive' / dressed plainly / shy / does not draw attention to herself / not interested in what's going on.
   c) Does not fit with the previous description of her / a change in mood / shows an interest in Andy / shows that she is sharp or intelligent / suggests she is judging him.
   d) He is polite or well-mannered / he has charm / he is starting a successful career / he is shallow or superficial / he is not interested in Miss Conway.
   e) She does something to make herself noticed / they get to know each other / they fall in love / they argue / it turns out that they know each other / any other reasonable conjecture.
2. a–y, b–z, c–x

   [1] for each up to a maximum of **[3]**

English Language 1 – pages 161–164

Page 161: Creative Reading 1

1.

A naive/unreliable narrator	A
An omniscient narrator	D
A reliable first-person narrator	B
An intrusive narrator	C (also omniscient)

[2] for each up to a maximum of [8]

Page 162: Creative Reading 2

[1] for each correct answer in 'How we learn' and up to [2] for a reasonable explanation in 'What we learn' up to a maximum of [15].

1.

Character	How we learn about the character	What we learn
Hyde's housekeeper:	a)	She is a bad person / she cannot be trusted / she is polite.
Magwitch:	b)	He is aggressive / rough / frightening.
Darcy:	e)	People are generally impressed by him when they first meet him but quickly change their minds because of the way he behaves.
Mrs Reed:	d)	She is bad-tempered / aggressive / cruel / uncaring.
Victor Frankenstein:	c)	He is behaving strangely / he is sick / he is hysterical. He worries his friend.

Page 163: Narrative Writing

The following answers are examples of the sort of thing you might write. Your own answers will be completely different. [1] for each reasonable answer.

1. a) First person; yes. b) Formal, using Standard English.
    c) Female; 82; Small, neat, well dressed; Grew up on a farm and married a farmer, now living in a bungalow in a village; A widow, with two children who live abroad, friendly with the neighbours but no close friends; Speaks in a Cornish accent but uses Standard English. [maximum 8]
2. a) In the village post office. b) Yes, she goes abroad.
    c) Now. d) A year. e) Yes (except for some memories in flashback). [maximum 5]
3. Exposition: Doris leads a quiet life in a small village with her two cats. Inciting incident: She wins the lottery. She decides to visit her children but not tell them she's a millionaire. Turning point: She goes to see her daughter in France, who is too busy to be bothered. She books her a ticket to Australia. In Australia her son lets her stay but after a while he puts her in a horrible home. Climax: She buys the nursing home, improves the lives of its patients and returns home, where she spends the rest of her money on herself and on charities. Coda/ending: Doris is living happily in the village with her cats and a man she met in the nursing home. She has spent all her money and not given any to her children. [maximum 5]

Page 164: Descriptive Writing

The following answers are examples of the sort of thing you might write. Your own answers will be completely different. [1] for each reasonable answer up to a maximum of [20] overall.

1. a) Third.
    b) Past.
2. a) Gaudy rides, milling crowds.
    b) Screeching child, loud dance music.
    c) Spicy sausage, burning wood.
    d) Tangy mustard, sweet toffee.
    e) Sticky candyfloss, slimy mud.

3. a) A blur of swirling colours and harsh noises.
    b) Candy-striped stall; fluffy toys piled high.
    c) Blue nylon fur, plastic brown eyes.
4. a) The crowd rumbled and rolled like a storm-tossed ship.
    b) An explosion of excited laughter.

English Language 2 – pages 165–166

Page 165: Reading Non-fiction 1 and 2

1. Up to [2] for each answer similar to the following up to a maximum of [20]:

	Text A	Text B
What is the writer's attitude to Little Mickledon?	Likes it. Finds it 'charming and tranquil'.	Does not like the peace and quiet: 'totally cut off'.
What is the writer's opinion of the B & B?	Finds it 'delightful' and gives positive impression of the owners.	Finds it a 'disappointment', criticizes several aspects and does not like owners' attitude.
What impression do you get of the writer?	Someone who likes peace and quiet. Someone who focuses on positive aspects.	Someone who likes to be in touch. Someone who likes to criticize / likes to find fault.
How would you describe the general tone and style?	Positive/enthusiastic/ vague	Negative/critical/ honest
Comment on language features.	Uses words like 'relax', 'calm' and 'tranquil' to give an impression of peace and quiet. Uses archaic words/ spellings (Olde, yore) and puts quotation marks round 'civilization'.	Colloquial – addresses readers with imperative ('Be warned'). Uses adjectives to give an unflattering picture: 'grubby', 'pitiful', 'hippy'.

Page 166: Writing Non-fiction 1 and 2

1. The following are only suggestions. There are many other points you could make. [1] for each up to a maximum of [10].

Pros	Cons
Studying for exams is much more important.	It helps you understand the importance of things like punctuality and politeness.
The work being done is not interesting or meaningful.	It helps you choose your future career.
Students on work experience are just free labour.	You can learn new skills.
In the time you cannot get a realistic idea of what the work is like.	You might make contacts which would lead to paid employment.
You've got the rest of your life to experience work.	You get to meet a wide range of people.

2. **[1]** for each of the following up to a maximum of **[5]**:
   - opening with 'Dear Sir' or 'Dear Editor'
   - setting out the opening correctly
   - using a formal tone
   - clearly stating the purpose of your letter
   - putting your point of view strongly and clearly
   - using a rhetorical or literary device
   - accurate spelling and punctuation.

3. **[1]** for each of the following up to a maximum of **[5]**:
   - using an intriguing/amusing headline
   - using a strapline
   - using an appropriate informal tone
   - clearly stating the purpose of your article
   - putting your point of view strongly and clearly
   - using a rhetorical or literary device
   - accurate spelling and punctuation.

Shakespeare – pages 167–168

Page 167: Context and Themes

1. Up to **[2]** for each reasonable answer up to a maximum of **[12]**.
2. Up to **[2]** for each reasonable answer up to a maximum of **[12]**.

Page 168: Characters, Language and Structure

1. **[2]** for each quotation and **[2]** for a reasonable interpretation up to a maximum of **[12]**.
2. **[1]** for each correct answer and up to **[2]** for a reasonable explanation similar to the suggestions below up to a maximum of **[12]**.
   a) Oxymoron. Its use suggests confusion about love and how the themes of love and hate are intertwined in the play. **b)** Metaphor. The speaker (Shylock) picks up on an insulting comparison and extends it to warn that he can 'bite.' **c)** Rhetorical question. The speaker (Cassius) is trying to get Brutus to think about whether Caesar's name should be synonymous with power and so questions his power. **d)** Pathetic fallacy / personification. The speaker claims that the wind and thunder have told him about Prospero, reflecting his own fear as well as Prospero's power.

The Nineteenth-Century Novel – pages 169–170

Page 169: Context and Themes

1. Up to **[2]** for each reasonable answer up to a maximum of **[10]**.
2. **a)** **[1]** for each reasonable answer up to a maximum of **[5]**.
   b) Up to **[2]** for each reasonable answer up to a maximum of **[10]**.

Page 170: Characters, Language and Structure

1. **[1]** for every box completed with a reasonable answer up to a maximum of **[25]**.
2. a–x, b–v, c–y, d–z, e–w
   [2] for each correct answer up to a maximum of **[10]**

Modern Texts – pages 171–172

Page 171: Context and Themes

Below are examples of the kind of answer you might have given. Up to **[5]** for each reasonable answer similar to these, depending on how full your answer is.
1. **a)** *An Inspector Calls* is set shortly before the First World War, in 1912, in a 'large city' in the Midlands. The family is middle-class and wealthy, Mr Birling being a self-made man who has married someone from a higher social class. They are 'comfortable' and smug but the Inspector reveals the dark underside of their world.
   b) The world of *Never Let Me Go* seems to be just like the real world of just a few years ago. However, there are

aspects of this world which are not real (as far as we know). Breeding people to provide spare parts is not something that is done officially now, although there are cases of people having children to provide genetic material for existing children who are sick.
   c) *DNA* was written as part of a national scheme to produce new plays for schools and youth groups. The writer states that the names and even genders of the characters can be changed to suit the group performing the play. Some might say this leads to a lack of definition in many of the characters.
2. **a)** **[1]** for each theme up to a maximum of **[4]**.
   b) Up to **[2]** for each reasonable answer up to a maximum of **[8]**.

Page 172: Characters, Language and Structure

1. **[1]** for every box completed with a reasonable answer up to a maximum of **[25]**.
2. **[1]** for each reasonable answer up to a maximum of **[10]**.

Poetry – pages 173–176

Page 173: Context and Themes

1. **a)** 'Follower' **[1]** **b)** 'Singh Song!' **[1]** **c)** Sonnet 29 ('I think of thee!') **[1]**
2. **a)** Extract from 'The Prelude' **[1]** **b)** 'Kamikaze' **[1]**
   c) 'Remains' **[1]**
   For questions 3 and 4, the following answers are suggestions. You may have listed other poems. **[1]** for each title listed appropriately, up to a maximum of **[12]**.
3. **a)** 'Before You Were Mine'; 'Eden Rock'; 'Follower'; 'Walking Away'; 'Mother, any distance'. **b)** 'When We Two Parted'; 'Neutral Tones'; 'Porphyria's Lover'; 'The Farmer's Bride'.
   c) 'Follower'; 'Singh Song!'; 'Before You Were Mine'; 'Letters from Yorkshire'. **d)** 'Love's Philosophy'; Sonnet 29; 'Winter Swans'; 'Singh Song!'
4. **a)** 'The Charge of the Light Brigade'; 'Exposure'; 'Bayonet Charge'; 'Remains'. **b)** 'Poppies'; 'War Photographer'; 'The Émigrée'; 'Kamikaze'. **c)** 'London'; 'My Last Duchess'; 'Checking Out Me History'; 'The Charge of the Light Brigade'.
   d) Extract from 'The Prelude'; 'Checking Out Me History'; 'Poppies'; 'The Émigrée'.

Page 174: Language, Form and Structure

1. **[1]** for each technique identified and **[1]** for each reasonable explanation (the explanations below are suggestions only), up to a maximum of **[40]**.
   a) Alliteration, pathetic fallacy. The alliteration of 'l' and 's' (also called sibilance) helps to make the line sound gentle and sad. The image of the earth starving adds to the sense of bleakness and despair. **[4]**
   b) Repetition, archaic language. The repetition of 'long' increases our sense of the future stretching ahead. The archaic language perhaps makes it sound more important. **[4]**
   c) Pathetic fallacy, onomatopoeia, enjambment. The image of the earth gulping for breath suggests the mood of the poet at the beginning of the poem. 'Gulping' might reflect the sound of the muddy earth beneath his feet. The enjambment reflects the continuity of movement and mood. **[6]**
   d) Caesura, metaphor. The caesuras might give a sense of separation, as well as giving emphasis to the two single-word sentences that follow. The two metaphors give us a picture of the poet and his mother's roles in the relationship. He is flying away and she is holding him to the ground. **[4]**
   e) Dialect, rhyming couplet, enjambment. The use of dialect gives a sense of the speaker's heritage and identity. The rhyming couplet gives the poem a light-hearted tone in contrast with its serious subject

matter, as well as reflecting the childish or simple nature of what he was told. The enjambment also makes the lines seem childish, as the poet uses 'and' to build a list. [6]

f) Assonance, simile, end-stopping. The repetition of the long 'o' adds to a sense of calm. Comparing the darkroom to the church makes the photographer's work seem spiritual and important. The end-stop makes us pause, almost as if pausing before entering the church-like room. [6]

g) Enjambment, caesura, simile, onomatopoeia/alliteration. The enjambment gives a sense of the continuous nature of one aspect of the storm, while the caesura reflects how it can suddenly stop and start again. The simile is almost an oxymoron, as 'spit' and 'tame' do not seem to go together. Perhaps the poet is implying that cats are never really tame and, similarly, the storm cannot be tamed. 'Spit' and 'spray' could be seen as onomatopoeia, the 'sp' sounds reflecting the noise made by the water. [10]

Page 175: Unseen Poetry

1. Up to [2] for each answer similar to those below. Other answers might be equally valid.
   a) It is set in a forest during a storm.
   b) No, it is irregular (free verse). The lack of regular patterns reflects the unpredictability of the storm.

c) 'Cackle with uncouth sounds' conveys the harshness of the sounds described. It could be called onomatopoeia.

d) In 'white liquid fire, bright white' the short 'i's are sharp and quick, like the lightning.

e) Describing the lightning as a 'white snake' adds a sense of danger as well as painting a vivid picture.

f) By adding a lot of details in this simple way, the poet builds a sense of the way the storm continues and shows no sign of stopping.

g) The repetition of this phrase and the shortness of the line give it greater impact, emphasizing that humans may think they have harnessed the power of electricity but they cannot really tame nature.

h) The power and wonder of nature – the insignificance of humans – the arrogance of humans.

i) He is in awe of nature – he is excited and perhaps frightened by the storm – it makes him feel insignificant – it makes him realize that humans are not really powerful.

j) Any answer rooted in the text. [maximum 20]

Page 176: Unseen Poetry

2. The answers below are suggestions. There may be other valid responses. Up to [2] for every box filled in with a reasonable response, up to a maximum of [32].

	'Storm in the Black Forest'	'The Vixen'
Setting (time and place)	In a forest during a storm.	The poem takes place in the woods on what seems to be a typical day for the vixen.
What happens in the poem	The poet describes the stages of a violent storm and how it never seems to end, making him think about man and nature.	The poet describes the behaviour of a vixen and her cubs, and how she reacts to danger.
Structure	Four stanzas of unequal lengths (one of only one line) and lines of different lengths, giving a sense of unpredictability.	One stanza of 14 lines, describing what happens in a controlled way. 14 lines, as in a sonnet, but not sonnet structure.
Rhythm and rhyme	No regularity – again reflecting the storm.	Iambic pentameter – smooth and regular. Rhyming couplets – simple structure, each couplet describing one small action.
Vocabulary/register	Language of richness (bronzey), danger (snake), movement (wriggling) and science (electric) combine to convey awe and wonder.	Everyday, straightforward language.
Use of sound	Alliteration and assonance used to suggest the sounds of the storm.	Sounds made by vixen conveyed by onomatopoeia. Alliteration in line 13.
Imagery	Metaphor and personification used to give vivid impression of the power of the storm.	Literal imagery: the poem describes the scene.
Themes and the poet's attitude	The power of nature; the arrogance of man; the wonder of nature. The last stanza draws a 'lesson' from the experience. He is excited and frightened by nature and impressed by its power. He feels humans are comparatively powerless, though they think they are powerful.	Tension between nature and man; motherhood; the beauty of nature. He is impressed by the vixen's care for her cubs. He sees the danger posed by humans from her point of view. The ending gives a positive, hopeful view of life.

Practice Exam Papers – pages 177–200

Page 178 English Language Paper 1 – Section A: Reading

1. Any four from:
   - mirrors
   - cakes
   - sweetmeats
   - chocolates
   - wedding cake.

   [1] for each up to a maximum of [4]

2. Look at the mark scheme below, decide which description is closest to your answer and then decide what mark to give it up to a maximum of [8].

Marks	Skills	Examples of possible content
7–8	You have analysed the effects of the choice of language. You have used an appropriate range of quotations. You have used sophisticated subject terminology appropriately.	The first sentence, although quite long, is a simple sentence and does not make the shop sound especially attractive. The simile 'like the butt of a cigar' is not appealing, being something thrown away, and not appropriate for children. The writer seems to realize this when he says 'One should rather say', as if correcting himself, and his new simile 'like the butt of a firework' is better. You can imagine children gathering round the butt of a firework and looking at the colours. This leads into a detailed description of the contents of the window, focusing on the bright colours…
5–6	You have clearly explained the effects of the choice of language. You have used a range of relevant quotations. You have used subject terminology appropriately.	He uses long sentences to list all the sweets and chocolates, putting across their attraction by using imagery. It glows 'like the butt of a firework', which is something children would like. He makes it seem alive by saying the light is 'dancing'. The sweets seem unobtainable to the children, whose noses are 'glued' to the window but do not go in. They are called 'gutter-snipes' so are probably poor, in contrast with the richness of the shop window.

3. Look at the mark scheme below, decide which description is closest to your answer and then decide which mark to give yourself up to a maximum of [8].

Marks	Skills	Examples of possible content
7–8	You have analysed the use of structural features. You have chosen an appropriate range of examples. You have used a range of subject terminology accurately.	The description of the shop window in the first paragraph makes an ordinary setting seem enticing and almost exotic. Introducing the 'gutter-snipes' makes us think of people wanting something they cannot have, so when the focus moves to Angus, we have a sense of his wanting something too. The second paragraph gives his background, establishing something about his character and what he does. In the third paragraph, another character is introduced as he moves into the shop…
5–6	You have clearly explained the effect of structural features. You have chosen relevant examples. You have used subject terminology accurately.	At first the focus is on the shop window, giving a sense of how attractive it is to children. When it moves from the children to the young man we wonder what the attraction is for him. After we learn about him, we find out. The third paragraph describes the attractive young waitress. In the final paragraph he places his order and, after a pause, suddenly asks her to marry him, leaving the reader wondering about their relationship.

4. Look at the mark scheme below, decide which description is closest to your answer and then decide which mark to give yourself up to a maximum of **[20]**.

Marks	Skills	Examples of possible content
16–20	You have critically evaluated the text in a detailed way. You have used examples from the text to explain your views convincingly. You have analysed a range of the writer's methods. You have used a range of relevant quotations to support your views.	The writer introduces Angus by describing him looking into the shop window with the children, thus associating him with the children. He too wants something that maybe he cannot have, something that has a 'fiery charm' for him. The description of the wedding cake, 'remote and satisfying', is a clue about what this is. In the second paragraph, the description of his appearance and background makes him sound eccentric and full of contradictions. He is 'listless' and 'resolute' at the same time. He has been disinherited by a rich uncle apparently for being against Socialism, whereas you might expect the opposite. His actions in the shop are just as eccentric.
11–15	You have clearly evaluated the text. You have used examples from the text to explain your views clearly. You have clearly explained the effect of the writer's methods. You have used some relevant quotations to support your views.	The description of Angus gives odd details, such as that he was 'disinherited for Socialism' by his rich uncle. The writer builds up a clear picture of what he looks like, as he does with the young lady. At first it seems as if their relationship is just that between a waitress and a regular customer as he passes her 'merely raising his hat' and then just orders a bun. However, when he proposes to her, as if he is ordering something else, the reader wants to know more about them.

Page 179 English Language Paper 1 – Section B: Writing

5. Look at the mark scheme below, decide which description is closest to your answer and then decide which mark to give yourself. This task is marked for content and organization, and for technical accuracy.
   Content and Organization [maximum 24]

22–24	**Content** You have communicated convincingly and compellingly throughout. Your tone, style and register assuredly match purpose, form and audience. You have used an extensive and ambitious vocabulary with sustained crafting of linguistic devices. **Organization** Your writing is highly structured and developed, including a range of integrated and complex ideas. Your paragraphs are fluently linked with integrated discourse markers. You have used a variety of structural features in an inventive way.
19–21	**Content** You have communicated convincingly. Your tone, style and register consistently match purpose, form and audience. You have used an extensive vocabulary with evidence of conscious crafting of linguistic devices. **Organization** Your writing is structured and developed, including a range of engaging and complex ideas. You have used paragraphs consistently with integrated discourse markers. You have used a variety of structural features effectively.

Technical Accuracy [maximum 16]

13–16	You have consistently demarcated sentences accurately. You have used a wide range of punctuation with a high level of accuracy. You have used a full range of sentence forms for effect. You have used Standard English consistently and accurately, with secure control of grammatical structures. You have achieved a high level of accuracy in spelling, including ambitious vocabulary. Your use of vocabulary is extensive and ambitious.
9–12	You have usually demarcated sentences accurately. You have used a range of punctuation, usually accurately. You have used a variety of sentence forms for effect. You have used Standard English appropriately, with control of grammatical structures. You have spelled most words, including complex and irregular words, correctly. Your use of vocabulary is increasingly sophisticated.

[maximum 40]

Page 182 English Language Paper 2 – Section A: Reading

1. A, B, F, H [maximum 4]
2. Look at the mark scheme below, decide which description is closest to your answer and then decide what mark to give it up to a maximum of [8].

Marks	Skills	Examples of possible content
7–8	You have given a perceptive interpretation of both texts. You have synthesized evidence from the texts. You have used appropriate quotations from both texts.	In 1891 the libraries in Marylebone are new, although the buildings they are in are unsuitable, one being 'plain and insufficient', contrasting with the King's Park library, which was built over 100 years ago but is 'roomy' and 'generously proportioned'. The number of people using this library is falling, reflecting the fact that the area is not 'thriving', while in Marylebone, where the libraries are 'in two of the most populous parts of the parish', 'the demand increases daily'.
5–6	You have started to interpret both texts. You have shown clear connections between texts. You have used relevant quotations from both texts.	The libraries in Marylebone are not funded by the council. King's Park is run by the council but the council does not want it and says it is not attracting enough people. They also say it is only really pensioners who use it, whereas the Marylebone libraries are used by 'persons of all sorts and conditions'. In Marylebone the buildings are cramped and unattractive but the King's Park library is 'roomy' and 'beautifully decorated'.

3. Look at the mark scheme below, decide which description is closest to your answer and then decide which mark to give it up to a maximum of [12].

Marks	Skills	Examples of possible content
10–12	You have analysed the effects of the choice of language.You have used an appropriate range of quotations. You have used sophisticated subject terminology appropriately.	The tone is extremely polite and to a modern reader might even seem sycophantic, the writer's signing off with 'We beg, Sir, to remain yours obediently'. It seems odd that they would be 'obedient' to a newspaper editor but it must have been the convention of the time, as it reflects the courteous tone of the whole letter (for example, the use of modal verbs: 'May we be allowed'; 'We would'). The use of long, complex sentences also makes the tone seem reasonable and polite…
7–9	You have clearly explained the effects of the choice of language. You have used a range of relevant quotations. You have used subject terminology appropriately.	The tone is very gentle. They start with a question, which explains what they want in a very polite way. In the second paragraph they say what they are not going to do, giving the idea that people already agree with them. They give a long explanation, in the past tense, of the history of their libraries. They use statistics as evidence to impress the reader with their 'success', a word they keep repeating.

Page 183

4. Look at the mark scheme below, decide which description is closest to your answer and then decide which mark to give it up to a maximum of **[16]**.

Marks	Skills	Examples of possible content
13–16	You have compared ideas and perspectives in a perceptive way. You have analysed methods used to convey ideas and perspectives. You have used a range of appropriate quotations.	The two sources have different purposes. A's is to report on the campaign to save the library and B's is to persuade people to support public libraries. However, A includes both direct and reported speech from several people who are trying to keep the library open and who use emotive language, such as 'heart' and 'devastating', together with personal anecdotes, clichés ('drop in the ocean') and rhetorical techniques such as rhetorical questions ('how can the Mayor…?') to persuade. Source B also uses rhetorical techniques but is more subtle. The letter starts by saying what it is NOT going to do, implying confidence that the argument for public libraries has been won. Its tone is calm and measured, its arguments backed by evidence. This is similar to the way the council spokesperson in source A puts her case…
9–12	You have compared ideas and perspectives in a clear and relevant way. You have explained clearly methods used to convey ideas and perspectives. You have used relevant quotations from both texts.	Witherspoon is reporting the views of others while Debenham and Hollond give their own point of view. More people who are against the library closure are quoted than people who are in favour, so in the article you get a stronger impression of their point of view. They all use emotive language. The council's response seems cold and uncaring, focusing on 'statistics'. The letter is very unemotional and uses logical arguments and facts and figures to argue for public libraries – a bit like the council's arguments in Source A.

Page 183 English Language Paper 2 – Section B: Writing

5. Look at the mark scheme for page 179 question 5 above, decide which description is closest to your answer and then decide which mark to give yourself up to a maximum of **[40]**. This task is marked for content and organization, and for technical accuracy.

Page 185 English Literature Paper 1 – Shakespeare and the Nineteenth-Century Novel
Section A: Shakespeare

For all questions, look at the mark scheme below, decide which description is closest to your answer and then decide which mark to give yourself up to a maximum of **[30]**.

Marks	Skills
26–30	You have responded to the task in an exploratory and critical way. You have used precise, appropriate references to support your interpretation. You have analysed the writer's methods using subject terminology appropriately. You have explored the effects of the writer's methods. You have explored links between text and ideas/context.
21–25	You have responded to the task in a thoughtful, developed way. You have used appropriate references to support your interpretation. You have examined the writer's methods using subject terminology effectively. You have examined the effects of the writer's methods. You have thoughtfully considered links between text and ideas/context.

This question is also marked for AO4 (spelling, punctuation and grammar) up to a maximum of **[4]**.

Marks	Description of performance
4	You have spelled and punctuated with consistent accuracy. You have consistently used vocabulary and sentence structures to achieve effective control of meaning.
2–3	You have spelled and punctuated with considerable accuracy. You have consistently used a considerable range of vocabulary and sentence structures to achieve general control of meaning.

Your answers could include some of the following points.
1. *Macbeth*
   - Macbeth is seen here preparing for battle; he is a soldier again.
   - Speaking in soliloquy, he says he has no fear.
   - He is aware of what he has done.
   - Ambiguity in 'she should have died hereafter'.
   - Repetition of 'tomorrow' and imagery used to describe time.
   - Imagery conveys one man's insignificance and the pointlessness of life.
   - Macbeth as a brave commander at the start of the play.
   - Influence of the witches and Lady Macbeth.
   - His conscience and feelings of guilt.

- His murders, cruelty and tyranny.
- His heroic defiance and bravery at the end of the play.

2. *Romeo and Juliet*
   - Juliet's desire for Romeo to stay, pretending it is still night.
   - Imagery of light and dark – they can only be together in the dark.
   - The marriage is consummated and so is a real marriage – important later in the play.
   - Romeo's use of nature imagery/personification.
   - Imagery reflects the enormity of their passion.
   - Awareness of danger – love and death.
   - Earlier, Juliet insisted on marriage as proof of Romeo's love.
   - Marriage seen as political tool by Capulet.
   - Marriages arranged by parents.
   - Marriage as holy – spiritual and sexual fulfilment.
   - Nurse's disregard for the sanctity of marriage as well as for Juliet's feelings.

Page 186

3. *The Tempest*
   - Powerful images of spirits chasing the men.
   - Comic version of revenge – the plot to kill Prospero as a comic sub-plot.
   - Prospero using magic, as he does to capture and control those who took his kingdom.
   - Language used to describe torture, including alliteration, conveys delight in inflicting pain.
   - Audience left wondering what Prospero will do with the others who are at his mercy.
   - For most of the play Prospero seems intent on revenge.
   - Caliban seeks revenge on Prospero.
   - The last act shows Prospero choosing to forgive.
   - Forgiveness and reconciliation more powerful and more satisfying than revenge.

Page 187

4. *The Merchant of Venice*
   - He sees Antonio as a 'fool' for lending without interest, recalling that moneylenders had to be outsiders.
   - He has no interest in appearing merciful as society might expect.
   - Repetition of 'my bond' shows anger.
   - He recalls his former treatment by Antonio.
   - Calling him a dog implies Jews are seen as less than human.
   - The jailer has allowed Antonio to 'come abroad' – Antonio, the insider, is not seen as a criminal.
   - His description of how he will not behave implies that such behaviour is expected from him towards Christians. He is rebelling against this.
   - Antonio's earlier treatment of him showed that anti-Semitism is the norm.
   - Scenes with Jessica and his servants show how Jewish society is separate and different from the rest of Venice.

5. *Much Ado About Nothing*
   - Benedick has not yet appeared, but we anticipate a clash and/or romance with Beatrice.
   - Beatrice asks if he is with Don Pedro, indicating an interest in him.
   - Something happened the last time they met but we never know exactly what.
   - Contrast between the messenger's account of Benedick as a 'good soldier' and Beatrice's.
   - She does not seem to want to hear anything good about him.
   - Leonato's reference to a 'merry war' makes us expect battles of wits – but is there real dislike or is it all a joke?
   - They argue and misunderstand each other but their friends think they are suited.
   - Compare/contrast their relationship with the more conventional wooing of Hero by Claudio.
   - Their reactions to Claudio's treatment of Hero.

Page 188

6. *Julius Caesar*
   - Brutus's love for Portia shows a strong marriage.
   - Portia argues that love requires trust.
   - She feels she has been 'left out' of the conspiracy because of her sex.
   - She has to 'prove' she is as brave and trustworthy as a man.
   - Her way of proving it (taken from Shakespeare's sources) is shocking to Elizabethan and modern audiences but was thought admirable by Romans.
   - She defines herself by her father's reputation. She sees herself as better than other women.
   - Compare/contrast with Calpurnia, Caesar's wife.
   - Her suicide – seen as honourable in the context of ancient Rome.

Page 189 English Literature Paper 1 – Shakespeare and the Nineteenth-Century Novel.

Section B: The Nineteenth-Century Novel

See mark scheme above for Section A. This question does not carry additional marks for spelling, punctuation and grammar. Your answers could include some of the following points.

7. *The Strange Case of Dr Jekyll and Mr Hyde*
   - The story is told by Poole, introducing another narrator.
   - Another piece of the jigsaw for Utterson and the reader.
   - Poole very close to Jekyll but is convinced it is not Jekyll.
   - Poole's reaction one of fear, his hair standing up – feels he has seen something evil.
   - Compares the man he saw to a rat – Hyde is often compared to animals. He is also referred to as 'it', as if he is no longer human.
   - Jekyll has physically shrunk – 'more of a dwarf' – matching other descriptions of Hyde.
   - Stevenson is building up gradually to a full description of transformation.
   - Utterson and others assume Hyde is a separate person. They see Jekyll as 'good'.
   - Consider Dr Lanyon's narrative and his reaction.
   - Consider Jekyll's own narrative and his motivation – to separate good and evil.
   - The story shows that this is impossible – what else does it say about good and evil?

8. *A Christmas Carol*
   - Here Dickens uses shock and horror, surprising the reader at the end of the chapter.
   - The two children are personifications of Ignorance and Want (poverty).
   - The language used to describe them is vivid and repulsive.
   - However, the description is not very much exaggerated – it is what very poor children would look like.
   - The ghost uses them as a warning of what might happen if poverty and lack of education are not dealt with – revolution.
   - Dickens uses Scrooge's transformation to explore ideas about responsibility.
   - Using the Christmas ghost story, a popular form, Dickens gets his messages across in an entertaining way.
   - Being charitable and socially responsible is part of the spirit of Christmas – it does not stop you enjoying yourself.
   - This chapter shows a wide range of people at Christmas, many poor.
   - The Cratchits are used to show what life is like for poor families and how easy it could be to improve their lives.

Page 190

9. *Great Expectations*
   - The voice is that of the adult Pip looking back on his childhood.
   - He makes us aware of the child's innocence and naivety, realizing for the first time that his parents are really dead.

- There is some irony in the adult narrator's description of the child's fear.
- Pip recreates his feelings as a child – a mixture of comedy (the church being upside-down) and terror.
- His descriptions of the landscape, creating atmosphere and setting the tone.
- For most of the novel we, like Pip, are kept in ignorance about Magwitch.
- The reader empathizes with Pip but can see that he makes poor judgements.
- The novel as a 'Bildungsroman' – the story of Pip's education in life.

10. *Jane Eyre*
- As narrator Jane shares the feelings she had at the time with the reader.
- Here she analyses her feelings, which she does throughout the novel.
- She opens with a rhetorical question and answers it.
- She analyses Rochester's character, calling him 'proud, sardonic, harsh' but also listing his good qualities.
- She is concerned with morality. It is important for her to think he is no longer immoral.
- It is now clear that she is in love with him, a feeling that has been developing throughout the novel.
- Jane rescues Rochester on several occasions – almost as if he has to be less powerful for her to love him.
- Symbolism of the fire and Rochester's attitude to Jane after it.
- His marriage to Bertha and his deception – Jane's reasons for leaving Thornfield.
- Jane's return to Thornfield and their mutual love.

Page 191

11. *Frankenstein*
- Physical description of Elizabeth's 'loveliness'.
- This is followed by a description of her nature, painting her as an ideal woman.
- Frankenstein in love with her – has she any other purpose in the novel?
- The other woman mentioned, Justine, is also seen as good, innocent and an object of love.
- Neither Elizabeth nor Justine has any real power, relying on men to help them.
- They are both innocent victims of Frankenstein and his creature.
- Female characters are secondary in the novel and do not take an active role.
- However, they are almost always seen as good and pure.
- Consider how this reflects female roles in the Gothic tradition and in early nineteenth-century society.

12. *Pride and Prejudice*
- Contrast in reactions of Mr and Mrs Bennet.
- Elizabeth's reasons for rejecting Mr Collins.
- Ironic/comic tone of passage.
- Use of dialogue to convey attitudes of Mr and Mrs Bennet and their characters.
- Serious point given to unlikely character to make in a comic way. Who will maintain her if she is not married?
- Contrast Elizabeth's refusal with Charlotte Lucas's acceptance of Mr Collins.
- Marriage must be for love but must also make sense financially and socially.
- Other examples of marriage: Mr and Mrs Bennet, Lydia and Wickham, Jane and Bingley.
- Marriage of Elizabeth and Darcy as an ideal.

Page 192

13. *The Sign of Four*
- The mysterious atmosphere created by description of the moonlit night.
- Passage focuses on the discovery of the body, which changes the investigation to a murder case.

- Description of body brings home reality of violent death.
- Language used to describe the scene and Watson's reaction creates sense of horror.
- Detailed description of room sets up murder as a puzzle.
- The note introduces the mystery of the 'sign of four'.
- Novel explores the effect of murder on people and society.
- Explores what makes people murder.
- Murder gives Holmes a chance to demonstrate his skills.
- Consider the conventions of the detective story.

Page 194 English Literature Paper 2 – Modern Texts and Poetry. Section A: Modern Prose or Drama

Use the mark scheme for English Literature Paper 1 (above). This question is also marked on your spelling, punctuation and grammar (maximum **[34]** in all).
Your answers could include some of the following points.

1. *An Inspector Calls*
- Eva Smith as a representative of the working class.
- Is she one person or several people?
- The inspector shows the photo to the Birlings separately.
- She is involved with all the Birlings.
- The situations she is in are almost stereotypical.
- The Birlings' treatment of her reveals their characters and attitudes.

2. *An Inspector Calls*
- The Birlings and their house are comfortable and middle-class – they are smug.
- Their main concern is making and spending money.
- Mr Birling is not concerned about his workers or their lives.
- Mrs Birling does charity work but does not appear to really care.
- The children are only interested in spending money.
- They cannot see what Eva has to do with them.
- To different degrees they are made to see how selfish they are.
- Refer to the Inspector's speech about responsibility.

3. *Blood Brothers*
- The fact of their being brothers demonstrates the importance of class in their futures.
- They behave and speak differently.
- Edward has opportunities that Mickey does not have.
- Is it just money or is there more to class?
- There does not seem to be any social mobility in the play.
- The differences between them are quite crudely drawn.
- The two boys are not different in nature – their differences are the result of upbringing.

4. *Blood Brothers*
- The opening immediately tells us the deaths are inevitable.
- Mrs Johnstone is very superstitious. Mrs Lyons mocks at first but changes.
- The narrator often refers to superstitions.
- The idea that events are pre-ordained has more to do with social class than fate.
- What happens is the result of choices characters have made.
- Do they refer to fate and superstitions as a way of avoiding responsibility?

5. *The History Boys*
- The character of the charismatic unconventional teacher is common in fiction.
- Bennett, through other characters, shows an awareness of this.
- He does not belong in the modern world of school (even in the 1980s).
- He is a complex character as a teacher – inspirational and fun but with ambivalent attitudes to the value of education.
- He is witty and can be incisive but sometimes is just saying things to be clever.
- Compare/contrast with personalities and styles of other teachers in the play.
- His 'groping' and the reactions to it – the tolerant attitude towards it is not what we would expect today. Is it realistic?

6. *The History Boys*
   - Why has Bennett made the choice to have all the boys studying history (unlikely in real life)?
   - Is it just a way of passing exams?
   - Mrs Lintott and Irwin have different approaches. Irwin wants to question everything.
   - Is this any better than accepting everything?
   - The idea that there is 'no need to tell the truth'.
   - Irwin's subsequent career involves him in making history.

Page 195

7. *DNA*
   - The other teenagers physically abuse Adam.
   - There is psychological bullying in the group. John Tate bullies to keep power.
   - Phil's treatment of Leah could be seen as bullying.
   - When John Tate gives up he is seen as weak.
   - What is meant by 'bullying'? How are possible meanings reflected in the play?
   - What is the difference between bullying and leadership?

8. *DNA*
   - He only appears briefly but has a central role.
   - He tries to control the others through fear.
   - He threatens and patronizes others.
   - He tries to ban the word 'dead'. Why?
   - He loses control as things get serious.
   - The reports of him 'losing it' later suggest he feels guilt.
   - Compare/contrast with Cathy, who is truly ruthless.

9. *The Curious Incident of the Dog in the Night-Time*
   - Christopher accepts his father's version of events, as does the audience at first.
   - His desire to solve the mystery leads him to the truth.
   - Judy speaks through letters.
   - Her version of events is very different.
   - She gives the other side of living with Christopher, admitting she could not cope.
   - She presents a nostalgic view of family life.
   - In the end she returns and commits to Christopher.

10. *The Curious Incident of the Dog in the Night-Time*
    - Christopher is in a Special Needs school.
    - It is not spelled out in the text but he appears to have been diagnosed with autism.
    - We do not see him interact with other pupils but his stories show he thinks they are stupid.
    - He is extremely good at Maths and is entered for exams.
    - His relationship with Siobhan is crucial.
    - It is not clear what (if any) benefit Christopher gets from his education.
    - It does not go into issues around autism / special needs / education. The situation is accepted as it is.

11. *A Taste of Honey*
    - The mother–daughter relationship is central.
    - She argues with her mother about everything and resents their way of life.
    - She knows nothing about her father and is worried by what her mother tells her about him.
    - There is a role-reversal, Jo seemingly more mature than Helen.
    - Jo is critical of her mother but puts up with her.
    - Jo is motivated by not wanting to be like her mother.
    - She feels she can do without her but in the end has no-one else.

12. *A Taste of Honey*
    - Helen is an irresponsible parent.
    - Jo appears more responsible but does not always think about consequences.
    - The boy disappears after getting Jo pregnant – he takes no responsibility.
    - Jo's father did not take responsibility for her; Helen implies he was incapable of doing so.
    - Jo matures by facing up to her responsibility for the baby.
    - Geoff steps in when Helen has left but goes when she returns. Is he serious about looking after Jo?
    - When Helen returns she seems to be willing to help but changes when she learns the baby's father is black. Will she return?

Page 196

13. *Lord of the Flies*
    - Ralph is typically British, according to the conventions of the time.
    - He would not be out of place in the adventure stories which influenced Golding.
    - He is good-looking, charismatic and popular.
    - He is elected democratically and tries to run things fairly.
    - He is practical, building shelters and looking at ways of being rescued.
    - Contrast with Jack – Jack becomes more powerful as Ralph becomes less powerful.
    - Although tempted to join Jack's gang, he resists savagery.
    - At the end he still believes in 'civilization and good behaviour' but has experienced evil and savagery.

14. *Lord of the Flies*
    - Golding's characters are English public schoolboys, representatives of the 'civilized' world.
    - At first they behave as they would expect adults to, electing a leader and making rules.
    - Rivalries, fights etc. are usual in schools but here they get out of hand.
    - The role of Jack and the hunters.
    - The symbolism of the conch and the beast.
    - Changes in the way the boys speak.
    - Stages in the escalation of violence: killing the pig, Piggy, Simon.
    - What happens at the end? Has civilization broken down or have we just learned how superficial the idea is?

15. *Telling Tales*
    - 'The Invisible Mass of the Back Row' starts in Jamaica and moves to England.
    - The narrator describes sights, smells and tastes of the West Indies.
    - In school she is taught a version of history and culture she does not recognize.
    - Moving to England, she feels the difference in cultures but makes friends with girls from similar backgrounds.
    - In England she finds out more about black history and identity, and finds her voice.
    - The narrative is in Standard English but most of the dialogue is in Jamaican dialect.
    - Compare with Carla finding Polish identity in 'My Polish Teacher's Tie'.
    - Compare with the narrator's return to Japan in 'A Family Supper'.
    - Compare with Elizabeth's sense of identity in 'The Odour of Chrysanthemums' or the narrator's in 'Chemistry'.

16. *Telling Tales*
    - Carla introduces herself at the beginning.
    - She tells the story in the past tense, in chronological order.
    - The tone is colloquial, as if she is explaining what happened to someone she knows.
    - She reflects on her own feelings and motives.
    - Through the story she reveals more about her background as it becomes more important to her.
    - She feels different from the teachers / almost invisible to them.
    - Compare with narrator of 'The Invisible Mass of the Back Row' finding her voice but with a different attitude.
    - Compare with 'Chemistry'. Carla is more in control and more perceptive; the boy in 'Chemistry' is an unreliable narrator.

17. *Animal Farm*
    - He is loyal and hard-working, and not intelligent.
    - He does not get involved in ideas and politics.
    - He is exploited by both Mr Jones and the pigs, though he does not see it.

- In terms of the Russian Revolution he represents the non-political working class or 'proletariat'. The revolution was supposed to be for them.
- He is presented as a sympathetic character.
- He is essential for the running of the farm.
- His death shows how little he is valued.

18. *Animal Farm*
- *Animal Farm* as an allegory of the Russian Revolution.
- *Animal Farm* as a fable – not just about one historical event but a moral tale about all revolutions.
- At the start Orwell clearly shows the need for change.
- Major's vision of fairness and equality is inspiring.
- The rebellion has the backing of all and appears to be spontaneous.
- There is a need for leaders, which creates a love of power and corruption.
- Is Orwell saying all revolutions must fail or just describing where they have gone wrong?

Page 197

19. *Never Let Me Go*
- They are called guardians, not teachers. What is the difference?
- In some ways they act like conventional teachers, but some things they do – such as the 'sex lectures' or the gallery – are odd.
- They know about the children's future but only give little bits of information.
- They are part of the system and controlled by the system.
- Miss Geraldine is the most popular guardian and is a stereotype of the popular female teacher.
- Miss Lucy's talks with Tommy show her doubts about the school. She is 'idealistic'.
- Miss Emily's views are ambiguous. She works within society as it is.

20. *Never Let Me Go*
- Madame and her gallery are sources of speculation to the students.
- Most students are keen to get work in the gallery, but are not sure why.
- Tommy thinks the art work is used to decide whether couples can get 'deferrals'.
- The gallery becomes the focus of Tommy and Kathy's hope.
- Kathy, Tommy and Ruth go to a real gallery in Norfolk. It is here that Ruth's hopes of finding her 'model' are dashed.
- The gallery is part of the focus on being 'creative' at Hailsham – an attempt to make the students more human or to prove they are human, perhaps.
- Think about Miss Emily's rather confusing and self-justifying explanation at the end of the novel.

21. *Anita and Me*
- Some of the neighbours' behaviour is casual, even unknowing, racism.
- The dog's name causes Meena to question racist language: 'it's like a swear word'.
- Sam's behaviour at the fete is more openly racist – Meena feels personally hurt.
- Casual racist language used against Meena's mother.
- Racist violence against Aunty Usha is reported and Sam's racism culminates in beating up Mr Bhatra.
- The reference to 'Paki bashing' suggests an acceptance of racism which Meena has not been aware of.
- First-person narrative gives empathy to Meena and the reader shares her growing awareness.
- References to *To Kill A Mockingbird*, and the marked similarity of the ending to that novel's ending.

22. *Anita and Me*
- Mrs Worrall represents the positive side of the Tollington community.
- Her baking fascinates Meena, who is more interested in it than in her mother's cooking.
- She is welcoming and not prejudiced.
- Her family life is seen as sad. She cares for her husband but has no contact with children.
- British families are implicitly criticized in comparison to Indian families.
- Nanima represents the family's Indian roots.
- She cannot speak English and dresses traditionally.
- She shows the importance of the family and reconnects Meena to the family.

23. *Pigeon English*
- Narrator uses dialect expressions such as 'Asweh' and 'hutious'.
- Harri is regularly in touch with his father and sister in Ghana.
- Memories of life in Africa and differences from his present life.
- Importance of the church as centre of the community for Africans.
- Religious/moral principles and traditions.
- Culture of school / the estate.
- Gang culture giving sense of belonging.

24. *Pigeon English*
- Much of the action takes place in school.
- Harri's attitude to school and learning.
- Relationships in school – Dean, the gang, Poppy, the teachers.
- School seems innocent at first, seen through Harri's eyes, with normal activities like playing games and making friends.
- However, we realize it is a dangerous place where bullying and violence are accepted.
- Life in school reflects life on the streets.

Page 198 English Literature Paper 2 – Modern Texts and Poetry. Section B: Poetry

For both questions 25 and 26, look at the mark scheme below, decide which description is closest to your answer and then decide which mark to give yourself up to a maximum of [30].

Marks	Skills
26–30	You have compared texts in an exploratory and critical way. You have used precise, appropriate references to support your interpretation. You have analysed the writer's methods using subject terminology appropriately. You have explored the effects of the writer's methods. You have explored links between text and ideas/context.
21–25	You have made thoughtful, developed comparisons. You have used appropriate references to support your interpretation. You have examined the writer's methods using subject terminology effectively. You have examined the effects of the writer's methods. You have thoughtfully considered links between text and ideas/context.

25. Your answer might include:
    - Direct address to the loved one – 'When We Two Parted', 'Love's Philosophy', 'Winter Swans', 'Neutral Tones'.
    - Appeal to the loved one – 'Love's Philosophy'.
    - Use of sonnet form – compare with other forms used.
    - Regular and controlled rhyme and metre – 'When We Two Parted', 'Neutral Tones'.
    - Intense love – 'Love's Philosophy', 'Porphyria's Lover'.
    - Mutual love – 'Winter Swans'.
    - Use of natural imagery – 'Neutral Tones', 'Love's Philosophy', 'Winter Swans', 'The Farmer's Bride'.

26. Your answer might include:
    - The poet witnesses the suffering but is not personally involved – contrast 'Remains'.
    - Suffering both physical and psychological – 'Remains', 'Exposure'.
    - Regularity of form, metre and rhyme – 'The Charge of the Light Brigade', 'Storm on the Island', contrast with other poems.
    - Repetition – 'Remains', 'The Charge of the Light Brigade'.
    - Suffering caused by the powerful – 'Ozymandias', 'The Charge of the Light Brigade'.
    - Suffering of ordinary people – 'The Émigrée', 'Bayonet Charge'.
    - Urban setting – 'The Émigrée', 'Remains' – contrast 'The Prelude', 'Storm on the Island'.
    - Angry tone – contrast 'Kamikaze', 'Exposure'.

Page 200 English Literature Paper 2 – Modern Texts and Poetry. Section C: Unseen Texts

27.1 Look at the mark scheme below, decide which description is closest to your answer and then decide which mark to give yourself up to a maximum of [24].

Marks	Skills
21–24	You have explored the text critically. You have used precise references to support your interpretation. You have analysed the writer's methods using appropriate subject terminology. You have explored the effects of the writer's methods on the reader.
17–20	You have responded thoughtfully to the text. You have used appropriate references to support your interpretation. You have examined the writer's methods using subject terminology effectively. You have examined the effects of the writer's methods on the reader.

Your answer might include comments on:
- Poem in three regular stanzas.
- Impact of short rhyming couplet in lines 5 and 6 of each stanza.
- It starts with a grand, general statement and then gives examples.
- The third stanza addresses the reader directly.
- Death is a 'leveller' because it is the same for everyone and all are equal.
- Personification of Death ('his icy hand').
- Identification of classes of people by things associated with them ('Sceptre and Crown', 'scythe and spade') – called 'metonymy' in literary criticism.
- The poem reads like a warning.
- The language reflects decay: 'dust', 'wither'.
- There are many words associated with surrender and powerlessness: 'tumble', 'yield', 'stoop', 'captives'.
- For most of the poem the tone is negative – it seems as if no human activity is worthwhile as it all ends in death.
- The last two lines give hope of a kind, an idea that 'the just' can leave something behind.

27.2 Look at the mark scheme below, decide which description is closest to your answer and then decide which mark to give yourself up to a maximum of [8].

Marks	Skills
7–8	You have explored comparisons of the writers' use of language, structure and form, using appropriate subject terminology. You have convincingly compared the effects of the writers' methods on the reader.
5–6	You have thoughtfully compared the writers' use of language and/or structure and/or form, using effective subject terminology. You have clearly compared the effects of the writers' methods on the reader.

Your answer might include comments on:
- The first is about death in general, the second about the death of an individual.
- Stevenson speaks of how he would like to be remembered; Shirley implies no-one will be remembered.
- Stevenson expresses contentment with both life and death. Shirley's view of death is not comforting.
- Both focus on what remains: the grave; the dust.
- Rhythm, rhyme and alliteration give Stevenson's poem a cheerful tone. Shirley's is more ponderous, with a heavy beat.
- Both poets use the second person, 'you', but for Stevenson 'you' seems to be a loved one, while for Shirley it is anyone who reads the poem.

This page has been left blank

ACKNOWLEDGEMENTS

The author and publisher are grateful to the copyright holders for permission to use quoted materials and images.

P.30–31 *Nineteen-Eighty-Four* by George Orwell (Copyright © George Orwell, 1949) Reprinted by permission of Bill Hamilton as the Literary Executor of the Estate of the Late Sonia Brownell Orwell. P.88–89 *The History Boys* by Alan Bennett (Faber and Faber Ltd). P.88–89 © Simon Stephens, 2004, *The Curious Incident of the Dog in the Night-Time*. Reprinted by permission of Bloomsbury Methuen Drama, an imprint of Bloomsbury Publishing Plc. P.90–91 *Never Let Me Go* by Kazuo Ishiguro (2010), Faber and Faber Ltd. P.90–91 *Lord of the Flies* by William Golding (Faber and Faber Ltd). P.90–91 *Anita and Me* by Meera Syal, Flamingo (1997). Copyright © Meera Syal. P.90–91 © Willy Russell, 2001, *Blood Brothers*. Reprinted by permission of Bloomsbury Methuen Drama, an imprint of Bloomsbury Publishing Plc. P.100 From 'Kamikaze' by Beatrice Garland: Copyright Templar Poetry in *The Invention of Fireworks* (Templar, 2014). P.100, P.101 *Singh Song!* from 'Look We Have Coming to Dover' by Daljit Nagra (Faber and Faber Ltd). P.100, P.101 Extract of *Checking Out Me History* copyright ©1996 by John Agard reproduced by kind permission of John Agard c/o Caroline Sheldon Literary Agency Ltd. P.100, P.101 *Follower* from 'Death of a Naturalist' by Seamus Heaney (Faber and Faber Ltd).
P.116–117 'Florence' by Joyce Rackham, from *The Times* (13 October 1982). P.174 Extract from 'Walking Away' from THE GATE AND OTHER POEMS by C Day Lewis reprinted by permission of Peters Fraser & Dunlop (www.petersfraserdunlop.com) on behalf of the Estate of C Day Lewis. P.174 'Winter Swans' Copyright © Owen Sheers 2005. Reproduced by permission of the author c/o Rogers, Coleridge & White Ltd., 20 Powis Mews, London W11 1JN. P.174 'Mother, any distance' by Simon Armitage, Copyright © Simon Armitage. P.174 'Checking Out Me History', John Agard, *Alternative Anthem: Selected Poems with Live DVD* (Bloodaxe Books, 2009). P.174 'War Photographer' Copyright © Carol Ann Duffy 1985. Reproduced by permission of the author c/o Rogers, Coleridge & White Ltd., 20 Powis Mews, London W11 1JN. P.174 *Storm on the Island* from 'Death of a Naturalist' by Seamus Heaney (Faber and Faber Ltd).

All images are © Shutterstock.com

Every effort has been made to trace copyright holders and obtain their permission for the use of copyright material. The author and publisher will gladly receive information enabling them to rectify any error or omission in subsequent editions. All facts are correct at time of going to press.

Published by Collins
An imprint of HarperCollins*Publishers*

1 London Bridge Street
London SE1 9GF

© HarperCollins*Publishers* Limited 2020

ISBN 9780008112561

First published 2015
This edition published 2020

10 9 8 7

All rights reserved. No part of this publication may be reproduced, stored in a retrieval system, or transmitted, in any form or by any means, electronic, mechanical, photocopying, recording or otherwise, without the prior permission of Collins.

British Library Cataloguing in Publication Data.

A CIP record of this book is available from the British Library.

Publishing Manager: Rebecca Skinner and Emily Linnett
Commissioning Editor: Katie Galloway
Author: Paul Burns
Editorial: Susan Milligan
Cover Design: Kevin Robbins and Sarah Duxbury
Inside Concept Design: Sarah Duxbury and Paul Oates
Text Design and Layout: Jouve India Private limited
Printed in Great Britain by Bell and Bain Ltd, Glasgow

MIX
Paper from
responsible source
FSC® C007454
FSC
www.fsc.org

This book is produced from independently certified FSC™ paper to ensure responsible forest management.

For more information visit:
www.harpercollins.co.uk/green